Advance P

"I loved this book. I knew these chara my fellow teachers in a private school that hired p already had a real life outside of academe (even I had that, thanks to the Peace Corps), and some of my own classma from my college days. Garfinkle catches exactly the passionate and reckless moods of the anti-Vietnam War movement among young people in those years, the deadly naiveté, delight in rebellion, and idealistic misunderstanding of where events just had to go from there. The rendering of those times is keenly accurate, to my experience at least, and very evocative.

"And there's that best-friend pairing that we've all seen, maybe been part of at one time: the anxious, hopeful young woman full of doubts and longings, and her best friend the diva, the drama queen, the performer of outrages looking hard for trouble to get into. What an inspired idea, to bring the latter back to life as a ghost, an angry, unsettled child, that haunts the milder soul's more adult life!

"Writing a really good ghost story is a lot harder than it looks. But Garfinkle pulls it off with élan and produces a wonderful story about lives unlived, for one reason or another, shifting perspectives, what (if anything) we owe our dead, and how we reflect each other, hold each other back, and provide the take-off for others' sprints into maturity. There's also some tasty detail about the lives of working actors on a soap-opera gravy train, that as a film and theater enthusiast, I found delightful."

Suzy McKee Charnas, author of *The Vampire Tapestry*
and the Holdfast Chronicles

"All of us have questions and regrets about things we've done, but Jo Bergman is literally haunted by her past. This remarkable novel kept me on tenterhooks as I watched Jo seesaw among the different lives she would have experienced had she made different decisions. Gwynne Garfinkle has nailed both the fraught nature of the 1960s and early '70s and the difficult path of a woman struggling to be her whole self despite the ghosts of her past and the challenges of her present."

Nancy Jane Moore, author of *For the Good of the Realm*

"Here is a book that took me back in the same way a ghost of her past takes Joanna back, again and again. Gwynne Garfinkle's ghost story realistically recreates a traumatic moment in America's past. I was more than impressed with the realism of a period that I personally lived through. Garfinkle asks the reader what would happen if you could go to a pivotal moment in your past and relive it, searching for a different outcome? Would you, could you? In the end would it make it any better? Garfinkle's deft prose takes you on this journey with suspense and gentleness, tackling both regret and hope with equal sincerity. This book lives not only in the softer side of the horror genre, but as a work that instructs us to confront our own choices and how they irrevocably impact others. If you want a thoughtful and intriguing journey, buy this book."

Beth Plutchak, author of *Liminal Spaces*

"Garfinkle (*People Change*) delivers a fascinating, disorienting ghost story set in the 1970s. Actor Joanna Bergman has carried shame and remorse over her friend Cynthia Foster's death since it happened four years ago. As protestors against the Vietnam War, the duo would have done anything to stop the bloodshed—but when Cynthia and Joanna plotted to blow up a New York City draft board, Joanna backed out at the last minute. Her hesitance spared her life, and Cynthia died in the explosion. Now, the war is over, and Joanna has her first stable acting gig on the daytime soap Hope Springs Eternal and is developing feelings for her costar, Martin Yates. She's guiltily moving on with her life, until Cynthia's angry ghost appears to her and forces Joanna to relive that fateful night, turning over alternate choices she could have made and how things might have gone differently. The tale moves swiftly between reality and the paranormal, successfully making the reader question if Cynthia's ghost is just a projection of Jo's psyche or something more concrete. Fans of counterculture narratives and ghost stories will want to take a look."

Publishers Weekly, Sept. 2021

Can't Find
My Way Home

Can't Find
My Way Home

by

Gwynne Garfinkle

Aqueduct Press
PO Box 95787
Seattle, Washington 98145-2787

www.aqueductpress.com

Library of Congress Control Number: 2021943552

ISBN: 978-1-61976-212-1

First Edition, First Printing, January 2022

10 9 8 7 6 5 4 3 2 1

Cover Illustration © Can Stock Photo / Tanantornanutra
Title Page © Can Stock Photo / magann

Book and cover design by Kathryn Wilham

Printed in the USA by McNaughton & Gunn

Acknowledgments

Many thanks to L. Timmel Duchamp and Kath Wilham at Aqueduct Press for understanding what I was going for with this ghost story about activists and soap opera actors, and for helping to make it a better book. I'm so pleased that my novel found a home with this wonderful press.

Daytime dramas were produced very differently in the 1970s than they are today. When I started writing this book, some soap operas were still in production in New York; now the remaining U.S. soaps all come out of Los Angeles. I'd like to thank Lara Parker, Peter White, and Rory Metcalf for answering my many questions about old-school NYC soap opera production.

I did far more research into the 1960s-70s anti-war movement and other activism and events of the period than I can enumerate here, but I do want to mention Jeanne Córdova's memoir *When We Were Outlaws*, as well as two documentaries I found particularly useful: *The Weather Underground* (dir. Bill Siegel and Sam Green) and *Guerrilla: The Taking of Patty Hearst* (dir. Robert Stone).

Thanks to everyone who read and critiqued this novel as I wrote and revised it, and especially to Lisa M. Bradley for her insightful comments and moral support. For encouragement and camaraderie, thanks to Sonya Taaffe, Lyman Chaffee, Sofia Samatar, Patty Templeton, C.S.E. Cooney, Francesca Forrest, Julia Rios, and Victoria Janssen.

Thanks to Carolyn Soyars and Eileen Lucero for many years of friendship.

Special thanks and gratitude to my mother, Audrey Garfinkle, for all her love and support.

Finally, I'd like to acknowledge the tireless and often unsung creators of daytime dramas through the decades, especially the brilliant writer and producer Claire Labine (1934-2016).

For my father, Louis Garfinkle (1928–2005),
the first writer I ever knew

"What do you want to be when you grow up, Joanna?" my best friend Cyn asked as we lay on our backs on her bed listening to Phil Ochs. It was a few days before the new year. We were both seventeen.

"An actress," I said without hesitation.

"Well, I figured that much. But what kind? Do you want to be a movie star?" She said *movie star* with dreamy excitement trembling in her voice, though she usually affected nonchalance.

"I don't know about that." I couldn't quite picture myself as glamorous and larger than life. Besides, I wasn't pretty enough to be a movie star. "I like theater. It's scary, but I like it."

We both had on minidresses (hers a couple of inches shorter than mine) and tights, our shoes kicked off on the floor. I loved Cyn's room, with its big Jimi Hendrix poster, the LPs propped against the wall, and the closet and dresser full of clothes I would have liked to borrow if Cyn hadn't been so petite. (Though even if they'd fit me, they wouldn't have looked nearly as good as they did on her.) Most of all, the room was full of Cyn's bright, tense presence.

"You should be a movie actress, Jo," she insisted. "If I could act, that's what I'd want to do." That made sense. Cyn *was* pretty enough, and she had charisma to spare.

The album side ended, and the needle replaced itself at the beginning. Phil Ochs began to sing "Tape from California" with gorgeous nasal plaintiveness.

"What do you want to do when you grow up?" I asked.

Cyn was silent. I turned my head and watched her ponder, staring up at the ceiling, her long blonde hair spread about her face. Then she shook her head and turned to look at me. "Something important. I don't know what exactly. Something that'll make everyone sit up and take notice."

"You will," I said. "Of course you will."

She smiled. "We both will."

I thought to say that we didn't seem to want the same thing, though she seemed to think we did. Instead I closed my eyes and listened to Phil Ochs sing about New York City exploding.

Chapter One:
The War Is Over
(September 1975)

The day Cyn came back, I was about to walk home from the studio after the read-through for tomorrow's episode of *Hope Springs Eternal.* The best thing about acting was that I got to be somebody else. Corollary to that: I got to not be myself. That was always a relief. So what if this gig wasn't theater? Most of the actors in the company had theater backgrounds (some much more extensive than mine). My dad hated that I was doing a daytime drama. But it was steady acting work. Far better than being a temporary secretary.

The lobby at the studio was small and unobtrusive, with a couple of small couches, a plastic chair, and, toward the back of the room, a desk where the security guard sat reading a paperback of *Jaws.* I had almost reached the glass door that led to the street, when someone said, "Hey, Joanna," and I turned.

It was Martin Yates, my new costar. "Glad I caught you," he said. "Want to get a drink?"

I wasn't sure what I'd expected him to say—maybe that I'd left something in the rehearsal room, or that the director had just learned we'd been using the wrong version of tomorrow's script—but an invitation wasn't it. "I need to learn my lines for tomorrow," I said, waving my script. I still wasn't used to having so many lines and so little time to learn them.

Martin waved his script back at me. "Me too. Plus I promised my little girl I'd help her with her math homework. God help me. She seems to think I'm the one qualified to help her, when my wife is the brains of the family."

I had met Martin's wife at a cast party months ago. All I could remember was a pleasant brunette with a Brooklyn accent. "I thought your daughter was in the third grade."

"She is."

I started to laugh. "Surely you can handle that! It's not exactly precalculus."

"Hey, it's been a lot longer since I've taken math than it's been for you, okay?" he said, grinning. "So how about that drink? We've just established you're far too young to be all work and no play."

I eyed him. This wasn't a come-on, was it? He smiled with an air of absolute innocence: soap opera leading man Martin Yates, in well-fitting jeans and a red shirt that showed off his slender but powerful build. I flushed at the thought of kissing him at the end of the week, much less with three cameras hovering. It would be my first love scene since I'd joined *Hope Springs Eternal*.

Just then Clarissa Bauer came up behind us, startling me, and said, "Marty, the last thing we want to do is discourage new cast members from working hard."

That was more than a bit galling, since I'd never worked as hard at anything as I had since I got this job. I'd been with the company for six months, but I suspected I'd always be the new girl as far as Clarissa was concerned. She was a dark-eyed, thin-nosed, thin-lipped woman somewhere in her forties; she wore a navy pantsuit and possessed a kind of austere beauty, like the wicked queen in *Snow White*.

"Don't worry," Martin said. "Joanna isn't cut from the same cloth as Heather O'Connor."

Clarissa shuddered. "She whose name will live in infamy!" she intoned. I laughed; Clarissa shot me a dirty look. "Heather O'Connor used to share my dressing room," she told me.

I'd heard plenty of stories about Heather's tantrums and inability to take direction. She'd been fired just before I joined the company. "I know," I said. "She does shampoo commercials now?"

"That's what she's well-suited for. She has lovely hair." Clarissa peered at me. "You have lovely hair as well, Joanna."

"Thanks," I murmured, though she was looking me up and down with narrowed eyes and a pursed mouth as though she found fault with my outfit (jeans, a white blouse with tiny purple flowers, and a brown velveteen jacket). I'd never been able to figure out why Clarissa disliked me, except maybe that she disliked ingénues on principle, especially ingénues who shared her dressing room.

To my surprise, Martin put his arm protectively around my shoulders. I caught a whiff of spicy aftershave. I didn't usually like cologne on men, but he smelled good. "We were gonna go around the corner for a drink," he told Clarissa. "Join us?"

"No, thank you, Marty. I mustn't be late to the theater. Have a good evening!" She headed through the glass door. Martin still had his arm around me. It felt strong and comforting.

"I thought Clarissa's play closed last weekend," I said.

"Next weekend, and I wouldn't mention it to her, if I were you." He gave my shoulders a squeeze, then let go of me. "So, Chauncy's?"

He had bulldozed my objections to going for a drink with him. But I did want to go. "Chauncy's, it is," I said, and let him usher me outside.

The studio was a nondescript, two-story building of pale brick nestled in the middle of a block of similar buildings on the Upper West Side. The late afternoon was pleasantly cool and cloudy. We walked around the corner to Chauncy's. I had visited the bar a few times with Susan Harding and Babette Wilder, who played mother and daughter on *Hope Springs Eternal* (though I was pretty sure they weren't far enough apart in age for that to be biologically possible). The place was small and comfortably run-down. A transistor radio behind the bar played Elton John, "Someone Saved My Life Tonight," not too loudly. The bartender, a strapping guy with curly black hair, yelled "Hey, Marty!"

"Hi, Jim. Do you know Joanna Bergman? She's with the company."

Jim had served me drinks before, but he sized me up as though he wasn't sure. "Nice to meet you, Joanna."

Martin ordered Scotch and a mug of beer, I just a Scotch. We sat in a booth. The front section of the *Times* lay on Martin's side of the table. He pushed it aside. "Joanna Bergman," he said with a smile, and sipped his beer. "So, are you Scandinavian?"

I stared at him. "What?"

"Well, your last name...and you kinda look like Liv Ullmann."

I wanted to say, But she's so beautiful. "I saw her in *A Doll's House* this spring."

"At the Vivian Beaumont? I wish I'd managed to see that."

"She's one of my favorite actresses, especially in *Scenes from a Marriage*. *Persona* kinda freaks me out, though."

"Oh, I think *Persona's* a masterpiece," he said. "What I wouldn't give to get to work with Ingmar Bergman. The impossible dream..."

"Me too. I'd even learn Swedish! But anyway, I'm not Scandinavian. I'm Jewish. German and Polish, mostly."

His mouth dropped open—then he grinned. "Really? Me too. Russian Jewish on my mother's side. Irish Catholic on my dad's."

"Oh!" We gazed at each other, reframing our assumptions. I'd always thought he looked a little like John Cassavetes, with his dark hair and eyes, olive complexion, and lean build. I wasn't sure what I'd thought he was, but Jewish had never occurred to me. "Well, we're all vaguely Christian on *Hope Springs Eternal*," I said. "I guess it's natural enough it didn't occur to either of us."

He laughed. "True enough. I grew up pretty confused about the whole thing. Not to mention the fact that I got a double dose of guilt, Jewish and Catholic."

He said it jokingly, but then his smile faded. I wondered what Martin had to feel guilty about. We both fell silent.

Martin drank some beer. "Listen, I wanted to tell you that I was glad when I saw where the writers were going with our storyline. Even though I'll probably get a lot of hate mail. The fans are crazy about me and Babette. I've never been able to figure out why."

Neither had I, but it didn't seem politic to say so. "I hadn't been sure that was where they were going with our storyline until a couple of weeks ago," I said. "I thought maybe Sam and Jean were just going to stay platonic and investigate Eric Read." Jean Christopher was an aspiring journalist, and her cousin Vicki's husband Sam Jameson, a private investigator, was helping her look into the shady dealings of the town mayor, who happened to be Vicki's mother's second (or was it third?) husband. I thought of the storyline as Watergate, Soap Opera Style.

"I know what you mean," Martin said. "The buildup has been fairly subtle. I don't think they would have gone in this direction if you and I didn't have chemistry."

I sipped my drink and wondered again if he was coming on to me. But his tone wasn't flirtatious, just matter of fact. We did have good chemistry. It filled our scenes with tension and energy, even when we had to recite pages of exposition about Mayor Read.

"Anyway, I'm glad we'll be working together more," he said. "I could use the challenge. You know what I mean."

"I'm glad to be working with you, too, Marty." Before I'd worked with Martin, I'd viewed him as an attractive loudmouth. But I was discovering he was also a thoughtful, diligent actor. Generous—he was good at giving you what you needed.

"Nothing against Babette," he hastened to add, looking sheepish. "She's a great girl. It's just…"

It was just that she couldn't act. I was a little surprised Martin had noticed, because Babs was probably the most gorgeous woman I'd ever met, and he and Babs seemed to be good friends. "I just wish Babette had half as much personality on screen as she does off," I said. "If she did, she'd be pretty terrific."

"That's it exactly." He looked grateful, then embarrassed for some reason. He glanced down at the newspaper. "Patty, Patty, Patty," he muttered. "Damn news is full of nothing but Patty Hearst, or should I say, Tania. And when it's not Patty, it's another fruitcake trying to shoot Ford. What a circus."

I picked up the newspaper, and Patty Hearst's mug shot confronted me, a matter-of-fact, self-righteous gaze. I wondered what Cyn would have thought about the Symbionese Liberation Army. There had been something both riveting and ridiculous about them, kidnapping an heiress who proceeded to spout their rhetoric ("Death to the Fascist Insect," whatever that meant), don fatigues and a beret and brandish a carbine, change her name to Tania, and take part in a bank robbery. Watching the story unfold on the nightly news had been like watching a soap opera. It wasn't clear whether Patty Hearst's conversion had been genuine or the result of brainwashing. But I could imagine the SLA's bravado, their sense of theater, appealing to Cyn. Could almost picture a submachine-gun wielding Cyn swaggering through a bank, chewing the scenery.

"And since when do women take it into their heads to assassinate the President?" Martin asked. "What a weird trend."

I looked up from the newspaper. "I'm not sure two women constitute a trend."

"That Sara Jane Moore looks like a dumpy *hausfrau*, not an assassin," he said. "Squeaky Fromme's the pretty one, albeit psychotic."

"Watch out, Marty. Apparently some dumpy *hausfraus* carry guns."

Martin grinned like a bratty kid. "Was I being a male chauvinist, Jo?"

"Just a tad," I said, smiling, though I felt irked.

"Well, you must admit, the whole thing's laughable," he said, and threw back his Scotch. "Stupid self-styled revolutionaries." His tone was self-satisfied, smug.

I looked again at Patty Hearst staring down the camera. The sounds of the bar—"Fame" by David Bowie bumping and grinding on the radio, a guy and a girl gabbing and laughing in a booth near the door—all started to recede behind the dull roaring in my ears.

Martin picked up the newspaper and pushed it aside. "But enough about all that," he said with a huff of laughter.

I took a sip of whiskey. It burned all the way down, a satisfying minor pain. The song trudged to its conclusion, its sped-up ethereal *fame, fame, fame*s dipping down low, lower, lowest. I ransacked my brain for something to talk about, something pleasant and neutral. I looked over at Patty Hearst's slightly crumpled mug shot. "Who knows what Patty Hearst's trip is," I said. "I think the SLA are kinda nuts, though that doesn't mean they deserved to burn to death on live TV."

"Granted," Martin said. "That was pretty horrible."

Pretty horrible barely began to cover it. I had sat transfixed in front of the TV during the shootout between the SLA and the police on a residential Los Angeles street. Amid the rat-tat-tat of bullets and the tear-gas haze, one of the police's tear-gas grenades ignited a stash of ammunition in the SLA safe house, and it went up in flames with everyone inside. No one tried to put out the fire. At first it hadn't been clear if Patty

Hearst was in there too. I'd imagined her burning to death with the others.

"Pretty horrible," I echoed, and took a sip of my drink. Memories had me by the throat like tear gas. I struggled to pick up the thread of the conversation. "I don't agree with the SLA's tactics. But that doesn't mean that I think everyone who ever did something extreme to try to change things for the better…" I couldn't finish. Did I believe we'd been in any way justified? When I let myself think about it, which wasn't often, I thought we'd been collectively insane, all four of us. The way we used to talk about revolution! The memory made me squirm, like recalling a disastrous romantic obsession. It wasn't exactly *What did I see in him?*, because I remembered precisely how I had viewed the revolution, a maelstrom of joy and freedom, the end of war, the end of ugly old white men ruling the world—but *Did you really think that was going to happen?*

"I think I get what you're saying," Martin said gently. "But one thing you learn as you get older is that change is about patience. These types are all about the grand gesture, all style and no substance."

"Sort of like actors?" I asked.

"At least actors aren't hurting anyone. Well, some performances can be painful, but the audience usually recovers." He wore a little-boy grin. He was trying to smooth things over, to make me laugh.

I did laugh, briefly. I ran my fingers over the cracked leather of my seat and touched the exposed foam within. "What we do doesn't hurt anybody, but does it really help either? Right or wrong, some people have dared to risk everything for a better world. I think it takes real bravery, of the kind I, for one, don't have."

"Brave? Stepping in front of a train, jumping off a building, that's real brave. It's also stupid. Shooting innocent people, like the SLA did? Trying to shoot the president? You think that helps people?"

"Of course not. I'm not talking about that! I'm talking about fighting to stop injustice, to stop the war. I'm talking about not going on like it's business as usual when people are dying." What was I doing? I hadn't talked like this in years.

"You do know that the war is over, right?" He spoke slowly and ponderously, as though I might be a bit dim.

"Of course I know the war's over!" The fight left me. "It's over now." How the war had poisoned everything. It had burned into our minds, taken over our imaginations. And now the war was over, and Cyn was still dead. I stared into the inch of Scotch left in my glass.

"Hey, Jane Fonda," Martin said, and I looked up and saw that he was smiling slightly. "Remind me never to talk politics with you. At least not when you're drinking."

A laugh escaped me. "I'm not drunk, Marty. I'm..." I shook my head. "I don't know what I am. Sorry." Why was I arguing with him about this stuff? It wasn't as if I even disagreed with him. It was just that he had jabbed an old wound. Still, after six months of playing cousin-confidante-sidekick to Babette, I was finally getting a juicy storyline, a romance with a married man—and the last thing I should be doing was picking a fight with my new costar.

But Martin just smiled, his eyes heavy-lidded, as if he were entirely relaxed and enjoying himself. "Don't apologize. It was kinda entertaining." He sipped his beer. "Forgive me if I'm stomping all over your romantic notions of revolution."

Wow, my new costar was infuriating. "I do not have any ro-mantic notions of revolution! Maybe I did once, but not now."

A commercial came on the radio, and someone turned the dial. "Fight the Power" came on, mid-song, and Martin froze. Then we both burst out laughing. It felt good, as if a door in me that had been jammed shut had suddenly, without effort, swung open a crack.

"Wow, have I been put in my place!" Martin said. "By you *and* the radio." He danced a little in his seat, a self-mocking shimmy, and I had the sudden wish, as if we were in a romantic comedy or a musical, for him to get up, offer me his hand, and dance me around the bar.

Then a vague uneasiness that registered as a prickling sensation at the back of my neck made me turn.

The girl standing by the bar looked just like Cyn—exactly, impossibly like Cyn. I hadn't seen her come in. She had sleek, short hair like Mia Farrow in *Rosemary's Baby*, a haircut that accentuated her sharp little features. She wore jeans and the black peacoat I remembered. She stood stock still, legs planted firmly in an upside-down V, that ramrod straight posture Cyn had adopted in her final year.

It couldn't be her. It couldn't be. But how could it be anyone else?

She stared straight at me as if she were posing for a mug shot. Then she turned and strode to the door, was gone so quickly it was as if she'd never been there.

For a few seconds I stared at the dark wood of the door. Then I got to my feet. "Excuse me," I muttered at Martin's astonished face and made for the door. I pulled it open and nearly collided with Ed, one of our cameramen, a beefy guy with muttonchops and a mustache. "Hi, Joanna…" he said as I hurried past him. It was dusk. There was a taxicab parked at the curb, but no one in the backseat. I ran down the block and looked up and down, then turned and did the same in the other direction. "Cyn!" I shouted at no one. She wasn't there. What had I expected?

I went back inside the bar. Martin was chatting with Ed, who stood next to the booth smoking a cigarette. Martin threw back his head and laughed. I had the urge to sneak away, but then Martin saw me. I walked back to the booth and sat across from him.

Martin looked at me strangely. "I wasn't sure if you were coming back."

Ed looked from Martin to me as if he might be intruding. "Well, have a good evening, folks," he said and headed for the bar.

"Sorry, Marty," I said. "I thought I saw someone I knew."

"Must've been someone important."

"It couldn't have been her." What was wrong with me? Of course it hadn't been Cyn. It had been some blonde girl who'd happened to be there when I'd been thinking about Cyn.

"You okay?" Martin asked.

"Sure." I downed the rest of my whiskey. I felt cold all over.

"Hey," he said softly, "we're gonna be working together a lot, so...what we were talking about before? The whole revolution shtick. I'm sorry if I offended you."

I could still see Cyn's afterimage when I looked at him, as though I'd been staring at the sun. Only slowly did his face, real, substantial, blot out hers. "You didn't offend me, Marty." Well, maybe he had, but somehow that didn't matter now.

"But it's clearly a subject you take personally. How come?"

Wouldn't it be a relief to tell someone? But he'd said *revolution shtick*. He would never understand. Or would he? "It's complicated," I said. Of course I couldn't tell him. It could ruin everything.

To my surprise, he reached across the table and took my hand. "You don't have to tell me if you don't want to, Joanna. I just wanted to make sure we're okay." His hand was warm, and his face was suffused with kindness.

"We're okay," I said. I'm okay, I thought. I'm okay I'm okay I'm okay. I didn't see her. I didn't hallucinate her either. It was just some blonde girl, and we'd been talking about *the whole revolution shtick*. I wanted to keep hold of Martin's hand.

13

Chapter Two:
Piece of My Heart
(1968–1970)

If I could have told it to anyone, how would I have begun the story? Martin Luther King Jr. was already dead, and Bobby Kennedy. I was sitting against the wall in the brown-carpeted hallway outside the high school auditorium. So wrapped up in stage fright, studying my paperback of *Saint Joan*, that I jumped when a girl said, "Hello, Joanna." I looked up, and there was Cynthia Foster and this tall, muscular boy with dark hair and very blue eyes.

"I gotta get to practice," the boy said. "Good luck." He gave Cyn a quick kiss on the lips and took off down the hall.

"Is he your boyfriend?" I asked.

"Thomas?" She smiled mysteriously. "He's very tall and very strong."

I gave her what I hoped was a knowing nod. "You're trying out for the role of Joan?"

In answer, she waved her copy of the play. Damn it, I wouldn't stand a chance against such a pretty, popular girl as Cynthia Foster with her long, sleek blonde hair and long legs in a much shorter skirt than the one I had on. Cyn was petite, but she had presence. Charisma. Damn it, I wouldn't stand a chance against someone with charisma. I might as well give up right now. Then I wouldn't have to audition—except that I really wanted to be in this play. I couldn't think of anything I'd ever wanted as much, except to have a guy who loved me who would walk down the halls of the school with his arm around me.

There were three other girls waiting to audition. Cyn ignored them and sat beside me on the carpet. "I hope I don't have to wait too long," she said.

"A couple of girls have already tried out," I said. "I'm really nervous." I hoped saying it out loud would make me feel better, but it made my stomach do a loop de loop. Why was I subjecting myself to this? Why did I want to be in this play anyway?

"I'm not nervous," Cyn said.

"Really? What's your secret?"

She shrugged. "It doesn't really matter to me, one way or another. It seems like it'd be fun. But it's just a play. Just make-believe."

"Hmm." It matters to me, I thought. Why?

"It would be fun to be up there, on stage," Cyn said. "I do like attention. I must admit, I like it a lot." And she grinned.

∞

I hadn't been in a school play since way back in the fourth grade, when I'd been one of three dancing ragamuffins in *A Christmas Carol*. I'd never taken any dance classes, but I practiced my routine at home until it was perfect, and I loved my costume of artfully pieced rags in different colors. To my great disappointment, I only got to do one performance—during the day for the other kids—because I came down with the flu before the evening performance. Lying in bed with a fever and a stuffy nose, I imagined the other two ragamuffins doing the routine without me.

Brisk, kindly Miss Anthony taught the fifth grade and presided over the school's musical productions. I looked forward to being in her class and pictured the whole year as being full of music and dance performances in the school auditorium. The first day of fifth grade I was desolate to discover Miss

Anthony had left the school. That was the end of my fledgling theatrical career

Then, in senior English, Mrs. Waterson praised how I read aloud from *Macbeth* and suggested I try out for the school production of *Saint Joan*. I tried to dismiss the idea but found I couldn't stop thinking about it.

∞

Two days after my audition, I scanned the sheet of paper taped to the auditorium door. I couldn't believe my eyes.

"Good for you!" someone said, and I turned. Cyn was smiling at me. "I knew you could do it, Joanna. Joanna of Arc!"

"Thanks," I said, wondering if she was really okay with not getting the part.

As if she'd read my mind, she said, "I'm already pretty busy with the debate team. Hey, want to come over after school?"

We fell into being best friends as if it had never been otherwise.

∞

It had been a long time since I'd had a best friend. I'd been a dreamy, shy little kid. My best friend Millie Turner, a mousy girl who was only uproarious and sarcastic when we were alone together, moved away at the end of third grade. After that, I carried *Little Women* around with me at school as a security blanket and shield. I loved that Jo March and I shared a name, even though hers was short for Josephine. I was outwardly quiet, but I identified with Jo's rebellious ways.

When I started junior high, it didn't help that my dad was an English teacher at my school, though I wasn't in any of his classes. Being a teacher's daughter gave me a reputation as, at best, a goody-goody, at worst a fink. Besides which, I had little in common with the other kids, since I was bookish and had crushes on movie stars from the thirties and forties. My dad was pleased that I loved to read, but my mom worried about my lack of a social life.

Then the Beatles hit, and suddenly I had a shared interest with the other girls. There were countless lunches in the cafeteria discussing which Beatle we liked best. (John was the one I respected most, but I had a crush on Ringo.) At home I spent endless hours listening to Beatles albums (and, a little later, Dylan LPs). My dad seemed crestfallen at my new preoccupation. He didn't understand it. My mom was just glad I was getting invited to parties.

Still, I wasn't close to any of these girls like I would be with Cyn.

∞

We sat on the floor in Cyn's living room, close to the color TV, even though the radiation could hurt you if you were too close to the screen. The horror of the images drew us in. The dead body sprawled face down on the ground, the blood on the soldier's face, the burning huts, the blood the guns the explosions. The corpses, American and Vietnamese. It made me feel crazy, witnessing all of it. And then they would go to a commercial for floor wax or coffee.

Cyn seemed so cool and self-sufficient, but her eyes fixed on the TV screen were full of shocked disbelief. "Joanna, how can they show *that* and then sell things like it's *normal*? It makes me want to throw up."

"My little brother is scared the war will still be going on when he's old enough for the draft. His best friend's older brother is over there."

"How horrible."

"They always made war sound so heroic, fighting the Nazis and all," I said. "But what if this is what it's always been?"

"The North Vietnamese aren't Nazis," Cyn said, and I held my breath, afraid she would say, *The Americans are the Nazis.* I'd lost family I'd never known, distant relatives on my father's side, in the camps, and Cyn was vaguely Protestant. I wasn't sure I could explain to Cyn why it would be wrong to call

17

Americans Nazis. I just knew I didn't want her to say it. But instead she said, "Our tax dollars at work."

"Our tax dollars," I agreed. "It's so wrong." *Wrong.* The word was inadequate, puny. I heard my own voice, inadequate and puny, in opposition to the monumental horrors of war.

∞

At the same time—and it was the opposite of the war, which made me feel sick and helpless—being in the play was the most exciting time of my life so far. I loved working with the other actors and the director Mr. Aiken and even the kids painting sets and working the lights and the curtain, all working to make something beautiful and moving. Of course the play was about war too (the Hundred Years' War, which we might have studied in history class at some point, but I didn't remember much).

"This afternoon after rehearsal, I told Mr. Aiken I was having trouble relating to that part of the play, because I don't believe in war," I told Cyn after school. We were sitting on her bed listening to *Tape from California.*

"Good for you," Cyn said. "What did he say?"

"He said Joan was fighting against an occupying army."

Cyn was silent. Then she said, "So it's like Vietnam?"

"That's what I said. Mr. Aiken said, 'Maybe.'"

"Maybe he's afraid to come out against the war to his students. Maybe he's afraid he'd get fired."

We listened awhile to Phil Ochs singing "White Boots Marching in a Yellow Land" with his wistfully hopeful twang. Cyn thought Phil Ochs was better than Dylan. "I keep trying to imagine what it was like to be Joan," I said. "She was only nineteen when they burned her at the stake. I mean, I can't really relate to the religious stuff in the play either."

"Because you're Jewish? I wish I were Jewish. But even being Catholic like Joan is better than being Methodist. Being Methodist is so boring."

"The thing is, I *can* relate to Joan hearing voices that told her to buck the system. And how she had the guts to be a martyr for what she believed in, even when she was scared."

Cyn's eyes shone. "Wow, that is amazing," she said. Then she grinned. "So, is there anyone in the cast you have the hots for?"

"What?"

"Come on, there must be somebody."

"Not really…" I stared at the big poster of Jimi Hendrix on the opposite wall. Actually I did have a crush on the boy who played the Dauphin. He was slight and pimply, but brilliant in the role of the weak and cowardly Charles. I wasn't sure why I didn't tell Cyn. Maybe because he was nothing like any of the guys Cyn dated, or because one of the girls making the costumes was his girlfriend.

"Saving yourself for Hendrix?" Cyn asked with a laugh. Then she serenaded me over the Phil Ochs record: "Hey Jo, where you going with that gun in your hand?"

∞

Backstage opening night, my heart was pounding so hard, I wondered why I'd ever wanted to do this. My fellow cast members bustled around me adjusting their costumes and muttering lines to themselves. Maybe I would die of fright before I even got on stage. But Cyn and my parents were in the audience. I had to do this somehow.

I stared at myself in the mirror in my Joan getup: a brown suede tunic, brown cigarette pants and leather boots. I'd get to carry a sword and wear a breastplate spray-painted silver in some of the later scenes. My hair was in a tight braid down my back. I'd wanted to cut my hair short for the role, but my usually easygoing parents vetoed the idea. (Cyn said, "That's too bad, but you do have beautiful hair. The hell with art.")

I stared into the mirror, straightened my spine, and whispered, "Light your fire: do you think I dread it as much as the life of a rat in a hole? My voices were right."

∞

When I strode across the stage, a power surged up in me, and I became the calm at the eye of the storm. I got to speak Shaw's beautiful words and make them my own. During the trial scene, when I tore up my recantation and cried out the words I'd whispered at the mirror (mere hours ago, lifetimes ago), people in the darkened auditorium gasped audibly. I got to be Joan of Arc, to sacrifice everything and still be safe. I got to live another life and keep my own, and that was even better than the applause at the end of the play. But I loved the applause. How I loved the applause. I would've said it was better than sex—a phrase Cyn liked to use—but I hadn't had sex yet, unless you counted solo orgasms in bed at night.

Cyn found me backstage afterwards. She had on a purple velvet minidress, and it seemed like every guy in the place did a double take at her entrance, including Mr. Aiken and my Dauphin crush. She ignored them all. "You did it!" she cried and threw her arms around me. She was small-boned but strong. Then she held me at arms' length. "So how does it feel to be a star?"

I laughed. "Oh, sure, I'm a big star."

"Of course you are. No one else here could do what you did up there, and they all know it. And if they don't, they're a bunch of idiots."

∞

I thought about trying out for drama school instead of applying to four-year colleges, but my dad said no. "You can take drama classes in college," he said. "You shouldn't put all your eggs in one basket. I want you to get a proper education."

"Don't let him get you down, Jo," Cyn said. "The main thing is that we both go to college in New York City. I can hardly wait to get out of Rochester."

We both got into the School of New York. Cyn's parents set her up in an apartment off-campus, and she wanted me to be her roommate, but my parents insisted that I live in one of the residence halls.

The day before classes started, Cyn and I walked hand in hand in Washington Square Park, taking it all in, the hippies and chess players, musicians and politicos. I could hardly believe we actually got to live in New York City. Everything was here, including the world of theater I hoped to be a part of someday.

There was a draft board near campus. It was a few doors down from a bakery where we went between classes sometimes. We'd see guys going inside the draft board, some holding themselves straight and tall, others with shoulders slumped as if they were going to their executions. It always sent a chill between my shoulder blades. The building was nondescript—red brick with big windows—but a place of death.

The political scene at SNY was a wild smorgasbord of pacifists, anti-war liberals, radicals ready to smash the state when they could and some windows in the meantime, counterculture types more interested in smoking dope than making revolution, radicals who believed smoking dope was part of making the revolution, Black Nationalists, Puerto Rican Nationalists, and women's liberationists. I found it hard to negotiate, but Cyn dove right in.

At our first peace rally at SNY, we were mashed close together in a crowd of students in the quad, while another student with long unkempt hair roared into a megaphone against the war, against the state, against Tricky Dick and his pig lackeys, for the victory of the Viet Cong and the freedom of Huey P. Newton, for the People, the revolution, the new world we would forge. "Power to the people!" Cyn yelled, and all around us young people cheered and shouted. Cyn smiled fiercely at me. She had never looked happier or more alive, and I was swept up into joy, into history.

But the next day there was more news of war, more Tricky Dick with his jowls and his lies. The place of death remained open for business.

"Don't go in there," Cyn said one afternoon to a ridiculously young-looking boy with greasy dark hair and bad skin. We'd been about to go inside the bakery for coffee when we spotted the kid staring fixedly at the draft-board door. He jumped when Cyn spoke.

"What?" he asked.

"Don't go in there," she said.

"I have to," he said with a resigned little smile.

"You don't have to. You can burn your draft card. You can be a conscientious objector. You can go to Canada. There are lots of things you can do that don't involve killing and/or being killed." Her tone was soft and earnest. Her tone wasn't soft and earnest very often.

The kid was transfixed by Cyn, with her short skirt and her long hair and her passionate urgency. He glanced back at the draft board, then looked at Cyn again. I held my breath.

Then he turned and went inside the draft board.

"Damn it!" Cyn said. "I almost had him."

"You tried," I said. "His mind was already made up."

She shook her head. Then she gave the draft board the middle finger. "God, I hate that fucking place."

"So do I."

∞

Cyn didn't have a steady boyfriend, though there were always guys around her, guys who wrote for the college newspaper or gave impassioned speeches at the anti-war demos or argued with Cyn about the fine points of Marxism or Maoism. Some of them she slept with once or twice and told me about afterwards: *He's far sexier when he's giving a speech*, or *He's good in bed, but he confuses macho posturing with being a revolutionary.*

Leonard was my first real boyfriend. We met in Freshman Comp, my first semester. He was an intense, homely boy from Newark who wrote poetry and confided that his father told him he was worthless. After our first blissful month as a couple, he'd sometimes shut himself in his dormitory room and not want to talk to me for days at a time, until I felt panicky. "He's being an idiot," Cyn said. "Who does he think he is?" But I was all too relieved when Leonard emerged from his room smiling and saying he still loved me.

"What's your boy like in bed?" Cyn asked when Leonard and I had been together a couple of months.

"None of your business," I replied.

"That bad, huh?"

"I didn't say that!" I had no one to compare him to. I experienced more pleasure on my own, but I got pleasure from his pleasure. Somehow I didn't want to explain this to Cyn.

"I tell *you* everything," Cyn said.

"That's different. I love Lenny."

She peered at me. "Maybe there's more to him than meets the eye."

∞

For the Vietnam Moratorium that November, Cyn and I went to Sheep Meadow in Central Park and lay on our backs on a blanket amid thousands of people, everyone clutching a balloon. Black balloons symbolized those who had died in the war, white those who would die if the war continued. Cyn and I both had white balloons. All of us on the ground were supposed to be corpses. "Taps" played on a bugle. Lying there in the cold, the strangest sense crept up on me of how small and breakable our bodies were, Cyn's and mine and everyone's around us. How easy it would be—a bomb, a bullet (a concentration camp, a gas chamber)—to die. How we were no different from the people dying in Vietnam. Only an accident of birth separated us from their fate.

"Hey," Cyn said, and I turned my head to look at her. "What's wrong?"

"I was just thinking how easy it would be to die," I said. "To be a corpse for real. All of us lying here."

I thought she would laugh it off, but a shiver went through her shoulders. "Stop that. This is just political theater. You of all people should know that."

Her fear made me less afraid, because it was distracting to see Cyn afraid of anything. "I know," I said. "It's true, though, isn't it?"

"Now you've got me freaked out! Just stop it. We're going to live forever."

"No, we're not," I whispered.

A few minutes later we all let go the strings of the balloons and watched them float into the cloudy sky. Like souls going to heaven, I thought, though I didn't believe in heaven.

∞

"Cynthia's very experienced, isn't she?" Leonard asked one night when he and I were naked in his bed.

"I suppose she is," I said.

"Don't you ever wish you were more experienced?"

That stung. "I guess I never thought about it. I just want to be with you, Lenny."

I had gone on the occasional date in high school, mostly to movies and school dances, but I hadn't done more than kiss anyone. When Cyn and I started college, we'd gone to Planned Parenthood together and started taking the Pill, though I was still a virgin. Lenny had been my first. "You don't think a little variety might be fun?" he asked.

The panicky feeling returned. "Is that what you want? Variety?"

"I didn't say that." He stared at the ceiling. "I do think Cynthia is beautiful."

I wanted to say, *Please don't sleep with Cyn or anyone but me.* I wanted to say, *You're hurting me.* But monogamy was dead, and anyone who disagreed was uncool, unrevolutionary, uneverything that I wanted to be.

So it wasn't a surprise when, one night, I walked into Cyn's pot-fragrant bedroom during a party and found Leonard on top of her, his long dark hair flopping into her face, the pasty skin of his back looking particularly unappetizing as his skinny ass pumped between her spread legs. I watched in horrified silence, Janis Joplin singing "Piece of My Heart" on the stereo in the next room, until they noticed I was there.

"Hi, Jo," Cyn said. "Are you having fun at the party?" She was a bit stoned, probably. She, at least, was friendly. Leonard glanced back, stopped moving. He looked annoyed, as if I were a buzzing fly interrupting his pleasure. I left the room in tears. Eventually they found and comforted me. Eventually, after they'd finished.

Leonard wanted to sleep with Cyn again, but she had no interest. Whenever he looked at me, it was with an expression of guilty irritation that filled me with pain. I started avoiding his phone calls and dodging him on campus.

"You're well rid of him," Cyn said. "He's not political enough, and in bed he's nothing to write home about."

"You're right," I said. "On both counts." And we laughed. But for months after, I couldn't hear Janis Joplin without feeling sick to my stomach.

∞

One January morning, Cyn and I stood with a couple hundred protesters outside Hayes Hall, which housed the Mathematical Science Institute. "Ho Ho Ho Chi Minh!" we shouted. My nose kept running from the cold. I clapped my gloved hands in time with the chant to try to warm them. A bearded guy Cyn had slept with carried a large sign that read WAR MACHINE OFF CAMPUS.

"Pigs!" someone yelled, and sure enough, a line of cops with riot helmets and batons was advancing on us. A bolt of fear went through me.

The cops halted several yards from us. One of them lifted a megaphone, but I couldn't hear a lot of what he said over the chanting. "...All persons here are in violation of...hereby ordered to immediately and peacefully disperse..."

No one moved. "Ho Ho Ho Chi Minh!" Minutes passed. The cop with the megaphone gave another dispersal order. We kept up the chant.

A cop raised what I thought was a rifle, and I froze in terror. People screamed. He got off a shot, and pungent clouds wafted over us.

For an instant I was relieved: tear gas, not bullets. Then it hit my throat, and I doubled over coughing. So did Cyn. The crowd scattered. I couldn't catch my breath. Tears poured down my face. "Run!" Cyn cried. Through streaming eyes I saw a boy fall to the ground and a cop's baton descending on him. I straggled after Cyn's pale hair and black peacoat.

When we were clear of the gas and mayhem, I stood under a tree and coughed until I gagged. I dry-heaved again and again. Finally I stopped retching, and Cyn smoothed back my hair. Tears streamed down her face. "Come on, Jo. Let's get out of here."

"I hope that kid wasn't hurt bad," I said croakily an hour later on Cyn's couch, when we had showered and changed out of the tear-gas-reeking clothes. I was wearing a terrycloth robe of Cyn's. It was small on me. "Do you think they made arrests?"

Cyn shrugged. "Probably. Fucking fascists."

"I can't believe the school called the police on us."

She handed me a cup of hot tea with honey, then sipped her own. "Why not? It's clear all they care about is their war profits, not their students."

26

Just then I remembered something. "Christ! Auditions for *Hamlet* are tomorrow, and I can barely speak."

"We live in a fucking police state, and you still give a shit about auditions? It's not like..." She paused to clear her throat. "It's not like you even got in the last play you tried out for."

"Don't rub it in." I wanted to try out for Ophelia. Maybe my voice would be okay by tomorrow. "I told Franny Silver I'd meet her at the audition."

Cyn rolled her eyes. "That's a good reason to stay home."

Franny was in my Shakespeare class. We studied together occasionally. "Franny's nice," I said.

"Nice and boring."

"She's trying out for Ophelia too."

Cyn took a swig of tea. "Shakespeare's so irrelevant right now, Jo."

I didn't have it in me to argue when I could barely talk, so I just sipped my tea. Maybe Cyn was right. Then again, Shakespeare was as full of violence and war as the nightly news.

∞

After the audition, Franny and I sloshed through the rain to the student center. The place was packed with damp kids trying to warm up with a hot drink. We stood in line to buy cups of coffee. Then we snagged the only free table, a tiny one near the window, and hung our damp coats over the backs of our chairs. Franny had long dark hair that hung halfway down her back and large brown eyes. She had on a long flowered dress with a vaguely Renaissance look, but she still looked preppy rather than hippyish. "You're more likely to get the part than me," she said, ripping open a packet of sugar and pouring it into her cup. "You're the ethereal type. Maybe I should've tried out for Gertrude. Not that I'm sexy or mature or anything, but I'm tall. Maybe that would've worked in my favor."

I fingered the lace-trimmed bell sleeve of the dark purple velvet dress (also vaguely Renaissance-looking) I'd worn for the audition. "You think I'm ethereal?" I asked. I sounded like I'd just smoked a whole pack of cigarettes.

Franny smothered a laugh. "You poor thing! I must admit, your voice doesn't sound all that ethereal at the moment."

"Damn it. Hopefully they'll take into account that my voice isn't usually like this." I stared out the window at the miserable rain pelting the campus and remembered my gravelly recitation of Ophelia's mad scene. "Oh, who am I kidding? I didn't get the part."

"Who are we both kidding? Probably Elizabeth Wellesley got the part."

Elizabeth Wellesley had had a major role in every Shakespeare production the school had put on since I'd come to New York City. "Why does she get all the luck?"

"I hate her," Franny said, then smiled ruefully. "Well, I'd like to hate her, except she's really nice, and she can act."

"She *was* really good as Viola." The hot black coffee soothed my throat. "I shouldn't have even bothered today. I guess I hoped my voice would magically clear up when I walked on stage."

"Well, what can you do? It's tough luck having a head cold when you have an audition."

"It's not a cold, Franny. It's tear gas."

Her eyes widened. "You were at that protest yesterday? That's so scary."

I shrugged, now a seasoned veteran of a police riot. "It wasn't much fun," I conceded, and coughed on cue.

"My parents are always warning me not to go to protests. They're pretty liberal, but they don't want me to get my head bashed in."

Phil Ochs' song "Love Me, I'm a Liberal" wafted through my head. "If no one's willing to put their bodies on the line, how will anything ever change?"

Franny pondered. "Well, by voting. The democratic process."

I let out a snort. "Yeah, that's been working so well. The anti-war candidates didn't even make it to the general election, and now we having fucking Nixon."

Franny wagged a finger at me and grinned. "Such language! You sound like your friend Cynthia."

"War is the real obscenity." God, I really did sound like Cyn. I believed the words, but it sounded like I was reading a script.

∞

Sure enough, Elizabeth Wellesley got the part. I told myself it didn't matter. Only ending the war mattered. I had nightmares of gunshots to the head, burning villages, piled corpses. When I was awake, the nightmares rose up to find me in the pages of the *New York Times* and on the nightly news.

Cyn and I kept going to protests. Each time, I feared there would be tear gas and batons, but there was only more chanting, more holding up picket signs, all of it seeming entirely ineffectual except that not protesting would have meant tacit approval of the war. I kept thinking of my epiphany at Sheep Meadow: that there was no difference between us and the North Vietnamese, just luck. We could have been the ones shot in the head, napalmed, reduced to dead meat.

∞

"Fuck," Cyn kept saying as we stared at the TV screen. "Oh, *fuck.*" We had heard the news hours ago on campus, but somehow Walter Cronkite at the anchor desk made it real. The National Guard had opened fire on a crowd of protesters at Kent State. Four students were dead.

"I keep thinking that it could've been us," I said when the news broadcast went to a tire commercial. We were sitting on Cyn's sofa, our legs drawn up. We had been at a campus rally when the speaker railing against the invasion of Cambodia had been handed a piece of paper containing the news. People had wept and raged and shaken their heads in horrified disbelief.

"It could still be us, Jo," Cyn said, wiping her eyes with the back of her hand. She got to her feet and began to pace, hands balled into fists. "They're not even pretending they're not fascists anymore."

I remembered the cop raising his gun at the Hayes protest—the instant when I thought it would be bullets, not tear gas. I imagined cops aiming and firing on us as we screamed and tried to run. Bullets ripping through my body. Falling to the ground, bleeding and in pain, or dead instantly. That was what they had felt, those students in Ohio. A jolt of fear went through me. I hugged myself, still safe and alive, for now.

"Thank god we're striking tomorrow," Cyn said. "I have to *do* something. I have to do *something*, you know?"

"I know," I said, though I wondered if doing something would make me feel less afraid, or more.

∞

The next afternoon Cyn and I stood with dozens of protesters outside Masters Hall, a hulking brick classroom building in the north part of campus. That morning students had occupied it, along with other classroom buildings. From a third-floor window hung a banner that read WE STRIKE FOR JUSTICE! with a drawing of a clenched fist beneath the words.

It was a bright, sunny day, and I tried to angle my picket sign to block the sun from my face. My sign said: POWER TO THE PEOPLE. Cyn's said: SHUT IT DOWN! Cyn had on ripped jeans and a black t-shirt. (I had on a black t-shirt and jeans with no rips.) She was chatting a few feet away with Ed and Teddy, two radicals she'd slept with. Ed had a gaunt, beautiful face. Teddy's broad face was mostly obscured by a fuzzy beard. He kept saying something about "the fucking pigs" and laughing hectically. I tried to remember which of the guys Cyn had said was better in bed.

The school buzzed with a bright, dark energy. The student strike was a carnival and a wake simultaneously. So far there was no police presence. I'd even seen a few professors joining the strike. A shaggy-haired guy with an acoustic guitar sat on the grass in front of the building and sang Dylan's "Masters of War," while a clump of students sat and listened solemnly. Near them, a copy of the well-known anti-war poster lay in the grass: WAR IS NOT HEALTHY FOR CHILDREN AND OTHER LIVING THINGS. I couldn't tell if it belonged to someone or had been abandoned.

"Look at what's happening to Angela Davis!" Cyn exclaimed. "I would give anything to study philosophy with her instead of the fucking lackluster philosophy profs we have here. So of course UCLA tried to fired her, because god forbid she's a Communist, but the students are taking her classes anyway, even if it's not for credit. What does course credit matter? The university system isn't a place for revolutionary thought. We have to take it over."

"Burn it down, man," Ed said.

"Yeah, burn the fucker down!" Teddy yelled, and he laughed and laughed.

Franny came walking across the lawn. She paused and listened to the music, then saw me and headed over. "Et tu, Joanna?" she said with a bemused smile. She had on a white button-down shirt and a long flowered skirt, and she was lugging her collected Shakespeare and a notebook.

"You know classes are canceled, right?" I asked.

She looked wistfully at Masters Hall. "Yeah, but I guess I was hoping. I was really looking forward to hearing what Professor Michaels had to say about *The Tempest*."

Our Shakespeare class would have been about to start. Professor Michaels had a beautiful English accent, and he always set my mind alight with his observations. "Me too," I admitted. "But this is more important."

She widened her eyes at me. "More important than Shakespeare? Say it ain't so, Jo!"

"Very funny. Four kids died yesterday, Franny."

Her smile faded as if I'd slapped her. "I know that, and it's horrible. But canceling classes won't bring them back." Something caught her attention. "Look, it's Professor Michaels!"

I turned to follow her gaze. The professor was walking towards Masters Hall. With his short hair, lightweight gray suit and leather briefcase, he couldn't have looked more out of place. He tried the building door. When it didn't open, he turned, frowning, and saw us. I felt like hiding but kept my picket sign aloft as he walked toward us.

"I wonder how long this will last?" he said wearily in his beautiful, urbane accent. He always reminded me of Patrick McGoohan.

"Not too long, I hope!" Franny chirped.

Professor Michaels eyed my picket sign. "'Power to the people,'" he quoted with mild irony. "I wouldn't have expected you to be part of this crowd, Joanna." He didn't sound reproachful, just surprised.

"Well, we have to do *something*," I said. "The killing—it has to stop." I had never spoken to him except about Shakespeare. I felt flustered and inarticulate.

Professor Michaels gazed at me intently. Then he sighed. "Perhaps you're right. Perhaps, in the face of such horrors, business as usual is inappropriate. On the other hand, I can't help but wonder if the best way to meet such horrors is to continue with the business of this university, which is to think, to reason, to study art and literature and history. Isn't all of that the opposite of the mindless slaughter you're protesting today?"

I thought he was completely right and wrong at the same time. I didn't know how to respond. The guy with the guitar had finished "Masters of War" and was singing "Lay Lady Lay," a song I despised. It made it even harder to formulate a reply. "Maybe," I said finally. "But the business of the university isn't enough. Not today."

"Well, I think you're right," Franny told the professor. I felt like kicking her.

Cyn strode up, picket sign down at her side, and put her arm around my shoulders. "Come on, Jo," she said. "Rally in the quad." Then she smiled up at the professor. "Join us! Join the strike!"

A smile played on his lips. Was it my imagination, or was he blushing? "Thank you for the invitation, but I'd best be going. Joanna, Frances, I'll see you in class when it resumes."

We watched him go. "He's sort of sexy for an old dude," Cyn remarked.

"He's not that old!" Franny said.

Cyn glanced at Franny as if she'd only just noticed her. Then she turned to me. "Come on, Jo."

"You coming to the rally?" I asked Franny.

She shook her head. "You know what my parents would say."

Cyn did a double take. "You can't be serious!"

"We can't all be rebels," Franny said airily.

Cyn led me away. "What a little twit," she said when we were, I hoped, out of earshot.

∞

When it was her turn to speak, Cyn brandished the megaphone and stood ramrod straight in front of hundreds of students in the quad. "We're at war," she said. "Not just in Vietnam. Here, in the United States of America. The National Guard fired on white kids at Kent State. Make no mistake, no longer are the pigs only killing black militants. Don't think it can't happen to you, just because of the color of your skin. Don't kid yourself. If you oppose the war, if you oppose racism and imperialism, that makes you an enemy of the state. The truth is, they're afraid of us—afraid of *us*! And they should be afraid, because we're going to tear their house down!"

The crowd cheered wildly. Cyn raised her fist in the air. It was her moment, as *Saint Joan* had been mine. But this was real life, real death. I thought of Joan of Arc, and of those college kids who'd been martyred. What would we be willing to sacrifice?

Chapter Three:
Poetry Man
(September 1975)

The morning of my first love scene with Martin, I woke with a pounding heart and a dry mouth. What was more, when I walked to the studio in the mild autumn weather, my skin felt tender and too warm, and I started to ache all over. I couldn't be getting sick, not today.

"Larry took me to dinner at La Côte Basque," Babette was telling David Halpren when I walked into the rehearsal room. It was a large, windowless space on the second floor of the studio. There were folding chairs and card tables scattered about, and a table with a coffee urn and pastries by the door. Babs and David had Styrofoam cups of coffee before them on their table, but I didn't want to have coffee breath when I kissed Martin. Where was Martin, anyway? He usually got here before I did.

"Sounds like a wonderful date," David said. "Are you going to see him again?"

Babette and David were both startlingly good-looking, even first thing in the morning. Babs had on no makeup (most of the women in the company tended not to wear any to the studio, since they'd wind up in the makeup chair before taping anyway), but she was still stunning, with enormous blue eyes, auburn ringlets, and pronounced cheekbones. As for David, his clean-cut good looks translated well to the TV screen, but he was almost unnaturally handsome in person, like a Ken doll come to life. Unlike Babette, though, he was a good actor.

"I'm seeing him tomorrow night," Babette said. There was a tremulous softness to her voice that surprised me. "I like him, David. It's refreshing spending time with a man who isn't in show business. He's so down to earth."

I stood there, wondering if I should intrude on their conversation. Babs looked up with a smile and said, "Join us, Joanna."

"What does Larry do?" I asked, sitting next to her. She sometimes talked with a breezily cynical tone about some unnamed man she'd been seeing, but this clearly was a different guy.

"Can you believe he's a cardiologist?" Babette played a cardiologist on *Hope Springs Eternal*.

"How'd you meet him?" I asked.

"Oh, he came up to me in Bloomingdale's one afternoon and asked me out. He recognized me from the show."

I shook my head. No one in the outside world seemed to recognize me from the show, aside from a few people who'd asked for my autograph outside the studio. I was never mobbed by autograph seekers like Babette was—and never in my life had I been asked out by a complete stranger. I had a feeling that happened to Babette a lot.

"So how's your new place, Joanna?" David asked. His voice was smooth and bland as a radio announcer's.

I had just moved from the small, crummy apartment in Chelsea I'd shared with a roommate to a small but nicer place near the studio. "It's wonderful living someplace with an elevator," I said. "My last place was a third floor walk-up. Now I just need to fix the place up."

"You should have a housewarming," Babette said.

"First I need to get some furniture for the living room." A wave of fatigue swept through me. I unzipped my purse, found a tissue and wiped my nose. There was no denying it, I was coming down with the flu, with the unmistakable fever and chills that always reminded me of what had happened four years ago. Which reminded me of seeing Cyn at Chauncy's. But I hadn't seen Cyn. Of course I hadn't.

"I know some adorable furniture places," Babs said. "We could go together sometime."

"That'd be great, Babette." I rarely did anything socially with anyone from the show, so I was pleasantly surprised by Babs's overture—but I was distracted by the onrush of flu symptoms. I wiped my nose again and put the tissue back in my purse. I sniffled. Oh, this was just marvelous. I was going to sneeze all over Martin and forget my lines. Martin had to kiss me today, for godsake.

Just then Martin walked in, and my stomach did a backwards somersault. "Morning, all," he said and headed for the coffee urn. Apparently he didn't care about having coffee breath when he kissed me. Oh well, if he was going to drink coffee, I could too. I'd pop a mint or two afterwards. I checked my purse to make sure the mints I'd bought hadn't miraculously disappeared, then got up and poured myself a cup. "Morning, Marty," I said as he deliberated among the pastry choices.

He glanced up. "Hi, Hot Lips," he said, and grinned.

"Very funny." I smacked his arm and nearly made him spill his coffee.

"Hey!"

"Oops. Sorry." I lowered my voice. "Hey, Marty, I think I'm coming down with the flu or something. I hope you don't catch it."

He reached out and touched my forehead with the back of his hand, which was cool and soothing. "You do feel a bit warm. Poor kid."

"I don't want you to get sick too." What did I expect, for him to tell the director to call off the love scene?

"Occupational hazard," he said. "Anyway, I never get sick. Too mean to get sick, my wife always says." Then he looked at me sharply. "Unless…"

"Unless…?"

"You're not gonna throw up, are you?"

I assessed myself: I had a nervous stomach, but nothing horrible. "Oh, no, it's nothing like that."

"That's good. One time I was doing a screen test with a girl who was trying out for *Hope Springs Eternal*, and suffice it to say, it's too bad she wasn't trying out for *The Exorcist*."

"What, her head spun around? She levitated?" I marveled at my ability to joke at a time like this.

Martin chuckled appreciatively. "She puked all over one of my favorite shirts. Nice girl, though." He plucked a powdered donut from the pink cardboard box.

I wasn't going to vomit on Martin, so apparently everything was okay in his book. For a moment I felt downright relaxed. Then the director walked in, and my nervous system went back on alert.

The day's production schedule began. First we ran through our lines with our scripts on our laps. Then we went on set for camera blocking. Different sets were packed together on the soundstage. A hospital nurses' station was cheek by jowl with the living room of Jean Christopher's apartment. Next to the living room was Dr. Vicki Jameson's office, complete with medical plaques on the walls. The sets were a lot smaller than they appeared on TV, and, of course, they didn't have ceilings. Above, where the walls ended, were clusters upon clusters of lights.

Martin and I sat on the small sofa in Jean's living room, which had a braided rug on the floor and a manual typewriter on a desk in the corner. Vincent Lassiter, today's director, loomed above us. He was a stocky man with salt-and-pepper hair and a nose like a prizefighter. "No, you've gotta tilt your head like this, Joanna," he said, tilting his head to one side.

"Try it again." I tilted my head, and Martin started to lean in, and Vincent said, "No, no, no—like *this*!" I giggled uncontrollably as Vince took my face in his hands and guided me into position. "Otherwise it's gonna look like a train wreck."

Martin eyed me indulgently. "Having a bit of a nervous breakdown, are we?"

I nodded helplessly. Nodding only made me dizzy, which reminded me that I was going to have my first on-screen love scene when I was stuffed up and disgusting.

"Come here, you," Martin said. His cool hand cupped my cheek, and I snapped to attention. Love scenes were so strange, though we tried to pretend they weren't—kissing someone for art, or money, or both. It was strange to have Martin's face close to mine. Strange and also terrific. I tilted my head just so, and my eyes drifted closed, and he kissed me.

"You've got it," Vincent said.

After camera blocking, we broke for lunch. Then there was the run-through and the dress rehearsal. After that, Vincent sat between me and Martin on Jean's living-room sofa and gave us his notes. "Your feelings for Sam are genuine," he told me, "but this is also about Vicki. You love your cousin, you don't want to wreck her marriage, but you always wanted to be like her. You envied her looks, her career, her love life. In a way, being with Sam means you get to be her." Something about what he said made me uneasy. Maybe it was that I didn't think Jean envied Vicki exactly. Her beauty, sure, and the men she attracted—but Jean had never wanted to be a doctor, and she thought Vicki was a little uptight and conservative.

I had given Jean a little of my back story, mine and Cyn's. Jean had written against the war in her school newspaper in high school and college. She'd covered the anti-war rallies and marches, as well as the Black Power movement and women's liberation. Maybe she'd believed in the revolution, but wielding the pen and the typewriter insulated her from more direct action.

When it became apparent that revolution wasn't as imminent in this country as it had seemed, uncovering corruption à la Woodward and Bernstein became her quest. She didn't entirely understand that her actions had potentially negative consequences and that everything might not turn out all right.

"You don't mean for any of this to happen," Vincent was telling Martin. "It's just, you're so sick of arguing with your wife all the time, and this girl comes along, she's so open and so full of hope, it's like a new lease on life. You like who you are with her." Martin nodded seriously, with that look he got when he was internalizing some new aspect of the story or his character. Then he looked over at me and smiled with such open affection that I held my breath for a moment, unsure whether he was smiling at me or Jean. I decided it might be both, and I smiled back.

Finally we taped our scenes. I needn't have worried that I'd be okay to tape the show with the flu coming on. As soon as the stage manager said, "Scene one, take one," and clapped the slate in front of one of the cameras, I was fine. Even my sinuses cleared, like magic. A surge of well-being swept through me. I was free to be Jean Christopher, who was still idealistic, still emotionally wide open. Now that she had her own story, it was increasingly a joy to play her.

The three cameras glided across the floor trailing snarls of cables. Sam's black coat was slung over a chair. On the table before us were a pile of notes, a yellow pad, and two coffee cups. We sat on the sofa and drank coffee and uttered pages and pages of dialogue about uncovering Mayor Read's shady dealings. I had forgotten that we had to drink coffee during our scenes. Everyone drank so much coffee on this show. Was that true of all daytime dramas? These tales of adultery were all a pretext for getting housewives to buy coffee by the truckload, on the off chance that drinking it would lead to getting kissed by the likes of Sam Jameson.

We taped our three scenes in a row, since they were all on the same set. "It's amazing, isn't it, Sam—putting together the pieces of a story," I said towards the end of the third scene. "Piecing together the truth. It's the best feeling in the world."

"Sometimes it is, depending on what the truth turns out to be," he said. "The truth can be pretty ugly, Jeanie." No one else in Hopefield called me Jeanie. He said the word with such tenderness.

The cameras moved in close, science fiction monsters with their eyes on us. I focused on Martin, on his earnest gaze that made me feel safe and important. I smiled Jean's broad, joyful smile. "But uncovering the ugliness, bringing injustice to light…that's the first step toward making the world a better place," I said. "What could be more beautiful?" Maybe it was because of my fever, but the scene reminded me of the talk we'd had at Chauncy's, or a slightly romanticized version.

He smiled at me, and the most dazzling astonishment bloomed on his face. He was looking at me in a way that made my stomach do a slow flip and my body fill up with light. "Beautiful," he said, leaning towards me. We both hesitated— then we kissed in a long moment of perfection. We both had coffee breath, but it didn't matter.

∞

When we'd finished taping, I could tell my fever had gone up, but I felt euphoric. Babette and David had already taped their scenes in the hospital sets, and Martin and I found them chatting outside the door to the stairwell that led up to the dressing rooms. They still had on their doctors' outfits. Babs managed to look voluptuous in a lab coat. "Believe me, I know it's past time," she was saying.

"Moving forward can be frightening…" David replied, then trailed off when he saw us.

"Sounds like a serious philosophical discussion," Martin said with a trace of irony.

Babs shrugged. "Just talking about life."

"Oh, that," Martin said.

Babs rolled her eyes at him, then quickly turned to me. "So Jo, let me know when you want to go furniture shopping."

"I will," I said. "Thanks."

"That's right, you just moved," Martin said. "How's your new apartment?"

"It's nice. Underfurnished, though. Needs a lot of work." A Mae West voice in my head leered, *Come up and see me sometime.* I couldn't stop looking at Martin. His face and body, clad in Sam's jeans, red plaid shirt and black coat, seemed to give off a radiance. The harsh planes of his face were beautiful.

"I'm going to help Jo shop for her new place," Babs told Martin.

"Oh, you are, are you?" he asked. "Somehow I doubt Jo shares your fondness for red velvet."

Her eyes widened. "I have a beautiful apartment! Don't I, David?"

David smiled mildly. "Of course, Babette. It's very *you*."

"Oh, you're a big help!" she burst out, and the men laughed. I was starting to get the picture of Babette's apartment, feminine and glamorous as Babs herself, though I wasn't clear whether the effect was tacky or tasteful. Either way, it wouldn't be my style. I almost wished it were.

∞

Martin, Babette, and I went back to the rehearsal room for the table-read for Monday's show. After that, I went to my dressing room. My reflection in the mirror was flushed with fever, but I also glowed ridiculously from being kissed. I wagged a finger at myself and said, "Only make-believe." But I couldn't remember ever seeing myself look so beautiful, hazel eyes shining, lips curving into a smile I couldn't stop, my lips that his had kissed, would kiss again in other episodes, the joy of it, the utter silly joy. When was the last time I'd been kissed?

It must have been when I was with Ian, who I'd stopped seeing long before I'd joined *Hope Springs Eternal*—and Ian had stopped kissing me long before we'd stopped sleeping together. It had indeed been a while, and technically these kisses didn't count. Martin had to kiss me. It was his job. But I didn't care.

I had barely pulled off Jean Christopher's brown suede boots when there was a knock on the door. "You decent?" Martin called.

"Come in!" I said.

The door opened, and he peeked his head in—then he entered. "Hey, I was just thinking. If you need furniture, I might be able to help you out." He leaned with casual grace against the counter. "I still have a few chairs and a table from my old apartment. They're in the attic, and they should be in pretty good shape. Nothing fancy, but you might like them."

"Thanks! That'd be great."

"Don't thank me until I've taken a look to make sure they haven't been gnawed by mice or anything. If they're all right, I can bring them by sometime."

"How much would you want for them?"

"*Want* for them?" He looked at me as if I were nuts. "It'd be a gift. Or you could consider it a permanent loan."

"I'd really appreciate it, Marty." I felt it would be perfectly natural to reach up and touch his hand, or to stand up and touch his cheek, stroke his hair, put my arms around his neck and kiss him. In my feverish mind I was doing those things as we talked. Then I sniffled and reached for the box of Kleenex on the counter.

"Poor kid," Martin said. "Go home already. Get some rest."

"I hope you don't catch this bug."

"Don't worry about me. Just take care of yourself." He was looking at me with that warm, steady gaze.

"I will."

He opened the door, then turned and lingered in the doorway. "Great work today," he said, and smiled. "I'm so glad you're here."

"Thanks, Marty. I'm glad, too."

"I'm serious. Sam's not the only one with a new lease on life. Creatively speaking."

As I gazed at him, Martin and Sam merged, then separated again. "That's good to hear," I murmured.

"See you next week, kid."

When he'd closed the door behind him, I saw myself grinning like a fool in the mirror. I pulled the cream turtleneck over my head and unzipped my dark green skirt. I looked at myself in beige bra and white panties in the mirror. Maybe I did look a little like Liv Ullmann, though my hair was darker, and my eyes weren't blue.

I pulled on my brown wool sweater, then let out a cry: Cyn was standing behind me in the mirror. She looked just as she had at Chauncy's, with her short hair, black peacoat and jeans. I turned—there was no one there. I turned back and saw only my reflection.

A wave of dizziness went through me. I touched my hot forehead with the back of my hand. I didn't feel like I was running such a high fever that I could be hallucinating, but then, I had never hallucinated from a fever before, so how would I know? Cyn had been staring at me the way she had at Chauncy's. No, she hadn't. It was just the fever. It had to be. Or maybe…I'd been thinking of Liv Ullmann. There was that scene in *Persona*, the famous two-shot of Liv Ullmann and Bibi Andersson facing the camera. Cyn looked like Bibi Andersson with her short blonde hair. Maybe I'd been remembering that. Just remembering a scene from a movie.

I hurriedly stepped into my jeans and pulled on my own boots. I put on my coat and slung my purse over my shoulder. When I left the dressing room and pulled the door shut, I had the urge to go to Martin's dressing room and see if he was still there. Why? To tell him I'd seen my dead best friend in the mirror? It was just that I felt safe with him, and I felt so off-kilter right now.

I walked down the hall. His dressing room door was ajar. Before I could stop myself, I knocked softly, and it opened further. Martin had Babette pressed against the far wall. His hands were on her ass, her arms around his neck as they kissed. Of course, I thought. Of course! Then Babette saw me and let out a squeak. Martin turned and saw me. They leapt apart like soap opera characters.

"You didn't lock the door?" Babs asked Martin and shook her head. "It takes brains, Marty." She smoothed her disheveled hair. She still had on Vicki's light blue pullover and brown skirt, minus her hospital smock, which lay in a heap on the floor along with Sam's black coat.

Martin just stood there, expression blank. A laugh forced itself from his lungs. "Hi, Jo," he said. Then something that looked like shame dragged his mouth into a frown. His whole face darkened with it.

"Sorry," I said. "I did knock."

"Did you want something, Jo?" Babs asked brusquely.

"It's nothing," I murmured. "Sorry…" I turned and hurried down the hall towards the stairwell. I had to slow down and clutch the banister on my way down the stairs because my head was spinning with fever. As I pushed through the glass door of the lobby onto the street, I heard Cyn speak distinctly in my ear: *The flu didn't keep you home today, did it, Joanna? How interesting. I guess this actually matters to you.*

Chapter Four:
Love Will Keep Us Together
(September 1975)

"Not real not real not real," I chanted at my bathroom sink as I removed the day's makeup. Moving the cream across my cheeks and forehead seemed like an awful lot of work. The Noxzema felt cool on my skin, but I was so stuffed up, I could barely smell its odor of menthol and eucalyptus. I eyed my reflection in the mirror—just me, no Cyn. Seeing Cyn, hearing her, hadn't been real. I'd really seen Martin and Babette kissing, hadn't I? It seemed as unreal in its way.

I splashed water on my face, and it felt shockingly cold. Then I dried my face with a blue hand towel that seemed rougher than usual. I still needed to take off my eye makeup and reached for the baby oil on the counter next to the bottle of Love's Fresh Lemon. I remembered the purple egg of violet spray cologne Toni liked to wear. I wasn't used to living alone. In my old apartment, where Toni still lived, but with a new roommate, the bathroom counter had been a riot of lipsticks and mascara, combs and hairbrushes, perfumes and lotions. We had been struggling artists together—Toni was a dancer—and she'd been enthusiastic at first when I'd been hired by *Hope Springs Eternal.* She'd regaled me with stories about watching the show with her grandmother when she was a kid in Bed-Stuy. (It had been her grandma's favorite show, though as far as I knew it had never had any black characters.) But when I'd got into the routine of working at the studio while

Toni kept waitressing and auditioning, she had grown cold and resentful. I'd missed her even before I moved out.

It was almost too much effort to change into a nightgown, but I managed it. Then I got in bed and lay beneath blankets and a quilt with the bedside lamp on, wrapped in the almost comforting cocoon of my fever, a Kleenex clutched in my fist. I listened to the whoosh and honking of traffic and the muffled sound of the next door neighbor's radio: "Love, love will keep us together."

Thank god it was the weekend, and I'd have a chance to rest up and shake this bug, and I wouldn't have to see Martin and Babette for a couple of days. What a stupid cliché, becoming infatuated with an actor just because the characters you played were falling in love. But Martin was the least of my worries. Surely when my fever went down, I would know I hadn't seen or heard Cyn. Then why had I seen her at Chauncy's? I hadn't been sick then. Was I losing my mind? If so, maybe I hadn't really seen Martin and Babette kissing. Somehow that thought wasn't terribly comforting.

Every time I closed my eyes, I had the uncanny feeling that cameras were hovering over me and that the room didn't have a ceiling. I opened my eyes, and the beige ceiling loomed reassuringly over me in the half-light. I wondered how high my fever was, but the last thing I wanted to do was haul myself out of bed and take my temperature. I closed my eyes again and dozed. Oh well, if I needed to go to the hospital, all I had to do was walk into the next set. What? I opened my eyes, and I was in my narrow bed with the patchwork quilt, in my small bedroom that contained the chest of drawers I'd had since I was ten and a couple of bookshelves mostly crammed with plays. Cyn sat perched on the edge of the bed.

"Must be dreaming," I murmured and closed my eyes again. When I opened them, she was still there. Her skinny legs were bare and crossed at the knee. She had on a white tennis outfit. I hadn't seen her in such attire since we were in high school. I remembered her clobbering me at tennis the one time we played together. "You're still here," I said.

"I've been here for a while," she said. "Waiting for you to wake up."

I dragged myself upright to sit against the headboard. "But I'm still asleep. I must be."

"Why is that?"

"Because you're here," I said. "You're here, so I must be dreaming. Unless I'm hallucinating from the fever."

Cyn smiled slightly. "Your logic leaves something to be desired, Jo."

"You and your logic. The *Science of Logic*. Who was that, Hegel?"

"Hegel." She said the name as if it were something from a long way off, something she hadn't thought of in a thousand years. There was something unutterably sad about the way she said it, and I wanted to change the subject.

"So go ahead, Cyn. Tell me you don't approve of my being on a soap opera. I always knew you wouldn't."

She considered that for a moment, her head tilted to one side. "It's a kind of power, I suppose," she said finally. "And you're good at it, so you may as well do it."

"It beats being a temporary secretary, that's for damn sure." My voice came out croaky, and I cleared my throat.

"But you do know it's all about the commercials, Joanna. You're selling diapers and dishwashing liquid to bored housewives."

"And coffee," I said. "Don't forget about coffee. We're always drinking coffee in Hopefield."

Her face was moon pale in the lamplight, her short blonde hair like a skullcap, making her look like Joan of Arc. As if she'd read my mind, she said, "Not exactly George Bernard Shaw, is it?" Her small blue eyes glittered like undersea pearls.

Pearls that were her eyes, I thought—but that wasn't even the right playwright.

"Never got over that, did you?" I said. "My getting that part instead of you. For that matter, my getting anything you didn't."

Cyn laughed low in her throat. "In the grand scheme of things, *Saint Joan* doesn't seem like such a big deal."

I picked up the crumpled tissue next to my pillow and swiped at my nose with it. Then I croakily recited: "Can a poor burnt-up lass have a ghost? I am but a dream that thourt dreaming." I was impressed that I remembered the lines correctly in a dream. Or maybe I only thought they were correct because I was dreaming? It didn't feel exactly like a dream, except for the fever making everything unreal.

Cyn brought her small hands together three times in ironic applause. "You always were great at memorization, Jo. But there's only one thing I envy you for now. That's breathing, and all the stuff that goes with it. Like dancing, and drinking hot coffee, and fucking." She raised a pale eyebrow. "It's been a while for you, hasn't it, Jo?"

"I'll have you know I drank hot coffee this morning."

Cyn grinned, her sharp little nose and thin lips making her look like a ravenous fox. "How many mornings since you've had company in this teensy little bed of yours?"

"None of your fucking business."

Cyn laughed and wriggled delightedly on the bed's edge, but the bed didn't move. "Oho! And none of *your* fucking business either, apparently. Poor Joanna. Maybe you can screw that dude you had the scene with today. I'm pretty sure he wants to."

"'That dude' is married, Cyn."

"Who cares? Nobody owns anybody." She flicked a glance at me. "Almost nobody, anyway."

"And he has a gorgeous girlfriend on the side," I added.

"That redhead? She's nothing much."

I shivered. Had Cyn been spying on me at the studio? I'd seen her in the mirror. That had been part of the dream, right?

"Will you be quiet already?" I murmured, although it occurred to me that that was a pretty rude thing to say to someone I hadn't talked to in four years. It *was* nice having a friend in the apartment. "Not that I don't appreciate the visit, but I've got the flu. I need to rest."

"You can sleep when you're dead. And you can't get rid of me that easily."

"Don't wanna get rid of you. I never wanted that. Just want some rest, Cyn. We can talk in the morning." I lay down and turned onto my side, away from the lamplight, away from Cyn. I thought to turn round again, to reach up to turn off the lamp, but I didn't want to move. I felt like I was baking from the inside. Cyn was softly humming something, lulling me to sleep. What was she humming? Oh yeah, Nina Simone, "I Wish I Knew How It Would Feel To Be Free." We had always loved that song.

∞

Sun streamed through the blinds. I squeezed my eyes shut and snuffled uncomfortably. My nightgown was drenched and felt clammy. Shreds of a song played in my head. That's right, Nina Simone. Then I remembered, and I heaved myself upright. Of course there was no Cyn perched on the edge of the bed.

Then I saw it, at the corner where Cyn had sat. Neatly placed so its edges were flush with the edges of the bed. My old well-thumbed paperback of *Saint Joan*.

Chapter Five:
Street Fighting Man
(January–February 1971)

Cyn and I went to see *The Battle of Algiers* one night at a little theater near campus a week after the new year. On the movie screen, three Algerian women put on Western garb and makeup. One woman cut her hair short and bleached it. Drums pounded on the soundtrack. A man gave the women the handbags and their instructions. They carried the handbags past the French soldiers at the checkpoints. In a room, a man with wire-rimmed glasses set the clocks. The women had half an hour to place the handbags. In the cafe, French guys and girls danced to a jaunty tune cut short by the blast. The terrible beauty of it.

After the film ended, we walked into the lobby, the ululations of the Algerian women still ringing in our ears. And there they were, leaning against the concession stand: two guys, one tall and thin, with a pale mustache and wire rims, the other slender with dark, curly hair. They approached us. "Hey," the bespectacled one asked Cyn, "didn't I see you at the Free Angela rally the other week?"

"You may have," she said. "I saw you give a speech once, at one of the demos. That was a while ago." She'd managed to dress him down and compliment him in the same breath.

"I was out of circulation for a while," he said. "I'm Alex. This is Jeremy. Your first time seeing the film?"

Cyn had to admit it was. Point one for Alex. "I'm Cynthia. This is Joanna. Her first time seeing it too."

51

"I've seen it five times!" Jeremy blurted out, then looked at his shoes. I liked him from the start.

The four of us walked out into the cold Village night and ended up back at Cyn's place. Alex produced a joint that mostly he and Cyn smoked. Alex smelled of patchouli. Jeremy didn't. We exchanged cursory information. Alex had gone to SNY but dropped out his senior year. Jeremy was in his senior year there, majoring in biochemistry. Both guys had been members of Students for Peace and Justice before it was torn apart by sectarianism.

Cyn put *Rehearsals for Retirement* on the turntable, took Alex's hand, and led him into the bedroom. The door shut. Jeremy and I were left to smile awkwardly at each other in the overheated, pot-redolent living room. I wasn't nearly stoned enough. "Do you want some wine?" I asked. "I think Cyn has some."

Jeremy nodded. As Phil Ochs sang "Pretty Smart on My Part," I went into the kitchenette and found a half-empty bottle of cheap red in a cabinet. There were no wine glasses; I brought the bottle and a couple of tumblers into the living room.

Jeremy was sitting on the couch studying the cover of *Rehearsals for Retirement*. I put the tumblers on the coffee table amid a riot of political flyers and pamphlets: *Free Angela. Free the Panther 21. U.S. Out of Vietnam. Victory for the NLF!* I uncorked the wine, poured a bit and tasted it. Thankfully it hadn't gone off. I poured us each a healthy glassful, then sat on the other end of the couch. "Do you like Phil Ochs?" I asked.

"This record cover is strange." He handed it to me. The cover showed a gravestone in the grass. On the gravestone there was a photo of strapping, handsome Phil Ochs in a dark suit, standing in front of an American flag, a rifle slung across his back. Beneath the photo were the words: "Phil Ochs (American), Born: El Paso, Texas 1940. Died: Chicago, Illinois 1968. Rehearsals for Retirement." Phil Ochs liked to say that he'd died in Chicago during the police riot at the Democratic National Convention.

"It is strange," I agreed.

A moan—male—wafted out from the bedroom, then another. Great. I considered turning up the record. I considered suggesting going someplace else, but it was cold outside, and I'd only just thawed out. Jeremy and I assiduously pretended we hadn't heard anything.

He belted down some wine. "I was at that Angela Davis rally too. So were you, right?"

I nodded, flattered he'd noticed. "The charges against Angela are such a frame-up," I said. "They're making an example of her." This was something I cared passionately about, but I feared it came out sounding stupidly self-evident.

Jeremy looked at me for a long time. His eyes were large and dark. Finally he said, "What Cynthia said about seeing Alex speak at a demo a while ago but not since? He was badly beaten by the cops at a demo about a year ago. He was out of it for a while."

"How awful. Were you and Alex friends then?"

He shook his head. "I knew who he was. He and his friends were, well, not movement stars exactly, but visible—but he barely knew me. Then his friends went underground. He was in the hospital and then stuck at home with his parents in Bridgeport while he recuperated. I kept visiting and bringing him stuff to read. That's when we became friends."

"That was nice of you, to do all that for him."

He shrugged. "I guess I felt responsible for him, seeing what they did to him. Two pigs worked him over with batons. Kicked him, broke his ribs, fractured his skull. He was lying in the street. His face was covered in blood, and he was moaning. Then he passed out. I thought he was dead."

"How horrible." I remembered the panicky feeling of being tear gassed, the sight of that boy being clubbed by a cop.

Jeremy drank some wine. "Someone called an ambulance, and I waited with Alex. Then I rode with him to the emergency room." He was looking at me with a strangely intense gaze. "I believed in pacifism until that day. After that, I thought pacifism was just giving them free rein—giving them license to do what they did. And then Kent State happened, and Jackson State, and I knew I was right."

On the stereo, Phil Ochs was singing "I Kill Therefore I Am." I peered at Jeremy. Likely he'd been around during the student strike after the killings at Kent State, but I hadn't noticed him. He was quiet and unassuming, not like the usual loudmouth politicos around campus. Yet he had this to say, and I couldn't argue with him.

"I think nonviolence has its limits," I said. "I mean, nonviolence can be an act of violence too, if it permits violence to go on."

He nodded and nodded, as if that was exactly the right thing to say. He leaned toward me and spoke just above a whisper. "I taught myself to make a pipe bomb while Alex was recuperating. I kept telling myself I was gonna blow up a police station as a reprisal for what they did to him. But Alex said that was too big an action for me to do alone, and there were more important reasons to hit a target than what had happened to him."

"Wow." I didn't know what to say. Bombings of government buildings and the offices of war profiteers had been fairly commonplace for the past couple of years, but I'd never talked to anyone who admitted to being involved. I wasn't against it, at least on a theoretical level, if no one was injured—but still, talking about it felt dangerous. Dangerous or exciting? Maybe both.

"I guess I shouldn't have told you that," Jeremy said. "For all I know, you could be an agent."

"What, like a Fed? A member of the Red Squad?" I started to laugh. "You think Cyn and I trawl screenings of *The Battle of Algiers* looking for radicals to bust?"

He grinned. I liked the way his smile made me feel. "I was just kidding," he said. "I've seen you and Cynthia around campus for a long time. You don't really seem like FBI infiltrators."

I wished I could say I'd seen him around campus too. "So have you blown anything up?" I whispered.

He shook his head. "Even though protests don't seem to accomplish much."

"I know exactly what you mean."

We drank wine and listened to Phil Ochs until side one of the LP ended. I listened with trepidation to the silence, expecting more sounds to emanate from the bedroom—but all was quiet. Were they asleep in there? "I guess they're not coming out any time soon," I said.

Jeremy drained his glass. "I guess I'll go, then."

"Me too."

"I thought you lived here."

I shook my head. "I live at Hellman Hall."

"I'm at Brooke Hall. Want me to walk you home?"

We walked in silence to campus, slightly insulated against the chilly night by the wine. I kept sneaking glances at Jeremy. When we got to my door, I wondered if he would kiss me—but that was silly. This wasn't a date. Cyn and I didn't go on dates. The concept was so outmoded. "Thanks for walking with me," I said.

There was such sweetness to his smile. "See you around, Joanna." I opened the door and went inside.

∞

Cyn showed up at my dorm room late the next morning, a Saturday, with coffee and pastries from the place near the draft board. "Where's Miss Goody Two-Shoes?" That was Cyn's nickname for my roommate.

"I think she's at the library."

"Of course she is." Cyn's face was bright and mischievous. I knew she was dying to talk about the previous night. We sat cross-legged on my narrow bed and ate raspberry croissants. On the wall next to my bed I had taped a poster of Angela Davis, resolute and beautiful with her tall Afro, passionately speaking into a microphone; at the bottom of the page was the slogan "Free Angela and All Political Prisoners." (Cyn had the same poster in her bedroom, along with a copy of Angela's FBI "Wanted" poster and pictures of Che Guevara and a swaggering, now-dead Jimi Hendrix.) Angela shared my wall space with old movie pictures I'd collected: Katharine Hepburn and Cary Grant squaring off in *The Philadelphia Story*, Leslie Howard and Wendy Hiller squaring off in *Pygmalion*, shorn-headed Renée Jeanne Falconetti weeping in Dreyer's *The Passion of Joan of Arc*.

"So out with it," I said. "How was last night?"

"It was okay."

"Don't get crumbs on the bed! Just okay?"

She gave a laugh. "What do you want me to say? We balled. Then he told me the reason he's not underground is that the pigs beat him so badly at a demonstration, it took him the better part of a year to recover. And by then, his comrades were mostly underground."

"Jeremy told me."

Cyn looked surprised. "Alex might still go underground. *We* might have to, at some point."

Going underground sounded romantic, but it didn't seem real. Sort of like saying we might have to go to the moon someday.

"Anyway, then we fucked again. He wanted to stay the night, but I kicked him out. You didn't have to leave, you know. I'm sorry I stuck you with Alex's friend."

"That's okay. We had a good talk."

"Oh." She looked at me sharply. "You didn't fuck him, did you?"

"Where? When?" I wasn't as adept at casual sex as Cyn, though I'd tried it a couple of times at parties when I was drunk and/or stoned.

"Well, you might have," Cyn said. "On the sofa, while Alex and I were in the bedroom."

"So are you gonna see Alex again?"

"We're meeting up tonight."

"Aha!"

Cyn licked raspberry from her fingers. "Aha, what?"

"Maybe you like him more than you're letting on. Maybe he's the right guy for you."

"What, like the man of my dreams? *Please*. There's no such thing, Joanna."

"So you're saying you just want to be his friend, or what?" I tore off the end of my croissant and popped it into my mouth.

"I don't want to be his *old lady*. Next thing you know, he'll be expecting me to cook and make the coffee. I'm never going to be anybody's factotum." She grinned. "He's not bad in bed, though. You should give him a try."

"What?" Alex smelled of patchouli. I had never liked the stuff. "Cyn, why would I want to do that? Alex likes you. He barely even noticed me." I didn't want to tell her I liked Jeremy.

"Oh, come on. It'd be fun." She stroked my upper arm. Her voice became a caress. "Your skin is awfully soft."

What was this? More of Cyn's non-monogamy line? Or perhaps just another way to know me, too well. Or maybe just so she could say she'd done it with a woman. Whatever it was, I didn't want that kind of involvement with Cyn. We were close, and it was sometimes messy, but it would get messier and more tangled if we crossed that line.

"Hey, that tickles," I said, and moved my arm away.

Cyn regarded me with an opaque expression. Then she crumpled the empty pastry bag, got up, and tossed it in the trash. "I'm so bored with your goddamn bourgeois hang-ups, Jo," she said in a blasé tone, and I wondered if I'd imagined what had just happened.

∞

"Hey, cut that out," Cyn said about a week later, when Alex tried to kiss her hello as he and Jeremy walked in the door of her apartment.

"What's the matter with you?" Alex asked.

"You don't get to do that without permission," she said, arms crossed over her body. "It doesn't go without saying."

"Hi, Jeremy," I said. He smiled at me, then picked up Cyn's paperback of *Capital* from the coffee table.

"I thought you were all free love and smash monogamy," Alex said.

"Exactly. That means I'm not your territory, man."

Alex's glasses had slipped down his nose. He pushed them back up and regarded her with dignity. "Point taken. So you won't mind if I sleep with other girls?"

Cyn shrugged. "Why should I mind? Hell, I told Jo she ought to give you a whirl."

"Cyn!" I hissed, blushing. Jeremy didn't look up from *Capital*.

Alex's expression could only be described as aghast. "Look, Cyn, who you sleep with is your prerogative, but you don't get to choose my sex partners. No offense, Joanna."

"None taken," I said, relieved.

"Why should sex be such a big fucking deal?" Cyn demanded. "It's natural. Just animal instinct."

"So when are you and Jo gonna get it on?" Alex asked.

"What makes you think we haven't?" Cyn retorted.

Alex raised his eyebrows. "Wild," he said. Jeremy was apparently deep in contemplation of Marx, but I didn't quite buy it. For a frozen moment I thought Cyn would kiss or fondle me to prove her point, but she only sent me a wry smile. Then we all started to talk about the war, which was safer ground.

I thought Cyn might relent and let Alex stay the night, but after we drank some wine and listened to Neil Young, she yawned and said, "I have an early class tomorrow." I sent her an amused glance—her first class wasn't until ten. Smiling, she came up to me and whispered in my ear, "*You* can stay if you want." I shrugged and shook my head.

At the door, Alex made no move to kiss Cyn goodnight. She smiled up at him, then gave him a lingering kiss. Alex looked baffled and overheated as she herded us out the door.

"We'll walk you home," Jeremy told me when we were standing outside in the cold.

The three of us walked in silence. Then Alex said, "I'm gonna take off," and strode with his hands in his pockets into the darkness.

"What's with him?" I asked.

Jeremy gave a huff of laughter. "Cynthia has him not knowing whether he's coming or going."

"You don't think he's going back to her place? That probably wouldn't go over so well."

"I don't think he'd dare at this point," Jeremy said.

We fell silent. I felt nervous and keyed up at being alone with Jeremy. I couldn't think of anything to say. At the edge of campus, we passed a couple passionately kissing against a tree, despite the cold night. "Brrr," I said. "It sure is cold." How scintillating.

"You're cold? Here…" To my surprise, Jeremy took off his scarf and placed it around my shoulders. "Better?"

"Thanks." I looped the scarf around my neck. The thick cable-knit wool was warm and soft. I felt almost as if he'd put his arms around me. "This is a nice scarf."

"My mom knitted it for me." He gave a rueful laugh. "Wow, how uncool can I get?"

I laughed. "I don't think it's uncool. I think it's kinda nice, Jeremy."

"You're just saying that." His voice was warm and velvety in the half-dark.

"No, I'm not." I was surprised at how full of tenderness my voice sounded.

When we reached my residence hall, I unwound the scarf and draped it over Jeremy's slender shoulders. In the lights from Hellman Hall, he smiled, and it went through me like a kiss. I didn't want him to go.

"Hey," I said, "maybe I'll see you at school tomorrow."

"I hope so. When do you have class? Maybe we can get a cup of coffee or something."

After we'd compared schedules and planned when to meet, I went inside and floated up the stairs to my room. I knew that by Cyn's standards, what had happened between me and Jeremy was nothing. But it lit me up inside.

∞

"Hey, can you keep a secret?" I asked Jeremy. We were drinking coffee in the student center. We'd been meeting between classes two or three times a week for the past couple of weeks.

He leaned his elbows on the table. "Of course." He wore jeans and a brown sweater with a hole in the elbow. I was increasingly moved by his physical presence, his dark eyes, curly hair, and olive skin.

"Tomorrow I'm auditioning at the Studio of Dramatic Arts." Once the words were out, I almost wished I'd kept quiet. "Not that I'll get in. I mean, I got the lead in a play in high school, but nothing since. Maybe I was just a big fish in a small pond."

"What makes you think you won't get in?"

"I guess I don't dare let myself hope I will. I want it so much, you know? I feel like the only way I'm ever going to get anywhere with acting is if I really study."

"I think it's great you're auditioning."

"You do?"

"Of course! If it's something you really want. What does Cyn think?"

"She doesn't know. You're the only one I've told, aside from my parents, and I had to tell them, because I have to talk my dad into paying my way if I get in. He wants me to have a regular degree to fall back on—but he wanted to be a writer, and instead he's a junior high school English teacher. I don't want to give up on my dream without even trying, you know?"

He nodded. "How come you haven't told Cyn?"

"Oh, she'd try and talk me out of it. Call it bourgeois, self-indulgent. Don't you think that's what it is?"

"Not if it's what you love."

"Thanks." I basked in Jeremy's approval. It felt like we were in our own little bubble in the student center, no one but us. It was a good feeling.

Then Cyn walked in, clutching a spiral notebook and some books. I glanced at my watch—that's right, she had a philosophy seminar in five minutes. Her face went rigid when she saw us, just for an instant. Then she strode over, pulled up a chair and took a swig of my coffee. "Rally tomorrow in Times Square to protest the Laos invasion."

"Good," I said. "What time?"

"5:00."

"I might be a little late." My audition was at 3:30.

She peered at me. "Why? You don't have class tomorrow afternoon."

Jeremy and I exchanged glances. "I have an audition," I said.

"*Oh.*" She didn't bother to ask for details.

∞

"One, two, three, four! We don't want your fucking war!"

Umbrella aloft, I moved through the crowd looking for Cyn, Jeremy, and Alex in gaudy, glaring Times Square. I'd come straight from the audition and felt over-dressed in a demure knee-length skirt instead of the jeans I ordinarily would've worn to a demo. Ah, there they were, all of them yelling the slogan near a girl waving a slightly soggy NLF flag. I took my place next to Jeremy. We smiled at each other, then I joined in the chant. I waved at Cyn, who didn't smile but nodded at me with an expression I couldn't read. Was she mad at me for being late?

A guy with a megaphone began to speak about how Tricky Dick had promised to end the war but expanded it instead into Cambodia and Laos. "Nixon lies, and millions die!" he shouted, and the crowd took up the chant. I was full of righteous indignation, yet I kept going over the audition pieces I'd done—monologues from *Suddenly Last Summer* and *A Midsummer Night's Dream*—what I'd done right and wrong, and whether they had been the right monologues to use. I kept seeing the impassive faces of the man and two women watching me from the front row of the theater at the Studio of Dramatic Arts.

"Nixon lies, and millions die!" The slogan had been used for LBJ, and here we were using it for another president while the war ground on, ground people up, while we stood yelling in the rain.

Off to one side counterdemonstrators jeered: "If you hate America so much, why don't you leave?" "Traitors!" "Get a job!"

Between speakers, Jeremy turned to me. "So, how'd the audition go?"

"It's hard to tell. I was pretty nervous."

"I bet you did great," he said, beaming.

"Thanks. It feels kinda self-indulgent, worrying about whether I'll get in, compared to all this." It was raining harder, and the wind blew the rain across my face. I wiped at it. "I mean, it's not life and death."

Droplets of rain clung to Jeremy's shaggy hair despite his umbrella. "Aw, come on, Jo. What are we fighting for, if not for—I don't know—beauty and meaning. Or something," he concluded with a laugh.

"I think so too." Between what he'd said, and the rain droplets clinging to his hair in the growing darkness, the moment felt magical. I wanted to kiss him.

Then Cyn was at my side. "Hey, check out this guy, Jo," she said as a bearded guy took the megaphone. "He's a history prof at Queens College. I heard him give a speech last month."

∞

After the demo we headed back to Cyn's place. Cyn and Alex stood in the kitchenette drinking red wine and arguing about Hegel and Lenin. "If you'd really read the *Science of Logic*, you wouldn't say that," Cyn said.

"I have read it!" Alex spluttered.

I was sitting on the sofa with Jeremy. "There was this girl in the fourth grade I liked, and she had a stamp collection too," he said. "So one day I left two rare British stamps on her desk, but I didn't dare say they were from me." His Brooklyn accent sounded caressing.

"Aw, that's sweet," I said. He was still that shy boy. Both of us were shy, but there was something between us, something sweet and good.

Cyn strode over and plunked herself down on the couch between us. She gave me a strange, defiant smile. Then she turned to Jeremy and kissed him full on the lips. I froze, the blood whooshing into my head, the moment unreal and unstoppable. Cyn pulled off her sweater. She wasn't wearing a bra. Jeremy's eyes latched onto her small breasts. She kissed him again. For a moment I thought Jeremy would pull away. His arms went round her naked back. I had ceased to exist.

Alex was watching from the kitchenette with a stricken expression. I got up and walked toward him. He gave a startled laugh, and I turned—Cyn was dragging down Jeremy's zipper. Jeremy's eyes were rapt. I wished Alex wasn't here to see this. If only I saw, it wouldn't be as humiliating. Yes, it would. "I'm gonna go," I muttered.

Only then did Alex seem to see me. "Want some wine?" he asked.

"No."

"You sure?" Then he grabbed me by the shoulders and kissed me. He tasted of sour wine and smelled of patchouli. For a moment I thought, Why not? The kiss was sloppy and impersonal. Then I thought, No, it's what Cyn wants, and I pulled away.

"I can't," I said. "I've gotta go."

He looked over at the couch again. I wouldn't let myself look, tried not to hear the quiet sounds, the sighs. I headed for the door. We got out of there as if the place were on fire.

"I'll walk you home," Alex said.

"Okay." It was raining. We'd both left our umbrellas inside, but we didn't go back for them. The rain pelted my hair. I thought of Jeremy and the magical raindrops. What an idiot I'd been. We walked in silence. I might as well have been inside a cocoon, for all I noticed of my surroundings.

"Why do you think she did it?" Alex asked finally.

The question hadn't occurred to me. She did it because she wanted to. Or maybe so Alex wouldn't think of her as his *old lady*. "Why not?" I snapped. "Nobody owns anybody, right?"

He looked surprised. "So you're okay with it?"

I said nothing. I didn't let myself cry until I was in bed in my dorm room, and only when I was sure my roommate was asleep. Cyn did it again, I thought. I can't believe she did it again.

∞

The next morning I grabbed a cup of terrible coffee in the residence hall kitchen, then headed for the library, though I usually studied in my room. I was afraid Cyn might show up, and I didn't want to see her.

The corrosive pain subsided somewhat in the spacious, oak-paneled reference room lined with volumes and full of students bent over books and notebooks. I sat at a table and opened my Ibsen to *Hedda Gabler*, and everything fell away: Cyn and Jeremy, the endless war…Cyn and Jeremy. All that remained was great art, the theater, the life of the mind.

"There you are."

I looked up. Cyn had on a black turtleneck and jeans and carried an armful of books with *Capital* on top. With her short sleek hair, she looked like Jean Seberg in *Breathless*. "I have to finish reading this," I said. My Ibsen class wasn't until the next day, but I didn't think Cyn would remember.

Looking puzzled, she pulled up the chair next to mine. "Are you coming to my Marx study group at lunchtime?"

I liked what I'd read of Marx, but the study group got pretty abstruse, and right now it was the last place I wanted to be, especially if Alex and/or Jeremy would be there. And they would be, wouldn't they? Cyn had them both wrapped around her finger now. "Not sure," I said. "I might have too much studying to do."

"What could be more important than this?" She brandished her copy of *Capital*. A couple of students at the next table sent us annoyed glances. "You have to get serious, Jo."

"Look, I'll go if I can." I turned back to Ibsen.

"You're not upset about last night, are you?"

I closed the book. "Keep your voice down."

Her eyes widened. "Oh, come on. It didn't mean anything."

"Then why did you do it, Cyn? If it meant nothing?" I had to fight to keep my voice from rising.

She shrugged. "I don't know. I just felt like it, in the moment." She leaned closer. "Anyway it was nothing to write home about. He came as soon as I put him in." She whispered it, grinning, but I felt like it echoed through the high-ceilinged room.

My head felt so hot, I thought I would start crying or screaming at her, or maybe both. I wanted to say, You have ruined everything. "I see," I said.

"It's not like you and Jeremy ever do anything but talk. What are you always talking about, anyway?"

The words hovered on my tongue: *We talk about drama school. If I get in, there won't be a damn thing you can do about it.* But no, I wasn't going to tell her, not today. It was a small corner I kept to myself, something Cyn couldn't poke and grab at. "Oh, nothing that would interest you," I said in a blasé, Cyn-like tone, and I was gratified to see how disconcerted she looked. I opened my book again. "I need to get back to this," I said and pretended to read until she got up and left.

I didn't let myself look up until I was certain she was gone. Then I actually tried to read, but my heart was pounding, and I couldn't focus.

I found a pay phone near the library, pulled my little address book from my book bag, and dialed Rose Hall. A girl picked up after several rings, and I asked for Franny. A minute later she came to the phone. "Franny speaking."

"Joanna speaking," I said, and was startled to hear that my voice sounded steady and pleasant. "I'm glad I caught you. Are you free for lunch?"

"I am free as a bird."

And so am I, if I want to be, I thought. "Want to get a slice of pizza?"

So much for Cyn's lunchtime study group.

∞

At the pizza place on the edge of campus, Franny and I sat on tall stools at a round table and ate slices of cheese pizza dripping tomatoey grease onto paper plates, and talked about theater. We laughed easily and often. I felt like I could breathe for the first time in weeks, like I'd made a prison break from Cyn and her intense, demanding presence. At the same time, it felt like I'd misplaced something—a hand, perhaps, or a foot.

Something kept me from telling Franny I'd applied to drama school. Telling Jeremy had felt special, and then he slept with Cyn. Maybe I wasn't ready to trust anyone with any real confidences.

Franny and I were heading for our respective classroom buildings after lunch, when I saw Cyn coming out of the library. It occurred to me that she'd gone back to see if I was still there. When she saw us, Cyn froze, then straightened her spine and marched up to us. "I thought you had to read Ibsen," she said.

"I took a break," I said.

"Hello, Cynthia," Franny said in a bright, friendly tone.

Cyn ignored her. "We missed you at the study group."

"Sorry." The word came out before I could stop myself. I had nothing to be sorry about. She was the one who needed to apologize, and she wasn't going to.

"What study group?" Franny asked.

Cyn waved *Capital* under Franny's nose. For a moment I thought she might sock her in the face with it.

"Oh!" Franny said in a stilted tone that made me uneasy. "Groucho and Harpo are the only Marxes I know much about," she added with a laugh.

Cyn's glance swept over Franny in her pink cashmere sweater and long denim skirt, and her eyes narrowed with contempt. Then she looked at me. I could practically hear her say, *So you'd rather hang out with this little twit?* "See you later, Joanna," she said and strode off, clutching her books to her chest.

Franny watched her go. "For someone who isn't an actress, Cynthia sure knows how to make an exit."

I gave a laugh. "She is pretty theatrical, isn't she?" I felt a pang at my own disloyalty, then brushed it aside.

∞

For the next week, I avoided Cyn and the guys. Mostly I buried myself in school work. Franny and I had lunch together a couple of times and went to see *The Music Lovers*. (Neither of us liked the movie much, though we both loved Glenda Jackson.)

Cyn didn't try to contact me, and when we saw each other on campus, we'd stop dead in our tracks, then head in separate directions. Maybe Cyn thought she was letting me stew and that I'd come crawling back. I was still too angry to see that happening, though the feeling of something missing never dissipated. It was like a low whine in the background.

I ran into Jeremy in the halls one day on my way to 16th-century English lit. "Hi, Jo," he said and smiled tentatively.

"Hi," I said and kept walking.

∞

"My roommate's out with her latest *lover* again," Franny said wearily. "I know it's old-fashioned, Jo, but I'm not planning to lose my virginity until marriage."

We were sitting cross-legged on the braided rug in her room listening to a Barbra Streisand LP early one evening. I thought Streisand had a good voice, but she left me kinda cold, though Franny loved her. Her side of the room was neat and tidy, her bed made, with a patchwork comforter in shades of lavender spread atop it. A framed Art Nouveau poster of Sarah Bernhardt hung on the wall, and tragedy and comedy masks hung above her dresser. The roommate's side of the room was a welter of clothes and underwear strewn on the unmade bed, with more clothes plus mismatched shoes on the floor, and a poster of Mick Jagger plastered crookedly on the wall next to the bed. The room was chilly, the radiator making occasional sputtering noises in counterpoint with Streisand singing about some perfect lover man she hadn't met yet. "You're not a virgin, are you?" Franny asked.

I shook my head. I wondered if Cyn had slept with Jeremy again. The last thing I wanted to talk about was sex.

Franny let out an exaggerated sigh. "I know it's not very hip and groovy to be a virgin." She said *hip and groovy* like it was one word. "That's okay. We can't all be hip and groovy. Why even try?"

"Why even try," I echoed. Maybe it would be easier to have someone like Franny for a best friend. Maybe it would be restful, a relief. Surely a virgin wouldn't screw the guys you liked.

The side of the Streisand album ended. I got up, put the record back in its sleeve, reached for one of the LPs I'd brought and put it on the turntable. "Wait till you hear Nina Simone," I said. "She's incredible." Cyn and I had discovered her back in Rochester, when we'd found my dad's copy of *Nina Simone in Concert* in the record cabinet (the same copy I'd brought with me to SNY). We had spent hours listening to her albums together. We were especially spellbound by her version of "Pirate Jenny"—that deliciously chilling moment when the maid Jenny orders the deaths of everyone who treated her with contempt, and Nina Simone hoarsely whispers, "That'll learn ya."

I put the needle down on "Pirate Jenny" and settled back down on the rug. As we listened, Franny began to look uneasy, but I was too entranced to pay her much attention.

When the song ended, she said, "It's a bit *disturbing* for my tastes."

"I thought you'd like it. It's from *The Threepenny Opera*."

"Oh! I didn't realize. I'm not that familiar with Kurt Weill or Brecht."

I got up again, turned over the record, and played "Mississippi Goddam."

At first Franny smiled and bobbed her head in time to the jaunty piano tune. As the song gained urgency, the anger rising in Nina Simone's deep, rich voice, her smile faded, and she sat very still, hugging her knees. She looked like she'd tasted something bad. Before the song was even over, she leapt up and plucked the needle from the record. "I'm afraid she isn't for me, Jo."

"How come?"

She shrugged. "I guess I don't like being told I'm going to die for crimes I'm not even responsible for. It's not my fault I'm white, is it? I don't like the idea that Nina Simone would hate me for that. It isn't fair."

"It's not about you, Franny."

"At first I thought maybe she was just talking about the south. But no, she meant the whole country. I just don't find it entertaining. It's all very radical chic, I know. It's all very hip-and-groovy."

She thought she was being cute. I was getting more and more furious. "It's not about being hip. It's about freedom and equality." I had planned on playing her "I Wish I Knew How It Would Feel To Be Free," but Franny didn't deserve Nina Simone.

"Freedom to do what, kill whitey?"

I winced. "Freedom to live! To have opportunities. To get to do more than go fight in foreign wars when you're treated like a second-class citizen at home."

"Why are you getting so angry? I don't run things. I'm apolitical. I'm an actress, or anyway, I want to be. I like make-believe, just like you!"

It felt like an accusation. "Terrible things are happening in our names," I said. My voice shook.

"Maybe so, but we're still just kids. Why should it be up to us? I'm still figuring out who I am. Who am I to say I know better than the people running things?"

Appalled, I stared at her. I had never felt more like a committed radical than in that moment. "I want the world to change," I said quietly. "I want it to be better for everyone. 'To each according to his ability, to each according to his need.'"

"Is that from a Nina Simone song?"

"It's Karl Marx." I thought of Cyn clutching her copy of *Capital*, and the study group I'd avoided.

"So you're a Communist, like Cyn?"

"Neither of us are Communists, exactly. But revolutions have been happening all over the world. Why not here too?"

Franny shuddered. "God, I hope not. Angela Davis is a Communist, right? All over campus, I keep hearing 'free Angela' this and 'free Angela' that, but she tried to break those black convicts out of prison. She bought the guns they used when they kidnapped that judge and killed him. That's not justice."

"That's not what happened, Franny."

"Oh, were you there?" She sounded like a bratty child.

"If Angela had been in on the attempt to free the Soledad Brothers, why would she have bought the guns under her own name? It's so obviously a frame job. Angela said she's innocent, and I believe her."

"If she's innocent, why did she run from the law?"

I shook my head. "Are you serious? The law's treating her as guilty unless proven innocent. And now she might get the death penalty for something she didn't even do, because she had the courage to speak out against injustice."

"We're going to have to agree to disagree, Joanna." She said it as if she were above it all, as if none of it mattered. What was I doing here? Cyn was right about Franny, and I was too disgusted to stay a moment longer.

I got to my feet, took the LP from the turntable and put it back in the sleeve. "I'd better get going."

"Okay," Franny said. She actually sounded surprised. Maybe she thought none of this mattered to me either.

I couldn't wait to get back to Cyn.

Chapter Six:
The Revolution Will Not Be Televised
(March–May 1971)

"I wonder if they'll read the communiqué on the news," Jeremy said, tapping his foot nervously. He was sitting on one end of Cyn's sofa, with Alex next to him and Cyn next to Alex. I sat on the floor at Cyn's feet and tried to read Ibsen.

"Maybe," Alex said. "Probably they'll just quote Nixon going on about how stinking these violent revolutionaries are."

"Jo, put that book down," Cyn said.

It was the beginning of March, and we were waiting for the evening news to come on. The Weather Underground had bombed a men's room in the Capitol Building as retaliation for the invasion of Laos. Cyn and Alex and Jeremy thought it was the best thing ever. No one had been hurt, only property. It was marvelous political theater. If it had happened in a movie, I would've wholeheartedly applauded. Yet something about it didn't feel right. I told myself it was just my privilege, my white middle-class upbringing. I didn't want to be like Franny.

"I have to finish reading *Rosmersholm* by tomorrow," I said. True, but I also used the book as a shield against being in the same room with Jeremy. My week away from Cyn and the guys hadn't solved anything, except that now I truly felt I had nowhere else to go.

"We should drop out of school already," Cyn said. "How is studying some dead white author going to serve the revolution?" Cyn had welcomed me back without a word of reproach (all she'd said was, "Tired of that daddy's girl?", and I'd nodded), but she'd been sniping at me for days. I couldn't help but think it was her way of paying me back.

"Marx is a dead white author," I said.

"Are you comparing Marx to fucking Ibsen?"

"Well, he was considered pretty revolutionary in his day." I was baiting her, but her dogmatic tone set my teeth on edge.

"Joanna Bergman, too busy studying some dead Norwegian to pay attention to what's going on right under her fucking nose."

I started to laugh. "Some dead Norwegian!"

"You're missing the *point*. The whole school system in this country is reactionary and oppressive. The revolution is coming. Do you want to be left behind?" She looked genuinely agitated.

"Of course not! It's just…"

"It's just what?"

I hesitated. It felt like lying to keep it from her, even though it also felt like self-protection.

"You should tell her, Jo," Jeremy said, and the three of us turned to him in surprise. Well, it was clear where his loyalties lay now. All because he'd fucked Cyn that one time? Or had it happened again? I didn't want to know.

"Tell me what?" Cyn asked him, then turned on me. "Tell me *what*?"

"Thanks a lot," I told Jeremy. He couldn't meet my gaze. What a wimp. "I applied to the Studio of Dramatic Arts," I told Cyn. "It's a two-year program. If my dad agrees to pay tuition. If I get in. Chances are, I won't."

"You went behind my back?" she demanded. "You told *him*, not me?"

Jeremy looked like he wanted to sink into the sofa, while Alex watched us avidly.

"I didn't want to have to deal with your disapproval until after the audition," I said. "And after that, I didn't want to get into it with you unless I got in." I still held the Ibsen paperback open on my lap.

"Did you tell Franny Silver?" Cyn's eyes were dark with pain. "Is she going to that drama school too?"

"No, I didn't tell her," I said quietly. "As far as I know, she hasn't applied."

Cyn let out a relieved breath. Then she eyed me sharply. "So that's your priority? Being an *actress?*"

"It's not my only priority, Cyn."

"We should be doing nothing but making the revolution and trying to stop the war. We need to be doing *more*, not less. Otherwise we're just good Germans."

I was tempted to remind her that I was the one who had family who died in the camps, and of the four of us, Jeremy and I were the Jewish ones—but that wasn't the point. "Art is part of the revolution," I said.

"You keep telling yourself that," Cyn said.

"Are you really saying that Phil Ochs and Nina Simone aren't—"

She laughed derisively. "You're hardly Nina Simone, Jo."

"It's like that line in 'Mississippi Goddam': 'this is a show tune, but the show hasn't been written for it yet.' Imagination is part of it, Cyn. It has to be." I was too flustered to say it well, and anyway I was afraid that Cyn was right, that my desire to act was merely self-indulgent escapism. Why was it that when I was with Franny, I felt like a radical, but when I was with Cyn, I felt like a bourgeois would-be artist? Jeremy had said *What are we fighting for, if not beauty and meaning?* But he sure wasn't sticking up for me now.

"You're the one who lacks imagination, Jo," Cyn said. "You're still stuck in these little girl fantasies of being an actress. The high point of your life was a fucking high school play. It's time for you to grow up."

If she had slapped me across the face, it couldn't have stung more. No one said anything for a long moment. Then Alex murmured, "We'll all be underground within six months, or dead." I was pretty sure he meant it to be comforting.

"My parents won't support me if I drop out of school," I said. "What about yours, Cyn? Are they still gonna pay for this apartment if you're a full-time revolutionary?"

Cyn glared at me. She didn't like my pointing out that her parents had more money than mine and lavished it on her. "Like Alex said, soon we'll probably be underground anyway. That means no contact with our families."

Was she serious? I liked the fantasy of being outlaws on the run. Very *Butch Cassidy and the Sundance Kid*, or *Bonnie and Clyde*. (I tried not to think about how both movies ended in a hail of bullets.) But I had little idea of how it actually worked, or how completely we'd have to change our identities. I thought of the photo of Angela Davis taken when she'd been apprehended after months on the run; she looked incongruous with a pixie cut, her proud Afro stuffed inside a short-hair wig. Even aside from giving up my dream of the theater, it would hurt my parents if I dropped out of sight. (Franny wouldn't even go to protests because her parents wouldn't approve. Did thinking of my parents make me no better than Franny?) Jeremy had told me how close he was with his family—but he looked resolute, the committed revolutionary. Then he gave a little jump and glanced at his watch. "It's time for the news!" He got up and switched on Cyn's small black-and-white TV.

I put the Ibsen paperback aside and stared, stunned, at footage of the rubble in the Capitol Building. The sight of the debris seemed in its way as improbable and astounding as the moon landing had been. There were broken windows and doors ripped off their hinges. Take *that*, I thought. The damage was mostly to a men's room and barber shop, nothing that would slow down the war machine—yet it was hundreds of thousands of dollars of damage, the anchorman said. He quoted briefly from the Weather Underground's statement: "We have attacked the Capitol because it is a monument to U.S. domination over the planet."

"Fuck, yeah!" Alex said. Jeremy let out a whoop, and we all laughed. In that moment, I put aside my misgivings, and everything seemed possible.

When the broadcast went to a mouthwash commercial, Cyn said, "See, Jo? It's happening. It's really happening."

Alex lit a celebratory joint, and we passed it around.

"I want in on this action," Cyn said.

"Me too," I heard myself say, and Cyn sent me an astonished smile.

"You know I'm in," Alex said.

"Me too," Jeremy said.

"It's high time we planned something," Cyn said. "Memorial Day is already coming around again, not to mention the anniversary of Kent State. I'm so sick of the same old demonstrations. They don't change anything, no matter how huge the crowds are. No one in power listens, because they don't have to."

"Violence is the only language they understand," Alex said.

"We need to gum up the works," Cyn said. "Even a little bit. Bring the war home, right?"

The drums from *The Battle of Algiers* began to pulsate in my brain. "Something symbolic," I said. "Destruction of property. If we could be sure not to hurt anyone."

"Hey, we're not like *them*," Alex said. "Anyway, they care more about property than people." He passed Jeremy the joint.

"Exactly," Jeremy said, and took a drag. "They're freaking out over an explosion in the Capitol men's room, which hurt no one, while they're committing wholesale murder overseas. Cowardly hypocrites."

"That is so true," I said, and Jeremy looked at me in grateful surprise. He leaned down and passed me the joint, and our fingers touched. I took a drag and held it in my lungs, then blew it out. "Too bad we can't hit that draft board," I said. "Goddamn place of death."

The words hung in the air. The four of us stared at each other.

"Wild," Alex said appreciatively.

"That's it, Jo," Cyn said. She took the joint, her fingers lingering on mine. "That's what we'll do."

My head was hazy with the grass. "Wait," I said. "How would we…"

Alex narrowed his eyes behind their wire rims. "I think I know a guy who can get us the stuff we need. And Jeremy knows what to do. Right, Jeremy?"

"Right," Jeremy said. "You know I've been waiting to do this for a long time."

They liked my idea. I wasn't like Franny, I was making the revolution. We were going to do something—really *do* something.

"Let's do it on Memorial Day," Cyn said.

"Memorial Day," Alex agreed.

My jubilation veered into stage fright. But Memorial Day was a long way off. Maybe the idea would be forgotten by morning.

∞

Cyn put *Let It Bleed* on the turntable and blasted it loud so we could talk about the action, "Gimme Shelter" lending an apocalyptic swagger to the proceedings. We didn't seriously think Cyn's apartment was bugged, but it seemed safer than my dorm room or Jeremy's, and Alex shared a tiny cold-water flat with roommates.

"I tried to bring a book bag into the draft board, and they searched it," Jeremy said.

"Which means planting the device in a bathroom is a no-go," Alex said.

"Maybe Jo and I should try going in," Cyn said. "If they don't search our purses, we could bring in the device that way."

Alex shook his head. "Women at a draft board? If they searched Jeremy, they're certainly gonna search you. With the Capitol bombing and all the other incidents of the past couple of years, they're probably beefing up security."

"The janitor leaves by eight p.m., and there's no night watchman," Cyn said. "Couldn't we break in after the janitor leaves?"

"I wouldn't want to chance it," Alex said.

"Gimme Shelter" faded out, replaced by "Love in Vain." I was torn between disappointment and relief that we would have to call off the plan.

"We could pick a different target," Jeremy said.

Cyn shook her head. "No. It should be the draft board."

Alex got up and paced. Then he stopped. "There's a mailbox outside the building. We could plant the device under it. It wouldn't do as much damage, probably, but it would get the point across."

"What about innocent bystanders?" I asked. "Someone dropping something in the mailbox, or a car driving by."

"We can set the bomb to go off in the middle of the night," Jeremy said. "And we can call it in with enough time for the street to be cleared before the explosion—but not so much time that they can get the bomb squad there."

"It's a plan," Cyn said. "Alex will get the supplies, Jeremy will assemble the device and set the clock. Jo and I will place the device."

"Cyn..." I said.

"No way," Alex said.

"I can place the device," Jeremy said quietly.

"That wouldn't be fair," Cyn said. "You and Alex have tasks already. I'll carry it, and Jo can act as lookout."

"I'll carry the device, and Jeremy will be lookout," Alex said.

"Why, because you and Jeremy are *male*?" she asked. "Your chivalry has no place in the revolution."

I couldn't help but smile at that, though I was cold all over. I imagined the bomb going off with us still there. I imagined the cops grabbing us. We weren't really doing this, were we?

"It should be the women who place the device, like in *The Battle of Algiers*," Cyn said. "Agreed, Jo?"

If this were a movie, the women should place the bomb. I felt like I was in a movie right now. "Agreed," I said, and Cyn smiled.

"Agreed," the men grudgingly said.

∞

We planned every detail of the action until we knew it letter-perfect. Some days I thought we'd just keep planning, like a much-rehearsed play with no opening night. Other days I knew it would happen. Of course I would not back out. No one else was backing out, were they? Cyn and Alex and Jeremy were elated, with a sort of nobility to them, a revolutionary fervor, a calm. We were going to our destiny. Part of something bigger than us. Making history.

We had, of course, talked about prison. I imagined my parents' sorrowful faces if that happened. How could I do that to them? Cyn thought of prison in big, romantic terms: of a spectacular trial, during which she would condemn the war, racism, and imperialism, followed by a period as a political prisoner, studying philosophy and writing revolutionary tracts in a cell. I didn't think she seriously thought we'd get caught, but I suspected part of her wanted it.

Four days before the action, I got a thin envelope from the Studio of Dramatic Arts. I took it into my room and sat on the bed. Finally I ripped it open and read it. I leapt to my feet and gave a whoop of joy. Then I just stood there, stock still.

I told no one I'd been accepted. What was the use? After the action, I'd tell everyone. If I was still alive. If I wasn't in jail.

∞

The bomb was in Cyn's bedroom closet. "Jeremy actually made me leave the apartment while he assembled the thing," Cyn said. "He was so nervous, I thought he might fuck up and blow a hole in my living room—but it's a thing of beauty. Wanna see?"

I nodded, though the idea of it sucked all the air from the room. I didn't even like firecrackers as a kid. I liked fireworks up in the sky, pretty sparkly lights, but the kind the neighborhood kids set off on the Fourth of July scared me. (*You could lose an eye, or a finger,* my mom had often said.)

Cyn opened the closet, and we peered down at the cardboard box on the floor. It contained a length of pipe closed off by steel caps at both ends, with a fuse at one end. "Wild, huh?" Cyn whispered, as if she might wake the thing if she spoke too loudly.

"Real *Battle of Algiers,*" I whispered. I felt faint and noticed I was breathing too fast.

"Isn't it!" With a last look, she carefully shut the door, and we went back into the living room. Two envelopes sat on the living room table: our communiqués, stamped and addressed to the Associated Press and the *New York Times.* It was Sunday morning. Everything was ready. Everything except the clock, which Jeremy would attach and set tonight.

Cyn had never looked happier. She looked like a saint with her cropped hair and her air of portentous doings, of risking all. When she hugged me goodbye, her body felt thin and strong, honed down, the body of a revolutionary, as perfect for the part as her shorn hair. "I'll see you tonight," she said and smiled at me, the most beautiful smile I had ever seen.

"See you tonight." As I left her apartment, the unease gripped me tight, tighter. I went home and felt utterly apart from the others at the residence hall. They were caught up in the stuff of everyday life: classes, boyfriends, diets. I thought they were lucky. I tried to work on my Ibsen final paper, but I couldn't settle down. I lay on my stomach on my bed, arms propped on my elbows, and kept staring at the same much-underlined page of *Ghosts*, not reading a word. How I wished this were just another ordinary day.

I didn't need Cyn to point out that this was a stupid, self-indulgent thought. In Vietnam, in Cambodia and Laos, this could be no ordinary day. For black revolutionaries, danger was real and every day. I, on the other hand, had the luxury of being able to choose to participate in this action.

Would the bombing help anything? I had been swept up by the drama, the story of Cyn and me and Jeremy and Alex fighting to end the war, fighting for revolution. But all I wanted to do right now was hide in my bedroom and read Ibsen. I turned and looked at the "Free Angela and All Political Prisoners" poster on the wall. It hit me forcibly how much I didn't want to be a prisoner.

"I can't do it," I said aloud. But I couldn't back out now. I went around it and around it in my mind until I was dizzy and exhausted. Some revolutionary I was. I put the book aside and lay down on the bed with the light on. I could see the bomb on the inside of my eyelids. I had to set the clock, and if I did it properly, I'd be able to get comfortable. There were a million little wires, and my hand got tangled in them. Wires sprouted more wires, and they kept changing colors. Then I was on a stage, and I had to set the bomb while saying my lines, and I couldn't remember them. I couldn't get the words out. My lines were disjointed and made no sense.

When I woke up, my nose was running from one nostril, and the other nostril was completely blocked. I needed to find a Kleenex, but I didn't want to move. I swiped at my nose with my fingers. I felt hot and dry, and the room had a bright, theatrical look to it, spot-lit by fever. I sniffled heavily. Then I sneezed three times in quick succession.

I heaved myself upright, and a wave of dizzy exhaustion hit me. Where was my purse? On the floor by my bed. I leaned down and retrieved it, found a crumpled tissue inside and applied it to my leaking nose. Then I subsided back onto the bed, snuffling and swallowing phlegm. Of all the times to get sick…

Something like elation came over me. I couldn't very well be the lookout in this condition. Then I felt ashamed. It wasn't as if the Viet Cong got a break from bullets and napalm when they caught the flu. Cyn would still want me to go. But I would be a liability right now. Wouldn't I?

I got up and crept downstairs, Kleenex in hand. Jennifer Bowe, a lanky, long-haired girl, was using the pay phone in the hall outside the common room. "Maybe…" she cooed, cradling the receiver. "Maybe, if you ask me nicely…"

I leaned against the wall and waited, dabbing at my nose. Staying on my feet was exhausting.

Finally Jennifer glanced at me. "Listen, honey, I have to go now. I'll see you tonight."

Tonight. The word sent a whoosh of nausea through me.

Jennifer hung up the phone. "All yours," she said. I waited until she headed out the front door. Then I put a dime in the pay phone and dialed Cyn's number. Two rings, three. What if she wasn't there, and I'd have to go tonight after all? Finally she picked up. "Hello?"

"Hi, Cyn."

"What's wrong? You sound awful."

"I'm sick. I have the flu."

"You were fine a few hours ago."

"It came on fast." I peered into the common room; no one was there. "I don't think I'll be able to make it tonight." I sniffled wetly and wondered if she thought I was malingering.

Her voice was cold and terse. "I don't believe this."

"I'm sorry, Cyn. We can postpone, right? I know we said Memorial Day, but that wasn't the main thing." What if she got Jeremy or Alex to go with her? I didn't want Cyn risking everything without me there with her.

"You want to postpone for a day or two?" Cyn asked.

"A few days, maybe. Until I'm feeling better." I didn't mean it. And I knew she knew.

"A few days," she said bleakly. Then there was a long silence.

"Cyn? Are you there?"

"I'm here," she said. "Get some rest, Jo."

"I'm sorry, Cyn."

She gave a harsh laugh. "Of course you are." She hung up.

I stood there with the dial tone buzzing in my ear. I'd never heard her sound so disappointed. For a moment I thought I would call back and say, Never mind, I'll be there tonight. Then another wave of exhaustion went through me.

"Hey, Joanna." Edie Tavris stood there, her hair in pink curlers. "You done with the phone? Wow, you look awful."

I hung up the phone. "I've got the flu."

She backed up a couple of steps. "Well, get some rest. And please don't give it to me."

I went back to bed. I told myself Cyn wouldn't go ahead with the plan without me. Even knowing she was disappointed in me, I was still relieved. I gave myself over to the flu.

∞

In the morning I phoned Cyn, but no one answered. I dragged myself out of bed every couple of hours to call her, to no avail. Was she avoiding me? She had never done that before. Surely she hadn't gone ahead with the action without me, and gotten busted? I felt too sick to walk to her apartment. Fetching orange juice and toast from the kitchen was almost too strenuous.

Toward evening my roommate Anne Browning and another girl from the dorm, Maggie Schneiderman, appeared at the foot of my bed. "Joanna, we're sorry to wake you," Maggie said. "We were just watching the news."

"There was an explosion last night at the draft board near campus," Anne said. "But we didn't know it was your friend Cynthia until we saw the news."

I braced to hear her say Cyn had been arrested. Instead she started to cry. I wanted to slap her. Everything felt like a dream.

"I'm so sorry," Maggie said.

"What do you have to be sorry about?" I asked. "You can't believe everything you see on the news." My voice sounded strange and far away. Then Edie Tavris came in and said my mother was on the phone.

I went downstairs in my pajamas and picked up the phone, and my mother said, "Joanna, honey, have you heard about Cynthia?"

Four or five girls stood in the doorway watching me. Then they all went back into the common room and clustered around the TV.

Chapter Seven:
Cracked Actor
(September 1975)

It was a dark, cloudy Monday morning. Everything felt a little unreal as I walked to the studio, the shreds of my dream of Cyn—or whatever it had been—clinging to me like cobwebs. (*Can a poor burnt-up lass have a ghost?*) Every block or two I'd snuffle or cough deeply, bringing me back into the simple world of the body fighting off illness.

When I walked into the rehearsal room, I cringed inwardly at the sight of Martin and Babette. Martin and David Halpren sat facing the door, Babette and Clarissa across the table from them. They all had cups of coffee, and Clarissa had a cigarette that tickled my throat.

"I would kill to have that part," Martin said, then looked up and saw me, and his smile faded. Damn it.

"What part?" I asked. Babette turned and saw me, and her face froze.

"Pacino's," Martin said. "In *Dog Day Afternoon*. Have you seen it?"

I shook my head and made for the coffee urn.

"He's such a gorgeous man," Babs said, and for a surreal moment I thought she meant Martin, then realized she meant Al Pacino. My script wedged under my arm, I poured myself some coffee and took a scalding sip, attempting to douse my cough before it could spring back to life.

Martin and I would have to kiss again at the beginning of our first scene today, which picked up where our last scene had left off—but then we would both pull away and call it a mistake. I remembered how stupidly elated I had been after we'd kissed, before I saw Martin with Babette. Everything seemed so awkward now, I almost wished we could skip the kissing.

"It's not my cup of tea," Clarissa was saying in her measured, theatrical voice. "Cops and robbers."

"Oh, it's so much more than that," Martin said. "Best movie I've seen all year."

Maurice Myles walked in, looking dapper in a gray suit. "Maurice! How *are* you, darling?" Clarissa cried.

"Good morning, darling," Maurice said, and they kissed each other's cheeks with loud *mwahs*. Maurice was a tall, middle-aged man with short pale hair, small eyes and a rugged jaw.

"We were just talking about *Dog Day Afternoon*," Clarissa said. "Have you seen it?"

"I can't say that I have," Maurice said. He had a mellifluous, patrician voice, with perhaps a touch of English accent, though I was pretty sure someone had told me he was from Boston. "Though I do find Mr. Pacino terribly attractive."

Babette laughed. "That's what I said!"

Martin got up and joined me at the coffee urn. He looked tired and tightly wound. "Hey, I looked at the furniture I told you about. It looks pretty good. A little dusty, but that's easily remedied."

That was quick. Was it some kind of bribe to make me forget what I'd seen? Why would he even care? Probably I was the last member of the cast to know about him and Babette. Maybe he was afraid I wasn't worldly and sophisticated like everyone else and might cause trouble for him. "Great," I said, forcing a smile. "Thanks."

"So we should figure out when I can bring the stuff over. This neighbor of mine has a van he lets me borrow sometimes. What's your schedule like this week?"

He was going to borrow a van? "After today, I'm not working again until the Thursday afternoon table-read," I said.

"How about tomorrow?"

"You don't have to go to all this trouble, Marty," I said, somewhat taken aback.

"It's no trouble. I just need to phone my friend about the van. He's a rock musician, but he mostly uses the van when he's on tour—which he's not, at the moment." He rattled off the info at top speed, as if he'd just drunk a whole pot of coffee. The image of Martin driving the Partridge Family bus, red and blue and yellow and white, popped into my mind.

David Halpren walked up and inspected the box of pastries. He looked his usual fresh, neat morning self in a blue pullover, white shirt, and navy pants.

"Say, three o'clock tomorrow?" Martin asked.

"If you're sure it's not too much trouble."

"I'll let you know when I've talked to my friend." He picked up a glazed donut and hurried off to sit next to Maurice. A moment later he was laughing heartily about god knows what.

"What was all that about?" David asked.

"Marty's gonna give me some of his old furniture. He's gonna bring it in his friend's van." David Cassidy began to sing "I Woke Up in Love This Morning" in my head.

"Sight unseen?" David asked. "What if you hate the stuff? Is he going to load it back in the van and take it home with him? Or leave it on a street corner, perhaps?"

I burst out laughing. It had never occurred to me I wouldn't like the furniture. What did I care what it looked like? It was only furniture, it was free, and it came from Martin. The whole thing was absurd. "Well, with any luck, I'll like it."

"Hope so," David said dryly. "By the way, now that we're practically neighbors, we ought to go to the movies sometime. I've been wanting to see *Dog Day Afternoon*."

His eyes were startlingly blue. Was he asking me out? "Sure, that'd be nice," I said as nonchalantly as I could manage.

∞

At lunchtime I sat in my dressing room, spooned up chicken noodle soup from a thermos cup and silently went over my lines. *Vicki's not just my cousin, she's my best friend. The kiss was as much my fault as yours, Sam. I should have stopped you, and I didn't.* (To which Martin had to reply, ironically enough, *I'm a married man, I ought to have more self-control. I love my wife.*) We had kissed briefly on the couch during camera blocking. It had been a little awkward, but I had still enjoyed it more than I wanted to admit, and I looked forward to doing it again this afternoon. When Sam and Jean kissed, it wasn't sleazy like Martin and Babette, even if Sam was cheating on his wife as surely as Martin was.

Clarissa ate celery sticks and studied her script on her side of the dressing room counter, on which sat, neatly arranged, a comb and gold-backed hairbrush, various toiletries, a bottle of expensive-looking perfume, and framed photos of Clarissa smiling amid other people. In one photo, she wore dark lipstick and a black, low-cut gown, and Maurice wore a tux. They had their arms around each other and smiled zanily. I liked the Clarissa in the photo much more than the Clarissa sitting at the counter. I knew she wished she had the dressing room to herself, because from time to time she'd glance over with an annoyed little moue. The feeling would have been mutual, except that today I preferred not to be alone in the dressing room, for fear that I would see Cyn in the mirror again.

I was finishing my chicken soup when there was a knock on the door.

"Enter," Clarissa said regally.

The door opened; it was Martin.

"Hello, Marty," Clarissa said. "What can we do for you?"

He looked from me to Clarissa and back again. Then he said, "So, about tomorrow. We're all set with the van. I need your address. And you'd better give me your phone number too, just in case."

A few days ago, I would've been pleased at the idea of Martin visiting my apartment—and part of me still was. Mostly I felt irritated, as if I were the one he was cheating on, and he was trying to make it up to me with a bunch of dusty furniture. I tore a strip of paper from the day's script and wrote my address and phone number on it. Clarissa watched as if witnessing a suspicious transaction.

Martin examined what I'd written. "You must be down the street from Halpren's place." Then, noticing Clarissa's scrutiny, he told her, "I'm giving Jo some furniture from my old apartment."

"Oh?" Her black brows arched. "From your bachelor days?"

"Well, not exactly," he soldiered on. "I think we still used it when my wife and I were first married. But by the time we moved into our house, Gloria was tired of the stuff."

"I see," Clarissa said, as if it were all terribly suspect.

"Jo has no furniture," Martin said a bit desperately.

"I have some furniture," I retorted, though I was starting to feel sorry for him.

"So, tomorrow at three o'clock," he said. He kept looking at the strip of paper with my address on it.

"Tomorrow at three," I said. "Thanks, Marty."

He left the dressing room and closed the door. Only then did I let myself smile.

"Well, well," Clarissa said.

"Well, well, what?" I asked.

She smiled frostily. "I could give you a piece of advice, but I doubt you'd listen to me. You're young and think you know everything."

"I don't think I know everything."

"Martin means well," she said. "He just doesn't think. That means you have to be the one to do the thinking. Understand?"

I was sure she knew about Martin and Babette, but I could hardly discuss it with her. "He's just giving me some furniture."

"Is that what they're calling it these days?" She sounded so much like the character she played that I burst out laughing. Clarissa, looking offended, turned back to her script.

∞

At one-thirty the next day I sat on the tan carpet in my living room and watched *Hope Springs Eternal*. The bulk of the episode was devoted to Vicki confronting her mother's husband, the supercilious Eric Read (Maurice), about his affair with Sylvia Cartwright (Clarissa). "You took vows before God when you married my mother!" cried Vicki (Babette at her most histrionic). "Doesn't that mean anything to you?"

When the show ended at two o'clock, I got up and scrutinized myself in the bathroom mirror. I had dressed carefully in jeans, a forest green sweater, and tennis shoes. I coughed a little and blew my nose (though I was feeling much better), brushed my hair, and reapplied lipstick, then sat cross-legged on my bed and waited.

On the other side of the bedroom wall, a small child burst into a sobbing tantrum. This seemed to happen a lot. The first time it happened, the morning after I moved in, I'd thought, half asleep, *I'll complain to the super*, and only when I was fully awake did I remember that you couldn't complain about a child crying the way you could about loud music or a yapping dog.

Martin had kids—a boy and a girl. I wondered if he thought about them when he was screwing around with Babette. In spite of which, the thought of being alone with him in my apartment made my heart race. I thought about how we'd kissed the day before on Jean Christopher's couch. I had liked it, in spite of the Babette weirdness. I had liked it a lot. "You are not Jean Christopher, and he is not Sam Jameson,"

I chastised myself. Then there was a knock on the door, and I gave a jump.

When I opened the door, Martin was standing there with a chair in each hand, and I started to laugh.

"I had to park a couple of blocks away. Figured I might as well save myself a trip." He wore his tan car coat over jeans and a red shirt. It was oddly wonderful to see him out of his usual context. He came in, turning sideways so as to bring the chairs with him, banging one against the doorframe in the process. He surveyed the small, white-painted room, empty of pretty much everything besides the TV, a shelf of books, a stack of LPs propped against a wall, and a dinky record player. He let out a low whistle. "You weren't kidding about needing furniture." He put down the chairs. "What do you think?"

They were plain wood chairs, straight-backed, honey-colored. "I like them," I said.

"Let's go get the rest."

I grabbed my keys and a jacket, and we went down in the elevator and walked the couple of blocks in the cool, cloudy afternoon, past a row of tenements peach and brown and pink, past the corner deli and more tenements, until we reached the van, which was not psychedelic, but plain and white and a bit battered-looking. Martin unlocked the door and slid it open, handed me a chair, and pulled out a small table.

We headed back up the street. A woman who looked like Gertrude Stein was walking an amiable-faced golden retriever who tried to jump up on Martin. "Hiya, doggy," he said, and leaned one end of the table on the pavement so he could pet the dog, though the woman glared at us as if we were furniture thieves who might want to steal her pet. Martin picked up the table, and we walked on.

A black guy and girl, both slender and wearing jeans and sneakers, strolled toward us holding hands. They wore identical looks of calm delight in each other, and though they barely glanced at me or Martin, I felt an inexplicable pride that he walked beside me. We walked together in my new neighborhood, and now that Martin was here, I felt somehow that it truly was my home.

Back upstairs, Martin arranged the table and chairs, then stood back and surveyed them. "What do you think?"

I moved the table forward a couple of inches, then an inch back. It was a long, low rectangle of pale wood. "They're just right, Marty. Thank you."

He shrugged out of his car coat. "Now you need a sofa. Red velvet or otherwise." The words hung in the air. Martin gave a sigh, draped the car coat over a chair back, and sat down. "Do you have anything to drink?"

"Sorry," I said, "I'm a terrible hostess. I only have milk and orange juice. Or water. Or I could make coffee?"

"No thanks," he said. Then he just looked at me until I sat across from him. "What you saw," he said finally.

I thought absurdly that he'd brought the furniture to set the scene for the conversation we were about to have. Just then I realized the furniture wasn't dusty in the least, and it smelled of furniture polish. "You didn't have to go to all this trouble, Marty. Just to talk to me."

"I'm happy to help. I mean, I was going to bring you the furniture anyway. But you seemed so shocked, the other day. That surprised me."

"Why? You figured I knew?"

"I didn't really think about it one way or the other. It's not a big secret—not at the studio, anyway. But then you seemed so shocked. I was afraid it might be a problem."

I had the urge to declaim, *You took vows, Martin! Doesn't that mean anything to you?*, and smothered a giggle.

"What's so funny?" he demanded.

I shook my head, but he kept looking at me like I was insane. "Did you watch today's show?" I asked finally.

"Before I drove here. So?"

I widened my eyes like Babette. "'You took vows before *God*, Eric! Doesn't that mean *anything* to you?!'"

His jaw dropped. Then he burst out laughing. That set me off, and then we were both cackling. "Okay, okay," he said at last, wiping away a tear. "What I was trying to say is, I guess I don't want to feel like you disapprove of me. Or like I've offended you in some way." He leaned forward and steepled his fingers. He looked so damned sexy in his jeans and red button-down shirt, so utterly corporeal. That he was alone with me in my living room, the first friend to set foot inside the place (unless you counted Cyn, which I didn't), seemed a marvelous stroke of luck, in spite of everything. "I just don't want this to get in the way of our working together, because working with you is terrific."

"I don't want it to get in the way of working with you either, Marty." He wanted my approval. I held back from telling him everything was okay, because I enjoyed feeling him yearn for something only I could give.

"Don't get me wrong," he said. "I'm not trying to defend myself here. I'm not proud of what I'm doing."

"Then why do you do it?" I wanted to say, why Babette? Aside from the obvious reasons—but maybe if you were a man, that was enough.

Martin shrugged. "It's just something we fell into. No grand romance. No grand anything, really."

"Does your wife know?"

He barked out a laugh. "Of course she doesn't." His face darkened, the way it had in his dressing room when I caught him and Babette. "Why do I do it? Because I'm a bit of a bastard, I guess. More than a bit, perhaps." He looked as if he expected me to contradict him. When I didn't, he slowly nodded, as if accepting the full weight of my judgment. I was surprised that it seemed to matter so much to him. I was about to relent and tell him he wasn't as bad as all that—but before I could speak, he said, "Hey, did you say you had orange juice?"

He followed me to the tiny kitchen with its faded but relentlessly cheerful blue-sprigged wallpaper. I poured each of us a glass of juice from the fridge.

He leaned against the blue tiled counter. "We've tried to call it off a few times. I'm weak, I guess."

I wondered if he knew about the guy who'd taken Babs to La Côte Basque. "Well, at least you didn't say your wife doesn't understand you."

I'd meant it as a joke, sort of, but he winced. "I hope we can still be friends, Jo," he said. Then he watched me and waited.

I finished my juice and placed the glass in the sink. "Of course we can, Marty."

"In spite of my moral failings?"

"Don't press your luck," I said, and smiled.

He smiled back, looking relieved. "Okay, I won't." He looked around the kitchen. "This is a nice little place. Can I see the rest of it?"

I showed him the white-tiled bathroom, then the bedroom. I felt shy as he stood in the bedroom doorway, looking in.

"So are you still gonna go furniture shopping with Babette?" he asked.

"I don't know. I haven't really talked to her since…" I trailed off. I didn't want to talk about that any more. We headed back to the living room.

"She has kinda froufrou tastes." He went to the window that looked out on a row of tenements. "She comes from money, you know. Her dad's a big-shot producer in L.A."

"Is that how she got this job?" I sat in one of Martin's chairs. I really did like them. They were friendly, somehow.

"*Hope Springs Eternal* is small-time, by his standards." He sat across from me. "She wanted to make it on her own. That's why she came to New York. Before that, she'd been Miss California. And she modeled."

Of course she did. "I like Babette. I just wish she were a better actress."

"You think she's bad now? Actually, she's improved a lot."

"Seriously?"

"Susan's helped her. I've tried. She might do better at a weekly series, someplace where she has more time to study her lines and do take after take until she gets it right." He eyed me. "I'd say we've thoroughly exhausted the topic of Babette. Let's talk about you, Joanna. You seeing anyone these days?"

The question took me aback. I shook my head. "Between the show and finding a new place to live, I've been too busy to think about that."

"Oh, come on. There's always time to think about that!"

"Clearly for you, there is."

I thought I might be pushing it a bit, but he smiled gamely and said, "Touché."

"I'm supposed to go to the movies with David tomorrow afternoon, though," I added.

He looked puzzled. "With David."

"Yes, with David. David Halpren."

"That's nice, Jo. Thing is, you're not really his type."

I gaped at him. "Thanks a lot!"

"That's not what I meant!" he said with a laugh. "What I'm trying to say is, he prefers men."

"Oh." When I thought about it, it made perfect sense. Why hadn't I realized? "Now I feel like a complete idiot." I hid my face in my hands. Martin was chuckling. Finally I looked up at him.

He was gazing at me fondly. "Don't feel bad. He's not in the closet, exactly, but he does keep things kinda quiet because he's considered such a heartthrob on the show."

"I see. That must be hard for him."

Martin shrugged. "I hope you're not too disappointed, kid."

"No, not really."

"I'm sure there are plenty of men who'd love to ask you out."

"Sure…" I ducked my head, blushing at his frank, good-natured gaze. I couldn't tell if he was flirting with me or just trying to be my friend.

Martin got up and walked over to the stack of LPs against the wall, bent at the knees and flipped through them: a couple of Rolling Stones albums, Joni Mitchell's *Court and Spark*, John Lennon's *Walls and Bridges*, some Nina Simone, Phil Ochs's *Tape from California* and *Rehearsals for Retirement*. All of them bore Cyn's mark, even the albums that had come out after her death. Watching him look at them made me feel exposed. "Of course you like Phil Ochs," he said, straightening up. Then he smiled as if something had just occurred to him. "You know, you would've loved my grandmother."

It seemed like a non sequitur, but somehow I knew he was paying me a compliment. "How come?"

"She loved Emma Goldman. Used to go hear her lecture in New York when she was young."

"She did?" That was pretty amazing, and I'd loved Emma Goldman since college—but did Martin associate me with the cliché of the bomb-wielding anarchist? He was smiling like he'd given me a present.

"My grandma, the anarchist! She was this little old lady from Minsk." He sat across from me again. "I was too young to know what the hell she was talking about. I just thought she idolized the woman the way I idolized Bogart or Joe Louis. But whenever she'd tell me stories about Emma Goldman—about her being arrested for opposing conscription, and I think there was something about birth control?—my ma would say, 'Mother! Don't tell him *that*!'"

I laughed. "That's such a nice story. I can't imagine seeing Emma Goldman in person. You know, when she came over from Russia, she lived in Rochester before she moved to New York City, like me." Like me and Cyn, I wanted to say. Maybe someone whose grandmother had loved Emma Goldman would understand what had happened back in '71.

"My grandma would've been horrified that I went into the army. Though she did support the United States participating in the Second World War, what with Hitler and all."

I stared at him. "You were in the army?"

He burst out laughing. "Now *you're* horrified! I never saw action, Jo. I was stationed in Germany."

"Were you drafted?"

"I enlisted straight out of high school."

"Why?"

He pondered for a moment. "I was this pudgy, bookish kid. I got sick a lot, stayed home from school. I didn't know how to talk to girls."

I tried to imagine Martin as a pudgy, awkward kid. Actually it explained a lot. I wanted to tell him I had been a quiet, bookish girl, but I didn't feel all that far removed from that girl.

"When I finished high school, I didn't have the first clue what to do," he said. "I wasn't good at anything. I just liked to read books and go to the movies. I didn't feel like going on with school. I sure didn't want to go into accounting like my old man. The army bought me some time. Not to say that I enjoyed it—I hated basic training—but the discipline was good for me."

I shook my head. He really was from a different generation.

"Then I came home, and I was ready to go to college, and I started acting..." He trailed off with a laugh. "Jesus, you're looking at me like I'm from another planet."

He'd caught me. "Well, you sort of are," I said.

"Thanks a lot!"

"It's not a bad thing. It's kind of neat, actually."

He tilted his head to one side and studied me. Then he smiled. "I see what you mean. The feeling is mutual, Jo."

This time I didn't look away. Getting to know this new, strange person was a wonderful feeling. I wondered if I could chance letting him know me better. "So even though you'd been in the army, were you against the war in Vietnam?"

"We're back to that, are we?" he said, grinning, but when he saw I wasn't smiling, he grew serious. "I didn't think about it much at first. When Gloria and I first met, she was protesting the war—you know, marching, leafleting? She was pretty much the first person I knew who opposed the war. She educated me on the history of the conflict. I was against it from that point on."

"I see." The fact that his wife had opposed the war, probably before Cyn and I ever met, made me feel guilty for being so attracted to Martin, even if it was mostly a carryover from Jean and Sam.

"And on that note, I guess I should be going." He stood and pulled on his car coat. I was surprised by how much I wanted him to stay.

We walked to the door. "Thanks again for the furniture," I said.

"You're welcome. I'm glad we talked." He put his arms around me and hugged me firmly. I held my breath for an instant, then hugged him back. His body felt strong and warm. We were alone together, and we weren't Jean and Sam, we were Jo and Martin. This was real. I closed my eyes.

When I opened them again, Cyn was standing behind Martin, in the spot where my teleprompter would have been. She watched us like a soap opera fan glued to the TV. Somehow it wasn't as much of a surprise as it should have been, as if we'd summoned her with our talk of Emma Goldman and the war. I gave a start, but Martin pulled away at the same instant and didn't seem to notice.

"Drive safely," I said, trying to keep my voice even.

"I will. See you on Thursday, right?" He leaned forward (from the corner of my eye I saw Cyn lean forward, watching) and kissed me on the cheek. I tried to hold onto the feeling of his lips on my cheek, and the way he looked at me afterwards, his dark eyes steady, their corners crinkling with his slight smile.

"See you on Thursday, Marty." As I shut and locked the door behind him, I felt like I was shutting myself away from all warmth and solidity and sanity.

Cyn was still there. She stood with her arms crossed.

"You're not real," I said. "This isn't real."

She wore a cream turtleneck, a dark green skirt, and brown suede boots. It took me a moment to realize it was Jean Christopher's outfit in the last couple of episodes I'd taped. "Why didn't you try and make him?" she asked, and gave a disgusted laugh. "I should've known you wouldn't seize the moment. That's your M.O. all over."

It was cold in the apartment. Cyn seemed to bring the cold with her. Or maybe it was me who was cold. I was breathing too rapidly. "This isn't happening," I whispered. "How can you be here?"

She shrugged. "You're not asleep, and you don't still have a fever, right? You're getting over the flu. The flu, your all-purpose excuse for getting out of things you don't want to do."

"But you died. You did die, right? You didn't—I don't know—go underground?" I clapped my hand over my mouth.

"That would get you off the hook, wouldn't it? If I hadn't really died. Oh, I died, all right."

"So I'm losing my mind."

"You think so? You seemed okay when that old dude was here. Aside from the way you fawned over him."

I closed my eyes tight, opened them again. She was still there. It was horrible. It was the opposite of horrible. "Cyn, I've missed you so much," I whispered.

Cyn shook her head vehemently. "Prove it!" she said. Then she was gone. I stood there gaping at the space where she'd been.

There was a crash in the kitchen. It sounded like an explosion shattering plate glass. I ran into the kitchen. The two juice glasses lay broken in the sink. That was all.

My heart was pounding. I felt sure a neighbor would come to ask about the crash. Or even the police. Had it really been that loud? Loud like the bomb that exploded at the draft board. I hadn't been there, but I had imagined it countless times.

I picked up a piece of glass and threw it into the trash. My index finger stung. Blood welled from a cut. I felt dizzy. Then—

I was standing outside the draft board in the middle of the night with Cyn. My nose was running, and I swiped at it. I was dizzy with fever. I was supposed to be the lookout, but I couldn't stop looking at the wicker handbag Cyn carried with the bomb inside, à la *The Battle of Algiers*. I wished I'd never seen that film. If I hadn't, maybe I'd be safely nursing my flu in my room at the residence hall.

Cyn turned and smiled at me. "Here goes," she whispered and placed the handbag in front of the mailbox. Then she nudged the bag under the mailbox with her foot. For an instant the flash illuminated her short pale hair. The blast knocked me backwards, the loudest sound I'd ever heard roaring in my ears. I hit my head against the wall.

I came to sprawled on my back on the pavement, my ears ringing. I was moaning. My head hurt, and there was pain like a knife in my leg. "Cyn," I said. "Cyn?"

I managed to hoist myself into a sitting position against the wall, though shards of glass bit into my hands in the process. Broken glass was strewn everywhere. When I looked at my leg, I thought I might throw up—something was sticking out of my thigh. I reached out and touched my leg, then recoiled. My jeans leg was soaked with blood. My breath came in short gasps. Cautiously I touched the thing that was sticking out of my thigh. It was hard and sharp. I was afraid to try and pull it out. Shrapnel, I thought.

Then I looked up and saw Cyn lying by the curb. She looked like she had been dropped from a great height. "Cyn?" I called. "Cyn!" She didn't move. It was too dark to see her clearly. I tried to tell myself she was just unconscious. "Cyn, please wake up. They'll be coming for us. We need to get away."

Her dark figure was so still. I tried to move toward her, but I nearly passed out from the pain in my leg. I felt light-headed and sick. I started to shiver, my teeth chattering. I was so cold. I needed to sleep.

Sirens, coming closer, startling me awake. Where was I? Vietnam? I knew I needed to run, but I couldn't feel anything.

The siren choked off at its loudest point. Running footsteps. "What a fucking mess," a man's voice said. Too late. Sleep now. Rest.

In my ear, Cyn's voice: "No, that's wrong."

I came to with a great shuddering breath, as though back from the dead. I was standing at the sink looking down at two broken juice glasses. In a panic I reached for my thigh. My leg was fine. Only my index finger was bleeding, and it left a red blotch on my jeans. A moment ago I had been bleeding to death. Was I going crazy? It had felt so real.

I went into the bathroom and pressed a Kleenex to my cut finger. Blood spread along the tissue—a small, manageable amount of blood. My face in the mirror looked pale and freaked out, but unharmed. "Cyn, did you send me back there?" I asked. "Please don't make me go back there. I don't want to die. I don't want to die." She didn't answer.

Chapter Eight:
No More Songs
(May–September 1971)

We huddled around the TV in the common room at the residence hall. Walter Cronkite said that Cynthia Foster had planned to blow up the draft board, that she or members of her group had phoned in a warning, had mailed a statement to the Associated Press and the *New York Times*. He didn't read the statement that we had carefully crafted and haggled over. He just said the bombing was in retaliation for the war in Vietnam. "A former student of the School of New York, Alexander Kloski, is wanted for questioning in connection with the bombing." I waited for him to say my name and Jeremy's.

They showed footage of the draft board. They must have cleaned up Cyn's blood before they let the cameras roll. The bomb had blown out the windows of the draft board and several other buildings on the block. The Chinese laundry. The bakery! It hadn't occurred to me that other buildings could be affected. Had the others known that was a possibility? I stared at the TV. We had done this. It had never seemed quite real, even when Cyn and I looked at Jeremy's bomb. It had always seemed like a fantasy. But Walter Cronkite said it happened. I could see the broken glass on the sidewalk. Cyn was really dead, and Alex was wanted by the cops, and for all I knew, Jeremy and I would be next.

The other girls' eyes were big with shock and sorrow and, let's face it, titillation. "Was Alexander Kloski Cynthia's boyfriend?" Edie asked me.

I wanted to snort with laughter as Cyn would have done. I just shook my head.

"I don't understand fighting for peace with violence," Anne said earnestly. I wanted to tell her how naive that was, how nonviolence could be nothing but complicity with violence, how committed we were to the struggle—but what did those words even mean now?

"You didn't know what Cynthia was planning, did you?" Edie pressed. Had she heard any of my phone conversation with Cyn yesterday? I couldn't believe those were the last words we would ever say to each other.

"Edie, for god's sake!" Maggie said. "Leave her alone. She's lost her best friend."

Then my throat closed up, and I was crying and coughing while the girls murmured their sympathies.

∞

Cyn's high school yearbook photo was in the *Times*. Where had they gotten that? She looked like any pretty, long-haired, smiling blonde. The headline read: COED KILLED BY BOMB OUTSIDE DRAFT BOARD, LOWER MANHATTAN. I imagined what she would say: "Not quite what I was aiming for, but look, Jo—I'm in the fucking *New York Times*!"

The girls mostly left me alone because I was a coughing, weeping mess, and they didn't know what to do besides pat my shoulder, hand me a Kleenex, and back away. My roommate slept in a sleeping bag in another girl's room—so she wouldn't catch the flu, she said, but I thought it was also because she didn't know how to deal with the sniveling best friend of the blown-to-bits radical.

∞

Two days after Cyn's death, there was a knock on my door around nine in the morning. I'd been up for hours, anguish making it impossible to stay asleep for long. My empty suit-

104

case was open on my bed, and I was staring into my side of the closet, willing a black dress to appear. The idea of shopping for a dress for the funeral was overwhelming. The knocking started up again, louder and more insistent, and I managed to tear my gaze away from the ridiculously bright and cheerful clothes in the closet. I opened the door. Two men stood in the doorway. Both were clean-shaven, with short hair and casual suits. One was stocky and looked around my dad's age, the other taller and younger, with red hair and freckles. They flashed their badges. I couldn't quite breathe. "We're looking for Joanna Bergman," the older cop said.

"That's me," I said, and was racked by a coughing fit. I felt so exhausted, like I was going to die, and I thought how ironic that would be, or how fitting, that the flu would carry me off after Cyn's spectacular, horrific death.

"Can we come in?" the younger cop asked. They didn't wait for me to answer. I followed their gaze: they had spotted the Angela Davis poster on the wall.

"You going someplace?" the older cop asked, gesturing at the suitcase on the bed.

"Rochester," I said.

"What's in Rochester?"

My throat was so tight, I could barely get the word out: "Funeral."

The older cop's eyes briefly softened. The younger cop was looking around the room. He plucked a book from my shelves— the copy of *Soledad Brother* Cyn had loaned me. He looked from the book to the poster—"Free Angela and All Political Prisoners"—and back again. His big hands riffled through the paperback. *Soledad Brother: The Prison Letters of George Jackson.* Was I going to prison? I wanted to ask about a search warrant. I kept thinking about the black dress I needed to buy.

"Did Cynthia tell you what she was planning?" the older cop asked. "Did she mention any accomplices? How about Alex Kloski?"

"No," I kept saying. I felt like I was going to faint. I felt more like Judas with each No.

"They're your friends, right?"

"Cynthia was my best friend." Should I say I wanted a lawyer? Call my parents and get them to find me one? I didn't want them to know the cops were here. Maybe mentioning a lawyer would make me look guiltier.

The younger cop shook my copy of Chekhov plays as if something incriminating would drop out. The older cop asked where I was when Cyn was at the draft board.

"I was here, in bed. I had the flu. I still have the flu." I kept sniffling and coughing and wiping my raw nose with a tissue. I thought they would never leave. They didn't mention Jeremy. I hadn't spoken to him since before Cyn died. I was afraid to contact him, for fear the cops would be watching.

Anne appeared in the doorway and stopped, eyes huge. "What's going on? What are you doing with my guitar?" The younger cop was vigorously shaking her acoustic guitar.

The older cop flashed his badge at her. "Are you Joanna's roommate? We'd like to ask you a few questions."

"But I don't know anything!" She looked terrified, as if they were about to read her her rights and slap on the cuffs. What if they did that to me, and I wouldn't be able to go home for the funeral? At least then I wouldn't need a black dress.

The older cop ushered Anne into the hall and closed the door—so we couldn't get our stories straight? The younger cop peered into the closet and yanked the clothes on their hangers along the rod. Then he squatted down and inspected the shoes on the closet floor. As he picked up one of Anne's loafers, turned it upside down and gently shook it, I imagined how Cyn would have joked: *That pig has a shoe fetish!* Then I remembered the bomb in the cardboard box on Cyn's closet floor, and I broke out in a sweat.

The door reopened, and the older cop came back in. Anne hovered in the doorway. The cops conferred in low voices, and I held my breath. Could Anne have said anything incriminating?

The older cop turned to me. "You haven't heard from Alex Kloski?" he asked. I shook my head. He wrote something on a pad of paper, tore out the page and handed it to me. "If you hear from him, give me a call."

I stared down at the phone number and the scrawled words "Detective Rynan."

"Miss Bergman? Did you hear me?"

I looked up and nodded at the detective. His salt-and-pepper hair was greasy and thinning. He scrutinized me for a long moment, while I squirmed under his gaze and wondered if he knew I would never rat out Alex. Finally he gave a sigh. "Come on, Jim," he said, and he and the other cop strode past me and out the door. I stood there hugging myself, the piece of paper clutched in my fist. I was relieved they were gone, though part of me wanted them to haul me in and make me pay for what had happened to Cyn.

Anne came into the room, picked up her acoustic guitar and held it to her body protectively. She wouldn't quite look at me. "That was so scary," she said, as if to herself.

"I think the redheaded cop had a shoe fetish," I offered.

Anne stared at me then. "How can you joke at a time like this, Joanna?" Still clutching her guitar, she marched from the room.

∞

I had never been in a church before. This one was small, with blue stained-glass windows and a large gold cross behind the pulpit. I didn't want to look at the casket, glossy and black, with white lilies heaped on the lid. I sat with my parents and brother, a few rows from the front on the left side of the church. None of us spoke as we waited for the service to begin. I started to cough dryly, and my mother reached into her purse and handed me a cough drop. I popped it into my mouth. The medicinal cherry taste filled my mouth, and I stopped coughing. Guilt surged through me as it had yesterday when my mother took me to Sibley's to buy a black dress.

My mom had hazel eyes like mine, and shoulder-length hair dyed the light brown it used to be naturally, so that the color was just off from what I always expected. My dad looked older than the last time I'd seen him, less than six months before. He had gray hair and a receding hairline, bushy eyebrows above blue eyes, creases in his forehead. My parents had believed me when I said, *I had no idea. Cyn never told me what she was planning. We went to some anti-war protests.* How could they believe me? Maybe they just wanted to.

My little brother Rob sat next to our dad. He looked somber and a little scared, his face softened, girlish even, in grief. He'd always had a crush on Cyn. He leaned toward me and said under his breath, "I always thought I'd have to go to Rick's funeral, not Cynthia's."

"Rob," my mom said.

"I know what you mean," I said. Rick was the older brother of Rob's best friend. He'd been in Vietnam, but he'd come home again, apparently safe and sound. I wondered if he'd killed anyone over there.

"There they are," Rob whispered, as Cyn's parents and sister came out of some alcove near the front of the church. I had been surprised that there wasn't going to be a reception at the Fosters' house after the funeral, but seeing Cyn's parents, I understood. Mr. Foster's mouth was set in a grim line. He'd always seemed glacial and authoritarian, and much more preoccupied with his job than my father was with his—though I had never really known what Mr. Foster did, except that it was something financial. Mrs. Foster was blonde like Cyn, though her face was longer, with beautiful cheekbones. She was tastefully clad in expensive-looking black. Her elegant face seemed obliterated, her eyes tunnels of despair. I didn't want to look at her, but I couldn't stop, any more than I could stop looking at the casket, drawn irresistibly by the horror of it. I was glad only family was going to the grave site, though I knew I ought to be there. I imagined what might have happened if I'd gone with Cyn to the draft board, if the bomb had taken me as well as her, or instead of, and my mother's face destroyed like Mrs. Foster's. That was the only thing that got me through each minute, the notion that my life might still be worth something because my parents had been spared that horror.

Cyn's little sister Ginnie was taller than she'd been the last time I'd seen her. She had always been a vague figure, little sister battering on Cyn's door, freckle-faced brat to be ignored and mocked, though she'd seemed a good enough kid. Now her face was grave and bewildered. She did and did not resemble Cyn. It hurt to look at her.

The pastor appeared and took his place behind the pulpit, and Cyn's parents and sister sat in the front pew on the left. In the rows behind them sat Cyn's extended WASP family, about whom she'd rarely spoken, usually in tones of disdain. I thought one gray-haired woman was Cyn's grandmother, who lived in…Connecticut, maybe? There were people in other pews who we'd known in high school, mostly guys. I guessed they hadn't left Rochester, though Cyn had left them far behind years ago. Mr. Ellis, who'd been in charge of the debate team, sat alone in a pew on the right side of the church. Cyn had been his star. He still had a luxuriant blond mustache. He hugged his tweed-clad arms, a look of quiet rage on his face. High school seemed a thousand years ago. The idea of talking to any of these people felt beyond me.

The pastor was tall and thin, with gray hair and a round face. His voice was bland and amiable. "We are met in this solemn moment to commend Cynthia Foster into the hands of Almighty God, our heavenly Father..." I could practically hear Cyn's laughter. I remembered that she'd said being a Methodist was boring. I wished I could have thrown her a Jewish funeral, though I'd only ever been to my father's mother's service, and that had been so long ago, I could barely remember it. Or maybe Cyn would have liked a Catholic ceremony, with incense and wine and communion wafers.

The pastor began to recite a psalm. He didn't read it well, but the beauty of the words cut through my fog. "...If thou, Lord, shouldest mark iniquities, O Lord, who shall stand? But there is forgiveness with thee, that thou mayest be feared..."

Forgiveness. The word caught in my chest. My eyes latched onto the closed casket heaped with lilies. I couldn't breathe, thinking of Cyn in there. The coffin was so small. Cyn had been small. It was hard to remember that.

∞

That night in my childhood bed I dreamed Cyn was trapped alive in her coffin. She was banging on it with her hands and feet. "Joanna, get me out of here, goddamn it!"

Then the dream shifted, and it was me in there. It was my punishment for backing out of the action. I could hear Cyn's voice on the other side of the coffin. "The action went fine without you, Jo," she said. "We're going underground, Alex and Jeremy and I. Too bad you can't join us."

Even stuck in the coffin, I was so relieved that she was alive, I began to cry. "I'm so glad you're all right, Cyn. I'm so glad you're all right!" I woke up weeping.

∞

I flew back to the city the day after the funeral. The day after that, I went to Brooke Hall. A muscled blond guy answered the door. "Is Jeremy there?" I asked.

He strode away, bellowing, "Blum!"

Jeremy came to the door. He looked strung out, dark eyes staring, skin sallow. "You shouldn't be here," he said.

"I know. But I had to see you."

"I have a final tomorrow morning, and I'm way behind on studying. I think I'm gonna flunk out." He smiled sardonically. "As if that matters."

"Finals…" I said, shaking my head. I didn't know how I would manage to finish my Ibsen paper, much less take my exams.

We walked to Washington Square Park. My skin crawled with paranoia. Maybe that frizzy-haired girl in shorts was really a pig. Was that clean-cut guy reading a newspaper tailing us? Jeremy and I sat on a bench. He smelled of sour sweat. He had always smelled clean and sweet.

"Was there something wrong with the device?" I whispered.

"It was fine. I was sure it was fine." Jeremy spoke so quietly it was as if he was swallowing the words. "The blast was a little larger than I'd thought it would be. But she should have had plenty of time to place it and get away. I don't know what could've happened."

You idiot, I wanted to say. The blast was a little larger? It blew out all the fucking windows on the street. What else did you get wrong? "And you let her go alone?"

He stared at me. "What do you mean? You were supposed to be with her. We asked her if she wanted us to wait for you to show up, but she said you were on your way. Didn't you go with her?"

"I was too sick to come. Didn't she tell you?"

I hated the way he was looking at me. Judging me. He had never looked at me like that before. "You must have been at death's door to back out at the last minute, Jo."

We both flinched at his unfortunate choice of words. Why hadn't Cyn told them about my phone call? I didn't understand. Had she thought I would show up after all? I couldn't bear the idea of her waiting for me and then going alone to her death.

"I came down with the flu. I really did, Jeremy!" Knowing that wasn't the only reason I backed out, and fearing he knew it too. "Where's Alex?"

He shook his head. "He split. He's gone underground."

That's what Alex had wanted all along, to be Jesse James, outlaw on the run—but what if he got caught? Would he rat us out?

"The pigs questioned me the day after he left," Jeremy said. "Man, I thought I was finished." He laughed hectically. I caught another whiff of his sweat, sharp and rank. Alex had always been the musty-smelling one, with his patchouli.

"They questioned me too." I lowered my voice to a whisper. "Are they going to arrest us?"

"I don't know." Jeremy scanned the park yet again. "We shouldn't be seen together."

Had I expected him to hold me and tell me everything would be all right and at least we still had each other? We didn't have each other. We didn't have anyone. "You're right," I said.

∞

I didn't see Jeremy again. One morning, on my way to take my Ibsen exam, I came out of my daze of pain just in time to see Franny walking toward me out of my classroom building. I steeled myself for a barrage of sympathy and curiosity.

Franny paused long enough to meet my eyes. Then, with an almost imperceptible shrug, she picked up her pace. I turned and watched her hurry across the lawn. I almost expected her to break into a run. I imagined all the things Cyn would say: *Daddy's girl, little twit, coward.*

Somehow I managed to pass all my finals. That in itself seemed a betrayal of Cyn. I went home to Rochester for the summer. For weeks, months even, I waited for the other shoe to drop. Then it was September, and I started drama school, as if nothing had happened.

Chapter Nine:
Chords of Fame
(October 1975)

"Who would play me in the movie version of my life?" Cyn asked, and I gave a start. She was sitting in what had been the empty seat next to me in the middle of Cinema 1, as the end credits began to scroll over the wet tarmac of Kennedy Airport at night and the cop cars with their flashing red lights. I wanted to get up and run, but I couldn't with David Halpren sitting next to me. I'd been bracing to see Cyn again since I'd cut my finger yesterday. Bracing to go back to the draft board, back to pain and fear and death.

I glanced at David, who still faced the screen.

"Don't worry about him," Cyn said. "I'm not in his movie."

Airplanes screamed on the soundtrack. I was still half in the world of the movie, the botched bank robbery and its aftermath. *We'll take care of Sal*, the FBI agent had told Sonny, and Sonny had demanded, *Do you think I'd sell him out?* Then Sal was shot dead. I remembered Cyn lying on the pavement, her body indistinct and very still in the dark. But I hadn't really been there, had I?

"In the movie version of my life," Cyn said, "I would have a neat bullet hole in my forehead, and you would watch them wheel me past on a stretcher. Your hands would be cuffed behind your back, and you would suffer beautifully for the camera. The audience would love you. But that's just one version."

I remembered what Martin had said: *I'd kill to have that part.* "I didn't sell you out," I whispered.

"What?" David asked.

I shook my head. "Nothing," I murmured. I wasn't Sonny—I was Stevie, the guy who backed out of the bank robbery at the beginning of the film. *I can't do it, Sonny. Sorry, Sonny.* And surely I was right to have backed out, because when I was at the draft board with Cyn—no, *if* I had been there—I had died too—*would* have died. I wanted to beg her not to send me back there, but I couldn't with David sitting next to me. I focused on the almost empty cup of Coke in my hand. It was real, here-and-now.

"I miss popcorn and Coca Cola," Cyn said. "I even miss cherry cough drops."

There was an empty tub of popcorn at my feet. A cherry cough drop had just dissolved in my mouth.

"In another version of things, we could have gone to Algeria," Cyn said, as if it wasn't a non sequitur. "I always wanted to go there, ever since we saw *The Battle of Algiers*. We could go to Algeria, Jo." There was a strange note of hope in her voice. Hope like Sonny and Sal had, when they thought there was a way out, an airplane out of the country.

David tapped my shoulder. "Ready, Jo?" he asked. The people in my row were standing, waiting for me to file out. I got up and left Cyn in the dark, but I kept wondering what she'd meant.

∞

In the rehearsal room Friday morning Martin held forth about Muhammad Ali beating Joe Frazier. "Fourteen rounds! It was brutal." He mimed a few boxing jabs.

"I'm awestruck by your machismo, Martin," Maurice said primly, and Clarissa and I burst out laughing.

Martin grinned and put his arm around my shoulders. "You a boxing fan, Jo?"

Pretty much the only thing about Muhammad Ali I'd ever cared about was that he'd risked going to prison and losing his career to oppose the war. "Not really. Muhammad Ali beat Joe Frazier?"

He goggled at me. "'Muhammad Ali beat Joe Frazier?' It was the Thrilla in Manila, for god's sake!"

"Oh, right. I guess I heard about that." I had heard about it, but I liked eliciting that incredulous look in his eye. His arm around me felt warm, and his sweater was thick and soft. I was glad Babette wasn't here today. Clarissa's eyes narrowed at the sight of Martin's arm around me, though she was hanging on Maurice's every word as usual. Didn't Clarissa know Maurice was gay?

"You're such a *girl*, Joanna," Martin said. "Jesus, I need coffee." He pulled away and poured himself a cup.

"Hey, I saw *Dog Day Afternoon* the other day," I said. I wondered what David had thought about the gay subject matter of the movie. Funny that it hadn't occurred to me until now.

Martin took a cautious sip of black coffee. "Did you love it?"

I tried not to think of seeing Cyn in the darkened theater. *We could go to Algeria, Jo.* "I loved it," I said.

His answering smile was like sunlight spilling across my face.

∞

The day went by in a blur of enjoyable hard work. I had two scenes with Martin and Maurice, though I was mostly a spectator to their verbal sparring as Sam Jameson took Eric Read to task for cheating on his wife. I loved the panache with which Maurice uttered lines like "Perhaps you ought to concern yourself with your own marriage, Jameson—and as for you, young lady, you would be wise to stop meddling in matters that don't concern you," but sometimes it made it hard to keep a straight face.

After that, I had a dialogue-heavy scene with Martin. Focusing on hitting my marks and remembering my lines kept thoughts of Cyn at bay until Martin and I were taping our last scene of the day. We sat drinking coffee across a table at the Hopefield Diner while the cameras lingered on our faces. At other tables a few extras pretended to eat and silently chat. Martin gazed earnestly into my face. "Eric Read's not gonna take this lying down, you know. These allegations are no joke. But you're not going to let this go, are you, Jeanie?"

Beneath the Band-Aid, my cut finger let out a small bright querulous sensation, a ticklish stinging like a paper cut. I remembered the broken glasses in my kitchen. I remembered the explosion, the deafening blast. Stop it.

Martin was looking at me expectantly. "You're not going to let this go, are you?" he repeated.

Damn it, what was my next line? I tried to glance unobtrusively at the teleprompter, though it was a point of honor with me and Martin to know our lines cold (unlike Babette, whose eyes frequently latched onto the teleprompter). The next line obligingly popped into my head. "I'm not going to let Eric Read intimidate me," I said. "I'm gonna find out what he's into if it's the last thing I do!" Then I took a sip of coffee (terrible and cold) and set the cup back on the table. There was a smear of blood on the white cup.

Somehow my cut had reopened and was bleeding through the Band-Aid. There were drops of blood on the table, and even a little on the left cuff of my yellow shirt.

"Cut!" Vincent's voice rang over the PA. "What is this, a horror flick?"

"Jo, you're bleeding," Martin said unnecessarily.

"I *know*," I said. "Sorry, everyone!" We were never supposed to stop in the middle of a take unless something went drastically wrong. Going up on a line wasn't enough, but apparently this qualified.

"Nancy, get her cleaned up," Vincent said.

Nancy, the perpetually harried production assistant, appeared and grabbed my hand as if she were a nurse. She cleaned the cut with an alcohol-soaked cotton ball. "Press down on this," she told me, and I did. She tried scrubbing the blood from my cuff, but it only paled a little. She rolled both my cuffs under, then wiped the blood from the coffee cup and the table top. I felt like a child who had to be cleaned up after.

"I cut myself on a broken glass the other day," I said. "Sorry!" I'd cut my finger, and then I'd gone back to the draft board. What if it happened again right now? I remembered my jeans leg soaked with blood, the excruciating pain in my thigh. I recoiled, pulling my hand away from Nancy as she was putting on a fresh Band-Aid.

"You okay, Jo?" Martin asked. My heart was pounding. I remembered my death. *What a fucking mess.*

"Hold still, Joanna," Nancy said, gripping my wrist so hard it hurt. She stuck the Band-Aid over the cut. Then she trotted away. I took a deep breath, then another and another. All it did was make me feel cold and light-headed.

"Hey, Joanna." Martin's voice, as if from far away. "I take it you get squeamish at the sight of blood?"

I let out a laugh like a death rattle.

"Are we ready?" Vincent demanded.

"Just a second, Vince." Across the table Martin grasped my uninjured hand. "Jesus, you're as cold as ice. Snap out of it, okay? So we can get out of here in the next week or so? If you do, I'll buy you a Scotch." He smiled, and a bolt of heat went through me. He had a hold of me. For the moment, I was safe.

I squeezed his hand. "I'm gonna hold you to that Scotch," I said.

∞

When we finally finished the scene, Martin and I went to our dressing rooms. I changed into my street clothes and was leaving to meet him in the lobby when I nearly collided with Clarissa. She fixed me with her dark-eyed glare. "Thanks so much for wasting everyone's time this afternoon," she said. "I suppose you thought we had nothing better to do than wait around for you." She'd still had a scene to tape with Maurice after Martin and I were done for the day. I wondered who had told Clarissa the wait was my fault.

I gingerly touched the Band-Aid on my finger. "I'm sorry I inconvenienced you, Clarissa. It was an accident. Though it wasn't really that long a delay, was it?"

She shook her head disgustedly. "It's Heather O'Connor all over again. Thanks to your lack of professionalism, I'm going to be late for the theater."

I thought to say that in that case, she ought to quit wasting her time haranguing me in the hall. Then I remembered that the show she was in, a production of *Antony and Cleopatra* at the Pelham Theater, was closing this weekend. She had been jubilant when she got the part of Cleopatra, and everyone in the company (myself included) had agreed she was perfect for the role—but the show had received lukewarm reviews, and it was already closing. No wonder she was being nastier than usual. "You don't have to invoke Heather O'Connor's name," I said quietly. "I said I was sorry. And I'm sorry your show is closing." I regretted that last bit the second the words were out. Her eyes widened as if I were trying to twist the knife. Then she swept past me into the dressing room and shut the door.

I shook my head, remembering how, when I'd started at *Hope Springs Eternal*, I'd actually thought Clarissa might become my mentor. Instead, she plainly hoped I would lose my job like Heather O'Connor. Surely one slip-up wouldn't make that happen, when I was finally in a front-burner storyline— but what if there were more slip-ups? Could I find out what Cyn wanted and get her to stop what she was doing to me?

More than ready for that drink, I went downstairs and found Martin chatting with the security guard. When he saw me, he smiled, and a wave of relief went through me.

"Sorry about what happened today," I told him as we walked out the lobby doors.

"Oh, come on, none of that," he said. "It could've happened to anyone."

"Thanks for saying that. Clarissa really let me have it—" I fell silent as I became aware of the woman coming toward me on the sidewalk. She looked about my mother's age, with black hair, large dark eyes, and a plump figure. She stared at me with an expression both awed and indignant. "You're Jean Christopher, aren't you?" she said, as if it were an accusation.

"Yes, I play Jean Christopher." Would she ask for my autograph?

"You're terrible," she said, holding herself proudly. "Your cousin Vicki trusts you. I see the way you look at her husband. I know what you have in mind!" My love scene with Martin hadn't even aired yet. This woman would go berserk when it did. "You weren't there, but Vicki and Sam had the most beautiful wedding." A note of something like admiration came into her voice. "How can you live with yourself?"

"Good question," I said.

"Come on, Jo," Martin said. "Let's get that drink."

"Oh my god," the woman said, bursting into a smile. "It's Sam Jameson!" Suddenly she was all girlish coquetry. "I can't believe it. I love you!"

Martin gave her a little wave. She giggled bashfully.

"Hi, Joanna," a man's voice said, and I turned. A guy with curly black hair was coming towards us. He wore jeans, a t-shirt, and a denim jacket, and he was smoking a cigarette. For an instant I thought he was another *Hope Springs Eternal* fan. "Remember me?" he asked with a slight smile. It was Jeremy.

"Hi," I said uncertainly. What I wanted to say was, *Are you real?* The cigarette between his fingers was wrong. Jeremy didn't smoke tobacco.

"Do you know this guy, Jo?" Martin asked, flanking me protectively.

I had the urge to say no. "We went to school together," I said. I didn't want to tell him Jeremy's name. That would make it too real.

"It's great to see you again, Jo," Jeremy said, taking another step toward me. He had put on a little weight—maybe a little muscle—and it suited him. His hair was shorter than it had been, and there was something guarded in his dark eyes, something reserved in his demeanor that once had been shy but wide open.

"What are you doing here?" I asked.

"I saw you on TV." Jeremy looked at Martin, then at me again. I was afraid of what he might say in front of Martin. "I tried to phone you here, but they never put me through."

"You phoned the studio? You could have left a message." I turned to Martin. "Hey Marty, can I take a rain check on that drink?" I tried to keep my tone light.

Martin scrutinized me, as if trying to make certain I'd be okay. "Of course. Have a good weekend, Jo." He kissed me on the cheek in a way that struck me as proprietary—or was I imagining? Then he headed off down the street, and I was left alone with my past.

I almost couldn't look at Jeremy. Over the years he had become an abstraction. It was strange to think of him watching me on TV. "Jeremy," I said. "I can't believe it's really you."

"Can we go somewhere and talk?" He took a step closer and lowered his voice to a whisper. "It's about a mutual friend."

"A mutual friend?" I repeated, mimicking his whisper. Had he seen Cyn too? Surely not. Or did he mean Alex? Was Alex still underground? All at once the old paranoia, the feeling of being watched, was back. Then I realized the woman who'd taken Jean Christopher to task was still standing there watching, as if this were all part of *Hope Springs Eternal*.

Chapter Ten:
Winter in America
(October 1975)

I brought Jeremy back to my apartment because I couldn't think of anywhere else to take him, and I didn't want anyone else to see us together. "Nice place," he said, surveying my living room with a puzzled air. Apparently he thought a soap actress would live someplace more luxurious.

"I like it," I said. I wondered if Cyn knew Jeremy was here, and what she would think of that. Would she make her presence known? I checked my Band-Aid—no blood leaking through.

"Is it okay if I smoke?" Jeremy asked, pulling a pack of Camels from his jacket pocket. I wasn't thrilled at the idea, but he seemed nervous enough already without adding nicotine withdrawal to the mix. I found the orange ashtray in my kitchen cabinet—my only ashtray, which my ex-boyfriend Ian used to use—and placed it on the table Martin had given me. We sat facing each other on Martin's chairs.

"So this is a surprise," I said.

He smiled too brightly. "I couldn't believe it when I saw you on TV! I work at a hospital in Brooklyn, and a lot of the patients love soap operas. They'll say, 'It's time for my story.' So one day Mrs. Wolf was watching her story, and I heard your voice coming from the TV, and I looked up, and there you were! I was so proud."

Memories welled up of telling Jeremy about my theater ambitions—how he had once been so supportive. I found myself getting choked up at his praise. "Thanks, Jeremy," I managed to say. Smoke curled from his cigarette. The smell reminded me of Ian smoking in my old apartment. The remnants of my old attraction toward Jeremy stirred reflexively. "So what do you do at the hospital?" I asked.

"I'm a nurse." He started to laugh. "My brothers give me a hard time about it—always asking if I wear a nurse's uniform and cap."

"Aw, I think it's great."

"Thanks. I sure never thought I'd end up working at a hospital. But it's good for me to help people. I think I'm good at it. It's sort of the opposite of..." He paused, looking uncomfortable. "The opposite of what we did back then, but for the same reason. Trying to alleviate suffering."

"That makes sense." *What we did back then.* In a way I was desperate to talk to him about all that, but I wasn't sure I could bear it. "You said you wanted to talk about a mutual friend?"

Jeremy leaned forward, eyes gleaming. "*He* needs some help."

"So you're still in touch with him?" Somehow I couldn't say Alex's name. Did I really think my apartment had been bugged?

"He calls from time to time. I help him out with money when I can."

"Oh." Well, this was a first. Surprisingly, it hurt. "So that's why you showed up after all these years. To get money for him."

He couldn't quite meet my gaze. "I would've wanted to get back in touch with you in any case. I've often thought of you. I really was thrilled to see you on TV."

"Is he still underground?" It seemed a ridiculous word that once had seemed brave and exciting.

Jeremy nodded. "He moves around. He doesn't tell me much. He's still political."

Doing what, robbing banks like Patty Hearst? "Look, Jeremy, maybe you think I'm rolling in dough because I'm on TV, but it doesn't work like that. I'm still pretty new to the show, and I basically make enough to live on."

"That doesn't seem right. I mean, the women in the ward all watch *Hope Springs Eternal.*" He took a drag of his cigarette and blew out the smoke. It caught in my throat, and I coughed and coughed and waved at the air. Looking chagrined, he held his cigarette over his shoulder, but the smoke still headed toward me.

"Would you mind putting that out?" I asked hoarsely. "I'm getting over the flu." When the words were out, they reminded me of our awful last conversation. Did he remember? Looking regretful, he stubbed out his cigarette.

"Look, even a little bit would help," he said. "I'm not exactly rolling in dough either, but I can't leave him hanging when he's still fighting the good fight."

"What exactly is he doing?"

"He doesn't tell me details. But he and some like-minded people, fellow revolutionaries—"

The whole revolution shtick. "Oh, Jeremy, I can't. Not after what happened."

Jeremy's face fell, as if I were deflating all his revolutionary daydreams. I couldn't fathom how he could still have revolutionary daydreams after what had happened. "Couldn't you just think of it as helping him to survive?" he asked. "We're partly responsible for him being where he is now."

"That may be true, but I think we all made a huge mistake, and I don't want to make another. You yourself said it: you're doing the opposite of what we did back then."

"I didn't mean I can turn my back on him now, or that I think what he's doing is wrong. Anyway, he's doing it for the right reasons."

"I can't help but feel like this is what he wanted all along," I said. "To be on the run, like some desperado or something. Like *Bonnie and Clyde.*" Cyn's image, mixed with Faye Dunaway's, flashed in my mind. Neither of us had directly mentioned Cyn. She was the subtext.

He rumpled his hair distractedly. "He's my friend, Joanna. I can't abandon him."

"I hope he appreciates what a good friend he has."

His self-deprecating shrug was vintage Jeremy. "Will you at least promise me you won't tell anyone what I've told you?" he asked.

"Of course. I would never…" *Never rat you out*, I was going to say, but the phrase sounded too strange in my head to say out loud, an artifact of four years ago. Then I had a troubling thought. "Does he know you're asking me for help?"

He didn't answer, fidgeting beneath my gaze.

"Oh, Jeremy, that's just great! You're discussing me on the phone with a political fugitive?"

"We didn't say your name. You have nothing to worry about."

"Nothing to worry about! Are you kidding?" I imagined them discussing *our old friend who's now on a soap opera*, on a phone line that could well be tapped. Imagined Big Brother lurking outside my door or down on the street. Amazing how quickly the old paranoia reasserted itself. But it wasn't actually paranoia if the Feds arrested you for conspiracy. Why had I brought Jeremy back to my apartment?

His face darkened. "He's the one in trouble, Jo. It seems to me you're in pretty good shape. He's the one putting his life on the line."

"That's his choice. If he's still doing those kinds of actions." Bank robberies? Bombings? Could Alex actually still be doing bombings? Sometimes the news still reported that radical groups were setting off bombs, though not nearly as often as a few years ago. "I don't think most people in this country respond positively to those kinds of tactics, especially now that the war is over. People think the SLA are wackos, and look what happened to them."

He shook his head grimly. "What does the SLA have to do with anything? You can't blame him for their mistakes. I sure don't want to see him die on TV the way they did."

For a moment I couldn't breathe, the idea was so horrible. "You have to know that's the last thing I'd want. But if he's still engaging in militaristic tactics even though the war is over—"

"I didn't say he was!" He spoke so loudly, I began to suspect he thought my apartment might be bugged and he wanted to make sure that bit came through clearly. Then, more quietly, he added, "The war may be over, but the power structure is still racist and imperialist."

"And don't forget sexist. But you can't tell me you honestly still believe the revolution's coming, Jeremy. The revolution isn't coming. Not here, not now. Not the way we thought, anyway. I'm not saying I don't believe in social change, but that's not how it's going to happen here. It's going to be slower, less flashy, more incremental." Suddenly I realized I was echoing what Martin had said that afternoon at Chauncy's when Cyn had come back. What had he said? That change was about patience, not the grand gesture. It was hard to even say the word *revolution* aloud. I had to fight through the molasses-thick pain I'd been stuck in since Cyn died, the pain that had made it nearly impossible for me to think usefully about any kind of social change, much less revolution. Somehow I had managed to talk to Martin about it, that afternoon at Chauncy's. Is that why Cyn had come back—because I was coming unstuck at last?

Jeremy was looking at me with narrowed eyes. "That's easy for you to say, now that you're a TV star," he said, more coldly than I thought he was capable of. Before I could protest that it wasn't easy for me to say and that I was hardly a TV star, he rose, reaching for the pack of cigarettes in his pocket. "I'm sorry I wasted your time. It was good seeing you again, Joanna."

As much as Jeremy's sudden reappearance had thrown me, now that he was leaving, I felt desperate for him to stay. "You haven't wasted my time. Will you give me a number where I can reach you?"

He gave a laugh. "Don't call us, we'll call you, right?" He headed for the door. "I work at Brooklyn Memorial, in Orthopedics. You can reach me there."

I followed him. Why didn't he want me to have his home phone number? Then again, I hadn't offered him mine. "It was good to see you again, Jeremy," I said quietly.

He turned and looked at me. "That guy you were with at the studio? He's on *Hope Springs Eternal* too."

"Yes."

"The two of you are…"

"Friends. He's married, with two kids."

"I see." He didn't sound convinced. In that moment I missed Martin, maybe because he had never looked at me the way Jeremy was looking at me, with mistrust and disappointment. Then again, there was so much Martin didn't know about me.

I unlocked the door, and Jeremy opened it. I expected him to make one last plea for Alex. But he just smiled and said, "I'll see you on TV." Then he was gone.

The room smelled of cigarettes. I opened the window and breathed in the early evening air. I looked out the window. I didn't see any lurking FBI agents, just a woman laden with shopping bags getting out of a taxi. Then Jeremy appeared on the sidewalk and walked briskly away. I wished I could redo the last hour from start to finish, but I wasn't sure how I would have changed it.

"Well, that was terribly depressing, wasn't it?"

I whirled around. Cyn stood there posing in a Bonnie Parker getup, complete with yellow beret and matching sweater. "I never knew you fancied yourself as Faye Dunaway," I said, trying to sound unruffled.

"You've had quite a day, haven't you?" Cyn asked.

I slammed the window shut. "And now you're here to make sure it gets even worse."

"What are you mad at me for?"

I faced her. "You scared me to death the other day. I'm still not over it."

"Oh, please. I'm the one who's dead, not you."

I was breathing too fast. "How long do you plan to keep punishing me?"

Gracefully she sat in the chair where Jeremy had been. "I didn't realize my presence was a punishment. I thought you said you missed me."

"Did you have something to do with Jeremy contacting me? Did you make it happen?"

"Do you think I'm all-powerful?"

I sat in the chair opposite her. "It just seems like a big coincidence that Jeremy would show up again right after you did."

"You know why he showed up. He saw you on TV and saw dollar signs. He never was terribly bright, as witness my demise."

My demise. The words sucked all the air from the room. "God, Cyn. When you sent me back, I saw you on that sidewalk. It was dark, but somehow I knew you were gone. Did you suffer? When I was lying there—I mean, it couldn't have been real, but it hurt so much. I've never been in so much pain. And then I wasn't, and that was a relief."

She was silent, her face impassive. Finally she said, "It hurt worse than anything ever could, but only for an instant. Then I felt nothing. What was worse was the millisecond before. Everything was so slowed down, I swear I can remember the instant between the flash—the detonation—and the pain. In that instant I thought, *Oh, fuck.* Honestly, that was my last thought. Not terribly inspiring, was it?" She gave a laugh.

I put my face in my hands.

"No, don't do that, Joanna. I need you to face things."

I pulled my hands away and looked at her. Now she had on the clothes she'd worn the last time I'd seen her alive: worn jeans and a black t-shirt. "Is that why you're here?" I asked. "To make me face things?"

"Make you? Help you, maybe."

She wanted to help me? It sure didn't feel that way. "Do you think I should give Jeremy some money for Alex?"

"Alex?" She said the name as if she were trying to remember who that was. "Why should I care about that?"

"I thought maybe that was why you mentioned *The Battle of Algiers* at the movie theater. Do you want me to support whatever's left of the revolution? Is that what would give you peace?"

She laughed derisively. "The revolution? I don't even know what the hell that is. I seem to remember dying for it. I seem to remember that it mattered to me. Now it all seems absurd. No, worse than that, it seems insignificant and faraway and make-believe. But *this*—" She gestured at herself, then at me. "*This* is real, Jo. But when you talk about giving me peace, what you really mean is, you want me gone, right?"

"It's not that simple. I just don't want to feel off-balance all the time and terrified and like I'm losing my mind. Is that too much to ask?"

"You have everything, Joanna. Stop feeling sorry for yourself. You owe me." Then she was gone.

Chapter Eleven:
Nowhere To Run
(October 1975)

On Monday I didn't have to be at the studio until late afternoon. When I got to the rehearsal room, carrying the scripts I'd just retrieved from my dressing room, Martin was sitting at the table alone with a cup of coffee and his scripts. He waved and said, "They're running late."

"I'm glad it's not on my account this time," I said.

"How's the wound?"

I held up my hand and wiggled the fingers. The Band-Aid was off, and the cut was healing.

"Bravo," he said. Then he smiled at me, a broad, warm smile, and the fear and strangeness that had gripped me all weekend, obsessing over Cyn and Jeremy and my imagined-or-not death experience, loosened its hold. It was a delicious relief.

I poured myself half a cup of coffee and sat next to Martin. "So how'd it go with your old boyfriend?" he asked, and my reprieve was already over.

I took a sip of acidic black coffee. "He wasn't my boyfriend."

"Really? That's the vibe I got." He asked about you, too, I wanted to say. "So how'd it go?" he persisted.

"To be honest, it could've gone better."

"I'm sorry, kid." He eyed me. "Are you okay?"

Not even remotely. But it wasn't as if I could talk about any of it with him, much as I might want to. "Sure," I said, though I didn't sound terribly convincing.

He studied my face. Finally he shrugged and opened one of his scripts. "So this is a big week for us."

I hadn't had a chance to look at my pages yet. "Really? Are we going to sleep together?" It was customary to discuss storylines in the first person, but my face grew hot.

"Not this week. But there's some heavy making out on Friday." He spoke matter-of-factly, as if it were no big deal.

"Oh." That was all I could manage to say.

He grinned. "Don't sound so horrified!"

I laughed, my cheeks burning. Did he really think horrified was how I felt? "The fans are sure gonna hate me now," I said. "Speaking of which, that was unbelievable the other day—that woman lecturing me as though I actually was Jean Christopher!"

"Get used to it, kid."

"You mean, this happens a lot?"

He sipped his coffee. "Let's just say that sometimes people have a hard time differentiating between reality and fantasy when the fantasy's coming into their homes five days a week. These characters seem as real to them as their own families. Maybe even more real."

Babette and Susan walked in. "He wants me to meet his kids," Babs was saying, then clammed up when she saw Martin.

"So soon?" Susan asked, then saw Martin and clammed up too. Susan Harding played Beverly Read, heroine of *Hope Springs Eternal* and mother of Vicki Jameson. She had been on the show for over a decade, and she was the only actor in the company with her own dressing room. She had shoulder-length, ash blonde hair and was more petite in person than she looked on screen, where she appeared formidable indeed.

"Hello, Joanna, Martin," Susan said. "Elsbeth and company will be here momentarily."

"Hi, Jo," Babette said, and pointedly didn't greet Martin. She sat at the other end of the table, as far away from him as she could get. Martin watched her from beneath narrowed lids, then shook his head with a bitter smile and started leafing through his script. Were they having a fight, or was it possible they had broken up?

Elsbeth Howard, today's director, came in with the associate director and the script supervisor, and we got to work. In today's episode Vicki confronted Sam about his feelings for Jean, and Beverly told Jean to stay away from her daughter's husband. "Sam and I are friends," I read.

"If that's true, then why play with fire?" Susan read in beautiful, measured tones. "For my daughter's sake—for the sake of your cousin and her marriage—please put some distance between yourself and Sam." I always loved working with Susan, though I was a bit intimidated by her seemingly effortless professionalism.

"Tell me the truth, Sam," Babette read woodenly as we neared the end of the final act. "Are you in love with my cousin?"

"I haven't wanted to admit it to myself," Martin said. "But yes, I'm in love with her. I love Jean Christopher." My breath quickened as if he'd declared his love for me. I was such an idiot.

"Okay, Shirley," Elsbeth said in her raspy voice. "How are we, time-wise?"

"We're right on target," our script supervisor said. "For once!" Shirley timed our reading of the script with a stopwatch. If we ran long, cuts had to be made.

"Great," Elsbeth said. "See everyone in the morning."

"Hey, Joanna," Babette said, "did you still want to go shopping for a sofa?"

"Sure," I said, surprised. We compared schedules and settled on Wednesday for the sofa expedition, while Susan hovered smilingly.

Martin touched my shoulder. "See you tomorrow, kid," he said, and was out the door before I could reply. I suppressed the urge to run after him. I had hoped we might get that drink we hadn't had on Friday, but maybe that would've been too awkward with Babs around.

Babette rolled her eyes. "What a baby," she said to Susan. Then she turned to me. "Sorry, Jo. I know you and Marty are friends. I don't want to put you in the middle."

"Why, what's going on?" I asked.

"I came to my senses, is what's going on."

I felt all too elated. Why was it so hard to remember that Martin still had a wife?

"Hey, what are you doing right now?" Babs asked. "Susan and I were going to go for a drink. Want to join us?"

∞

I expected that we'd go to Chauncy's, but instead we went to Le Fanal Bleu, which Susan said had been the longtime favorite watering hole among *Hope Springs Eternal* veterans. It was a cozy little restaurant, quiet and dark. We sat around a table and a fifty-ish Frenchman with thinning hair and a kind, rugged face brought us martinis and a basket of hot bread. Simple as it was, it all seemed so sophisticated. In my jeans and orange sweater I felt underdressed compared to Susan, casually elegant in tan pants and a thick, expensive-looking chocolate brown sweater, and Babette, predictably stunning in a green wrap dress. I wondered when I would start to feel like a grown-up.

Babette chattered on about Larry. "As I was saying before, Susan, he wants me to meet his children. They're teenagers, a boy and a girl. Apparently Larry and his ex-wife are on fairly good terms."

"Meeting the kids sounds serious," Susan said.

"You and Larry haven't been seeing each other very long, have you?" I asked.

Babette shrugged. "That's just the way Larry is—kind of old-fashioned. I find it refreshing, after some of the guys I've been with. Some men have a terrible time turning forty," she added loftily. "Larry's forty-two, but *he's* not having a midlife crisis." She popped the olive from her martini into her mouth.

So was Martin forty, or about to turn forty? And having a midlife crisis? He didn't seem forty somehow. Apparently that was the problem, according to Babette. Was she warning me off Martin, and, if so, was it because she still wanted him, or was she just being nice?

"So I hear you have a love scene with Mr. God's Gift this week," Babs said. How did she know about that already? Somehow I didn't think she'd read through the week's scripts. "I was petrified the first time I had to do a scene like that. Don't worry, Marty will take good care of you. He's like that, when you're in his good graces." She buttered a hunk of bread. "Wait'll you have to do an actual bedroom scene."

My stomach did a backflip at the prospect.

"Love scenes are mostly about choreography," Susan said.

"My first bedroom scene, I fell off the bed," Babs said gaily.

"You did not!" Susan exclaimed.

"Well, I would have, if David hadn't grabbed on for dear life at a crucial moment."

We all laughed. Just then I became aware of eyes on me. By the door, a lanky man in a dark suit was staring at us. A Fed? I held my breath.

The man burst into a smile and headed for our table.

"Larry!" Babette cried, and they embraced. He pulled up a chair next to Babs, and she introduced us. Jesus, I needed to stop being so paranoid.

"Why, you're Beverly Read!" Larry told Susan. "And you're Jean Christopher!" He had dark, graying hair, and looked a bit like Jimmy Stewart or maybe Henry Fonda. "I'm not used to meeting people I recognize from TV." Something about him made me think he might be from the Midwest.

"You'll have to get used to it, honey," Babs said in a tone of simple, sweet affection I'd never heard her use before.

We chatted for a few minutes, and then Babs and Larry left together. I wondered if she would spend any time learning her lines tonight. I was starting to understand why she made such frequent use of the teleprompter.

"Well," Susan said when they'd gone, "he seems like a lovely man."

"He really does!" I felt a trifle nervous being alone with Susan, who I admired so much.

"I'm glad for her." Susan took a sip of her martini, then turned the full force of her gaze on me. "So Joanna, how are you liking being part of the company?"

I felt put on the spot. "It's harder work than I'd expected, but I like it a lot. I never watched daytime dramas before I got the part, and I must admit I had preconceptions about the type of actors who did this kind of work. I hadn't realized there would be so many fine actors in the company."

I feared this would come off as insulting, but Susan nodded. "It can be frustrating not to receive the same kind of respect as actors in theater, film, and prime time," she said. "But those of us who actually work in daytime know better, don't we?"

Her *we* gave me such a sense of belonging. I thought of Clarissa's scornful treatment, and it occurred to me that I had looked in the wrong place for a mentor. "How did you get started with *Hope Springs Eternal?*" I asked.

"I did some theater work when I first came to New York. But my first big part was for television, when I was about your age. *The Lucky Ones*—a daytime drama, long since defunct. I thought I knew a thing or two about theater, but television was another thing entirely!" Laughter bubbled from her. "I forgot my lines so often, it's a wonder I wasn't fired my first week. I was so nervous. And the show went out live!"

"Oh god, *live?* It's nerve-wracking enough now."

"*Hope Springs Eternal* used to go out live as well! Anyway, *The Lucky Ones* got canceled, but the network liked me, which is how I ended up at *Hope Springs Eternal*."

"How long ago was that?"

Susan paused for effect, then leaned across the table. "Fifteen years ago," she intoned.

"*Wow.* What's it like, playing the same character for so long?"

She stared into her martini glass, then looked at me. "It's mostly wonderful. Like a longtime friendship. The company really is like family, and as you know, having steady work as an actor is nothing to sneeze at."

I wondered what it would be like to play Jean Christopher for so many years. It was an oddly comforting thought, a sense of continuity. At the same time it gave me a feeling of claustrophobia. Theater had always been my plan. I had looked down on soap operas, but I had been wrong about that. I respected Susan as much as any actor I had ever worked with. Not that I didn't want to continue with theater, though I couldn't imagine doing that right now, between whatever was going on with Cyn and all the lines I had to learn for *Hope Springs Eternal*.

"So tell me about yourself, Jo," Susan said. "Are you involved with anybody?"

That seemed rather an odd non sequitur. I shook my head. "Not in a while. My last boyfriend was an alcoholic. We were together, on and off, for a couple of years." I was surprised to find myself telling Susan about Ian, but she was easy to talk to. "He's a brilliant actor. But he never really noticed me, you know? Even when we were together, he was the only one in the room."

Susan gazed at me with sympathy. "That sounds lonely."

"It was, but sort of freeing, too."

"Isn't that interesting? I wouldn't have thought of it that way." She raised her glass and drank. She wasn't traffic-stoppingly gorgeous like Babette, but she had such fine cheekbones, such intelligent blue eyes. "Ah, well, it's easy to meet men at your age. Although I am seeing a wonderful man."

"An actor?"

"Lord, no." We dissolved into cackles of laughter. I thought she would tell me about the guy she was seeing, but instead she said, "And speaking of men," and then I knew where she was steering the conversation. "Martin Yates is charming and good-hearted, and you're fortunate to be paired with him, on an acting level. He can also be a damn good friend. But on any other level, I feel I ought to caution you to steer clear."

She had uttered the speech so smoothly, I would have felt like applauding if I weren't blushing so furiously. "With all due respect, Susan, didn't we just do this scene?" I asked with a laugh. "'Don't play with fire' and all that?"

She didn't smile. "You can tell me to mind my own business."

Oh great, I'd offended her. "No, I appreciate your concern! But it's not as if Martin would ever..."

Now she did smile, albeit wearily. "Oh, believe me, Joanna, the idea has certainly occurred to him."

It hit me with full force how much I wished that were true.

"I just don't want to see another friend get in over her head," Susan said.

"I understand."

Suddenly Cyn's voice was in my ear: "Please tell me you're not going to listen to that old bag." It was hard not to flinch.

"I hope I haven't made you uncomfortable," Susan said with a girlishly confiding look.

I tried to keep my expression composed. "Not at all. I appreciate the advice."

"She's had him too, you know," Cyn said. "She's just trying to cut down on the competition. She's over the hill, and he likes 'em young and pretty."

I don't believe you, I thought. You're lying. But looking at Susan's lovely, aging face (though she couldn't be much older than Martin), I realized with a sinking feeling that Susan might well have had a fling with him. For all I knew, Martin might have slept with every female in the company.

"She doesn't want to be your friend," Cyn said. "Neither does the redhead. Don't be so fucking naive, Joanna."

They do want to be my friends, I thought. My eyes filled with tears.

Susan looked stricken. "I didn't mean to hurt your feelings, Jo."

I shook my head. My throat was tight, and Cyn would not shut her fucking mouth: "You need to toughen up, Jo. Don't let that old broad push you around. Listen to me. Are you listening to me?"

"Excuse me," I said. "I'll be right back." I headed towards the back of the restaurant and found a little hall with his and hers restroom doors.

The ladies' room was small and clean, with one sink and two stalls, both vacant, and a cloying disinfectant odor that prevented me from taking a steadying deep breath. I looked in the mirror and half expected to find Cyn staring back at me, but all I saw was my own face. God, I looked like an overwrought twelve-year-old.

"Okay, Cyn," I said. "If you wanna talk to me, make it quick."

Nothing happened. I turned on the cold-water tap and washed my hands with the sliver of soap on the sink top. Then Cyn was behind me in the mirror. "You can't wash away the stain, Lady," she said.

I spun to face her, the tap still on, my hands dripping. "Stop it, Cyn. Just stop it. Why do you want to ruin this for me?"

"Oh, I don't know. Why would I?" She wore faded jeans with rips at the knees, a "Free Angela Davis" t-shirt, and an army jacket.

I shook my head violently and turned back to the sink. I turned off the tap and pulled a paper towel from the wall dispenser. "You don't want me to have any friends, is that it? You want me to be all alone, aside from you?" I dried my hands and threw the paper towel into the wastebasket.

She stood there, arms folded across her ribcage. On her chest, a full-Afroed Angela Davis gazed resolutely into the distance. I couldn't remember Cyn wearing that shirt. I wondered if she knew Angela had been freed years ago. "They can never really know you," she said. "I'm the only one who really knows you, Joanna."

Except Jeremy, I thought, and that didn't go so well. "I have to go. Susan's waiting."

She flinched as if I had struck her. "You really are utterly disloyal, aren't you? You don't even want to try to make things right. You are a fucking sellout, and your sorry excuse for a life is no excuse for what happened to me. How do you think your new friends would feel about you if they knew?"

"Shut up. Shut up!"

The bathroom door flew open, and a young woman with curly blonde hair and a pink dress came in. She looked around the room, taking in the fact that I was alone.

"Are you *okay*?" she pronounced with exaggerated care, wobbling on her high heels. Before I could reply, her gaze latched onto the mirror. "What happened?"

I turned and stifled a gasp. The center of the mirror had cracked into a starburst, as if Cyn had hit it with her fist. My face fragmented in the broken glass. "Broken," I whispered.

I felt my life fragment and reshape itself.

"Oh no," I whispered.

I tried to hold on.

It was the middle of the night at the draft board. I stood, keeping watch, a block away from Cyn. Snuffling from the flu, but I felt alert enough. I didn't want to be near that bomb, even now. My heart was pounding. A bit of exhilaration mixed with the fear. We were about to get away with it after all. Cyn was right, Alex and Jeremy were right, and we were about to be heroes of the revolution.

Cyn glanced over at me. Then she placed the wicker handbag in front of the mailbox. She straightened. We were home free. She did something with her foot. The explosion lit up the night, lit up Cyn like Joan of Arc. Knocked me off my feet. God, so loud and long. Loud like the voice of God or an atom bomb. Finally it stopped. "What the fuck was that?" a man's irate voice demanded, from where? Blocks away, I thought, but I couldn't tell over the ringing of my ears. His voice sounded small and tinny. I felt as if I'd just lived through a cyclone or an earthquake, nothing I'd helped create. But I had helped make this happen, and the cops would be coming.

I scrambled to my feet. I didn't seem to be injured. "Cyn? We need to get out of here." I crept toward the dark figure on the pavement, broken glass crunching beneath my feet. I stared down at what was left of her.

When the cops and the ambulance arrived, I was still screaming.

Chapter Twelve:
I Wish I Knew How It Would Feel To Be Free
(1971–1975)

A few cells down from mine at Brightdale Correctional, Alice was crying again, a high, keening wail that echoed through the dark cell block. It woke me from a dream in which I'd ended up going to drama school after all and was trying to memorize a passage from *Hedda Gabler*. On waking, it seemed to be the real passage as I remembered it, not dream-gobbledygook: *All the same, I'm in your power. Tied to your will and desire. Not free. Not free, then!*

"They killed him," Alice wailed. "They killed him! How could they, how could they? Oh god, oh god…"

Women from the other cells sleepily began to speak. "I'm so sorry, sister. So sorry." "Fucking murderers." "Shut up! Will you all shut up?" "Alice, I'm sorry for your loss, girl, but please let us get some sleep." "She's got a right to grieve!" "I'm not saying she don't. I'm saying I've got a right to *sleep*."

I hoped none of the guards would come by and bang on the bars and tell us to settle the fuck down. If that happened, the adrenaline would keep me from falling back to sleep until it was almost time to get up.

I turned onto my back and pulled the thin blanket up to my chin. The dream had been so vivid, like it was my real life and this waking was just a nightmare. But no, this was real, Alice sobbing because her man had been shot to death at Attica—the horror of it, indiscriminate slaughter quelling the prison uprising. Most of the time I was numb, but when Alice wept and carried on, it was like ripping a scab off a wound. The men at Attica dead, George Jackson dead. Cyn dead. What did fighting for a better world get you but a violent death and an early grave?

I wondered if Jeremy and Alex were all right, and where they were. I didn't really blame them for splitting town while they had the chance. The DA had offered me a deal in exchange for naming my accomplices. (They knew Alex was involved, but not, apparently, Jeremy.) I'd said no deal, despite my parents' pleading and cajoling, and got fifteen to twenty years. I'd proven I was no rat. But what was I now, in here? Not an actress. Not a revolutionary. I did as I was told. I waited in line for food and for the shower, the exercise yard and the common room. I worked in the laundry. I got locked back up in my cell. This was my life now.

Alice's sobs began to die down. Maybe I could fall back to sleep. Maybe I would dream of drama school and *Hedda Gabler*. Hopefully I wouldn't have the nightmare again, the one where Cyn was blown to bits in front of me.

∞

"What you reading?" Ruthie asked one afternoon in the common room. She was a small, wiry black woman who looked about thirty. Some of the women were clustered around the black-and-white TV set watching a soap opera. Others chatted and smoked and played cards. I sat in a corner in a plastic chair. The women usually left me alone. I felt as if I gave off an aura of pain like a force field.

I showed Ruthie my paperback of *Capital*. Cyn's copy, actually. My mom had told me Mrs. Foster wanted to throw out all of Cyn's political books, or maybe burn them, but she'd relented and thought I might want them.

"You a Marxist?" Ruthie asked.

I shrugged. I'd been reading the same sentence over and over, while soap opera characters flirted and argued and jockeyed for position.

Ruthie pulled up a chair and sat next to me. "What're you in for?"

I wasn't used to talking, but her question wasn't something I could answer with a shrug. "Conspiracy."

"Conspiracy to do what?"

"We exploded a bomb outside a draft board."

"I can understand inside a draft board, but outside? What good does that do?"

The stock phrases rattled around in my head. *Bring the war home. No more business as usual.* "Not much, actually," I said.

She gave a laugh. "Sounds like you didn't think it through."

"We thought we did."

She rested her chin on her knuckles and eyed me. "Don't talk much, huh? You stuck-up, or shy?"

I pondered that. "I just don't have much to say."

"I guess I can dig that."

"What are you in for?" I asked, to be polite.

"Shot my old man." She said it with a matter-of-fact swagger.

"How come?"

"Caught him messing around with my best friend."

"Wow." It was almost a line from "Hey Joe." I wondered if she'd killed her old man or just wounded him. Somehow it seemed too personal to ask. "Why did you shoot him and not your friend?"

"Good question. Guess I didn't think it through either. It was pretty dumb, because now I don't get to raise my kid."

"That's rough," I said. "My best friend slept with my boyfriend. More than one of my boyfriends, sort of. I didn't shoot her. But she died anyway." I was surprised to hear myself talking. It was as if a bottle had been uncorked. "Thing is, I don't miss those guys, but I do miss her."

"I hear that," Ruthie said. "You have a man on the outside? Any kids?"

I thought about Jeremy. "No," I said. "There's no one."

∞

It was a muggy June afternoon in the exercise yard, but it might as well have been Christmas and New Year's combined. "I can't believe it! I can't believe Angela's free!" the women kept saying, beaming.

Yvonne Bayley stood in the middle of the yard and began to sing "Eyes on the Prize." She was the only woman at Brightdale I'd heard of before I got here. She was a Black Panther, imprisoned on what she claimed were trumped-up murder charges. Considering the way the Panthers had been persecuted, I found that easy to believe. She was a round-faced young woman with a tall Afro. Usually she looked serious, but today joy bloomed on her face as she sang and clapped her hands. Other women, mostly black but some Puerto Rican, a few white, joined in, singing and clapping: "Keep your eyes on the prize, hold on."

I stood off to the side by one of the barbed-wire fences and watched and listened. I wished I could tell Cyn that Angela Davis was free. I wished I could tell her I was in prison with Yvonne Bayley. She would've been so impressed.

Helen came and stood beside me. She had a pasty face, stringy dark hair and black-rimmed glasses. "I don't see what the big deal is," she said under her breath. "I bet if I was some high and mighty Commie Negro chick, they'd let me go too. Know what I mean?" Did she think because I was white, I'd agree? Or maybe because I didn't talk much, she figured I was a pushover.

"An all-white jury acquitted her," I said quietly. "You think that's because she's black and a Communist? She spent a lot of time in jail for crimes she didn't commit. She lost her job because she was a member of the Communist Party."

Her lip curled. "Oh, you're one of *those*. That's right, I heard why you're in here."

"I heard why you're in here too," I replied. "You're in here for dope, and you think you're better than Angela Davis?"

Lots of women were in here for possessing or selling dope. Helen fixed me with a poisonous look. Then she punched me in the face. I was so surprised, I burst out laughing, even though it hurt. I just stood there laughing in her face, as she got more and more apoplectic. She grabbed my hair and pulled.

"Hey, let go!" I yelled, but she gritted her teeth and pulled harder. I grabbed her hair and yanked. It was greasy and thin.

"Let go of me, you Commie bitch!" Helen hollered. I kicked her in the shin. The whole thing seemed ridiculous and oddly choreographed, like we were in a women's prison movie. Just as I became aware that the singing had trailed off and that we had an audience, the guards pulled us apart. I had a hank of Helen's hair in my fist. I didn't think she'd pulled out any of mine. We both got slapped into solitary until the next day.

I sat on the bed in the tiny cell and grinned. The skin under one eye was tender and swollen. I lifted my fist in a salute to—to what, exactly? Even though I felt embarrassed to have called attention to myself—a white girl disrupting the celebration of Angela's freedom—I felt more cheerful than I had since before Cyn died.

The next day, Ruthie grinned at me in the cafeteria line. "That was pretty damn hilarious, girl. Who'd have thought you had it in you?"

"Certainly not me," I said. Further down the line, Helen glared at me. I glared right back with my newly minted tough-girl sneer. I wore my black eye like a badge of honor.

∞

My mother was aghast when I sat across from her at a table in the visitors' room. "What happened to you?"

I had hoped my black eye would have faded before her visit. I didn't have any makeup to conceal it. "It was nothing, Mom. Just a little skirmish."

She looked so proper and housewifely in her blue shirt-dress, which was so much more becoming than my shapeless blue prison dress. "A skirmish? Did one of those…" She looked around nervously at the other inmates and visitors. "Did one of *those women* attack you?" she whispered.

At the next table, Ruthie sat with her mother, a heavyset, unsmiling woman, and her son, a gangly boy, all elbows and knees. He kept looking around uncomfortably. Ruthie couldn't take her eyes off him. She gazed at him with tremulous pride. Her mother couldn't take her eyes off Ruthie. At another table, Dolores and her sister chattered in rapid-fire Spanish. By the door stood the guard, stolid and white and mustached. He looked deeply bored.

"No, Mom," I said. "A white woman punched me. Does that make you feel better?"

She grimaced. "Joanna, that's not funny."

"Sorry." Time to change the subject. "How's Dad?"

"He's sorry he couldn't come. He has the flu."

"Tell him I hope he feels better soon." I missed him, but I was glad I didn't have to see his look of baffled disappointment. "I had the flu the night Cyn died. I almost didn't go."

For a moment my mother wouldn't look at me, her face incandescent with pain. "I know I shouldn't speak ill of the dead—"

"Then don't."

"If only you'd had a different best friend, none of this would have happened. She led you down this path."

"It was our decision, Mom."

She shook her head. Easier to blame Cyn than me, I supposed. I couldn't wait for her to leave, though I would miss her when she did. I suspected she felt the same.

∞

Time here moved molasses slow and shockingly quick. I had been inside for four years. I started working in the prison library, a lot more interesting than the laundry. One afternoon in the common room, some of the women were arguing about which soap opera to watch. There had been a time when all anyone wanted to watch was the Watergate hearings, but that was long past. "Come on, I have to know if Sam's gonna cheat on Vicki!" someone said.

I was sitting off to the side reading Alice Childress in a book called *Plays By and About Women*. At long last I had started reading plays again, whatever the prison library had. I was even thinking about writing a play. Not that anyone would perform it, but I had to do something with my life. Nixon had resigned, and the war was over, and I was still inside. I would be inside for a long time. The revolution apparently wasn't happening.

"Of course Sam's gonna cheat," said Yvonne Bayley, the last person I expected to have an opinion on the matter, and I looked up from my book. "He's a man, isn't he?"

The women in front of the TV erupted with opinions: "Uh huh." "You got that right." "But Vicki and Sam had such a beautiful wedding!" "That Sam's a stone fox." "Yeah! He can cheat with me any day!" "Aw, I wanna watch *Hearth and Home*. That's my story."

"Sister, I can't believe you watch that retrograde, ultra-white bullshit," Yvonne's best friend Bernice said. She was an imposing woman with close-cropped hair and a way of squinting her eyes when she uttered a righteous pronouncement that made it seem the only intelligent position.

"Hell, it may be retrograde, ultra-white bullshit, but it's *fun*," Yvonne said. "Besides, it reminds me of my grandma. Hey, it's started! Somebody turn it up."

I had never watched an episode of a soap opera. I disliked them on principle. But the fact that Yvonne liked this one made me curious. I moved my chair closer to the TV.

In the platonic ideal of a middle-class living room, a somber, dark-haired man who looked a little like John Cassavetes stood facing a voluptuous woman with large, mascaraed eyes and pronounced cheekbones.

"I come in second to your career, Vicki," the man said. "I thought that when we got married, you'd be willing to put time and effort into this partnership. I guess I was wrong."

Bernice is right, I thought. This show is so politically retrograde. God forbid a woman should focus on her career.

"That isn't fair," the woman said, tossing her ringlets. "I have put time and effort into our marriage! Meanwhile you've been spending every free moment with your new best friend, Jean Christopher. My own cousin!" The actress managed to be simultaneously wooden and melodramatic.

The man's mouth was a tight line, his arms hugging his strong chest. The guy wasn't half bad as an actor, and I could see why the women thought he was a fox. Looking at him reminded me of how long it would be before there was any possibility of my having sex with a man again. "At least Jean makes time for me," he said quietly, pronouncing each word with equal emphasis, each word a blow, "which is more than I can say for my wife."

The women in front of the TV went wild. "Ooooo!" "He did not just say that to my Vicki!" "Don't let him get away with that, girl!"

"I want the truth, Sam," Vicki said. "What's been going on between you and Jean?" There was a tight close-up of her face, her huge eyes fringed by long lashes. The image faded to black, and a plaintive flute began to play what was apparently the show's theme song, a mid-tempo, string-laden number. It sounded familiar—I must've heard it on other days when I was trying to ignore the TV. Animated rain streaked across a night sky, illuminated by bursts of lightning. Then the sky cleared and brightened, a sun rose over the hills, and the words HOPE SPRINGS ETERNAL appeared in the middle of the screen in fancy script. What crap.

When the show resumed, a girl around my age was sitting on a small living-room sofa scribbling on a pad of paper. She had long hair and an earnest expression. There was a knock on the door, and the girl got up to answer it. An older blonde woman with a commanding air stood there. "Why, Mrs. Read—" the girl said.

"Hello, Jean," the woman said and swept past her into the apartment.

The women in front of the TV laughed raucously. "Oh Jean, you are so *dead!*" "You can't mess around with Beverly's daughter's man and get away with it."

I began to feel an uneasy sense of déjà vu. That living room, with the braided rug on the floor, the typewriter on the desk, and piles of notes on the coffee table, the expensively dressed blonde looking daggers at Jean—it all seemed so familiar. "I hear you've been spending a good deal of time with my daughter's husband," Beverly said. This actress was good. She gave off an air of flinty intelligence, a hard-edged glamour like one of the forties movie heroines I had loved to watch on TV when I was growing up.

"Sam and I are friends," Jean said.

"If that's true, then why play with fire?"

The words echoed in my head. There was something I had forgotten. Something I was remembering. Something Cyn had said? Something Cyn was, impossibly, saying right now into my ear: "This fucking show again? You are unbelievable."

What was happening to me? Slowly I got to my feet. I felt vertiginous, but I couldn't take my eyes off the TV. There was something about the long-haired girl on the black-and-white screen. "She's taken my place," I whispered.

Then I was standing in the bathroom at Le Fanal Bleu, staring into the broken mirror. "I said, what happened to the mirror?" a girl was saying with the elaborate over-enunciation of the inebriated. Her reflection behind mine in the mirror: curly blonde hair, pink dress.

"It cracked," I said absently. Had Cyn cracked it? Cracked my life, and I had followed one of the paths spider-webbing from the starburst center. Or I'd thought I had.

"I can *see* it cracked," the girl said.

I turned to her. "How long have I been standing here?"

She goggled at me, then laughed. "You're more loaded than I am!" She headed unsteadily into a bathroom stall, which she closed with a thwack. The bathroom filled with the sound of copious peeing.

I hugged myself and stared into the cracked glass. I was no longer wearing my blue prison dress. It was so strange to see myself wearing lipstick and eye shadow, jeans and the pumpkin-colored sweater I'd bought at Bloomingdale's. And that was the least of it. I'd spent the last four years—no, apparently the last few seconds—in Brightdale Prison. Now I was back in my life as an actress in beautiful, beautiful Manhattan, in the bathroom at Le Fanal Bleu. Susan was waiting for me. I would see Martin again tomorrow. Martin, who I had just been ogling on the TV at Brightdale! But what about my fellow inmates? Were they real, and still in prison? Brightdale was real. I'd heard of it before I was arrested—before I hallucinated I was arrested—before whatever had happened. Had I known Yvonne Bayley was at Brightdale? The experience was beginning to fade like a dream, but it hadn't felt like a dream.

Something else made me uneasy. The episode we'd been watching on TV, with some actress who wasn't me playing Jean Christopher, was one we hadn't even taped yet. We'd done the table-read for it this afternoon, which felt like ages ago. If I'd really been at Brightdale, I'd stayed a couple of weeks too long, but managed to wind up back at the right time and place. What if I got stuck somewhere else and couldn't get back?

Had Cyn done all this? How could I keep myself here and now, and not get shunted off to die on a sidewalk or get locked in prison or god knows what else?

The toilet flushed, and the girl stumbled out of the stall and made a beeline for the sink. I got out of her way. I had to pull myself together. It was time to rejoin Susan and act like everything was perfectly fine.

The dark, cozy French restaurant looked unbelievably glamorous after Brightdale, as did Susan in her tan pants and chocolate brown sweater. She smiled at me. It was so good to see her again, in real life and in color, not on that black-and-white TV. "What was *that*?" she asked.

I took my seat. "What was what?"

"You sort of *swaggered* up to the table."

"Did I?" I tried to laugh it off. Was I still the girl who'd stared down Helen in the cafeteria? It was hard to behave as if I'd only been gone for a minute. It was hard to stop worrying, even for an instant, that I might not get to stay here. It seemed unbelievable that I could go anywhere, do anything I wanted, and no guard would be able to tell me what to do. I felt as if I hadn't had a good-tasting meal in years. I reached for the basket of bread. "You know, I think I'd like to order some food."

"The onion soup is awfully good," Susan said, still looking at me a bit quizzically.

I savored each spoonful of soup and gooey cheese as if it might be my last.

Chapter Thirteen:
Wild Is the Wind
(October 1975)

Please, I thought, *please let me stay right here, right now.* The three cameras circled Martin and me as we stood kissing desperately in front of the coffee table in Jean Christopher's small living room. I caressed the back of Martin's neck and pulled him closer.

For days I had been bracing to see Cyn or, worse, to get shunted off to some other version of my life. But nothing had happened at the studio on Tuesday, or when Babette and I went sofa shopping on Wednesday, or during yesterday's table-read for the episode we were now in the middle of taping.

Martin's lips were soft, and his breath smelled of mint and coffee. I paid attention to the position of our heads so I wouldn't block his shot, and I gauged how long the kissing was supposed to last—a luxuriously long time. In a corner of my mind, the women of Brightdale huddled around the black-and-white TV and watched ravenously. I kissed Martin for all of them.

When it was time, I made myself pull away. "Sam, this is wrong," I murmured.

His ardent expression faded into bewilderment. "But Jean..."

"I can't do this to Vicki, no matter how I feel about you!" Slowly and deliberately I turned my back on him and stood stock still. "You should go."

"Maybe it's wrong, but I love you. I love you, Jean. I need you to know that." His voice shook. Hearing him say the words made my breath quicken and tears come to my eyes. Gently he put his hands on my shoulders and turned me to face him. He looked so serious and so full of need. No one had ever looked at me (at Jean? at Jo?) like that before. He pulled me into another kiss, and my arms went around his neck.

"Good work." Vince's voice over the PA.

We let go of each other. I felt weak in the knees, and looking at Martin made me shy. He regarded me from beneath heavy lids. Grinning wolfishly, he slowly wiped the edge of his mouth with his thumb. "You're hot stuff, Bergman," he said, and the crew broke up laughing.

∞

"Working with Babette is excruciating," Martin said. He took a swig from his mug of beer. "Sam and Vicki's marriage is falling apart, and she's giving it all the emotion of a fucking grocery list."

"I know what you mean." I sipped my Scotch. We sat across from each other in a booth at Chauncy's. I was glad it was just the two of us, not a larger group from the show. I could still feel him kissing me.

"So I tell her, 'Give me *something*, for god's sake,' and do you know what she says? 'I'm saving it for the cameras'!" He gave a disgusted laugh. "And I say, 'Saving it for the cameras? Yeah, you've been saving it a *long time*.'"

I burst out laughing. "I'm sorry you're having such a hard time working with her."

He sipped his Scotch with a morose air. "If it's not readily apparent, Babette and I are kaput."

I considered feigning surprise, but decided against it. "She told me as much."

"Did she? She told *me* she's dating some dentist or something."

"He's a cardiologist, Marty." Was this why he'd brought me here—to spill his guts about Babette? "I met him the other day. He seems really nice."

He gave a startled blink. "Well, it's none of my business, right? I just hope she's happy."

"You do?" My tone couldn't have been more incredulous.

He gaped at me, then he laughed. "Actually, I do, Joanna. When I stop being so goddamn selfish for a minute. It's just awkward. I'm sorry to lay all this on you."

"Well, I do consider Babette a friend, so I'd just as soon not discuss her with you. Anyway, what am I, chopped liver?" Had I really said that out loud?

His eyebrows lifted. Then he smiled. "You are most certainly not chopped liver. What you are is sensational."

My stomach did a lazy flip. "Thank you," I said, and sipped my beer.

"I've said it before, but it bears repeating: I love working with you. I love that you take it so seriously." He was looking at me with such warm appreciation. Martin's appreciation felt like the best thing in the world.

"Of course I take it seriously," I said. "I love this job." Until the words had left my mouth, I hadn't known I felt that way. How had this happened? It wasn't just because I got paid to kiss Martin, lovely though that was. Part of it had to do with the talk I'd had with Susan at Le Fanal Bleu—realizing how much I respected her and wanted to be like her, and how much there was to respect about the work we did, once I'd confronted my prejudices about soap operas. Then there was the time I'd spent at Brightdale, where I'd seen how much our stories meant to the women there. Even if it hadn't truly happened, it had felt real, felt true.

"You find it really satisfying as an actor?" Martin pressed.

"Absolutely. Don't you?"

He stared gloomily into his beer mug. "Sometimes. It's just, this isn't how I expected my career to turn out. I miss doing Shakespeare and Ibsen and Chekhov. I almost didn't audition for *Hope Springs Eternal*, you know. I only wanted to do theater, but I had a family to support. It was supposed to be a short-term role. I never expected to stay so long."

I wondered if I would end up feeling like Martin did if I didn't regain my focus on theater. "Clarissa does both. Why don't you?"

"Then I'd have no time for my family. At least this way, I'm home most nights."

Why was it so hard to remember that he had a wife and kids?

He gave a sigh. "You know, I swore I wouldn't be like my old man, but maybe it's inevitable."

"What is?"

"My father was an accountant. Can you imagine a more joyless occupation? He worked, he came home. Had dinner with us, went to bed. Got up the next morning, went back to the office. That was his life. Then he dropped dead at forty-five." He sipped his beer. "My mother said he'd been the life of the party when they met. Hard to imagine. Everyone said he died so young, but to me he already seemed like an old man. Partly because I was still in college. Forty-five might as well have been seventy-five to me back then. Doesn't forty-five seem old to you?"

I shook my head. "Not in a bad way. Just, you know, life experience. Knowledge."

"Life experience. Knowledge!" He gave the words an ironic edge. "That's a nice way to look at it," he added with a laugh. "See how you feel about it when you're my age. I turned forty in July. I'm sure not where I thought I'd be by this point. It's not that I'm not grateful. I know how lucky I am. It's just, there's still a lot I want to do before I die."

Maybe this was what Babette had meant about Martin having a midlife crisis. I finished my beer. "You're a wonderful actor, Marty. If you miss the theater, I think you should do something about that."

There was something wistful in his smile. "Thanks, kid."
He regarded my empty beer mug. "Didn't mean to get so
heavy. Another drink?"

∞

We left Chauncy's when we'd each had a second Scotch
and he'd had a second beer. It had gotten dark. "Want me to
walk you home?" he asked.

"Sure."

I felt keyed up being alone with him on the dark street.
We walked in silence. Then he asked, "Whatcha doing this
weekend?"

"I might go to a movie. Maybe the new Wertmüller."

"It's supposed to be sexy." He eyed me. "You going by
yourself?"

"I like going to the movies by myself sometimes," I said
breezily, though I wished he'd offer to go with me, improbable
though that was.

"You're so damned independent, aren't you? Don't need
anything from any man."

"Thanks a lot!" I smacked him on the arm.

"Hey, what was that for?"

"I need plenty. It's not my fault if men aren't always crawling out of the woodwork to provide it!"

"Okay, okay!" We reached my building. "Jesus, I didn't
mean to offend you. I just don't like the thought of you being lonely, that's all. You deserve…everything. Whatever you
need, you should have it."

"You're drunk." I wasn't exactly sober myself.

"But you do," he persisted.

"I do what?"

"Deserve every happiness."

"Stop it. You're gonna make me cry." I looked down at the
dark pavement. I was pretty sure that whatever I deserved, *every happiness* wasn't it.

"Aw, don't cry," he said, and I looked up at him. He was so beautiful. Maybe I didn't deserve to be standing here with him being so nice to me, but here we were.

"Okay," I said. "I won't."

"Goodnight, Joanna." He put his arms around me. The hug lasted a lot longer than I'd expected. I breathed in his spicy scent. He pressed into me, and my arms stole around his back. It felt unbelievably good. I wished I were sober so I could feel it better. Then he pulled back. "Goodnight," he said again, and gave me a brief kiss on the lips, then another. Then he kissed me properly, a glorious Scotch- and beer-tasting kiss.

Sam and Jean had not kissed like this—not this wet and sloppy and magnificent. I gave a sigh of astonished pleasure and pulled him closer. I wanted to live inside his mouth forever. Before, kissing him, I'd had to keep myself together, what with the acting, the cameras, the time constraints. Now I could let go, and it felt like I was dissolving. How lucky I was. Lucky to be kissing Martin. Lucky to be out of prison. This was the best of all possible worlds.

Slowly he pulled back and held me at arms' length. He looked dazed and overheated under the streetlights. "I'm more than a bit inebriated," he said.

"So am I." I discovered my handbag was still slung over my shoulder. It was a wonder it hadn't fallen to the sidewalk unnoticed. "Do you want to come up?"

A taxi drove by. Martin looked around as if suddenly remembering we were on a public street. He gave my shoulders a squeeze, then let go. "Gloria and the kids will be expecting me."

"I understand." A blip of guilt registered, but it was drowned by the intense feelings of well-being washing through me.

"You're sweet." He cupped my cheek. His expression was grave and cherishing. "Have a good weekend, Joanna."

"You too."

He kissed me again, an emphatic but all too brief and closed-mouthed kiss. The girl who had been locked up for four years pulled him close and kissed him passionately one more time. "Have fun at the movies," he said, and waited for me to open the front door. Then he gave a little wave and walked away. I wanted to watch him go, but I went inside and pushed the button for the elevator. It opened instantly, and I got on.

"I can't even think of the last time you looked this happy," Cyn said, leaning against the back of the elevator and regarding me with amusement. She was dressed in a sky-blue pantsuit that hung on her small bones. After a moment I realized it was the pantsuit Babs had worn to our sofa-shopping expedition. So Cyn had been there that day, watching us. That was disconcerting—or it would've been, if not for my drunken rapture. Even Cyn couldn't diminish that just now. "He must be an awfully good kisser," she remarked.

"You have no idea, Cyn. You have no idea!" I started to laugh. She laughed too, and the sound of our laughter echoed in the elevator.

I let myself into the too-warm apartment. I dropped my jacket on one of Martin's chairs and sat on another. The orange suede sofa Babette had helped me pick out would be delivered next week. What would Babette think if she knew about me and Martin? For that matter, what would Martin's wife think? But I couldn't care about Gloria right now. I had only met her the once. She seemed like an abstraction, and it wasn't as if Martin hadn't already cheated with Babette and god knows who else. Briefly I let myself wonder if Susan really had slept with Martin—but even if she had, what did that matter now?

Beneath my jeans, my panties were sodden. Fantasies of the future ran through my head. Martin and I drinking at Chauncy's, then coming back to my apartment to make love. Martin and I kissing in my dressing room when Clarissa wasn't there—then I kneeling before him and unzipping him, making him bite his lip to keep from moaning. Life was opening to me, with all the talk and sex and booze and art I wanted. Tonight I had tasted it. "I can't believe it," I said. "I can't believe it's actually happening."

"I hate to burst your bubble, but he's never going to fuck you, you know." Cyn was sitting on the third chair.

"You don't know that."

"Well, maybe if he's a lot drunker, or really stoned. Otherwise, no. If he were going to, it would be happening right now."

"But you said he wanted to."

"Oh, he did. Then he got to know you better."

"Thanks a whole hell of a lot. You're just saying that because you're still angry with me. You are, aren't you?"

She shrugged. "What does it matter if I am? You don't care how I feel. All you care about is that dude."

"Or maybe you're just annoyed because you can't take him from me the way you always like to do." The alcohol made it easy for me to toss that off. It almost sounded like something Clarissa's character Sylvia Cartwright would have said.

"Jesus. You can't still be upset about that. Jeremy? And what's his name, that stupid boyfriend of yours?"

"Lenny. And no, I'm not still upset about that, because while I may have to share Martin with his wife, I don't have to share him with you." I uttered the words with gusto, but they came out harsher than I'd intended.

She shook her head bitterly. "So you finally admit you're glad I'm dead. I knew it all along!"

"That's not what I said. I only meant…" Was she right? Was I glad she was dead? The idea was too horrible to contemplate. "Look, I'm sorry I said that, okay? I'm drunk. And anyway, haven't I been punished enough?"

"Punished?" She spat out the word incredulously.

"All those years at Brightdale. That was you, wasn't it? How did you do it?"

Gwynne Garfinkle

She wouldn't look at me. Finally I gave a sigh, got up, and turned on the TV. Walter Cronkite was talking about a Grand Jury indictment of a state trooper in the Attica killings. I sat down again and unzipped my boots. I remembered that woman at Brightdale who kept sobbing about her lover, shot dead at Attica. What was her name? Was she real? I didn't want to think about Brightdale. I didn't want to think about anything but Martin.

"Attica, Attica!" I said, remembering Al Pacino strutting along that Brooklyn sidewalk. Maybe I would go see *Dog Day Afternoon* again this weekend—the movie Martin and I both loved. I looked at Cyn, but she remained stone-faced.

They went to a commercial. A familiar-looking girl massaged suds through her hair. Then she tossed her long brown hair from side to side in slow motion. "With hair this clean and lustrous, you'll be turning heads wherever you go!" she announced with a superior smile. It was Heather O'Connor, who had played Maurice's daughter on *Hope Springs Eternal* and had been fired just as I was hired. I'd seen a few of her episodes in the days between my audition and starting the show. Clarissa was right—she did have lovely hair. I couldn't wait to tell Martin I'd seen her commercial.

After a commercial for eye drops, the news resumed. "In Los Angeles today, two members of the People's Armed Resistance were arrested in connection with a bank robbery." Two people were being hauled away in handcuffs: a tired-looking woman with dirty blonde hair and a man I recognized with wheaten hair and a scraggly beard. I thought he must be an actor, though he looked different from what I remembered. "Alexander Kloski and Sharon Gilmore, members of the self-styled revolutionary group the People's Armed Resistance, were apprehended by police as they drove away from the Landings Savings Bank in Studio City. Two other alleged bank robbers escaped in another vehicle and are still at large."

"Alex," I whispered.

A black-and-white photo appeared on the screen: intense face, long silky mustache, granny glasses. Alex as I remembered him. "Kloski has been a fugitive since the 1971 bombing of a New York draft board that left one young woman dead. Over the past four years, the People's Armed Resistance has claimed responsibility for a number of firebombings, including…"

"No," I said. "No, no, no. Not now. Please, not now." What if the FBI knew about Jeremy's connection to Alex? Could the Feds link me to them?

"I can't believe you're going to go to that fucking bourgeois drama school," Cyn said distinctly. Her eyes were fixed on the TV. "This will get your head on straight. Alex knows someone who can get the dynamite, and Jeremy can make the bomb—but I want it to be the two of us at the draft board. You and me, Jo. We'll be like Fidel and Che, Bonnie and Clyde. It'll be the greatest movie ever. We'll show them, Jo…"

"Cyn," I said, "look at me."

She didn't seem to hear me. As if hypnotized, she knelt on the floor and crawled toward the TV.

"Cyn, the war is over. Angela Davis is free. Cyn, are you listening?"

She shook her head. "I remember, Jo," she said, facing the TV. "Everything has already happened to me. I need it not to have happened."

"Oh god, Cyn!" I got up and knelt on the floor beside her. I tried to put my arms around her, but no one was there.

I sat on the floor, my knees drawn up to my chin, and stared unseeing at the TV, all my fantasies of the future replaced by another set, just as vivid: prison walls, my parents' baffled, disappointed faces, the end of everything. Would I be punished again? Would I be punished at last?

Chapter Fourteen:
Get It While You Can
(October 1975)

I woke Saturday morning to a pounding headache and the previous night's news about Alex crashing down on me. I tried to fall back asleep, but it was no use. I got up, put on jeans and a sweater, and went out into the drizzly cold to get a newspaper.

Back upstairs, I took some aspirin and put the coffee on. I toasted a slice of rye bread, spread it with butter, and took the plate and the coffee into the living room. It still felt like a gift to be able to make toast and coffee in my own apartment, to come and go as I pleased. I couldn't take it for granted.

I sat on one of Martin's chairs, the folded newspaper on the table before me. The front page talked, predictably enough, about New York City's budget woes. At first I didn't dare open the newspaper, as if I would find my own name inside. Finally I paged through it. Alex was a few pages in. There was a photograph of him and Sharon Gilmore, whoever she was, both of them disheveled and wild-eyed, flanked by cops. The article said they were being held without bail. I scanned the story for a mention of Cyn. There was her name, glowing on the page. "Mr. Kloski had been a fugitive since May 1971, when he was sought by law enforcement in connection with the bombing of a draft board in Lower Manhattan. Cynthia Foster, then a student at the School of New York, was killed when the bomb she was placing outside the draft board detonated."

The article listed a number of bombings carried out by the People's Armed Resistance, including offices of ITT and

Shell Oil, and a police station in San Francisco. No one had been injured in any of their bombings. I studied the photo of the bearded man in handcuffs. Despite everything I'd said to Jeremy about the revolution not coming, and despite the fact that I couldn't quite fathom how Alex had had the heart for such actions after Cyn's death, something in me admired Alex's dedication. He had not abandoned the fight for a better world. And if I could no longer trust the means he used to achieve that end, it was also true that I had given up the fight, shocked into inaction by Cyn's death, and that wasn't something I was proud of.

The story didn't say whether Alex or Sharon Gilmore would be tried for any crime besides the bank robbery. Would the police question Alex about Cyn's death? I thought about tracking Jeremy down at the hospital in Brooklyn where he worked. But what if the Feds were watching him? Was I being completely paranoid, or not paranoid enough? Jeremy must be freaking out. Did he blame me for not giving him money for Alex? (In that other reality, he and Alex had split town and left me to rot in prison—not that they'd had much of a choice, but it still rankled.) Had Jeremy really thought I could bankroll Alex's group? Whatever small amount I could have given would have been a drop in the bucket compared to whatever they'd been trying to garner with a bank robbery. A bank robbery! It was unreal. Last night I'd thought happily about going to see *Dog Day Afternoon* again. But it was about a botched bank robbery. I wasn't sure I would ever want to see it again.

My hands were cold, and I was hyperventilating. I tried to breathe slowly and evenly. I tried to focus on the memory of Martin holding me—but it seemed like a dream, or like a scene we'd acted. Was he thinking about me? Maybe he would call. I didn't even have his phone number. Maybe it was listed? But Gloria might answer, or one of their kids. Endless vistas of time stretched between now and Monday morning, when I would see him at the studio. Endless vistas of time? I couldn't count on that either—not when I'd twice been shunted off to other versions of my life.

What would Martin think of me if he found out what we had done in '71? Part of me longed to tell him, because otherwise, he could never truly know me. Only Cyn really knew me. Cyn and Jeremy and, I supposed, Alex. Alex, in his jail cell. I pushed the newspaper aside and wept.

∞

When I walked into the rehearsal room on Monday morning, Martin was chatting at a table with Maurice. He took a bite of powdered donut, put it down and sucked his fingers. The long nightmare of the weekend was over. In a moment he would look up and smile at me.

"I forget when they said her first day would be," Maurice said. "Sometime this week."

"What's she look like?" Martin asked. Then he looked up and saw me, and his face froze, just for an instant. He gave me a strained little smile that made me feel sick. I went and poured myself some coffee.

"Oh, fresh-faced, wholesome," Maurice replied. "Long chestnut hair."

"Is she beautiful?"

His words filled me with panic. Suddenly I hated the idea of him even thinking about another girl. His wife, sure, but no one else.

Maurice shrugged. "Very pretty, at any rate. She's fresh from Juilliard. Dorothy Wainwright seems very taken with her."

Our executive producer never seemed very taken with anyone, as far as I could tell. "Who are you talking about?" I asked.

"Amy Gundersen," Maurice said. "She's our new Kathy Read. My new daughter." He grinned. "I'm so proud!" he exclaimed mock-effusively.

Martin laughed. "The proud papa!" He still hadn't said hello to me. Then again, I hadn't said hello to him either. Everything seemed so fraught.

"What a coincidence," I said. "Guess who I saw on TV the other night? Heather O'Connor. She was doing a shampoo commercial."

"Of course she was," Martin said. Then, in a slightly lower tone, "Did you end up going to the movies this weekend?"

I sat across from him, next to Maurice. "I saw *Swept Away*," I said.

"Was it sexy?"

The way he said the word did things to me. If we'd been alone, would I have dared to tell him about the Italian lovers having endless sex on the deserted island, about the rich woman begging the sailor to sodomize her? "Parts of it were sexy. But the first hour or so was all about class war and the sex war, and then it veered into sex and romance."

"The sex war, huh?" He was looking at me strangely.

"See, this Communist ship-hand gets cast away with this rich-bitch type, and the tables are turned because she has to wait on him. He ends up slapping her around, but apparently she loves that, because they fall madly in love."

"Just a light comedy, eh?" Maurice said with a laugh.

"Right," Martin said, looking bemused. "Doesn't sound all that sexy, actually."

It wasn't my fault that was the plot of the damn movie. I'd left out the part where the lovers ended up back with their respective spouses.

Martin's gaze shifted. "Good morning, ladies!" he said heartily, and I turned. Susan and Clarissa had just walked in.

"Good morning, gentleman," Clarissa said with airy irony. Then her expression warmed. "Good morning, Maurice!"

Maurice got up to greet Susan and Clarissa. "So, my dears," he said, "today's the big day!" The bulk of today's episode was devoted to tumultuous scenes about the Beverly/Eric/Sylvia triangle. Susan, Maurice, and Clarissa stood around the coffee urn chatting excitedly about their storyline, leaving me and Martin alone. Susan looked over at us and smiled slightly with a perturbed crinkle between her brows, and I wondered if she could tell something had happened between me and Martin. Susan had been right, after all, about Martin being interested in me, and I had gone against her advice. I didn't want her to be disappointed in me.

I turned and looked at Martin. For an awful moment, silence stretched between us. Then he said, "Speaking of Communist ship-hands and class war, did you hear about that bank robbery in L.A.? Yet another quasi-revolutionary group at work. What were they called?"

I felt as if interrogation lights were trained on me. The name of Alex's group vanished from my brain. "I don't know."

"You didn't hear about it? I thought it'd be right up your alley. They were called the People's...something. The People's Army? The People's Revolutionary Army? It's always something to do with people and an army, isn't it?" He laughed.

Then I remembered: it was the People's Armed Resistance. As if from far away, I heard myself force a laugh.

He peered at me. "Hey, I was just teasing."

"I know." I wanted to put my arms around him and clutch him tight until this sick, cold feeling passed. I wanted to run.

∞

It was hard to settle down to work after that. I felt on edge, even when Martin/Sam looked at me meltingly and professed his love. When we kissed on Jean Christopher's couch during dress rehearsal, we bumped noses, hard. Martin let out a gust of laughter. "Jesus, I should get hazard pay."

I rubbed my nose. I felt like bursting into tears.

"You okay, kid?" he asked.

I pressed my lips tight together and nodded. He was so beautiful, and nothing was going right.

"Let's try that again," he said. "Ve-ry carefully."

A laugh escaped me. We approached each other inch by inch and cautiously angled our faces to kiss without injury. Then we pulled back, and I waited for him to speak. He just looked at me. Finally he said, "It's your line."

"Oh, right!" I couldn't remember my line. For the life of me, I couldn't.

"It's incredible..." Martin said, and at first I thought he meant, it's incredible that you can't remember your goddamn line. Then I remembered it was my goddamn line.

"It's incredible, you know?" I said. "Being with you." I managed to get through the rest of the scene, but it was like slogging through quicksand.

The taping was even worse. I kept having to sneak glances at the teleprompter. I tripped over my words. There were painful pauses as I tried to remember my lines. And still the cameras kept rolling, recording my every mistake, while Martin, damn him, knew his lines cold.

∞

"God, I was terrible today!" I said afterwards, when we were walking to the dressing rooms. Maurice, Susan, and Clarissa were still on set.

"Aw, it wasn't so bad," Martin said.

"I kept blanking out. I hate that!"

"You do know the tricks, don't you? You can hide your lines up your sleeve, or write them between your fingers." He stretched out his fingers and mimed writing on one. "If you use red ink, it won't show up on camera."

"I know, but it seems like cheating somehow. You never resort to those kinds of tricks."

"For some reason, I'm a quick study. And you usually know your lines cold."

"I'm glad you know that, Marty." I'd been thinking that I wanted to be like Susan, and now I couldn't even remember my damn lines. Who was I kidding?

Martin was studying my face, making me want to hide. "You've been awfully tense all day," he said. "How come?"

"It's because…" Suddenly I was fighting back tears again. There was so much I couldn't tell him. It kept piling up. I shook my head.

We reached my dressing room. I opened the door, but he just stood there. "I hope it's not because of anything I did," he said.

Great, he thought it was because we'd kissed the other night. "It's not, Marty."

"Promise?"

"I promise," I whispered. I didn't sound terribly convincing. "It's a problem with an old friend."

"That guy you went to school with?"

Oh, shit. "No! Not that friend." Yes, Jeremy too. Everything was a land mine today. "I wish I could tell you, Marty. I really do." This was getting me nowhere. "Hey, want to come in for a minute?"

He hesitated, then said, "Sure."

We went inside. I wanted to lock the door behind us, but I didn't quite have the chutzpah. Apparently I did have enough chutzpah to put my arms around him and kiss him hard.

Martin pulled back slightly with a puzzled look. "I'd have thought you'd be tired of kissing me after the day we've had."

I stroked the side of his face with my fingertips. "It's funny how much easier this is without the crew around."

That made him laugh, a wonderful laugh that made me feel relaxed for the first time all day. Then he put his arms around my waist and kissed me, and it was better than any Italian movie love scene or *Hope Springs Eternal* love scene. I felt triumphant.

We came up for air just long enough for him to pull out my chair from the counter, sit down, and pull me onto his lap. "Is this what you wanted to do all day?" he breathed.

"Among other things," I said, and he chuckled low in his throat and slid his tongue into my mouth again. It occurred to me, somewhere in the dim reaches of my brain, that I really should have locked the door. Then I stopped thinking for a delicious, indefinite length of time—until the door opened.

It was Clarissa, still wearing her Sylvia Cartwright costume, a bold rust-colored print dress. She let out a heavy sigh. "Oh, Marty. You never learn, do you?"

He was trying to stand up before I'd even hopped off his lap. He looked like a little boy being lectured by his mother. "I'd better go," he murmured to me, and I nodded.

Clarissa was still standing, arms crossed, in the doorway. "Lipstick, Marty," she said, and he gave a little jump, looked in the mirror, and wiped at his mouth. Then Clarissa deliberately walked past him, toward her chair. He headed for the door and closed it behind him.

Clarissa eyed me. "For god's sake, Joanna, must you look so proud of yourself?"

I looked in the mirror: I did look proud, and my lipstick was all kissed off. My mouth felt swollen, and I was wet between the legs. All I wanted to do was find Martin and go to my place. Maybe he was waiting for me. I remembered what Cyn had said: *He's never going to fuck you.* But Cyn had clearly been wrong.

"Are you listening to me?" Clarissa was saying. "The man has cut a swath through the female cast, and you're all too willing to add yourself to his collection."

"Are you speaking from experience?" I asked without thinking.

Her eyes flashed. "Believe me, I had no desire to be one of his trophies."

"I see." I wondered if she'd ever had the chance. I also wondered if she realized how much she sounded like Sylvia Cartwright. Or maybe it was that Sylvia Cartwright sounded like Clarissa?

With a wounded moue, she reached for the pack of cigarettes on her side of the counter. "I'm trying to express concern, Joanna. I see I needn't have bothered." She sat down, crossed her legs and lit a cigarette. "He's not going to leave his wife, you know."

"I know." It occurred to me that while I didn't feel proud to be fooling around with a married man, neither did I long for him to leave Gloria.

"You don't know a thing." She took a drag of her cigarette and exhaled luxuriously. "You're just another ingénue more interested in her costar than in the work."

"You don't know anything about me."

"Don't listen to me, then. But if you value your place in the company, maybe you should."

Why was I wasting my time letting Clarissa get to me, when Martin might be waiting? I grabbed my jacket and handbag and got out of there. Maybe Martin would be in his dressing room. Maurice might be there too, but I headed there anyway. When I didn't hear anyone inside, I knocked on the door.

The door opened, and Maurice stood there in his undershirt and trousers. "Joanna, my dear," he said. "How can I help you?"

I peered past him into the room. Maurice was alone. "I was just looking for Marty."

"Oh, he's been and gone."

"Oh." Had he gone home? Maybe he'd gone to Chauncy's. "Okay. Thanks, Maurice!" I smiled at him brightly and headed for the stairs.

I made it to Chauncy's in record time, but he wasn't there. So much for my visions of us having a drink or two and then hightailing it to my apartment for an afternoon in bed. Only then did I realize I still had on Jean Christopher's skirt and blouse. I'd have to go back to the studio for my clothes. I sat at the bar and ordered a Scotch. I wanted Clarissa to be gone when I went back. The taste of the whiskey reminded me of Martin. Cyn's words came back to me again: *He's never going to fuck you.*

Chapter Fifteen:
Fire and Rain
(October 1975)

In the dream, there was a camera pointed at me. I couldn't remember what scene we were shooting, so I riffled through my script, but the lines were gibberish. When I looked up again, the camera was a submachine gun mounted on some kind of rack, and Ed the cameraman was training it on me. I was frozen in fear, but Cyn grabbed my arm and pulled me into the next room.

"You know how to use this, right?" Cyn asked, handing me a submachine gun. She pointed her own weapon out the window and shot off several rounds. An answering rat-tat-tat came from outside.

I turned the gun around and around in my hands. I couldn't find the trigger. "Cyn, this is your show, not mine. I must've been brainwashed."

She had on a black beret and army fatigues. "Don't give me that, Jo. We're in this together."

She was right. I was Joan Christopher, and I was about to burn to death on live TV. I hoped my mother wouldn't be watching. The room filled with smoke. Flames burst through the window. I wanted to run, but my legs felt like lead. Cyn was trying to get to me, but she went up like a bonfire. I screamed her name and woke, heart pounding.

"I'm right here, Jo," she said, seated beside me on my new orange suede couch. She still had on the fatigues from the dream, and her face was pale beneath the black beret. A script was open on my lap.

The room was cold. Outside there was a loud pattering against the windows—gunfire? Flames crackling? No, it was a rainstorm. I had on jeans, a pullover sweater, and slippers. The table was littered with newspapers. The TV was on, with the sound low—some black-and-white movie with Basil Rathbone. It was Tuesday night, though how late, I didn't know. With his aquiline nose and resonant voice, Basil Rathbone had been one of my youthful movie crushes. I'd felt early sexual stirrings watching his Sherlock Holmes movies on TV as a kid.

"You were having a bad dream," Cyn said and reached out to stroke my hair. I felt a chill breeze across my temple.

"It wasn't another version of my life? That's a relief." Just a dream. As if waking to the ghost of your best friend was "just" anything.

Cyn lifted the script from my lap and began to read: "Grow up, Jean. Some of us have grown-up responsibilities. I've been trying to juggle my job and my marriage, while you've been gallivanting around town playing girl reporter... You and Sam and your precious feelings! You're behaving like adolescents." Her voice rose. "Don't tell me you're sorry. You're not sorry—"

"God, stop," I said. "You read Vicki's lines even worse than Babette does."

Cyn gave a laugh. "Fuck you."

"It's a terrific scene. Or it would be, if Babette could handle it. Or if *I* can handle it, for that matter." Tomorrow would probably be okay—it was just the table-read, and I'd have the script in front of me. But maybe on Thursday I should take Martin's suggestion and write my lines on my hand. Even considering it made me feel ashamed. At least I would see Martin tomorrow. Maybe we could continue where we'd left off before Clarissa had interrupted us.

"You said you were brainwashed," Cyn said.

"What?"

"In your dream. Is that really what you think?"

"Maybe you should stay out of my dreams." The sound of rain battering the windows redoubled, and I shivered. "Maybe we all were brainwashed. Some kind of four-way hypnosis." It occurred to me that if this were true, Alex had stayed hypnotized, and maybe Jeremy had too. It couldn't be that simple.

"And then you snapped out of it just in time to chicken out?"

"I didn't chicken out, Cyn. I honestly had the flu."

"Maybe. At the time, I was sure you were *acting*." She fixed me with her clear, gray-blue gaze. "You had the flu the other week, and it didn't keep you from your precious TV studio."

On TV, Basil Rathbone engaged in some fancy swordplay with—was that Errol Flynn? It must be *Captain Blood*. Saber rang against saber. Then Flynn stabbed Rathbone, and he fell dead in the sand, waves lapping over his face. I got up and switched off the TV. "Okay, I'll admit I was glad I got the flu so I didn't have to go through with it. I was too scared, Cyn."

"You were scared you wouldn't get a chance to go to drama school!"

I sat next to her again. "I was afraid we'd go to jail. I was afraid someone would get hurt."

"Someone did get hurt," she said quietly.

"I don't just mean us—I mean some innocent bystander. Anyone could've been there when the bomb went off."

"As it turns out," Cyn said, "no one was there but me."

It was still unbearable that she had died alone. "But there were those other times when I did go with you," I said. "The time I died. The time I went to prison."

"And yet here you are, safe and sound. So those times don't count, do they?"

"If they don't count, why did I have to go through them?"

She shrugged. "Maybe you'll get it right next time."

"Next time?" I exclaimed. "Please, I can't deal with a next time. Why are you doing this to me? *How* are you doing this to me?"

The sound of the rain abruptly ceased. The room seemed unnaturally quiet. Then a car horn sounded in the street and made me jump.

Cyn was silent for a long time, her lips pressed together. Finally she said, "How could you bail on me, Joanna? How could *you* do that to *me*?"

I was at a loss for words. It was a question I'd never expected I'd have to answer. "I didn't expect you to go alone. I thought if I bailed, so would you, at least temporarily."

"You didn't think the guys would go with me instead?"

"Maybe. I sure never thought you wouldn't tell them I wasn't coming. Why didn't you?"

"Don't you know?" she asked. I shook my head, and her eyes widened with exasperation. "I don't believe you. How can you not know?"

"Just *tell* me," I said.

She fumed silently, as if having to say the words would add insult to injury. Finally she burst out with it: "I was fucking humiliated! It was the most important day of my life, and you let me down. You were supposed to be my best friend!"

"I'm sorry." My voice was small and abashed. It had never occurred to me that I'd had the power to humiliate Cyn. It had always been the other way around. And now she was dead, and she was still calling the shots. Get it right the next time? How could I keep there from being a next time?

"I almost couldn't get rid of the guys after Jeremy set the clock," Cyn said. "They kept asking if they should wait for you to show up. I kept telling them, 'She'll be here.' Finally I yelled at them to stick to the fucking plan. 'I don't need you to hold my hand. I'm a revolutionary!'" She gave a laugh. "That did it. Anyway, it wasn't like the bomb was going to go off while I waited for you. There were hours left on the timer. Or there were supposed to be."

"What do you think went wrong?"

She looked so small and fragile despite her paramilitary garb, her legs drawn up on the sofa. "My hands didn't shake or anything like that. I set the little wicker handbag on the cement, and when I started to nudge it under the mailbox with my foot, the thing just went off. I don't know what went wrong. Jeremy knew more about bombs than I did. But what I did, I did right. I'm sure of that."

I wasn't sure if Cyn would have admitted to making a mistake, much less one that had cost her her life.

"But the point is, you should've been there, Jo," she murmured. "You should have been there."

It was nothing I hadn't told myself for the last four years, but how much worse to hear her say the words. "I know I let you down," I said. "I know I can't ever make it right. But you know what would have happened if I'd been there."

"Do I?"

"I watched you die, then I was arrested. I suppose I could have watched you die and then run away, so I wouldn't be arrested. Then there was the time I died too. Was that better?"

"To have died together..." There was a strange note in Cyn's voice, a quaver of longing. Then she seemed to shake herself awake. "That's not what I thought would happen, Jo. I thought we'd have to run. I thought we'd be on the run together."

Even now the idea held a certain romantic appeal, though it would have canceled out the life I was trying to build. "Alex ran. I guess he had the life you dreamed of, until they busted him." According to today's papers, Alex and Sharon Gilmore were in jail awaiting trial, and two men I'd never heard of had been arrested in connection with the bank robbery.

"Alex!" She tossed off the name dismissively.

"Maybe I'll be busted too. Do you want me to go to prison again, if that other time wasn't real enough for you?"

"Why would I want that?" she demanded.

"So I'd be punished for letting you down. Would that help you to—I don't know—rest?"

She glared at me. "Is that what you want, for me to *rest*, so you can forget me again? Stop trying to figure out how to get rid of me. Because I sure as hell don't want *you* to rest. I want you to get it right." Then she was gone. The script for Thursday's show, still open to the page she had read aloud, lay on the sofa where she'd been.

What did she mean, get it right? Get it right next time, she'd said. When I'd been at Brightdale, I couldn't remember any other life, except in bits of dream and déjà vu. How could I get it right if I couldn't remember getting it wrong? And what would getting it right even look like?

∞

When I got to the rehearsal room on Wednesday afternoon, Babette and David were already there, as well as a day player who played a nurse. Martin walked in with Elsbeth just before it was time to start the table-read. He gave me a quick smile, but we didn't get a chance to talk. Afterwards he said, "See you tomorrow," and left as soon as we were done. Had he hurried out because Babette was there, or was he avoiding me?

On Thursday morning I painstakingly wrote as many of my lines as would fit between the fingers of my left hand with a red pen. I felt more incompetent with each stroke of the pen. At the studio I held my fingers together so no one could see.

Babette mishandled the Jean-Vicki confrontation as I'd thought she would. When she wasn't melodramatically declaiming her lines, she was whipping her head around to peer at the teleprompter. Not that I could fault her after my performance the other day, and with my lines written on my hand. "Don't tell me you're sorry!" Babs cried. "You're not sorry.

You're…not…" She gracefully slid to the floor of Jean's living room.

The scene picked up with Sam arriving at Jean's door just after Vicki's fainting spell. Martin and I knelt over Babette. "Vicki, please wake up," he said.

Her eyelids fluttered open. She tried to sit up, but her head lolled woozily from side to side. Martin scooped her up in his arms and carried her to the sofa. With Babs's arms around his neck and her shapely calves perfectly displayed below her skirt, it looked like a love scene. Then Martin tripped on the edge of the rug and dumped Babs onto the sofa.

"Cut!" Elsbeth yelled over the PA. "Terry, tape down that rug!" At least it wasn't my fault this time.

Babette stood, smoothing down her skirt. "I'm not a sack of potatoes, Marty."

"Jesus, it was an accident!" Martin said. He and Babs glared at each other, then burst out laughing. I decided I'd liked it better when they weren't speaking to each other.

∞

After the taping, Martin was chatting with the day player, a blonde in a nurse's uniform. I couldn't seem to extricate myself from the conversation Babette and David Halpren were having about the big impending visit between her and Larry's teenage kids. "What if they don't like me?" Babs asked.

"You're being ridiculous," David said, as two crew members carried away Jean Christopher's sofa. "What's not to like?"

Martin laughed uproariously at something the day player had said. "I'm sure they'll like you," I said absently.

"I hope so," Babette said. "It means so much to Larry."

Martin headed off the set with the day player. I watched his departing back with a growing sense of panic. I wasn't coming in tomorrow, and Martin and I hadn't been alone since we'd been interrupted by Clarissa.

When Babette and David started talking about the *Hope Springs Eternal* twentieth anniversary party that was going to be held at the Brand Hotel, I excused myself and went upstairs. I knocked on Martin's dressing room door, and he opened it. He had changed from Sam's clothes into his own jeans and blue shirt, but the shirt was unbuttoned. "Hi," he said, looking surprised and not particularly pleased to see me.

"Can I come in?"

"Of course."

I entered and shut the door. He looked at me expectantly. His beautiful hairy chest shorted out my brain. "I was wondering if you wanted to go get a drink," I said.

He buttoned his shirt. "I'd like to, but I've gotta get to the table-read, and then Gloria and I are having some friends over for dinner."

"Some other time, then."

"Sure," he said. There were framed photos of Martin's children on his side of the counter. In one photo Gloria (better looking than I'd remembered) hugged a little girl and littler boy. Gloria wore jeans and a checked shirt and smiled tiredly. The kids looked impish, as though they were planning to take over the world and it would be great fun. They looked like both their parents, with dark hair and eyes. I wanted to tell Martin they were adorable—I knew how he would react, that proud father's look—yet I couldn't, not when I was trying to be the other woman.

On Maurice's side of the counter there were a number of photos. One was of Maurice and a younger man standing side by side, lanky and dapper in suits.

"I hate what they're doing with our storyline," Martin said, and I turned to look at him. "Sam flip-flopping from Vicki to Jean and back again. It makes him look like a spineless idiot."

I leaned on the counter. "What do you think is going on with Vicki fainting? Are they giving her some illness?"

Martin looked like he'd tasted something sour. "I have a sinking feeling Vicki's pregnant."

I gasped and clapped my hand to my mouth. Martin burst out laughing, and I joined in. Then I had a horrible thought. "If Vicki's pregnant, do you think Sam's going to reconcile with her?"

He gave a sigh. "I don't think that's what the writers were planning, but I've heard rumors that the network wants Sam and Vicki back together. God knows why they're so popular. I think we're a lot more interesting."

"But if there's no more Sam and Jean? My contract is up in a few months."

"Come on, kid. This is all pure speculation."

"Marty, I don't want to lose this job. I love this job." I remembered what Clarissa had said: *if you value your place in the company.* Did she have some inside knowledge?

He looked stricken. "Please don't worry, Jo. We don't know anything, not really." He put his hands on my shoulders and massaged them, and suddenly there was nothing in the world to worry about, it felt so good. I leaned forward and kissed him.

He kissed me back briefly, then pulled away. "Jo, maybe this isn't such a good idea."

"Why not?"

"…and here are the dressing rooms!" Maurice's voice, like a fanfare.

"I didn't know Maurice was working today," I muttered.

"The table-read," Martin said as the door opened. Maurice stood in the doorway with Babette and a willowy young woman with long brown hair. Where had I seen her before?

"I didn't know you were here, Martin," Maurice said.

Martin reached up and wiped at the corner of his mouth. Babette looked at Martin, then at me. Her eyes were canny and surprised, as if she were seeing me for the first time. Her reaction was so much more understated than it had ever been for the cameras.

"This is Amy Gundersen, my new 'daughter,'" Maurice said. "Amy, this is Joanna Bergman, who plays Jean Christopher, and Martin Yates, who plays her paramour, Sam Jameson."

Amy smiled. "I recognize you both! I watched *Hope Springs Eternal* while I was waiting to find out if I got the part." She had large blue eyes and an earnest look.

Martin smiled broadly and stepped forward to shake her hand. "Welcome, Amy. Maurice speaks highly of you."

"You know, I auditioned for the part of Jean Christopher," Amy told me. "But I didn't get to screen-test then. So I was thrilled when I got the part of Kathy Read."

I stared at her. That was where I'd seen her, wasn't it? On the black-and-white TV at Brightdale. She had been playing Jean Christopher. She had taken my place. "Welcome," was all I could think to say.

"Well, it's about time for the table-read," Babette said.

"Right," Martin said and headed out into the hall. I followed. "Have a good weekend, everyone," I said.

Martin turned, his smile fading. "That's right, you're not working tomorrow. See you next week, Jo." He reached past me and shut the dressing room door. Then they all walked away, chatting and making the new girl feel welcome.

I went into my dressing room and just stood there, picturing Amy on that TV at Brightdale. Picturing the way Martin had looked at Amy just now. Then I wiped the red ink from my fingers with a little cold cream. I hadn't even needed to look at my lines during taping. All writing them on my hand had done was to make me feel like a failure. I took off Jean's orange pinafore dress and off-white blouse. Another weekend awaited me, another weekend of leafing through newspapers looking for the latest on Alex and trying to figure out how to stop what Cyn was doing, another weekend of feeling alone and crazy—unless I wound up in some other version of my life, and that would be even worse.

My eye was drawn to the framed photograph of Clarissa and Maurice in evening wear, grinning with their arms around each other. I thought of Martin's family photos, Maurice's photo of himself and his boyfriend.

"Why don't you have any photographs in here?"

I jumped—Cyn was standing next to me. Like me, she had on only a bra and panties, though I didn't think she had ever worn a bra after we left Rochester.

"Cyn, I wish you wouldn't show up here." I reached for my jeans and sweater hanging in the closet.

"Where are the photos of you and me? Did you *burn* them or something?"

I stepped into my jeans. "Of course not." They were in a box on the top shelf of my bedroom closet. The box was taped shut. "I still have them."

"Too ashamed of me to have them on display?"

I pulled the sweater over my head. "Ashamed of you? Why would you think that?"

She shrugged. "I was never an actress. Never any of the things you apparently wanted to be so badly. It's pathetic the way you suck up to that married dude and all the people who work here. They're not your friends." She picked up the photograph of Clarissa and Maurice. "It's like this old hag, in love with a homosexual. She's never going to get anywhere, and neither are you."

I stepped into my shoes. "Put that down. You don't know what you're talking about."

"Oh Joanna, I know exactly what I'm talking about!" She turned and smiled at me, a sad, luminous smile. The picture slipped from her fingers and landed with a crash on a fancy bottle of perfume. The photograph and the bottle toppled to the floor.

I knelt, picked up the photograph and turned it over. A network of cracks spider-webbed across Clarissa's and Maurice's grins. "Oh no, Cyn, look what you've done!" A heavy sweetness, accusingly reminiscent of Clarissa, filled the room. A corner of the perfume bottle had broken off, and the liquid was seeping out onto the floor. Was it the smell that was making me dizzy? The room was getting dark. I could see Cyn a couple of blocks away, setting the wicker handbag on the cement. "No, I'm not going back there," I said. I was in two places at once, in the dressing room and on that late-night street.

"Hurry, Jo," Cyn said—the Cyn standing above me in bra and panties. But it was too late. The other Cyn nudged the handbag with her foot. The explosion was deafening, the roar, the shattering glass, and still I resisted, still stayed in the present, in the dressing room.

"Why didn't you try to help me?" Cyn demanded. Standing there in her underwear, but all blood and bone. I covered my eyes. "Why didn't you at least try?"

I was slipping back, the horror's pull irresistible. I couldn't hold on any longer.

"No," I kept saying,

"Oh no, oh no, Cyn…" as I stood over her body on the sidewalk. I was shaking, breath coming in gasps, ears ringing from the explosion. I could barely look at her. The darkness half-hid what had happened to her, but not the blood scrolling out from under her, not how she'd come apart. I wanted to scream, wanted to sob, but something stopped me. Soon the cops would come. There was nothing I could do for her. I swiped at my runny nose. There would be time to cry and fall apart, but right now I had to get away.

I didn't run, just walked as quickly and soundlessly toward campus as I could. Heart racketing in my chest. I kept almost blacking out, having to stop and make myself breathe in and out through my mouth until I could go on. I heard sirens in the distance.

I found a pay phone a few blocks from my residence hall. Fumbled in my purse to find my wallet. Deposited a dime and dialed the number, though my hand was shaking. One ring, two...

"Hello?" A wholly awake voice. Was it him, or one of his roommates?

"Alex?"

"Jo, is that you?"

My throat got too tight to speak. My whole body was shaking.

"Joanna, are you there?"

"It went wrong," I managed to say.

"What do you mean, it went wrong? Pigs?"

"No. The device. It went off. She's dead. Oh god, she's dead!"

Silence on the other end. "Okay. Okay. Let me think." He sounded calm and utterly at a loss.

I huddled in a corner of the phone booth. I was so cold. What if someone found me? "Alex, what do we do now?"

"You know what we do. Plan B."

"Plan B," I said. Plan B meant underground. It meant getting a bus out of town and probably never coming back. How annoyed Cyn would be that we'd gone underground without her. I held the phone receiver so tight, my hand hurt.

Chapter Sixteen:
Subterranean Homesick Blues
(October 1975)

L.A. was a bad idea. That was what I kept thinking, like a drumbeat, while Jeremy fucked me in the sleeping bag the morning of the bank robbery. It was half-light in the apartment in Inglewood. Alex and Sharon were having sex in their sleeping bag, over by the kitchenette. We were on the other side of the sofa, near the front door. Alex and Sharon had started first, then Jeremy had touched me cursorily and climbed on top of me. I felt both annoyed and aroused. It was as if, after all these years, he was still trying to prove himself to Alex, though he fucked me slowly and quietly, because actually he liked his privacy. It occurred to me that, if things went wrong today, this might be the last time we'd get to do this.

Cecil and Kamau were still asleep in their rooms, as far as I knew. I'd just as soon not have either of them walking in on us. Alex and Sharon were going at it vigorously, with grunts and moans. Alex, I remembered, was passionate and single-minded in bed, though the first time we'd had sex, he'd moaned Cyn's name when he came. In a way I'd understood.

Jeremy began to move more urgently. The room was a bit lighter, sun leaking through the closed blinds. I could look into his eyes. They were beautiful and open to me, though I was too wound up to feel open.

Alex came with a guttural moan. It turned me on. Maybe I'd be able to come after all. I wasn't sure if Sharon had. I closed my eyes and remembered Alex fucking me while Jeremy lay watching next to us in the bed, his hand moving slowly on his cock. That had happened when we first went on the run. We'd been scared shitless and grieving Cyn, and we'd tried to prove on each other's bodies that we were still alive. That didn't work so well anymore—not for me, anyway.

I squeezed my eyes shut and ground up against Jeremy. I remembered Alex's face as he came inside me, remembered Alex pulling out and Jeremy pushing inside me. That did it: I came with a gasp and didn't care who heard me. When I opened my eyes, Jeremy was looking delightedly down at me as if he'd made it all happen. He moved harder, faster, then froze above me, his mouth trembling.

When Jeremy collapsed next to me, Alex said, "Rise and shine, eh?"

"Fuck you," I muttered. Jeremy chuckled and hugged me to him. I wished I had a Kleenex to mop myself up. I wished I could go back to sleep, but the pre-action adrenaline had taken hold in spite of orgasm. I almost wished we were doing a bombing today. Bombings were a known quantity. Nothing had ever gone wrong with any of my bombs. But a bank robbery? Too many variables.

Our group had done bombings to protest, among other injustices, the murder of George Jackson, the Attica killings, the military coup in Chile. I had learned to build and set bombs, partly to continue the work of revolution, which was all I was good for underground. But also it was as if some irrational part of me believed that, for every bomb of ours that went off with no injury to anyone, Cyn might, in the slow accrual of destruction, be put back together again, good as new. Jeremy had never built or set a bomb again, though he had participated in planning actions and scouting locations. It wasn't that we didn't trust him to get it right, now that we were more knowledgeable than he had been with Cyn's bomb—but his hands shook at the mere idea.

Alex got up and walked naked across the ratty gold carpet. I watched his pale, wiry body through narrowed lids. He went into the john and shut the door. Sharon got up—like me, she had on an unsexy, threadbare nightgown—and padded to the kitchenette, dragging a hand through her disheveled, dark blonde hair. This day was going to begin whether I liked it or not.

One of the bedroom doors squeaked open, and Cecil came into the living room. He had on jeans and nothing else. He was slender and brown-skinned. "Morning, Lulu," he said, scrubbing at his eyes with his fists. "You making coffee?" Lulu March was Sharon's alias. I didn't know Cecil's or Kamau's birth names. Cecil had been a Black Panther in Chicago. He'd named himself after Cecil Taylor, the jazz pianist.

"Morning, Cecil," I said, disentangling from Jeremy and sitting up.

He smiled. "Morning, Emma. Ready for some expropriation?"

That made me laugh. "Ready as I'll ever be." I reached up to smooth my hair, which was chopped short and dyed blonde—not as pale as Cyn's had been, but lighter than Sharon's. My nom de guerre was Emma Shaw (Emma as in Goldman, Shaw as in George Bernard).

Sharon banged the coffee pot onto the stove. "What do you mean by that, Em? You agreed to the plan, despite your objections. We're well-prepared. We're ready to act."

Sharon could be so tiresomely dogmatic. At her most doctrinaire, Cyn at least had had style. I couldn't help but think of Sharon as the anti-Cyn: uncharismatic, sexually loyal to Alex. Maybe that was why Alex had latched onto her when we met up with her in Seattle in '72. Sharon had gone to Radcliffe, graduated at the top of her class, and gone underground in '70. When I'd asked her about her alias, she'd said it was after Louisa May Alcott and Jo March, and we'd bonded over *Little Women*—but she wouldn't call me Jo, even in the middle of that conversation. "Yes, Lulu," I said wearily. "We're ready to act. Absolutely, perfectly ready."

Sharon glared stolidly at me.

"Just a little stage fright, right, Em?" Cecil said.

"Right," I said, though his words gave me a pang from my other, aborted life.

Alex came out of the bathroom. "Cassidy, put some clothes on, man," Cecil said with a guffaw.

"I didn't know you were such a prude," Sharon said, smiling.

"I'm no prude. It's just a shock to the system so early in the morning."

"Okay, man," Alex said, grinning in his blond beard, and reached for his jeans on the floor. Just then Kamau came in, also wearing only jeans, a gun tucked into his waistband, cigarette in hand. A strapping, muscular man, Kamau almost always carried a gun in the apartment (generally a Colt Official Police .38 Special). He was a Vietnam vet and had served time for armed robbery, something I didn't like to think about, especially today.

"Hey, Kent," Kamau said to Jeremy. (His nom de guerre was Kent Wayne, after two comic book characters, plus a nod to Kent State.) "Cecil. Cassidy." As usual he acknowledged only the men, though his eyes flicked over me and Sharon. Then he did speak to Sharon: "Hey, is there coffee?"

I didn't get why everyone was dying for coffee. Weren't they as nervous as me? I felt like I'd drunk five cups already. I lay back in the sleeping bag and tried not to breathe the cigarette smoke and remembered watching the SLA shootout on live TV, that house going up in flames with all of them inside. We'd been in the Mission then. I wished we'd stayed there. Not that I agreed with the SLA's methods or much of their ideology, but I couldn't help but think of how they'd managed to hide out for ages in San Francisco, and when they got to Los Angeles, the cops got them. Then again, Patty Hearst had been arrested in the Mission less than a month ago. Maybe time was just running out for all of us.

Jeremy turned on his side to face me. "You okay, sweets?" he whispered. He would never let the other men hear him call me that.

I turned on my side to face him. "I miss our apartment," I whispered.

He let out a sigh. "Me too."

We'd only left San Francisco two weeks ago, but it felt like another lifetime, lost to us. I'd waitressed, he'd worked at a bookstore. We'd lived cheaply, but there had been leisurely spaghetti dinners and time alone together, reading, talking, drinking wine, making love in our bed. Alex and Sharon had lived a few blocks away in a similar setup. But then Alex had started to say, *We're getting soft*, and Sharon had chimed in: *Cozy and bourgeois.*

"We can find a place of our own here," Jeremy murmured.

"I suppose so." I didn't like any part of L.A. I'd been in so far, though primarily that had been this mostly black, downscale neighborhood, with a liquor store on the corner, and the mostly white, moneyed stretch of Studio City that contained the bank we were going to rob. "If we make it through today."

"We will," he said.

"I hope you're right. It's just, do you ever think, *this* is my life?"

He studied my face. Then he nodded with an ironic little smile and a lifting of his eyebrows, a very Jewish expression that caught at my heart, or what was left of it. I touched his stubbly cheek. I hoped we would make it through.

∞

Later that morning we took the freeway to Studio City. Alex drove the stolen Dodge Dart, Cecil his VW van, which would be the switch car. Sharon sat in the front with Alex, I in back with Jeremy. Sharon and I had on neat jeans and long-sleeved shirts, and Alex and Jeremy wore sports jackets and looked more well-groomed than they had in weeks. None of us said a word. Alex turned on the radio, and John Denver thanked God he was a country boy. Alex turned the dial, and an announcer's smooth voice spoke: "…the SLA, William and Emily Harris are set to be arraigned in Los Angeles Superior Court for kidnapping, burglary, and assault." Alex switched off the radio.

As the sprawling, unfamiliar city whizzed by, I pondered why I'd agreed to this action. I'd begun to wonder secretly if the People's Armed Resistance was becoming irrelevant. Our clandestine network was spread throughout the country, and aboveground sympathizers helped us with funds when they could—but sometimes it felt like we were on our own. I hated that we couldn't participate in aboveground organizing or social programs. With the war over, bombings seemed outmoded. Alex had floated the idea of assisting the Black Freedom Brigade with some actions in L.A. and elsewhere. I'd feared bank robberies would make us look like gun-happy lunatics. I'd suggested taking some time to hash out our priorities. Sharon had sided with Alex, of course. So had Jeremy, which hadn't been much of a surprise. I'd been overruled. I could have opted out—but that would have meant leaving Jeremy and being left stranded, alone.

Sometimes I thought about Emma Goldman, my namesake, deported for her anarchism, in exile from the United States, and I thought I understood how she'd felt. I hated that going back to New York wasn't an option. I had never stopped missing it, with a palpable ache, akin to the way I felt about my parents and my brother. We'd spoken on the phone a handful of times over the years. They didn't understand my life. I understood it less and less.

Alex pulled up around the corner from the Landings Savings Bank, which was on a wide, busy boulevard. I flashed back to Al Pacino walking into the Brooklyn bank with his carbine in a box with a ribbon. Jeremy and I had gone to see *Dog Day Afternoon* the week before. We'd loved it, but it seemed a bad omen. My carbine was on the seat between me and Jeremy in a large Bullock's shopping bag. The gun was real, and I knew how to use it, but it felt like a prop. Jeremy's gun (like Sal's) was in a briefcase, between him and the door. It was a pleasant, sunny L.A. morning, complete with palm trees. My heart was pounding in my throat.

I looked at myself in the rear view mirror, with my short blonde hair and sunglasses. I tried to wear Cyn's insouciant expression. She would have done all this so much better. "I'm Miss Bonnie Parker, and I rob *banks*," I said.

Jeremy let out a nervous laugh and leaned towards me. "We'll be okay," he whispered in my ear.

"You ready, Emma?" Alex asked. I nodded, got out of the car, and walked with my shopping bag around the corner.

I took a deep breath and pulled open the glass door of the bank. I smiled at the security guard standing near the door. He was an older white guy with a gray mustache. He smiled back with a kindly look.

There were customers at all the teller windows, and four people in line. Three of the tellers were women, the fourth a tall blond guy. The bank manager was nowhere in sight. I'd seen him sitting at his desk when we'd scoped out the place the other day. He was a frosty, business-suited man with short gray hair. Was he in back, out sick, coming in late? I wondered if I should go tell the others. The plan was that I should go back to the car in the next two minutes if there was a problem.

I headed for the wooden counter with the deposit and withdrawal slips. A red-haired man came in, stood next to me and filled out a slip. I fiddled with a deposit slip and watched from the corner of my eye as my comrades came in. Just as I was wondering if Alex would wait until at least some of the customers left, he pulled out his Smith & Wesson and brandished it at the security guard. "This is a bank robbery," he announced, and the rest of us pulled our weapons. One of the female tellers screamed. Everyone else went glassy-eyed at the sight of the guns. Jeremy had a carbine like mine, Sharon had a revolver like Alex's. I backed away from the red-haired customer and trained my gun on him. He gaped at me, his face flushing red.

"Up against the wall!" Alex said. I was surprised he didn't add, *motherfuckers.* The security guard and the customers lined up against the back wall, except for the red-haired man, who just stood there.

"Up against the wall!" I said, my voice startlingly loud and authoritative, and he obeyed. Then I told Alex, "No sign of the manager."

Alex blinked, momentarily disconcerted. He motioned for the tellers to come out from behind the counter and get up against the wall. "Where's the bank manager?" he demanded.

One of the tellers, a brunette who looked around my mom's age, said in a strangled voice, "Out of town. Visiting his daughter in Santa Barbara."

Alex nodded. "Fine. If everyone cooperates, no one will get hurt." He looked almost relaxed brandishing his gun. Jeremy and Sharon and I were silent, jerking our guns from side to side to cover the room. Alex got the keys from the security guard and locked the door, then drew the drapes. "You, come with me," he told the male teller, then looked at us. "We're going into the vault. Cover them."

I kept looking at the security guard. His face was ashen, and he looked bewildered and miserable. For the first time in my life, I felt like a terrorist.

Alex and the male teller reappeared, the teller carrying the bag full of cash. Alex took the bag. "Okay, all of you, down on the ground!"

The tellers and customers awkwardly got down on their hands and knees and then lay flat on their stomachs.

"We're done here," Alex said. "Let's move!"

We went charging out the door. As we turned the corner, an alarm sounded, loud and jarring. It took Alex a moment to get the key into the car door, but it felt like an eternity. "Come on!" I yelled. Finally we got inside and drove off. We were supposed to drive about half a mile to where Cecil and Kamau were waiting in the van, so we could ditch the hot Dodge.

Almost immediately a police car appeared behind us, lights flashing, siren blaring. "Fuck!" Jeremy said. "Oh, fuck…"

"Maybe we can shake them," Sharon said.

"Shut up," Alex muttered. "Gotta concentrate." He accelerated, blew through a yellow light, took a corner way too fast, and accelerated again. The cop car was gaining on us. Alex weaved through traffic. Two more cop cars appeared, following us. Alex turned onto a side street, then another. Now we were in a tree-lined residential area. Alex made a sharp right turn. "Shit!" he cried. We were in a cul-de-sac, boxed in, and going too fast. We skidded and crashed into the back of a parked car. My sunglasses flew off, and I was thrown forward against the back of Sharon's seat.

I looked around dazedly. We were in the quintessential suburban neighborhood, with one-story houses, garages and green lawns. "You okay, Jo?" Jeremy asked.

Cop cars kept roaring up and screeching to a halt, blocking us in. I wanted to tell Jeremy that was the stupidest question I had ever heard. "I don't know. Are you?"

"I think so."

"Alex?" Sharon was saying. "Alex!" She had blood running down her forehead, and he was slumped over the steering wheel. For once she'd forgotten to call him by his nom de guerre.

"Cassidy, you okay, man?" Jeremy asked.

Alex gave a moan and heaved himself upright. His glasses were broken and perched askew on the tip of his nose. "What's going on?" he whispered.

"We're fucked, that's all," I said, and looked out the back window at the battalion of cop cars with flashing red lights, the cops standing in the street with guns trained on us. A wave of adrenaline rolled through me, leaving me shaky.

"Maybe not," Sharon said, and I turned. She showed me the gun in her hand.

I thought of the SLA shootout, how everyone in that house ended up dead. "Don't be stupid," I said, but my tone was gentle. "If we try to shoot our way out, we're dead." My upper back was starting to hurt. I pushed the pain aside as best I could.

Sharon let out a sigh and set her gun on the dashboard, then turned to Alex, who seemed to be having a hard time holding his head up. "We're gonna surrender, babe," she murmured.

"Surrender?" Alex murmured, as if half asleep. "Never surrender…"

I looked into Jeremy's eyes, wide and frightened. He took my hand and squeezed it.

"Exit the vehicle with your hands above your heads," a voice boomed at us.

My heart was pounding. I didn't want to let go of Jeremy's hand. There was no guarantee they wouldn't shoot us anyway. Maybe it would be better to go out in a blaze of gun-toting glory?

I discovered I wanted to live.

"Exit the vehicle now, with your hands above your heads!"

I let go of Jeremy's hand, opened the car door, and stepped outside, hands above my head. A cop tackled me and threw me face down into the street. He put a gun to my head, and time stopped. The cold steel bit into my temple. "Don't shoot," I whispered, and thought of Al Pacino at the end of *Dog Day*

Afternoon, of Faye Dunaway's and Warren Beatty's bodies flopping and jerking with the barrage of bullets at the end of *Bonnie and Clyde*. Everything felt unreal. I wished I could push up through layers of sleep and wake up.

More cop cars kept screaming up and stopping. Alex cried out.

"Don't hurt him!" Sharon shouted. I heard a scuffle, and Sharon's voice, sounding out of breath: "Stupid asshole motherfuckers!"

My cop pulled the gun away from my head and hauled me to my feet. I never got a good look at him. He yanked my arms behind my back and slapped cuffs on my wrists. A woman was staring out the window of the peach stucco house I was facing. Watching the show. When she saw me watching her, she disappeared behind the drapes. Behind me a cop started kicking someone on the ground with soft thuds and grunts. I couldn't turn my head enough to see who it was, but I had a sick feeling it was Jeremy.

The cuffs cut into my wrists. I couldn't believe I was going to go back to prison. Back? I had never been in prison...

I saw Cyn's face. Flashes of it, with my haircut—no, I had hers. *Is this what you wanted, Cyn?* I thought. Then I heard her voice, as if she were right next to me: "Of course not, you idiot."

My head spun. Dressing room. Broken perfume bottle. Martin's voice: *It's always something to do with people and an army.* All at once I remembered everything, but I stayed where I was, handcuffs biting into my wrists. "Oh god," I whispered. "Get me out of here!"

On the ground Jeremy was moaning. "Get up, asshole," a cop said.

"Don't think he can," my cop said with a snicker.

"Oh god, Jeremy!" I cried, then realized I hadn't called him Kent. Not that it mattered anymore. In this life, he would be charged with armed robbery, his alias useless. In that other life, none of this had happened to Jeremy. He was a nurse. He had come to me for money for Alex. Please, I thought, if not for me, then for Jeremy, get us out of here. For a long, excruciating moment I was in two places at once, handcuffed in Studio City and in my dressing room on the Upper West Side. "Cyn, help me," I whispered, though I wasn't sure if she could, or if she wanted to.

Then my hands were free, and I was kneeling on the dressing room floor. The room reeked of perfume. Cyn stood looking down at me, Cyn with her short blonde hair (*my* short blonde hair?). She was in her underwear, her skin unmarked and pale.

"Are you trying to get me killed?" I demanded, scrambling to my feet.

She eyed me coolly. "You and Jeremy made a sickeningly cute couple."

Adrenaline still surged through me. "Is that all you can say?"

"I don't know what you're mad at me for. You're the one who keeps on getting it wrong."

"Getting it wrong! What the fuck does that mean?"

Her gaze latched somewhere to the side of my face. Her fingers drifted up to touch her own temple. "That's gonna leave a bruise."

"What?" I brought my fingertips to my temple. It was sore to the touch. I looked in the mirror. It was a shock to see my long brown hair. Even more of a shock: my temple was pinkish and swollen where the cop had jammed the gun against it. My wrists were red and abraded from the handcuffs. "That's impossible," I said—then noticed Cyn's reflection wasn't there. I turned. She was gone.

And here I was, saved from the pigs, saved from prison, unlike Alex and Sharon. And what about Cecil and Kamau? I didn't think theirs were the names I'd read in the newspaper, the other arrestees. But I had only known their aliases. It was so strange to have been intimate with Jeremy and Alex. It felt unfair to them, to know them in ways they didn't know me. It even felt unfair to have been Sharon's irritated comrade, when she didn't know me at all. Had Alex ever told her about me, in this version of our lives? At least Jeremy was safe, in this life. A nurse, not a bank robber.

The heavy smell of Clarissa's perfume brought me back to the present moment. I grabbed a fistful of Kleenex and mopped at the spilled perfume. Then I carefully placed the broken picture of Clarissa and Maurice on its back on the counter. Would Clarissa think I had broken her things? It wasn't as if I could tell her Cyn had done it. Maybe I could get the photo reframed and buy a new bottle of perfume before she could see the damage. It seemed ridiculous to worry about such things, after what I had just escaped. Part of me was still with my comrades in that other life, and I wondered if there was anything I could do for them. But this was my life too—no, not too, *this* was my life, wasn't it? How long had I been in the dressing room, anyway? There had been a table-read going on. I hadn't heard anyone come back this way.

I got to my feet and threw the perfume-reeking Kleenex into the wastebasket. I left the perfume bottle on the floor. I made sure my sleeves covered my abraded wrists and brushed my hair forward so it covered the mark on my temple.

I managed to make it down to the lobby without running into anyone. The security guard glanced up from his Robert Ludlum paperback. "Afternoon, Miss Bergman."

I made myself smile evenly. I remembered the security guard at the bank. "Afternoon, Charlie. See you next week."

He returned my smile. I hurried out the glass door like a criminal fleeing the scene.

Chapter Seventeen:
One Way Ticket Home
(October 1975)

"That's a nice little dress, Joanna," Clarissa said. "Youth truly is wasted on the young!" She lifted her champagne flute to toast the sentiment. My purple wrap dress was a little more low-cut than I was used to, and I feared it would unwrap itself if I wasn't vigilant. It had been over a week since my return from the underground, and I still wasn't used to wearing pricey or feminine clothes. It was deeply strange to have gone from being arrested in Studio City to sipping champagne at the *Hope Springs Eternal* anniversary party at the Brand Hotel. Clarissa had on a low-cut, slinky black number. Her dark eyes were dramatically mascaraed and shadowed.

"Thanks, Clarissa," I said, though I was pretty sure I'd just been insulted—but she was already sailing across the room toward Maurice and his boyfriend Ezra (the younger man from his dressing room photo). Clarissa hadn't mentioned her broken things to me. It seemed too good to be true. Yesterday the photograph of her and Maurice had reappeared, reframed, on her side of the dressing room counter, along with a new bottle of perfume. I was waiting for the other shoe to drop—with Clarissa as with everything else.

Glass of champagne in hand, I wandered through the crowded penthouse room. Martin wasn't here yet, and I was bracing myself to see him with his wife. We hadn't been alone together all week. I hadn't pressed the point, preoccupied with working out how to settle things with Cyn the next time I saw her. I reached up and touched my temple where the bruise was beginning to fade—then pulled my hand away, lest I rub off the makeup I'd used to cover it up. The marks on my wrists had disappeared after a couple of days. But what if next time I was injured more seriously, or couldn't come back at all? I needed to figure out how to stop getting shunted into dangerous versions of my life. I needed to stop *getting it wrong.* An idea had begun to take shape over the past week. I kept remembering what Cyn had said: *Why didn't you try to help me? Why didn't you at least try?*

Babette, predictably gorgeous in emerald green silk, stood with Larry and Susan, who had on a flowing, cream-colored gown. Susan waved me over. "…can't believe I've been with the show for fifteen years!" she was saying.

"You must've been a child when you started," Larry said.

Susan laughed. "You've found a good one, Babette."

"I know," Babs said, bestowing a melting smile upon him. I felt as if I were watching them through a scrim. After what I'd been through, this life didn't seem quite real. I tried to imagine how Joanna the revolutionary would view these people—and how she would view me. Would we all seem terribly frivolous? But she too had wanted to be an actress once.

Susan's eyes lit up. "I can't believe Jason Ryan is here. He played my first husband!" She headed off to embrace a rugged-jawed man.

"Jason Ryan?" Larry asked.

"He used to be on our show, years ago," Babs said. "He's on *The Grass Is Always Greener* now. An L.A. soap opera."

L.A.: the word jolted me. The day after I'd returned from the underground, I'd gone to the Riverside Library and looked at street maps of California, enough to satisfy myself that what I remembered of my life with Jeremy in San Francisco and our disastrous time in Los Angeles had been accurate and not some elaborate hallucination complete with giving myself the injuries I'd imagined a cop had inflicted. How could I know so much about the west coast, if it hadn't been real? In this life I had never left the east coast.

"Fifteen years," Babette was saying. "I wouldn't say this in front of Susan, but I can't imagine being on this show, or any show, for that long. Can you, Jo?"

The idea sounded better and better—if I could stay in this version of my life and fully inhabit it. I was beginning to suspect I'd never fully inhabited my life since Cyn's death. "It's not what I expected in drama school, but it's steady work," I replied.

"It's too much work!" Babs said, and Larry and I laughed. Then Babette's gaze fixed on something over my shoulder. Her smile faded and her grip on Larry's arm tightened. I turned. Martin, very handsome in a black suit, was coming towards us. He was alone. Maybe his wife hadn't come after all. He looked a little tense around the eyes and mouth. "Evening, ladies. Don't you both look great?" He eyed Larry, who was a few inches taller than him. "Hi, I'm Martin," he said cagily.

"Sam Jameson!" Larry blurted out. "I'm Larry," he added with a sheepish grin. Martin visibly relaxed, and they shook hands. If I'd had any doubt before, I was sure now that Larry had no clue about Martin and Babette's affair.

A woman with a drink in each hand walked up and handed what looked like straight whiskey to Martin. "Here, Mart," she said. She was a few inches shorter than Martin, sturdy rather than petite. She looked about Martin's age, with an olive complexion and dark eyes. Her dark hair was curly and short, and she wore a simple red dress. She wasn't beautiful, but she gave off an air of warmth and intelligence. She looked, somehow, a lot like Martin.

"Thanks, honey," Martin said with a quick sidelong smile. "Gloria, you remember Babette."

"Sure," Gloria said. "How are you?"

Babs gave her an apparently sincere smile and introduced her to Larry.

"I forget, have you met Joanna?" Martin asked, as if he had never had his tongue in my mouth.

"I think we met at a party a while back?" Gloria asked.

"We did," I said. When your husband and I barely knew each other. Before your husband and I kissed on camera and on a nighttime sidewalk and in our dressing rooms.

"Marty's told me so much about you. He says you're a terrific actress." Gloria had a contralto voice and a faded Brooklyn accent. She sipped a glass of red wine.

"Thanks." I wanted to say that Martin had told me a lot about her too, but he hadn't. The one significant detail I remembered was that she'd opposed the war. "Do you watch *Hope Springs Eternal?*"

Gloria laughed and shook her head. "Only once in a great while. It's a bit much for me to see my husband romancing beautiful women on my TV screen."

"It's a dirty job," Martin said, and Gloria punched him lightly on the arm just as I would have.

"One time," Gloria said, "our daughter Rosie told me, 'I saw Daddy kissing a lady on the TV.'"

Babette started to laugh uproariously, and Larry joined in.

"I guess I'd better start saving up for my kids' psychoanalysis," Martin said.

Babette was blithely smiling as if she'd never slept with Gloria's husband, as if all she'd ever done was kiss him for the cameras. I remembered sitting on Martin's lap in my dressing room and kissing him like the rest of the world had ceased to exist. I'm sorry, I thought. I'm sorry, I'm sorry. But what good did being sorry ever do anyone? Especially since I wanted to do it again.

"It's time for us to make the rounds," Martin said. His hand at the small of Gloria's back, he ushered her away.

"They make a nice couple," Larry said.

"Don't they?" Babs said, watching them go.

"I like her," I said, so quietly I didn't think anyone would hear—but Babs shot me a knowing look. Or did she look sorry for me?

I wondered why Martin cheated on Gloria. It was obvious how many years they had lived together, how much they had shared. The longest relationship I'd ever had was with Jeremy, in that other life. I had loved him, but I'd felt contempt for him too. I kept having the urge to contact him. But what would I say? We had never been lovers in this life. Should I try to help my jailed comrades? What could I do for them now? Anyway, Alex was the only one who even knew me.

"How do you plead?" a man's voice boomed. I looked around, but I couldn't figure out who'd spoken. Babette was saying something in Larry's ear, and he laughed and murmured a reply. I stood awkwardly a moment, then scanned the crowd for someone else to talk to.

Amy Gundersen was standing by herself drinking a glass of wine. I went up and said hello, and she smiled. "Oh, hi Joanna!" She had on a light blue dress that made her look very young and innocent.

"So how are you getting along at the studio? I remember how hard it was to get used to the pace of things." I talked as if I were an old hand.

Amy shrugged. "I find it sort of exhilarating! And I love working with Maurice. He tells such great stories about the theater. And he's so funny. Sometimes I can barely keep a straight face doing scenes with him!" She sipped her white wine. "You get to work with Marty a lot, don't you? I think he's a wonderful actor."

"Oh, he is," I said proudly.

"And he's so nice! He's really helped me to feel at home. He took me to that little bar down the street after work the other night."

"Oh. That's nice." When had that happened? Damn it. I finished my glass of champagne.

"How do you plead: guilty or not guilty?" That man's voice again, closer and louder this time. He sounded like he was playing the part of a judge. I glanced around, but Amy and I weren't standing that near anyone.

"...just feel so lucky to be part of this company," Amy bubbled. "Everyone's so terrific to me. And the work is so challenging. Speaking of which, I'm doing an Off-Off-Broadway show, too! It's *The Seagull*."

"Wow, you must be awfully busy." Too busy to spend time with Martin, hopefully. But he'd taken her to Chauncy's. I imagined him with his arm around her, introducing her to the bartender. What else had happened between them?

"It's a ton of work," Amy said. "But I can't pass up Chekhov. Anyway, Owen says I'd rather act than eat, sleep or breathe!"

"Who's Owen?"

"My boyfriend. I wish he was here. But he doesn't really feel comfortable around actors—not crowds of them, anyway."

Ah! That was all right, then. I beamed at her. "Well, I think it's wonderful you're doing theater *and* our show. I ought to do that too. The show just keeps me so busy!"

Prudence Fisher, our head writer, came up, looking over-warm in a gold lamé caftan. She was a tall, broad-shouldered blonde with a homely, pleasant face and wire rims. "Amy! It's so good to see you." Only then did she turn to me. "And Joanna. Having a good time?"

"Yes, absolutely!" I said over-brightly. Was I imagining it, or was Prudence looking at me strangely? Maybe my fears were right, and she was going to write me out.

"I just wanted to tell you how delighted I am that you've joined the cast, Amy," Prudence said. "You bring such a special quality to the role of Kathy Read."

"Thank you, Miss Fisher."

"Please, call me Prudence. How are you getting on?"

I excused myself and headed for the bar. I passed Dorothy Wainwright, our executive producer, talking with Susan and David. Dorothy was a small, forceful woman with sleek black hair framing her narrow face. Susan smiled at me, but Dorothy flicked a glance at me and looked away.

At the bar I ordered a Scotch and soda instead of more champagne.

"Hi, kid. Why so glum?"

I turned. Martin was smiling at me. "I'm not glum. I'm…" Glum didn't remotely cover it. I shrugged and took a sip of my drink.

"Well, you look beautiful tonight," he said.

Suddenly I was glad I'd worn this bothersome dress. "Thanks. So do you."

That had been the wrong thing to say. His smile faded. He put his empty glass on the bar and asked for a refill. *Maybe this isn't such a good idea*, he'd said. I was afraid to ask him what he'd meant.

Martin picked up his drink and clinked mine with it. There was something regretful in his expression. "Well, I'd better get back to Gloria."

"Okay." I wanted to tell him that I liked his wife, but that would have been the wrong thing to say too. I watched him walk away.

Nearby, Clarissa was hanging on Maurice, while his boyfriend rolled his eyes. Ezra was blond, with a boyish face and an athletic build.

"Darling, let's dance!" Clarissa crooned.

"You seem rather soused, darling," Maurice observed, but he obligingly twirled her a couple of times to the piped-in music. Then he let go of her with a gallant little bow.

"Please sir, can I have some more?" she asked, grinning like a little girl.

"Jesus," Ezra muttered, not too quietly.

Maurice took her by the shoulders and looked kindly at her. "Perhaps you've had enough for one night."

The delight drained from her face. She lifted her chin as regally as she could manage. "Don't be tiresome, Maurice."

"Could she be any more pathetic?" Cyn asked, and I jumped. She stood there looking incongruous in jeans and her "Free Angela Davis" t-shirt.

"There you are," I whispered. "I need to talk to you."

Then the room spun. Had I had too much to drink? I was standing in the courtroom, facing the judge. He had a visage like a judge at a Salem witch trial. "On the charge of armed robbery, how do you plead?" he asked.

I glanced at the lawyer who stood beside me—Sidney Glassman, well-known defender of radicals, with his broad, somber face and beaky nose. He nodded at me.

I wished the others were in the courtroom with me, especially Jeremy, but my case had been separated from theirs. "Miss Bergman?" the judge prompted. "How do you plead: guilty or not guilty?"

Was I doing the right thing, or should I go to trial with my comrades, try to justify our actions, explain our political motivations?

I remembered that security guard's ashen face at the bank. The ends did not justify the means. "Guilty, your Honor," I said.

Then I was back in the penthouse, and Clarissa was glaring at me.

"You're back," Cyn said. "Why on earth would you want to subject yourself to that courtroom?"

I couldn't very well retort that Cyn had subjected me to it, with Clarissa standing there. "What are you staring at?" Clarissa asked.

The judge, I wanted to say. "Nothing," I said. I had been in Los Angeles Superior Court, pulled into revolutionary Joanna's reality. What if I got pulled back there again? I had to do something to stop this.

"First you destroy my property, and now you stand here rudely gawking at me?" Clarissa demanded.

"Tell her to go fuck herself," Cyn suggested.

If that other version of my life claimed me, I would be stuck in prison somewhere in California for a crime that I didn't even believe in—and one that even Joanna the revolutionary hadn't wanted to commit. "Clarissa, I don't know what you're talking about," I said.

"Of course you don't," Clarissa said. "Of course you don't!"

This was uncannily like a scene from *Hope Springs Eternal*. Any moment now, Clarissa would slap my face. "Something of yours was destroyed?" I asked. "That's terrible. What was it?" Was she buying this at all?

Maurice cupped Clarissa's elbow. "Darling, please don't get exercised. This is a *party*."

Clarissa turned to him. "Maurice, you don't know what it's like to be beset by these damned ingénues..." I took that opening to head for the other side of the room. I nearly collided with Martin and Gloria, who were chatting with Vincent Lassiter and his wife, but I made a quick detour and went out onto the balcony, which was deserted.

The night air felt good after the overheated, smoky penthouse room. I looked out at the trees and grass and water of Central Park. A half-moon wavered through the clouds.

Cyn leaned on the parapet. "So that's his wife, eh?" she asked.

I glanced around, but no one was looking our way. "That's his wife, all right. But I can't talk about that right now. Tell me what you want from me."

"Oh, now you care what I want?"

"To save you, is that it? To try and save you?"

She rounded on me, her hands bunched into fists at her sides. "You have to want it. It means nothing if it's just to get rid of me again."

Could I make it happen? If I got back there, to the right place and time, could I remember what to do? And if it worked, would it get rid of Cyn's ghost or rewrite my life? It was a chance I had to take. I would go home and try it there, alone—

Another wave of dizziness hit me, and I was facing the judge again. "You are sentenced to ten years in prison," he was saying.

"Oh, no!" From the gallery, my mother's voice was a distraught moan. I turned to see her huddled weeping in her seat, my father grim beside her, and it filled me with shame to have hurt them. I wanted to tell my mom that, after all, this was no surprise—we had all known what the sentence would be if I pled guilty. Had she expected a miracle?

The judge banged his gavel. "Order!"

The ten years was only for the bank robbery. Other charges might be forthcoming for the bombings. Regardless, I was going away for a long time, again. *Again?*

I mustered all my will and pulled myself out of there. I was standing on the balcony looking down on Central Park. I breathed in the night air, looked out at the trees and grass and water, and reveled in my freedom. I didn't want to lose it again.

"Can't you stop doing that?" Cyn asked. She sounded genuinely concerned, and that scared me more than anything.

"You mean it isn't you who's doing it?" I demanded.

"I don't think so."

"You don't think so? What does that mean?"

207

She shook her head perplexedly. "It's never just me. It's you, too. It's both of us, together."

That made a certain kind of sense, if anything about this did. Maybe it was like acting. You and your acting partner did a scene together, but the scene was more than the sum of its parts. There was a shared energy between the players. There was something mysterious to it, if it worked. There was something beyond your control.

"Okay," I said. "I'm going to try." There was no time to go home first. I moved away from the edge of the balcony. It wouldn't do to fall off the building in the midst of my attempt. I lifted my Scotch and soda and drank it down. "Remember," I whispered, and held the empty glass at arm's length.

"What the hell are you doing?" Cyn asked.

"Trying to save your life, and mine," I said, and let the glass slip from my fingers. It shattered on the ground. For a long moment nothing happened, except that people in the penthouse turned to look at the klutz on the balcony. Martin was looking at me with concern. I couldn't look at him. He would hold me to this life. I wondered if I would even know him, if this worked. In spite of everything, I hoped so. I closed my eyes and visualized the draft board. That sidewalk. The mailbox. Now. It had to be now.

The sounds of the party faded like someone turning a volume knob. I opened my eyes and snuffled uncomfortably. It was the middle of the night. Cyn was a block away, the wicker handbag in her hand. We were about to get away with it, after all. She set the handbag in front of the mailbox. My heart was pounding. Something was terribly wrong. I didn't know how I knew.

I broke into a run towards Cyn. She turned and looked at me. "What's the matter?" she whispered when I was at her side. "Don't tell me you saw a cop?"

I shook my head. "It's nothing like that. It's just, something's wrong."

"Are you crazy? We're almost home free!" She looked at the handbag on the ground. "I just need to push this under the mailbox."

"No," I whispered. "Come on, let's go. Let's go!"

She stared at me. "What's wrong with you?"

I seized her hand. "I'm not fucking joking. Leave it!" I began to drag her away. She stumbled. She had to follow me to keep from falling over. I was stronger than her. Why had I never realized that before?

"Okay, okay!" Cyn pulled her hand free and followed me. When we were a block away, she stopped and said, "What is *with* you, Joanna—" and the bomb went off. The shock wave knocked us both off our feet. The sound went on and on, impossibly loud. Then it ceased.

"What the fuck was that?" a man yelled somewhere, over the ringing in my ears.

Cyn and I scrambled to our feet. "Are you all right?" she asked.

"Yeah. Are you?"

She nodded, though she was trembling. Or maybe it was me. "That was way louder than I'd expected," she said.

We peered down the street at the broken glass and shattered windows. "Come on, we've got to get out of here," I said.

She turned and looked at me. "How did you *know*?"

"I'm not sure." Maybe it had been nothing but malaise from my fever? "I just had a really bad feeling. Like déjà vu or something."

Her eyes were wide. "You saved my life!" she breathed. Then she gave a laugh. "I'm gonna fucking kill Jeremy."

That seemed hilarious. Suddenly we were both doubled over with laughter. I shook my head. "Stop it! Come on, let's go!"

We began to walk as quickly as we could without breaking into a run toward Cyn's apartment. Sirens sounded in the distance, and we huddled in a doorway, Cyn clutching my sleeve. She was still trembling. The sirens came closer, then passed.

"Okay," I whispered. "Let's get going."

"Wait," Cyn said. She reached up and cupped my cheek. Her hand was cool against my feverish face. Illuminated by the streetlight, her face was grave. Her gaze burned into mine. "We did it," she whispered. She pressed her lips dryly to mine. In that moment everything seemed unreal, and everything seemed possible.

"You'll catch the flu," I said.

Oh, how she smiled. "No, I won't. I'm fucking invincible." She grabbed my hand, and we headed for her place. Halfway there we started to run. I was suddenly full of energy, the flu forgotten. We were running, her hand in mine. We were so alive.

Chapter Eighteen:
Under My Thumb
(June 1971)

We didn't see Alex and Jeremy for a few days after the action. Cyn and I were both sick with the flu. Thursday night we all met at Cyn's apartment, drank wine, and celebrated our blow against the war machine—though the bombing hadn't gotten as much press coverage as we would have liked. Only the campus newspaper had printed our communiqué. The *New York Times* had devoted just one inside paragraph to the explosion, and the TV news reports we'd seen had been brief.

"The hell with the press," Alex said. "Bottom line, the windows of that fucking draft board are all boarded up. It's a thing of beauty."

"We gummed up the system," Jeremy said, grinning. "Maybe just a little, but we did."

Cyn and I were sitting on the couch, Alex and Jeremy at our feet. "Kind of a drag that the windows of the nearby businesses broke too," I said. "I hadn't expected that."

Jeremy's grin faded. "The explosion was a bit more powerful than I'd expected," he said.

"And one more thing, Jeremy," Cyn said. "If it hadn't been for Jo pulling me out of the way, I'd have been blown to kingdom come."

Jeremy blanched. "What are you talking about?"

"The device went off while we were still there," I said gently. "I had this weird feeling that something was wrong and got

211

Cyn out of the way, and when we were about a block away, the thing blew up."

"Fuck," Alex breathed. "Talk about a close call." He reached up and rubbed Cyn's jeaned knee. Jeremy looked straight ahead in stricken silence. I felt sorry for him.

Cyn briefly covered Alex's hand with her own, then pushed his hand off her knee. "Jo saved my life," she said and smiled beatifically at me. "My hero." Had she said it ironically? Not really. The way she was beaming at me made me blush. She hadn't looked at me with such admiration since I'd played Joan of Arc in high school. She looked like she wanted to kiss me again. Had she really kissed me, the night of the explosion? I'd almost started to think I'd imagined it.

"God, I can't believe it went off too soon," Jeremy said. "It could've killed you, and it would've been my fault. What could have gone wrong? You didn't bump it or jar it, did you?"

I remembered what Cyn had said after she and Jeremy slept together: *He came as soon as I put him in,* and I had to choke back laughter. Somehow Cyn having slept with Jeremy didn't hurt any more.

"No, I didn't bump it or jar it," Cyn said. "What's so funny, Jo?"

I shook my head. "I'll tell you later," I murmured, and she grinned.

I waited for someone to say, We'll figure out what went wrong, for next time. But no one did. Maybe we'd all decided there wasn't going to be a next time. I was almost disappointed.

∞

The next day, the last day of class before finals, Cyn was waiting for me when I left my afternoon Ibsen class. She had on sunglasses and a blue knit cap, though it was a warm day. "Let's take a walk," she said.

"I can't. I have to get to European history."

She leaned forward and spoke into my ear. "Alex and Jeremy are busted."

Suddenly the bustling hallway full of students heading to and from class seemed unreal. "Are you sure?"

"I heard it on the radio. We have to get out of the city." She grabbed my elbow and steered me towards the exit.

"But what about finals?" Even as I said it, I knew how ridiculous it sounded.

"Screw finals. We have to split."

"For how long?"

She shook her head. "Maybe when the heat is off, we can come back. Otherwise, this is it."

I tried to breathe evenly. "I can't believe this is happening. Are you sure you heard right?"

"Do you think I'd be here right now if I wasn't sure?"

"Maybe they won't come for us?" I whispered.

"Get real, Joanna." She pushed open the door. I didn't want to go through it. It felt final somehow.

Then we were outside, walking down the stone steps and across the grass. Only then did I notice the heavy shoulder bag Cyn was carrying. It looked stuffed full. "If we're leaving, I need to go back to Hellman and get some things," I said.

"You can't. The pigs could be waiting."

"But you got a chance to pack, at least!"

She coughed heavily. "I was at home when I found out. I was listening to the radio, and when I heard the news, I stuffed some things in my bag and came straight to you."

I glanced around. Students were everywhere, chatting, walking with their noses in books, living a normal day of pre-finals pressure. No one seemed to be paying attention to us, but Cyn was right. The cops would be looking for us. My skin prickled all over. "Where will we go?"

"Robert's in Denver now. He'd probably let us crash with him." Robert was an anarchist guitarist who had been one of

Cyn's flings when we'd first started college. I imagined being a third wheel in a strange city.

"Denver! So far away."

"We don't have to decide this minute. We should just get the first bus out of town. Then we can figure out a plan. Do you have much cash?"

I shook my head.

"That's okay. I have enough to hold us for a while."

We took the subway to the Port Authority bus terminal. On the train I kept seeing Jeremy's face. Alex could take care of himself, but Jeremy would be so scared. What if he ratted us out? No, I didn't believe he'd do that. Was it possible they wouldn't be convicted? It didn't seem likely. I wondered how much time they would get. God, this was real. We had set off a bomb, and Jeremy and Alex were in jail. Cyn and I had a chance to escape—but our lives as we knew them were probably over.

Port Authority was crowded and chaotic. "Keep watch for plainclothes pigs," Cyn whispered as we stood in the ticket line. She paid for two tickets to Middletown, Connecticut, even though it was in the opposite direction we'd talked about going, because there was a bus boarding in twenty minutes. Plus it was a college town, and we figured we could blend in. She bought a newspaper and some snacks, and then it was time to board. When we climbed on the bus, my stomach lurched. I felt like we were stepping off the edge of the world.

We sat near the back of the bus, which meant people were forever trundling past us to and from the toilet, and the toilet was forever flushing. Cyn sat in the window seat. I kept eyeing the other passengers with increasing paranoia, though no one seemed to scream out *pig*. One heavy white guy with an Afro and a jean jacket kept turning around and leering at us. A baby a few rows up started to scream. I felt like crying too. Cyn seemed to be holding it together much better. She had expected we'd go underground. I caught her smiling as she looked out the window. How can you smile when Alex and Jeremy are in jail? I wanted to demand—but I couldn't with all the people around. My paranoia began to spill over, and I wondered if it had really been that urgent that we leave. What if we just made ourselves look guilty by running? What if Cyn had made up the arrests? But why would she do that?

As if on cue, Cyn pointed to the newspaper page she was reading. The article took up about a quarter of an inside page. I scanned it. "Alexander Kloski and Jeremy Blum…held without bail…unknown whether they acted alone…"

I tried to control my rising panic. Had I really thought Cyn had made it all up? Maybe it would have been easier to think that.

∞

The room we checked into had ugly brown flowered drapes and brown carpeting, and the sink had a slow-running drain. I thought about the Bates Motel. At this point it would almost be a relief if some crazed knife-wielding clerk showed up and put me out of my misery—though the desk clerk at the inn had seemed kindly enough.

When I came out of the bathroom, Cyn was standing in front of the TV. It was black-and-white, and the picture kept rolling. She smacked the top of it a few times, and the picture stabilized. It was a little after seven, so we sat on our beds and watched Walter Cronkite. He talked about Vietnam and the draft and unemployment, but he didn't mention Alex or Jeremy or the bombing.

"Oh well, at least they're not broadcasting our photos nationwide," Cyn said, getting up and switching off the TV.

"You don't really think they'd show our photos on the local news?" I asked.

She shrugged, then sat on her bed with the newspaper spread out in front of her to study the article about Alex and

Jeremy. I sat next to her and read the story again. "God, I hope they're all right," I said.

"They're lost to us now," Cyn said.

"You say it like you don't even care what happens to them!"

"I do care. But there's nothing we can do for them besides drop out of sight. They would do the same thing if the tables were turned."

"I guess that's true. But aren't you going to miss Alex?"

Cyn gave a laugh. "You're such a romantic, Jo. Alex is my comrade, not my true love." She eyed me sharply. "Please don't tell me you're going to pine away after Jeremy."

"Why would I? There's nothing between him and me. You saw to that."

"Wow." She shook her head. "We're running from the law, and you want to fight about boys?"

I let out a sigh. "Actually, I don't."

"Good." She scrounged around in her handbag, produced a bag of corn chips, and offered them to me.

"I'm not hungry."

She shrugged and tossed them onto the bed.

"I wonder how long until our parents find out we're gone," I said. "Will the cops call them?"

"Probably." She gave a harsh laugh. "Oh, boy. My dad's gonna hit the ceiling."

My parents would be angry, too—but mostly I thought about how hurt and frightened they would be. "I wish I could call my mom. Just to tell her I'm all right."

"You can't."

"I know."

I got up and sat on my bed, which, like Cyn's, had a thick, rough coverlet with brown and orange and yellow flowers. I went through my book bag, which was, besides my purse and the clothes on my back, all I had left of my old life: an Ibsen paperback, a European history textbook, a spiral notebook with class syllabi in the pocket. I thought about drama school—how that possibility was floating away from me, maybe forever. I looked at Cyn, apparently engrossed in the newspaper. I was tired, and my nose was stuffy from the flu, and I just wanted to be back at Hellman, drinking chicken soup, even preparing for finals, back in my normal life. I held the Ibsen book to my chest and started to cry silently, though I knew it would only make me more congested.

It took a while for Cyn to notice. "Hey, what's wrong?" she asked.

I gave a laugh. "What's *wrong*?"

"I mean, besides the obvious."

I reached into my purse for a tissue and wiped my eyes and my nose. Finally I said in a small voice, "I wanna go home."

She got up and sat next to me. "Don't cry, Jo."

"Can't help it."

To my surprise, she started to stroke my hair. "We'll be all right," she murmured. "Everything's gonna be all right."

"Promise?"

"I promise." Her hand stroking my hair was soothing. I felt like a little girl being comforted. After a while, she gently pulled my hair aside and dropped a kiss on my neck, then another and another. Her lips were cool and soft. It made my breath hitch. I fought the urge to moan. It seemed wrong to moan in front of Cyn, wrong to be getting worked up. Where was this coming from? One minute she had been stroking my hair, and now my heart was beating between my legs.

"Is this okay?" Cyn asked. Such an unlikely question coming from her. I looked at her. She didn't look cool the way she had when she'd seduced Jeremy or led Alex into her bedroom, or even the way she'd looked in bed with Lenny. She looked so serious. There was a point of fear in her eyes. This really matters to her, I thought with a surprise that somehow wasn't surprise—and that realization moved me very much.

"Yes," I said. "It's okay." Then I kissed her. She made a surprised sound, then she pulled me close.

She was skinny and slight in my arms. She was smaller than me. That was odd. The guys I'd been with had all been at least a little taller than I was, and stronger. It was wet and intimate and strange to be kissing her, yet somehow, now that it was happening, it felt inevitable. I couldn't catch my breath. I felt both caught up and as if I were off to one side, observing, as we lay facing each other on the bed.

Neither of us knew what we were doing. She ran her small hands over me greedily, and she shuddered when I touched her anywhere, her upper arm or her back or her breast. At some point we took off our t-shirts and jeans but left on our underwear. I still wasn't sure why we were doing this, except that this was the perfect unreal capper to this unreal day, and all we had left was each other. After we had kissed and touched each other for what felt like a very long time, and she had brushed her hand between my legs several times but never lingered there, I became so frustrated I was ready to scream.

I hooked my leg over hers and began to move against her. She froze for a moment and then moved with me. I moved and moved, my mouth against hers. Then I broke the kiss and came with a cry.

Afterwards I rolled onto my back and closed my eyes, breathing hard. "Wow, that cleared my sinuses," I said with a laugh, and then I started to cough. When I opened my eyes, Cyn was propped on her elbow, and she was watching me. "Did you just get off?" she asked, as if it were impossible to believe.

"Wasn't it obvious?" I asked, feeling self-conscious.

"You weren't acting or something? Pretending?"

"Why would I do that with you? I've heard of women faking orgasm with a man, but..."

"You really came just from that?"

And she hadn't. It occurred to me that it was rude to leave her hanging. And how bizarre to be thinking about Cyn in such terms. "Yes. Can't you come that way? Do you need… penetration?" I realized we had never talked about it. As much as she'd always talked about sex, we had never talked about what got us off.

She didn't speak. Her face was flushed, and she looked both turned on and embarrassed. Now it was my turn to be astounded.

"Cyn, you've never…?" Cyn, the experienced one, the one without the bourgeois hang-ups.

She pressed her lips together. I could see her trying to come up with some superior pronouncement to explain this away. Finally she said, "Nope."

"That's terrible!" I said. "I mean, that's ridiculous."

"Fuck you," she said mildly.

"But it's easy," I said. "I'll show you." I pushed her onto her back and put my hand between her legs. I touched her as I had touched myself in bed for years. She closed her eyes and gave herself over to me. She spread her legs wide. Her body grew taut. A few times I thought she was almost there, but it didn't happen. My wrist was starting to get tired. Then her breathing sped up, she arched and cried out. I felt such a rush of power.

When she recovered, she looked at me. "My god," she said, and we both laughed. Then she said, "Let me," and pushed me onto my back.

As I drifted off to sleep hours later, naked and spent, I had the strangest notion that Cyn and I were going to go underground by sinking into each other's bodies. Then Cyn coughed, and I jolted awake in a strange room with a pounding heart, the bed linen rough against my skin. Cyn went back to sleep, her arm around my waist, but the dread of what tomorrow might bring latched onto me and kept me awake.

Chapter Nineteen:
How Can We Hang On To a Dream?
(October 1975)

The clock radio went off. Half-waking, I dreamed I was in New York, listening to a news report about President Ford refusing financial aid to the city. Then I woke fully and realized I really had heard the story. How I missed New York sometimes. "It's eight-O-five," the male announcer said smugly. I reached out and switched off the radio. Sunlight streamed irritatingly through the edge of the green flowered drapes. I'd stayed up too late reading last night.

"Let's play hooky today," Cyn said, lying on her side facing me, her voice thick with sleep. "Call in sick."

I turned onto my back, and the bedsprings complained. "I'd love another few hours of sleep, but I have to open the bookstore."

Her long brown hair, dyed nearly my natural color, was tousled around her face. "You and that fucking bookstore."

For almost two years we'd lived in this small one-bedroom apartment in Venice. The outside world knew us as Emma Shaw and Bonnie Van Ark. "I love that fucking bookstore, Cyn," I said, and pulled back the bedclothes.

Cyn grasped my shoulder. "I don't have to work the dinner shift tonight. We could go to a movie after work."

"The Feminist Theater Collective is meeting at seven. I'd really like to be there. Last week they told me I could sit in with the group if I wanted."

"That's far too public. For all you know, the Red Squad could be monitoring the bookstore."

"It's just a dinky little theater group, Cyn."

"Then why bother with it?"

I rolled onto my side, away from her. On the avocado-carpeted floor was the pile of books I'd bought with my employee discount at Womanpages: books by Adrienne Rich and Marge Piercy, Robin Morgan and June Jordan and Colette. And on top, the book I was currently devouring, *Flying,* by Kate Millett. My beloved books. The sight of them bolstered me. "Because it would make me happy, okay?" I said.

Cyn pressed against my back. "I can make you happy," she breathed. Her hand cupped my breast over my nightgown, and she kissed my neck wetly. It felt good, but it also felt like her way to win the argument.

"I've gotta get in the shower," I said in a matter-of-fact tone that stopped her cold.

She turned onto her back with a heavy sigh. "Get in the shower, then."

I got out of bed. Cyn lay there looking at me reproachfully. I stifled the urge to apologize and headed for the bathroom.

∞

In the small, pink-tiled shower, as I soaped my hair (cut short and dyed auburn these past four years— "Red Emma," Cyn and I used to joke), I argued with her in my head: *I love Womanpages. I want to be part of the Los Angeles Feminist Theater Collective. I actually feel alive again, part of the world, no longer stultified. Why do you want to wreck that for me? I hate feeling that the woman I live with is sitting in judgment on my every move. It's suffocating. Do you really think anyone is actually after us anymore? There's no more draft, the war is over, no one fucking cares about us.*

The last bit wasn't entirely true. I was in touch with my family. They knew I lived with Cyn, but not that we were lovers. At least, I didn't think they'd guessed. Cyn's parents, on the other hand, wanted nothing to do with her, the rebel, the embarrassment.

Even if no one was after us, Alex and Jeremy were still in prison, as far as we knew. Patty Hearst and SLA members Bill and Emily Harris had recently been arrested with great fanfare. We were lucky to be free. Was Cyn right? Would it be too risky to participate in the theater group? Was working at the bookshop too great a risk, or did Cyn just want to limit my involvement?

I rinsed herbal shampoo from my hair. I couldn't figure out why Cyn disliked the bookstore. Was she jealous that I had a more interesting job than she did? I had waitressed for a long time before I'd found the job at Womanpages. The jobs we could do were limited to places that would pay us under the table.

When I got out of the shower, I smelled coffee brewing. I put on jeans and a purple flowered blouse. Cyn was sitting at the living room table in her blue robe, sipping coffee and reading the newspaper. I poured myself coffee and a bowl of Cheerios and milk and brought them to the table.

"*Dog Day Afternoon* is playing at seven at the National," Cyn said.

"I told you, the theater group is meeting at seven." I pulled the paper toward me. "The movie's playing at ten o'clock, too. I could meet you there."

"I'm off work at five. I don't want to wait around until ten. Besides, I hate taking the bus that late." Cyn worked at a vegetarian restaurant in our neighborhood. The bookshop was in Westwood, so I took the car, and she bicycled to work, unless I dropped her off and picked her up.

"Come to the bookshop after work and watch the theater group," I said. "Then we can drive to the movie together."

She wrinkled her nose. "Not my scene. All those earnest lesbian-feminists."

"I'm a lesbian-feminist. And I've been looking forward to this all week."

"You can skip a week. Unless you're dying to spend even more time with Edward the Dyke."

That was Cyn's name for my coworker Sophie, after a booklet of poems by Judy Grahn. "Sophie doesn't stay for the theater workshop if she can help it. It's not her scene either." I spooned up cereal. "She's not even all that political. She's just always known she was gay." A wave of uneasiness went through me. I'd only been attracted to men before Cyn and I got together, yet I called myself a lesbian. Was it because I didn't know any women who called themselves bisexual? Kate Millett wrote in *Flying* about being pressured to declare herself a lesbian, because bisexuality was considered an evasion, a betrayal of the cause. On the other hand, the only great sex (hell, the only good sex) I'd ever had was with a woman.

Cyn narrowed her eyes at me. I couldn't believe she was jealous of Sophie. I wasn't remotely attracted to her, but she was the best friend I had besides Cyn, though she didn't know about my past. When I'd told Cyn that Sophie had broken up with her lover, Cyn had said, *Well, she can't have you.*

"Come on, Jo. Let's have fun tonight. You're always at the bookstore or some *women's* event. I miss you. And I'm a woman, if that counts."

A stab of guilt. No matter what was wrong between us, I didn't want to hurt her. "Okay, I'll meet you at the National before seven."

Cyn beamed. "Great!"

∞

It was a quiet morning at the bookstore. Womanpages was composed of a long, narrow, shelf-lined room and, down a few steps, a larger space at the back with more shelves, where readings and other events were held. Behind the front counter was a storage room that also served as an office.

A long-haired young woman stood at the fiction shelves and leafed through a May Sarton paperback. An older woman with short dark curls headed for the back of the store and browsed the sexuality section. Dominique, the owner of the store, was in the office with the door closed, probably dealing with bills or special orders. Sophie and I sat behind the counter.

"So are you looking forward to the theater group tonight?" Sophie asked. She was plump, with short brown hair, an upturned nose, and lively blue eyes. She had on jean overalls and a long-sleeved shirt.

I sighed. "Bonnie talked me into going to the movies with her instead. I guess there's always next week…"

Sophie rolled her eyes. "Man, Bonnie is so possessive."

I lowered my voice. "Back when she slept with men, she was all 'nobody owns anybody.' But with me, it's a whole other story."

"Because it actually matters with you." Sophie suddenly looked crestfallen. She had broken up with her lover over non-monogamy, because she couldn't handle the jealousy.

"Sorry, I didn't mean to bring up a sore subject."

She shrugged. "S'okay."

"You don't regret breaking it off with Anne, do you?" I asked.

"I miss her, but the situation was driving me nuts. I feel like I have my life back."

"That makes sense."

She peered at me. "Why? Are you seriously thinking about breaking up with Bonnie?"

The phone rang, and I grabbed it. A woman wanted to know if we had *Enormous Changes at the Last Minute* by Grace Paley. I found it on the shelf, came back, and told her we did. When I got off the phone, Sophie was ringing up the long-haired girl's purchases: paperbacks by May Sarton, Virginia Woolf, and Rita Mae Brown.

When the girl left, Sophie turned to me as if there'd been no pause in our conversation. "Well, my offer stands, if it comes to that." She had offered up her sofa if I ever wanted to move out.

"Thanks. I can't really imagine it coming to that."

"But you are imagining it, right?"

"Maybe." The idea of leaving Cyn felt like stepping into the unknown. It was a terrifying yet thrilling prospect.

∞

I left the bookstore before the theater collective arrived. I knew that if they started to show up while I was there, I'd want to stay even more than I already did. The movie theater was only a couple minutes' drive from the bookstore, and I got there early. Cyn wasn't outside the theater, and a flare of anger went through me. What if she was late and made me miss the workshop for nothing? Then I saw her hurrying up the sidewalk, a small, slim figure with long brown hair. She had on jeans, a gauzy pink shirt, and a jean jacket. She smiled when she saw me. I smiled back, and we got in line, but I was still half at the bookstore. I imagined the theater collective in a circle of chairs, the women shouting and whispering and truth telling. Last week the theme had been mothers and daughters. What would it be tonight?

∞

We sat near the back of the crowded movie house with our popcorn and Cokes. The film was marvelous. Al Pacino reminded me of someone. Jeremy, a little? He strutted along the Brooklyn sidewalk outside the bank, surrounded by cops, and shouted, "Attica! Attica!" No, it wasn't Jeremy. Some other guy. What did it say about me as a lesbian-feminist that I found Al Pacino so attractive? I didn't often find myself attracted to men these days—or, for that matter, to women besides Cyn.

Then again, I didn't often find myself in the proximity of men as gorgeous and charismatic as Pacino. *I would kill for that part.* Who had said that?

A wave of disorientation rolled through me. For a long moment I couldn't place where I was—was it Cinema 1?—and I had the strangest feeling that Cyn was no longer sitting beside me. I turned toward her in a panic, but she was staring at the screen, dreamily popping a kernel of popcorn into her mouth. The world righted itself.

∞

After the movie, we stopped at Dolores Restaurant for burgers. When we got home, Cyn was beaming. She'd gotten her way. I had loved the movie, but I was kicking myself for letting Cyn guilt-trip me out of doing something that mattered to me. I got my copy of *Flying*, sat on the chintz sofa, and disappeared into Kate Millett's world of sex and art and activism. Cyn put a Nina Simone LP on the turntable. Nina sang "Suzanne," and I smiled. Kate Millett and Nina Simone: I felt replete with women's art. But I wanted to make some too.

Cyn went into the kitchen and returned with a glass of red wine for each of us. She sat beside me on the couch and drew her legs up. She'd taken off her shoes. I hadn't taken off mine. "Aren't you glad we went out this evening?" she asked.

I wanted to keep reading, but I put the book face down between us on the sofa. I sipped my wine and said nothing.

"Aren't you glad?" she insisted.

"I had a good time. But I still want to get involved with the theater collective. I don't think it'd be a big risk."

"Not a big risk, to be acting in public? I thought you'd given up on those high-school dreams of yours."

I set my wine glass on the coffee table. "High-school dreams? As you may recall, you auditioned for the same part as me, and I was the one who got it. Maybe that's why you made fun of me when you found out I got into drama school—because you were jealous. Maybe you still are!"

She sipped her wine with a superior air that reminded me of when we were in college. "Oh, please. I never gave a shit about acting."

"Maybe not, but you were afraid I might have something you didn't, something apart from you. You were glad we had to go underground, because it meant I couldn't go to drama school. If we hadn't had to split town, who knows what I'd be doing right now?"

Cyn swung her legs around so her feet were on the floor. "And who you'd be doing it with, right?"

"That's not what I meant. And I never said anything about performing with the theater group in front of an audience. I know that's not possible. I just thought it'd be fun to participate in their improvisational exercises."

"I don't like it," Cyn said.

On the stereo, Nina Simone sang "Revolution," and her bravado swept me along. "Tough," I said.

Cyn glared at me. "So it's okay for you to put our lives in danger?"

"Oh, for god's sake. I'm always careful. Like last year, I didn't go to see Angela Davis at the Women's Building, even though I really wanted to, because we thought there might be surveillance."

"*You* wanted to see Angela Davis? I wanted to see her too! She was my hero, not yours!"

I stopped myself from protesting that she was a hero of mine as well. How ridiculous to fight over who loved Angela Davis best. "I didn't think you still cared about such things," I said.

"It hurts too much to think about. I put it all behind me, and you should, too." She sipped her wine, then spoke slowly and deliberately. "What would your friends at the bookstore think if they knew what we did in '71?"

I stared down at the pink and black Kate Millett paperback splayed on the sofa. "I don't know."

"Don't you?"

"They wouldn't turn us in."

"You think they'd be willing to go to jail for us like those dykes who wouldn't talk to the grand jury about Susan Saxe and Katherine Power?"

How I would hate to put Sophie or Dominique or anyone from Womanpages in that position. *Was* I putting them in that position? But Saxe and Power had been involved in a bank robbery that resulted in a cop's death. "Susan Saxe and Katherine Power are bigger fish than us," I said. "Probably no one is even looking for us anymore."

"You don't know that. We're still fugitives. I for one don't want to go to prison. Maybe it's time for us to move on while we still can."

Move on? I thought of the other places we'd lived, most recently Seattle. None of them had felt like home. We had kept to ourselves and moved on at the first inkling of trouble. We'd left Seattle when the cops came sniffing around on the trail of another pair of political fugitives, a man and a woman. We'd considered leaving Los Angeles last year, when the SLA (including two lesbians) were burned alive in a house not twenty miles from our apartment—but we'd decided to stay. I hadn't expected L.A. to feel like home, but ever since I'd started working at Womanpages, it had. I wasn't ready to give that up.

"You can move on if you want to," I said. "I'm staying."

My words detonated. Cyn stared at me. "You would choose that bookstore over me?" Her voice shook.

Hurting her made me feel sick. I hadn't expected this to come to a head tonight. I wasn't ready. Cyn was the only one who truly knew me. Sophie and the others might turn against me if they knew what I'd done. They might think me a male-identified leftist like some considered Susan Saxe, though she was a lesbian and called herself a feminist.

I stared at the black-and-white poster of Colette that I'd tacked on the opposite wall—Colette with her frizzy hair and her indelible stare of absolute authority. "I'm choosing my life, Cyn. My life as I choose to live it."

"Edward the Dyke has turned you against me. She can't wait to get her hands on you."

"That's ridiculous. Sophie and I are just friends."

She gave a harsh laugh. "You and I were just friends, once. Do you think you can do better than me? Do you think anyone would ever care about you as much as I do?"

"No, actually I don't. But I can't do this anymore." I couldn't believe I'd said it.

Cyn flinched as if I'd struck her. "Are you actually breaking up with me? All because I don't want you to get involved with that theater group?"

"You know that's not all it is."

"What, because I don't subscribe to your ideology? That's pretty ironic coming from you, Joanna."

"We just don't seem to share much anymore. We don't care about the same things."

"I'm sick of ideologies. I wrecked my life for a revolution that's never going to come." She reached for her glass of wine and took a swig, then looked like she was having trouble swallowing.

"I know how much you lost," I said gently.

"You have no idea! You think you can pick up your acting and carry on like the past four years never happened. I don't have that luxury. All I have left is you. And now I don't even have you anymore? I'm not a revolutionary or a fucking lesbian-feminist. I don't even *like* women, besides you. All I am is a waitress, serving up tofu and brown rice and smiling when the dudes come on to me so I'll get a decent tip. But if I can come home to you at the end of the day, it's enough for me."

I remembered what it was like when we first went on the run, sheltering with revolutionaries and would-be revolutionaries, hippies and druggies. How surprised Cyn had been to discover she had no power over these guys once they found out she wasn't going to sleep with them, and no, we weren't interested in a threesome. Loving me had cost Cyn dearly—maybe as dearly as the bombing had. "I'm sorry," I said.

Her eyes glistened darkly. "You're sorry? Out of nowhere you've decided you're leaving me, and you're sorry?"

"It's not out of nowhere, and it's painful for me too, but I think it would be best for both of us. We're holding each other back."

"What a load of fucking clichés. You just want to screw other people."

The thought of never having sex with Cyn again went through me with an almost physical pain. I nearly doubled over with it. But I couldn't tell her that. She would use it to hold on to me. "It's not about sex. It's not about love. It's about freedom."

"Freedom to fuck other people. The grass is always greener, right?"

Her words echoed strangely in my head. I wanted to tell her that for me, being a lesbian-feminist wasn't as much about sex as about being part of a community, a movement, something larger than the two of us locked in our claustrophobic relationship. It was about having a place in the world, belonging. But I knew all Cyn would say was that I belonged to her.

"You're not even going to deny it?" Cyn cried. "Maybe you need to fuck other women to prove to yourself what a big lesbian you are. The hell with that. The hell with labels! I always loved sleeping with men. Men were so *easy*. I gave that up for you, and you stuck a knife in my heart!" She put her head in her hands and laughed. Then I realized it wasn't laughter. She was sobbing, horrible gulping sobs. I sat frozen. I had never seen her so upset, not even when her parents cut her off entirely. I hadn't quite believed she could get this upset.

I reached out and put my hand on her shoulder.

She flinched away. "Don't touch me!" Her face was wet, but she was incandescent with fury. "You don't give a shit about me. Get the hell away from me!" She yelled so loudly I got to my feet and backed away from her.

"Cyn…"

"Leave me alone!" She stared at me as if she hated me. Then she got up, stumbled into the bedroom, and slammed the door. There was more sobbing. I had the awful realization that I had done it—I had broken what we had. What should I do now? I couldn't imagine us sleeping in the same bed tonight, or even in the same apartment. Suddenly I couldn't bear to be there a minute more. I was choking on her grief.

On the stereo Nina Simone was singing "To Love Somebody." I had the ridiculous thought that I should stay through the end of the song. Then I grabbed my purse and got the hell out of there.

I stood in front of our closed front door. I supposed I would drive to Sophie's house. I could sleep on her couch. It seemed wrong to leave Cyn, wrong to stay. It was a mild night, a bit damp. I walked to my parking space in front of the building. Then I stopped. Was I really going to leave Cyn sobbing all alone, thinking I was leaving her for another woman? Her words echoed in my head again: *The grass is always greener, right?*

Then I heard Babette's voice: *He's on* The Grass Is Always Greener *now. An L.A. soap opera.*

I ran back to the front door and yanked at the doorknob. The door was locked. Frantically I rooted in my purse for the keys. Had I left them inside? I pounded on the door. "Cyn!

Let me in!" I yelled. I'd forgotten to call her Bonnie. I didn't care if the whole neighborhood heard me. But it was too late. I found myself on the balcony of the Brand Hotel, hunting through my evening bag for a different set of keys. I found them—for all the good it would do. I stared at the keys in my hand. Then I looked up. Cyn's ghost was nowhere to be seen. Dressed-to-the-nines party guests were staring at me, and a waiter headed for me with a broom and dustpan. There was broken glass at my feet. I had done it. I had gone back and saved Cyn's life. And then I had thrown her away.

"What's wrong, Jo?" It was Martin, looking handsome in his black suit.

"She just dropped a glass, Mart," his wife said. "Joanna? You okay?"

I stepped away from the waiter sweeping up broken glass. I wanted to put my arms around Martin, bury my face in his chest and weep. My longing for him felt alien to me, but here it was, coiled inside my body. How was that possible? *Freedom to fuck other people*, Cyn had said. Was that why I had walked out on her, walked out of our life—for Martin? Or to be an actor? *I would kill for that part.* Oh god, what had I done?

"I killed her," I muttered. "Oh god, I killed her! I'm gonna be sick…"

"Hey, Gloria," Martin said, "can you get her to a bathroom?"

Instantly his wife was at my side. "Come on, Joanna," she said. "You've had a little too much to drink, maybe? Come with me."

Clarissa appeared in our path, a cigarette burning between her fingers. Her low-cut gown startled me. "Dorothy Wainwright is about to give her speech," she said. "Are you all right, Joanna?" She smiled a malicious, red-lipsticked smile.

I took a deep breath to keep from retching and got a lungful of cigarette smoke. I gagged and put my hand over my mouth.

"Excuse us," Gloria said. She grabbed my arm and navigated me through the crowded, smoky penthouse, past many more women in over-the-top feminine drag, and into the ladies' room. Susan was there in her cream-colored gown, reapplying lipstick. She did the tiniest of double takes at the sight of me and Martin's wife trooping in together, then she smiled.

"Enjoying the party?" she asked, and her smile faded. "What's wrong?"

I shut myself into the stall.

"Too much to drink, I think," Gloria said.

"Oh! Poor thing."

I gagged again and tasted sour red wine at the back of my throat. I wished Susan and Gloria would go away, so I could vomit without their hearing. I pulled my hair back—long brown hair again—and stood facing the toilet, which mercifully appeared to have been recently cleaned. I didn't want to kneel on the floor until I had to. The nausea began to ebb.

"Joanna, we're going back to the party," Gloria called. "If you're okay."

"I'm fine. Go ahead." To my horror, my voice sounded fine. Maybe I really was meant to be an actress.

I heard the door open and shut. Finally alone, I began to cry quietly. I had wanted to make Cyn's ghost go away, and I had succeeded. I had broken Cyn's heart, and now I could never make it right. It was as if it had never even happened.

Or could I make it right—get back to our life, our apartment in Venice, talk to Cyn? I had to try. But not here. I had to go home. Home to my apartment on the Upper West Side, where I lived alone.

I came out of the stall and looked in the mirror. Mascara was running down my face. The fact that I was wearing mascara—and lipstick and eye shadow, for that matter—took me aback, as did my low-cut purple wrap dress. No one who worked at the bookstore had worn makeup. Cyn had worn it to work sometimes because she said she got better tips that way. I had been a lesbian-feminist, and thus had worn no makeup. I had been a lesbian-feminist. What was I now? I grabbed some paper towels and did what I could to wipe off the runny mascara. Then I steeled myself and went out into the hall.

I stood in the penthouse doorway. Everyone was listening intently to Dorothy Wainwright: "*Hope Springs Eternal* was the brainchild of master storyteller Myra Chase in the early days of television. Little did she know that twenty years later it would be going strong..." The voice of the small, black-haired woman rang through the penthouse. It occurred to me that Dorothy was a lesbian. How did I know that? Somehow that other Jo was convinced of it.

Martin and Gloria stood together, their backs to me. Gloria had been kind to me. I didn't deserve her kindness.

Maurice and his boyfriend looked elegant in their suits. David Halpren stood alone, the best-looking man in the room. I wondered if there was some man he would have liked to bring to the party. Clarissa stood alone in her slinky gown. She turned and fixed me with her haughty gaze. I couldn't deal with her right now, or anyone here. I had to go home and try to make things right with Cyn. As Dorothy spoke of the past twenty years of *Hope Springs Eternal,* and of the years to come, I turned and walked to the elevator.

I took a cab back to my apartment. Almost I expected Cyn to be there when I let myself in. The next door neighbor's TV was blaring some sitcom.

I set my purse on the living room table—Martin's table—and went into the kitchen. I took a juice glass from the cabinet. My heart pounded as I held the glass, ready to drop it into the sink. Then I set the glass on the counter. What if I went all the way back to 1971, to the draft board? I couldn't go through that again, the explosion, four years underground. I tried to will myself back to our apartment in Venice. I closed my eyes and tried to picture our living room, but the details were beginning to fade. I kept seeing the pink and black cover of the paperback I'd been reading, but I couldn't remember what book it was. The raucous laughter from my neighbor's TV kept me from concentrating. I had the feeling I was stuck here for good. That was what I'd wanted, right?

I went into the living room and sat on the orange suede sofa. I was pretty sure our couch in Venice had flowered upholstery. I seemed to remember that Cyn and I had bought it at a thrift store. What would I have wanted to do differently, if I had managed to get back to that life? Would I have stayed with Cyn, no matter how unhappy I was, to keep her alive in that reality? Never become a professional actor, perhaps never come up from underground? Was my life in New York so important, if the trade-off was Cyn's life? In that other existence, she had lived four more years. She had loved me possessively, fiercely. I had loved her.

I stared at the dark TV screen and listened for her ghost, but there was nothing but the neighbor's TV and the traffic in the street below. This had been what I wanted—to be free of her. I didn't feel free, only empty.

Chapter Twenty:
Don't Let the Sun Go Down on Me
(October–November 1975)

"God, I hate this," I grumbled, eyeing the day's script. "Jean would not give up Sam this easily. And why isn't Vicki even considering an abortion?"

Martin, seated beside me at my dressing-room counter, was spooning up chicken rice soup from a thermos cup and studying his copy of the script. "This story is so damn anti-quated," he said. "There was an abortion on *Darkest Before the Dawn* a couple of years ago. Hell, Maude had an abortion. Why can't Vicki have one?"

"Because they want to break up Jean and Sam. And maybe write me out." I took a half-hearted bite of turkey on rye. I was too worried to be hungry.

"You don't know that. They could pair you with someone else. Maybe Halpren can be your new love interest. That could be quite a coup for you. He's very popular."

"But I wanna work with *you*, Marty." I sounded whiny and desperate, but I couldn't seem to help myself.

"I wanna keep working with you, too," he said warmly, though I detected a note of impatience. "But you should work with other actors. Expand your horizons, like Amy."

Amy Gundersen was getting plenty of air time, with lots of meaty confrontations with Maurice, her on-screen father. "You mean, the play Amy's doing? *The Seagull*, right?"

"Yeah, she's playing Nina. I saw it the other night."

"You did? How was it?" I tried to keep my voice even.

"It was a pretty average production. She was the best thing in it. But at least she's honing her craft."

His praise for her rankled. "You think we're not honing our craft here?"

He shrugged. "I guess we are." He lifted his cup and drank the remaining bit of chicken broth.

God, I hated this. I wanted to throw myself into my work. I wasn't used to being myself anymore. Too many versions of my life, half-forgotten, edited and reworked and discarded versions. Who was I now? All I knew was that I wanted to sink deeply, satisfyingly into the role of Jean Christopher, and I wanted Martin, on and off camera. Those were the things that made me feel anchored in the here and now (even when it was a make-believe here and now). But it was already Friday, and today was my only show of the week—and I was only scheduled to be in one episode next week. "Hey, want to go to Chauncy's after work?" I asked.

"I can't. I have to get home and take my kids trick-or-treating."

"Oh, right! It's Halloween." Even so, it bothered me that he'd taken Amy to Chauncy's and he wouldn't take me. I thought to ask him what costumes his kids were going to wear, but I was afraid he'd say one of them was going as a ghost, in a white sheet perhaps. The idea put a lump in my throat.

"Besides, are you sure you feel like drinking, after last weekend?" he asked with a grin.

"Very funny."

He peered at me. "Seriously, though, was there any special reason you tied one on at the party?"

"What do you mean?" It was no use explaining that I hadn't tied one on. I couldn't tell him what had really happened. The only one I could've talked to about that was Cyn, and she was gone. I had seen to that.

He scraped at the inside of the thermos cup with his spoon, though it was empty. "I just wondered if maybe you got drunk because my wife was there?"

I gave a laugh. "What? No! God, no."

"It only occurred to me when I'd sent you off with her to the ladies' room, and then I hoped I hadn't done the wrong thing."

We looked at each other—then we burst out laughing. It was a loose, ragged feeling. "Gloria was really nice to me at the party," I said. "Thank her for me, will you?"

"I will." There was a puzzled crinkle between his brows. "So you weren't drowning your sorrows? Though god knows I'm not worth being sorrowful about."

I shook my head and smiled. "You don't make me sorrowful, Marty. Quite the opposite. You help me forget my troubles." *Sorrowful* was starting to sound like a strange word. But it was true: I was full of sorrow.

"So you've got troubles?" he asked in a light, bantering tone.

The sorrow rose up in my chest. It was as if I were in mourning all over again. "We've all got troubles, haven't we?" Deflect, deflect. That was all I could do. It was such a lonely feeling.

He gazed intently at me. "You have been acting a bit wacky lately. I'm worried about you."

"You are?"

"What do you think? I care about you, Jo."

"Thanks," I whispered, fighting back tears. Would I ever stop mourning her?

"Aw, none of that," Martin said, and he leaned towards me and kissed my forehead.

"None of *that*," I said, and I kissed his mouth. He tasted of chicken soup. Kissing him was strange, after years with Cyn. So many details had faded, but kissing Cyn was still vivid. The smoothness of her face against mine, her gingery smell, the fierceness of her kiss. Martin was different—his rougher skin and slight stubble, of course, but also there was something friendly and leisurely about his kisses, as if he were listening to me and telling me something.

He broke the kiss. "Hey, save it for the cameras," he said with a smile, but I felt rejected. He turned back to his script. "Speaking of which, do you think we've got this scene down?"

I wanted to keep kissing him, but working with him was also a pleasure I ought to enjoy while I still had the chance. "I guess we have time to run through it again."

"Let's do it."

I began the scene. "Vicki's going to have a baby, and you're the father. I always knew this was too wonderful to last."

∞

After the day's taping, I ran into Clarissa as I was leaving my dressing room and she was heading to the rehearsal room for the afternoon table-read. She was carrying an armload of scripts. I had hoped I wouldn't see her this week. She burst into an unnerving smile. "Hello, Joanna! Feeling better?"

She'd obviously been saving up that line since the party. "Yes, thanks," I said, though I felt drained from Jean and Sam's tearful farewell scenes (the tears had been mostly mine, though Martin's eyes were wet as well).

"I was terribly concerned at the party. You must have been feeling unwell to have left in the middle of Dorothy Wainwright's speech. Alcohol can sneak up on one." I wondered if she had told Dorothy I got loaded and walked out on her speech. Would Dorothy really care? Walking out during the speech hadn't been smart, but I had been preoccupied with getting back to Cyn.

"I seem to recall you had the same problem at the party," I said. "I hope *you're* feeling better."

Her smile faltered. "I don't know what you're talking about!"

"I thought I heard Maurice saying you'd had enough. My mistake."

239

For a moment she was at a loss for words. Then she glanced down at her scripts, and her smile returned. "Well, I mustn't be late for rehearsal…"

She hurried off, and I headed home.

When I read my lone script for next week, I discovered why she had been smiling.

∞

Clarissa brandished the newspaper with the front page headline that read: "MAYOR READ CORRUPTION SCANDAL ROCKS HOPEFIELD." We were standing in Jean's living room, where Sylvia Cartwright had just barged her way in. "How dare you attack a fine man like Eric Read?" she cried, eyes flashing. "I promise you, you'll regret it!" She threw the newspaper aside. It landed on the table, upsetting Jean's piles of notes.

"Miss Cartwright—" I said.

She reared back and slapped my face. It stung a lot more than it had in rehearsal. "Not one word from you, you nosy little reporter!"

"Cut!" Vincent's voice said over the PA. "Good work."

I rubbed my cheek. Clarissa was grinning as if slapping me had been a long-hoped-for treat. I supposed it had been. "I hope I didn't hurt you, Joanna!" she said, all wide-eyed innocence.

"Not at all," I said, though my cheek still throbbed a bit.

Nancy appeared, clipboard in hand. "Miss Wainwright would like a word with you, Joanna. She's in her office."

My stomach did an unpleasant flip.

"I wonder what that's about?" Clarissa asked sweetly.

I headed off set and up the stairs. Maybe Dorothy Wainwright wanted to talk about my storyline. Maybe she wanted to assure me that I had an upcoming storyline. But she wasn't the reassuring type. I had never been inside her office, though it was down the hall from the dressing rooms. I knocked on her door and entered.

Dorothy Wainwright was sitting in a black leather chair behind a big desk. She wore a camel-colored pantsuit. She looked small behind the desk, yet she dominated the room with her dark, tense presence. She was leafing through a script. "Sit down, Joanna," she said with the barest flick of a glance, then scribbled something on a yellow pad. I sat across from her in a black and silver chair that was less comfortable than Dorothy's appeared to be.

I remembered lesbian-feminist Jo's intuition that Dorothy Wainwright was a lesbian. What had clued her in? Then again, she'd had lesbians on the brain.

Dorothy looked up with a thin-lipped smile that made me even more uneasy. "I wanted to talk to you about what's going to happen in the next few weeks."

"Okay." I nodded, one hand clutching the other in my lap.

"You've done a fine job, Joanna. Prudence Fisher in particular has been pleased with your work."

A cautious sense of relief wafted through me. "Thanks. I really love working here."

"Unfortunately, we feel that Jean's story has run its course."

"Oh." It occurred to me that I'd thought worrying about being fired would prevent it from actually happening.

"Vicki Jameson is a well-loved character, and Sam and Vicki are a popular couple. Jean was brought on to create obstacles to their relationship, and to stir up trouble for Eric Read, but now that the storylines are resolved, we don't quite know what to do with her."

"I guess I thought the relationship between Jean and Sam wasn't resolved. I mean, they're still in love with each other."

Dorothy shrugged. I soldiered on into her silence.

"Maybe Jean could do another investigation for her newspaper. Or she could be romantically involved with another man. I'd love to work with David Halpren."

"That's not the direction the story is headed. You're a talented actress, and we feel your talents could be put to better use elsewhere." For a brief, hopeful moment I thought she was going to ask me to join the cast of one of the network's other soap operas, but she didn't. I couldn't believe that just when I had begun to want a long-term career with *Hope Springs Eternal*, the opportunity was being taken from me.

"Maybe it seems as if I haven't been focused enough lately," I blundered on, barely knowing what I was saying. "I know I've made some mistakes. But I can do better, if you give me a chance."

Dorothy shook her head in an utterly dispassionate way. "We just don't see a place for Jean on the canvas. We'll be wrapping up her storyline in the next few weeks. The character will be killed off. I'm sorry to have to tell you this."

"I see." It was as if I'd found out I only had a few weeks to live. "How do I die?"

She gave a surprised blink. "I can't say." I wasn't sure if that meant she knew and couldn't tell me, or if she had no idea.

"Has Clarissa said something against me? She's always had it in for me." I knew before I'd finished speaking that this was a stupid thing to say.

Sure enough, Dorothy looked like she'd smelled something bad. "Joanna, this isn't high school. Whatever problems you and Clarissa have with each other have little bearing on the matter."

Little bearing, not no bearing. "Isn't there anything I can do to change your mind?"

"I believe I've made myself clear." She glanced at her watch. "I'm afraid I'll have to cut this short."

"I understand." I got to my feet.

"Good luck, Joanna."

In a daze I marched out of the office. I didn't want to see anyone. That would make it real. I darted into my dressing room—to find Clarissa, dressed in her street clothes, putting her costume on a hanger. Her thin brows lifted. "How was your meeting with Dorothy?"

"You got your wish."

"What are you talking about?"

I was afraid I was going to start to cry. "You got your wish!" I repeated and walked out.

Martin had finished taping before I had. Maybe he was in his dressing room. I knocked on his door. "Come in!" he said, and I opened the door.

He was sitting at the counter. Beside him in the other chair was Amy, munching an apple. They looked up at me with such innocent eyes.

I started to laugh. "Of course," I said. "Of course!" My day was complete.

Martin smiled gamely at me. Then his smile faded. "What's wrong?"

Amy regarded me with concern, Amy of the long brown hair and big blue eyes and Argyle sweater, long legs in jeans. She hadn't been taping today. Maybe she was here for the afternoon table-read. Or had she shown up just to see Martin?

"Amy, I need to talk to Marty," I said with as much dignity as I could muster, considering I couldn't quite catch my breath.

"I'll be in the rehearsal room in a few minutes," Martin told Amy, and she nodded. In that moment between the two of them, it was as if I had already vanished.

"I hope everything's okay, Joanna," Amy said, and then she and her half-eaten apple were gone.

"They're killing me off," I told Martin.

"What? They're..." The meaning dawned. "Oh, no. Really?"

I nodded, and then I couldn't look at him because I could feel my face collapsing. He got to his feet and pulled me to him. I put my arms around him. What was happening between us would not end, would it, because this gig was ending. Nothing was happening between him and Amy.

He sat me down in Maurice's chair, then sat facing me. "How'd you find out?"

"Dorothy called me into her office."

He winced. "You poor kid."

"She says my story has run its course." I gave a laugh. "Sounds like the flu, doesn't it? They're gonna kill me off in a few weeks."

"God, I'm sorry." He shook his head. "What can I say? I'll really miss working with you. But you're so talented. I'm sure you'll land on your feet."

Was that all he had to say? It seemed just yesterday that he'd said I'd given him a new creative lease on life. Would I even see him after I stopped working here? I was losing my job. How would I pay for my apartment? It wasn't as if I could move back in with my old roommate in Chelsea. I hadn't talked to Toni in months. I could collect unemployment, or maybe I could get another gig quickly. I'd have to call my agent. God, auditions. I'd have to go on auditions. I didn't want to go back to temp work. I was losing my job. How would I tell my parents? I let out a gust of breath and put my head in my hands.

"I know this is a shock," Martin said. "I'm so sorry, Jo. You don't deserve this. God, those network jerks should have their heads examined."

I looked up at him. "Thanks."

He took my hands in his. Only then did I realize how cold my hands were. "I'm sorry to have to leave you like this, but I've got to get to the table-read."

We stood, and he hugged me again. Then he kissed me, a firm cushiony peck on the lips. I wanted to grab him and kiss him hard and long, but somehow I couldn't when Amy had just been here. What if he rejected me? I couldn't take that right now.

We walked out of his dressing room, and he shut the door. "Take care, honey," he said. He'd never called me that before.

Mercifully, Clarissa was gone when I went back to my dressing room. I changed into my street clothes and managed to get downstairs without seeing anyone. I couldn't even meet the gaze of the security guard in the lobby. Then I found myself walking home on a gray November afternoon amid bustling people who, probably, hadn't just lost their jobs. "Well, Cyn," I said, "what do you think about that? In a few weeks I'll be dead too." I half expected her to retort that it wasn't remotely the same thing, but, of course, I had lost her too.

Chapter Twenty-one:
Rehearsals for Retirement
(December 1975)

When I walked into the rehearsal room on the Monday morning of my final week on *Hope Springs Eternal* and saw everyone sitting together at a table, I felt like a ghost. "Larry's sister is such a bitch," Babette was saying. "She treats me like an interloper because she's still friends with Larry's ex-wife, even though they've been divorced for years." Babs was freshly engaged to Larry, and she held out her hand and gazed transfixed at the sparkling rock on her finger.

Susan, listening indulgently to Babette, looked up and smiled at me. When Amy saw me, a look of pure hostility flashed across her face—then, bizarrely, she smiled and waved. Babette turned to see who she was waving at. "Oh, hi Jo," Babs said, and resumed her monologue. "Larry's teenage kids aren't much better. I don't know what's worse—his daughter freezing me out, or his son practically drooling at the sight of me."

I got a cup of black coffee and looked without hunger at the box of pastries. Then I came back to the table and hovered like a high school pariah. Babette kept yattering on about Larry's family.

"Have a seat, dear," Susan said, and I pulled up a chair next to her. "How are you, Joanna?" Susan overflowed with sympathy every time she talked to me, for which I was grateful, though it was a bit much.

"I'm about to spend half the week lying unconscious in a hospital bed," I said.

"Once I had to do that for *weeks*," Susan said. "I've never been so well-rested!"

I laughed. I would miss her.

"How was your Thanksgiving?" she asked.

"It was fine." In fact, it had been miserable. I'd eaten a turkey TV dinner in front of the television and wracked my brain trying to remember if Cyn and I had celebrated Thanksgiving when we'd lived together. Instead I'd remembered the gloppy mashed potatoes they served on Thanksgiving at Brightdale, which made me wonder if Alex had gone to trial yet. The evening news had talked of Squeaky Fromme's guilty verdict and Vietnamese refugees eating Thanksgiving dinner for the first time, but nothing about Alex, Sharon, or their comrades. I'd spoken to my parents and my brother Rob after dinner, but the main topic was the impending loss of my job, capping off the dismal evening.

"I was talking to Marty," Susan said, "and he said you didn't want a going-away party."

"I'd just as soon not." It would have seemed too much like a wake, but I couldn't tell Susan that.

Clarissa and Maurice walked in, chatting and laughing. Then they saw me, and their mirth subsided. Maurice sent a compassionate smile my way, but Clarissa wouldn't even make eye contact.

∞

At lunchtime I retreated to my dressing room. Fortunately Clarissa didn't. She had avoided me since she'd learned I was being written out, as if it might be contagious. I nibbled on a chicken sandwich and studied my lines. God, I hated these lines. They felt half-written, as if Prudence Fisher and her writing team had been forced by the higher-ups to overhaul the story they'd loved, and they couldn't pretend to feel invested in the new direction.

VICKI

Please, Jean, stay away from my husband for the sake of our child, if not for my sake. You used to care about me, didn't you? It wasn't all an act?

JEAN

I do care about you, Vicki, and I'm so sorry I hurt you. I know now that Sam belongs with you. I hope you can find it in your heart to forgive me.

VICKI

That's too much to ask right now. The truth is, I'm not sure I'll ever be able to forgive you.

Then, at the end of the episode, Beverly Read arrived at Jean's apartment building to find Vicki kneeling over Jean's prone body at the bottom of the stairwell.

There was a knock on the door, and Amy peeked in. "Hi. Mind a little company?" Before I could beg off, she came inside and shut the door. What on earth did she want? She walked over to the reframed photo of Maurice and Clarissa hugging each other in evening clothes. "What a great photo."

"Isn't it?" I looked wistfully at my own side of the counter. It would take me no time at all to clear out my stuff on Thursday afternoon. I hated the fact that Amy would still be here when I was gone. I had a flash of seeing Amy play Jean Christopher on the TV at Brightdale. *She's taken my place.*

Amy sat in Clarissa's chair. She looked lanky and girlish in jeans and a pink sweater. "We haven't had much of a chance to get to know each other. I just thought it'd be nice, before you go…"

"Oh. That's nice of you." Had I imagined her look of hostility this morning?

"Babette is such a trip, isn't she? All she ever talks about is her engagement."

That was true, but hearing Amy say it, I felt protective of Babette. I wondered if Amy knew about Babs and Martin. "Have you met Larry? He's very nice."

"I met him briefly at the party at the Brand. He does seem nice. I'm just not sure I believe in marriage." She uttered that pronouncement like a callow schoolgirl, then looked at me expectantly.

"How come?" I asked, though I couldn't have cared less.

She let out a sigh. "Owen thinks we should get married, and maybe he's right. We've been together since high school. But he doesn't understand about my acting. He says I shouldn't do theater while I'm doing *Hope Springs Eternal*, because it cuts into the time we spend together. He just doesn't understand how much I love acting. It makes me feel kind of lonely, you know?"

Apparently Amy had taken my impending departure as a cue to become my new best friend. "What does Owen do?" I asked.

"Oh, he works at a record store in the Village," she said, as if it were the most inconsequential job in the universe. "I just think it would be great to have someone I could share everything with."

Was she talking about Martin? Or maybe she was interested in Patrick, the new guy who played Kathy Read's boyfriend Tommy. "Are you thinking of breaking up with Owen?" I asked.

She looked startled. "Well, I don't know. I mean, not unless I knew that I had somewhere to go, you know?"

"So you're waiting for something better to come along? That's not really fair to your boyfriend. Maybe you just need to be alone for a while." It was surprising how easy it was to give advice when your own life was falling to pieces.

Amy looked at me as if I were insane. "What would be the point? I love Owen. I wouldn't want to break up with him unless I had a good reason."

A good reason like Martin leaving his wife? Was that really what Amy thought, or was I jumping to the wrong conclusion? Where Martin was concerned, my wildest suspicions were generally right on the mark.

"So tell me about you and Marty," Amy said, right on cue. Nope, it wasn't Patrick. Too bad.

"What about me and Marty?"

"When I first got here, I thought you and Marty had been friends for years, you seemed so close. Have the two of you...?"

I broke off a bit of bread from my sandwich and ate it. "Have we what?"

"*You* know." A steely and intrusive look came over her face.

I gave a laugh. "Look, I don't go around discussing my personal business with everyone."

"But I told you about me and Owen!"

"No offense, Amy, but that was your choice. This is my last week here. I have a lot on my mind, okay?"

She stared me down. "There is another man in my life besides Owen."

"I see." My face grew hot.

"But he has a complicated personal situation."

You don't know the half of it, I thought. I said nothing.

"Have you and Martin slept together?" she demanded in a clenched whisper.

I smiled with as much composure as I could muster. "I already told you, I'm not going to talk about it."

The door swung open. Oh, great—it was Clarissa. But for once I wasn't the object of her disdain. She looked pointedly at Amy. "Do you mind?"

"Mind?" Amy asked.

"My chair. You're sitting in it."

"Oh! Sorry." She jumped to her feet. "I'll talk to you later, Joanna."

"I don't think I'll have the time," I said. "I told you, this is my last week, and I'm going to be very busy."

Amy glared at me with hard blue eyes. "But we haven't finished—"

"That's quite enough, Amy," Clarissa said. "Joanna is a serious actress. This is her last week with the company, and she's giving the show her all. She doesn't have time for idle chit-chat. Perhaps you should take her example to heart." She swept past Amy, sat at the counter and crossed her legs.

Amy gaped at Clarissa. Then she murmured, "Sorry to have bothered you," at no one in particular, and hurried out the door.

I turned to Clarissa in amazement. "What was all that about?"

She lit a cigarette and took a leisurely drag. "Ingénues," she said, and smiled slightly. "Someday you'll understand."

∞

I came to the studio four days in a row, though on Tuesday and Wednesday I just lay with my eyes closed, first on a stretcher and then in a hospital bed, my face covered in sickly makeup, while Martin, Babette, David, and the day players in nurse uniforms did their thing around me. Then, on Thursday, Jean woke up long enough to say goodbye.

Martin and I were in the tiny hospital room set, cameras and crew wedged around us. I lay in the bed in a hospital gown, an IV taped to my arm. Martin gripped my hand and kept his eyes on me as if his steady gaze could keep me from vanishing. (I feared I was vanishing.)

"I'm so glad we met, in spite of everything," I said in a labored but distinct faux whisper. "It was always so easy to talk to you. I felt like I'd known you all my life."

"I feel the same way," he said, trying to smile encouragingly, though he looked terrified. "But listen, you're going to be fine. Do you hear me? You're going to be just fine." He squeezed my hand. "I love you, Jean," he said, as if he were praying.

It was the last time that I (Jean? Joanna?) would get to say the words, and I said them simply, joyfully. "I love you, too."

He leaned down and kissed me, and I reached up and caressed his coarse, thick hair. Then I looked into his eyes. "Be happy, Sam," I said, and let my hand drop.

His smile faded as he saw me fading. I let go of his hand, and my eyes began to close. "Come on, Jean," he said. "Stay with me!"

I remembered dying on the sidewalk outside the draft board. It seemed wrong to use that for the cameras. I had been cold and afraid on that sidewalk, but Jean Christopher wasn't afraid. Jean felt loved, and somehow that was enough. I smiled at Martin, then closed my eyes and went still. I breathed shallowly through my nose and tried to keep my chest and diaphragm from visibly moving.

"Jean? Jean!" His panicked voice rose, and I had to fight not to react. "We need a doctor in here!" he shouted.

"Cut!" Vincent said over the PA. "Jo, stay in position, would you?" We quickly moved on to the next scene.

"Time of death, 10:46 pm," David intoned as I lay motionless in the hospital bed.

"No, no, no," Martin said. "Keep working on her. Please."

"I'm sorry," David said. "We did everything we could."

"Oh, Jean…" Babette said melodramatically. "Jean, I'm so sorry!" My nose started to tickle. For my very last scene, please let the dead girl not sneeze. It took all my self-control not to wriggle my nose.

"How did this happen?" Martin demanded.

"It was an accident," David said. "A terrible accident."

"I don't believe that," Martin said. "If it's the last thing I do, I'm going to find out who did this to her." There was a fraught silence.

"Thank you, all," Vince said over the PA. I opened my eyes and took a gulp of air. The need to sneeze had passed. I pulled the IV from my arm. I had no more lines to learn. Jean Christopher was dead. I would miss her idealism and her openness. I would miss Sam Jameson and the way he'd looked at me like I was entirely loved.

"Come here, you," Martin said, and gave me his hand. His face was beautiful and tear-streaked. I pushed the sheets back and rose from the bed. Nancy handed me a robe to put on over my flimsy hospital gown. I donned it, then Martin hugged me.

"Jo," said David in his doctor's garb, "we're going to miss you."

Martin let go of me so David could hug me. Babette hugged me next—and after that, there was Nancy, and one of the nurse day players, and a couple of the cameramen. I felt myself unraveling. "Marty," I muttered, "I've got to get out of here."

"Okay," he said, "give the girl some air." He put his arm around me and shepherded me out of the hospital room and away, away from the sets forever. Then we walked upstairs to my dressing room. There was a bouquet of pink roses on my side of the counter, and a large envelope with "Joanna" written on it.

I sniffed a rose. "Now I really feel like this is my funeral," I said.

"Now, now," Martin said, "none of that. Open the card."

The card had a garland of flowers on it and a sappy rhyme in elegant script. Some people had just signed their names—I saw Clarissa's elegant signature—while others had written notes. Martin had written, in a bold, slanting hand, "Wishing you many exciting opportunities, love, Martin." Love, I thought. Then I saw Babette's note, in a round, looping hand that reminded me of high school yearbooks: "It was a lot of fun working with you. Let's keep in touch!"

"You want me to leave you alone?" Martin asked, leaning on the counter.

"Can you stay awhile?"

"Sure, if you want. It's a while yet before I have to get to the table-read."

It hit me afresh that I wouldn't be going to any more afternoon table-reads or morning rehearsals. And when would I see Martin again? He looked tired and a bit puffy from crying, and somehow that made him more attractive than ever.

"You look like I feel," I said, putting the card back in its envelope and setting it on the counter.

He raked a hand through his hair and let out a breath. "I feel kinda wrung out."

I looked at myself in the mirror, my face made up pale with dark circles under my eyes. "Wow, I look like the walking dead."

"Stop that," Martin said. "You're not dead. You're a talented young actress with your whole career, your whole life ahead of you. I'm angry and disappointed too, you know, but this could be the best thing for you. When's the last time you auditioned for a play?"

I hated feeling like he was comparing me to Amy. "It's been a while. But my agent knows I'm available now."

"Good. Who knows what projects will come your way? Theater, or prime time, or movies! You can't tell me that when you got here, you thought this would be the be-all and end-all of your career."

"No." It was hard to remember feeling that soap operas were beneath me, that this was just a brief stop on the way to bigger and better things. "It's just, I don't want to go, Marty." I walked up to him and put my arms around him.

"I know, I know." He held me. He felt so strong and alive. This couldn't be the last time we would be alone together. I looked into his eyes, his cue to kiss me. When he didn't, I kissed him. He kissed me back, sweet, frustrating pecks. I kissed his cheek, his neck, and heard him suck in a breath. Good. I kissed his neck wetly. Then I kissed him on the mouth again. This time he kissed me properly. I pressed my body against his. His hands moved up and down my back. My heart was pounding: *not dead, not dead.* I wanted to lock the door, but I was afraid to let go of him.

His lips brushed my neck, and I moaned. "Please," I whispered. "I need you."

He gripped my shoulders—then he was holding me at arms' length. "Jo, I can't."

"You can't?" I asked faintly. "But you want to, right?"

He was breathing heavily, his face flushed. "I'm sorry if you thought…" He let go of my shoulders and took a step back with a shamefaced grimace. "If I wasn't married, you're the kind of woman who…well, you're just not the kind of woman I could ever have a casual thing with. I care about you too much, and you deserve so much better."

"Why did you kiss me in the first place, that time outside my apartment? Was it because you were drunk?" I was terrified he would say yes, or worse, that he didn't even remember that night.

He couldn't quite look at me. "I don't know. No. I felt close to you. I do feel close to you. And sometimes the lines blur, when you're working with someone you connect with. But this would be wrong. I can't use you that way."

"What if that's what I want?"

His face looked the way it had that day I'd caught him with Babette—full of guilt and self-loathing. Now, when I needed him most, was he going to be ruled by his conscience? Or was he simply not interested because he was involved with

Amy? "I just can't," he said. "Please don't look at me like that. You don't want to be with a guy like me."

"Don't tell me what I want," I said quietly and distinctly.

"Okay, I'll tell you what I want. I want us to be friends."

All at once I felt very tired. "Oh, what does it matter? We probably won't even see each other again."

"Of course we will. If you want to, we will. You can call me any time." He looked so earnest, the big brother I'd never wanted him to be. "You have my number, don't you?"

I shook my head, and the fact that he had never given it to me felt like a crushing blow. He picked up a pencil from the counter and wrote on the back of the envelope of my going-away card. Then he handed me the envelope with a smile. I stared at his name and phone number and fought back tears.

"Talk to me, Jo."

I took a deep breath and managed to compose myself enough to look at him. "Oh Marty, you won't have time for me, between the show and your family and your *girlfriends*."

He winced. "Jo, you don't have to sleep with me to have my attention. I'm your friend. That's not going to change."

He was looking at me with such kindness. Kindness was such a small part of what I needed from him. Kindness couldn't keep me from feeling like I was vanishing, couldn't keep me from feeling cold and dead. "Okay," I whispered.

"Okay." He smiled, as if everything had been solved. "Will you be all right? Because I should probably get going."

"I'll see you," I said in a small voice.

"Soon," Martin said, and squeezed my shoulder.

When the door closed behind him, I started to cry. I still had the envelope with his number on it clutched in my hand. I tossed it onto the counter and took off the robe and the blue hospital gown. How pathetic I looked in the mirror in my underwear, face pale and tear-streaked, dark circles beneath my eyes. I wiped at my tears, but another fit of crying took me, and I buried my face in my hands.

I felt arms snaking about my waist from behind. They were cold and thin. I looked into the mirror. Cyn leaned her head so that it touched mine, her blonde hair against my brown. Her face was pale, with dark circles beneath her eyes, and she wore a blue hospital gown.

"I'm here," Cyn said. "Let's go home."

Chapter Twenty-two:
Hang On to Yourself
(January 1976)

"I'm so bored," Cyn said, lying on her stomach in front of the TV, bare feet in the air. "Let's do something."

I was sitting on the sofa with a cup of sweet, milky coffee and a buttermilk donut. I was still in my nightgown and robe, and the drapes were drawn against the cold, gray afternoon. "Would you put your feet down? You're blocking the screen."

Cyn wiggled her toes defiantly. "You really want to see this shampoo ad?" she asked.

Partially blocked by Cyn's jeaned legs, a woman tossed her long chestnut hair around the TV screen. "I suppose not," I said.

The credits for the soap opera that aired before *Hope Springs Eternal* began to roll. "Why don't you try out for that show?" Cyn asked.

"*The Grass Is Always Greener*? It shoots in Los Angeles."

"Oh."

"And since when do you want me to do a soap opera? I thought you looked down on them."

"It would be better than you moping around this apartment, waiting to run out of money. What are we going to do then—move in with your parents? I always hated Rochester. But for all we do these days, we might as well be there."

I drank some coffee. I'd put in a bit too much sugar. "My agent said not to expect any auditions until after the new year."

"I thought it was after the new year. What month is this?"

"January."

"What year is it?"

That took me aback. "Don't you know? It's 1976. It's the fucking bicentennial." The media trumpeted this fact every five minutes.

"1976," Cyn said in a puzzled tone.

It was two weeks into the new year. I had some money saved, and I'd started collecting unemployment. Still, if I was going to keep this apartment, I would have to find work soon. I ought to call my agent. The idea of auditions made me break out in a cold sweat, but I didn't want to go back to secretarial work.

Time had moved strangely since I'd left *Hope Springs Eternal*. The only thing that kept me on a schedule was TV: the soap operas I watched and the evening news. (The news talked often of Patty Hearst, but never of Alex. I wondered if his trial had begun yet.) My parents had offered to buy me a plane ticket to Rochester for the holidays, but I didn't have it in me to visit them with Cyn—and my failure—in tow, so I told them I had made plans with friends. My mom sounded pleased I was enjoying a social life, which only made me feel worse.

The credits to *The Grass Is Always Greener* faded to black. "Cyn, put your feet down!"

Cyn obliged. The show began at the hospital nurses' station. That hospital set looked so much more spacious on TV. The elevator doors opened, and Martin and Babette came out. Predictably a hollow, yearning sensation started up in the pit of my stomach.

"Now, Sam," Babette said, "you don't have to come with me. I work here, after all."

There seemed to be a smudge below Martin's right eye. "Vick, you aren't here as a doctor this afternoon," he said breezily. "You're here as a mother-to-be, and as the father-to-be, I have a right to be by your side."

Cyn let out an exaggerated yawn.

Babette smiled a glowing, pregnant-woman smile. Judging by the size of the pad inside her dress, the pregnancy was progressing unnaturally quickly. "It's just a routine checkup, Sam. Pregnancy isn't an illness. Nothing could be more healthy and natural."

"Nothing could be more beautiful," he said, and there was a close-up of his smiling face.

I leaned forward. "Why does Martin have a black eye?" There had been nothing in the previous episodes to account for it, but he had quite a shiner. It looked real. In fact, it looked like they'd tried to hide it with makeup.

Babette leaned towards him and gently touched his cheek below the black eye. "I can't believe the manager of Jean's apartment building opened the door in your face! Poor darling."

"They wrote it in," I said. "Martin got a black eye, and they wrote in an explanation. It looks like somebody punched him."

"Someone punched him?" Cyn asked. "What a surprise. What was it he said to you? Oh yeah—you're the kind of woman who, if he wasn't already married, he'd like to marry and cheat on."

"Shut up." I could tell myself that Martin was still thinking about me, because Sam was still trying to figure out who had killed Jean Christopher. "I wonder who killed me," I said as the cartoon sun rose in the TV sky and the words HOPE SPRINGS ETERNAL appeared.

"Lest you forget," Cyn said, "you're still alive. Let's go out, do something."

"It's freezing out." I didn't go out much, especially after my death scenes aired and a woman turned pale at the sight of me in Zabar's. *But I saw you die*, she said and dropped a tub of chopped liver. (Cyn said my death scenes were thoroughly unconvincing.)

After some commercials, *Hope Springs Eternal* resumed in Beverly Read's living room. Susan, seated on the sofa, poured herself a cup of coffee from an elegant silver pot. She looked every inch Beverly Read in a royal blue suit with a red and white scarf (bicentennial!). There was a knock on the door, and she went to answer it. "Kathy!" she said. "Come in."

The young woman at the door had long brown hair, but she wasn't Amy Gundersen. As she walked in, a male voice-over intoned, "Today the role of Kathy Read is being played by Annabel Becker."

"What the hell is going on?" I asked. "First Martin has a black eye, and now Amy's taken the day off?" Generally only hospitalization would make an actor miss a day on a soap opera. I couldn't shake the feeling that all hell was breaking loose at the studio.

Annabel Becker, whoever she was, wasn't having an easy time of it. "I…" Her eyes sought the teleprompter. "I was wondering if my father was here," she read. I was embarrassed for her.

Cyn sat up, blocking the TV, and turned to face me. She was wearing a blue Argyle sweater that looked incongruous on her. It looked familiar. "I don't understand why you want to watch this fucking show now that you're not on it."

"Let me watch my show in peace." I heard myself: my show. It wasn't mine anymore, except that I'd joined its devoted audience. I knew I shouldn't keep watching. I hadn't heard from anyone in the company since my last day. I missed being part of the show so much. I even missed Clarissa's nastiness, and Babette's engagement chatter, and the drama of Martin's overpopulated love life.

Cyn got to her feet in one graceful motion and strode to the sofa. She loomed above me as if she meant to strike me. Then she sat at the other end of the couch and stared angrily at the TV. Just then I realized what was familiar about the Argyle sweater she had on—it was one I'd seen Amy wear. What was going on with Amy, anyway? And why was Cyn wearing her sweater?

After *Hope Springs Eternal* ended, I changed the channel and watched *Darkest Before the Dawn* while Cyn gave me the silent treatment, but I couldn't keep my mind on the program. I kept thinking about Martin's black eye.

∞

That night I took the envelope of my going-away card from the bedside table and sat cross-legged on the bed. Cyn sat beside me.

"Do you mind?" I asked. "I'm nervous enough. I don't want an audience."

"Joanna Bergman, not wanting an audience? That's a first." She didn't move.

I turned my back on her and, heart pounding, dialed the number Martin had written on the envelope. It rang once, twice, three times. I almost hung up.

Then the phone picked up. "Hello?" It was Martin, sounding harried. I almost hung up again.

"Hi, Marty. It's Joanna."

"Jo! How are you?" My heart lifted at how glad he sounded to hear from me, but then he said, "Oh, wait a second." Someone—Gloria?—was talking in the background. "No, it's Joanna," Martin told her. "You can talk to her yourself if you don't believe me!...Listen, Jo, can I call you back in a few minutes?"

"Of course."

"Okay, I'll call you back. Bye."

"Bye." I hung up and sat there revving my engines.

"So?" Cyn asked.

I had forgotten she was there. "He's gonna call me back. I think he was in the middle of something." Gloria thought he was lying when he told her it was me. That couldn't be good.

"So you're going to sit by the phone?"

I didn't answer. Yes, that was what I was going to do. I sat by the phone and listened to the cars honking and roaring by. The kid on the other side of the wall had a screaming tantrum. The mother made soothing, then exasperated noises. Eventually the kid shut up.

Cyn fidgeted and finally sat back against the headboard. "He's not going to call back, you know."

It had been nearly an hour. Had he forgotten? If he was working tomorrow, he would probably go to bed early, but it was only just past eight.

You can call me any time, he'd said. What he hadn't said was that he'd actually talk to me. I'd been right, after all—he had no time for me. How pathetic I was, watching *Hope Springs Eternal* day after day, still feeling connected to him. But maybe he would still call. I lay down and closed my eyes. I had never changed out of my nightgown and robe. Maybe if I slept, I would wake to the phone ringing.

I felt Cyn watching me and opened my eyes. Sure enough, she was on her side, head propped on her hand. "I don't understand you," she said. "If I had your life, I wouldn't waste it. I would live, for god's sake. You walked out on me—"

"You remember that? Was it real to you?"

I had asked many times, but she never gave me a straight answer. She sat up. "You walked out on me so you could be free, and now look at you."

I dragged myself into a seated position. "I don't understand how you're still here. I saved your life. That was what you wanted, right?"

"And then you ended me. You walked out on that version of our lives, so it never really happened. It doesn't count." Her voice was cool and controlled—a little too cool and controlled.

"I didn't know when I broke things off with you that any of that would happen. I thought we would go our separate ways. I didn't know that your life, those four years, could just melt away. When I realized what was happening, I tried to stay. I tried to get to you."

"Apparently you didn't try hard enough."

"Honestly, Cyn, if I had known what would happen when I left you—"

"You would've stayed with me, for my sake? What a noble sacrifice. Fuck that." She got up and began to pace. Cyn with her short blonde hair. I thought of Cyn with the dyed brown hair, Cyn who had been given four more years and then had them taken away. Cyn whose heart I had broken.

"I'm sorry I hurt you," I said. I knew it wasn't enough.

She wouldn't look at me. "Don't flatter yourself. You weren't that good in bed."

I had a flash of the two of us on a bed somewhere—Portland?—Cyn's fingers moving inside me as she whispered frantically, *I wish I had a cock...I'd fuck you so hard...I'd make you come so fucking hard...I'd come so hard inside you,* until I'd gasped and clenched around her fingers.

"You were," I whispered.

Startled, she looked at me. "Well, that's your loss, isn't it?" She smiled bitterly. "Why am I still here? I'm keeping you company. Someone has to."

"But I don't understand how—"

"You wanted me here, didn't you? You needed me." There was a slight quaver in her voice.

"I don't know. I don't know."

"Would've served you right if I'd left you all alone, the way you're always leaving me." She sat on the edge of the bed. "I have to admit, I thought our life underground would be a lot more exciting." She shook her head. "I was a waitress, for god's sake! What a disappointment. But that was thrilling compared to *this.* Maybe it's just you, Joanna. Maybe you're just a bore."

"Hey, in another life, I robbed a bank."

She stared at me. Then we both started to laugh.

"Anyway," I said, "if I'm so boring, why do you keep coming back?"

"It's not like you give me a choice."

"What does that mean?"

She waved the question away. "If I were alive, I'd sleep as little as possible. I'd stay awake until I dropped. I'd want to do everything and see everything. I wouldn't waste a minute." She moved closer to me. "We could try again."

"Try again?"

"I want to be alive again. You want that for me, don't you?" Her eyes were fixed on me, her voice urgent and hungry.

"Of course. But..." Did she want us to go back to our life in Venice? She'd just said it had been a disappointment, but it hadn't been so bad. In some ways it had been great. Back to Venice. Why not? I would never have to go on another audition. I would never be humiliated by Martin again. A surge of emotion went through me—hope, or despair? "I don't want to go back to the draft board," I said. "I can't go through that again."

"That's not what I have in mind." She smiled mysteriously.

"What then?"

"You'll see. Come on, Joanna. It's got to be better than this." There was that spark of daring in her eye. I felt myself give way.

"Okay," I said. "You win."

Her laughter echoed strangely in my ears. She moved forward so that our noses almost touched, her blue-gray eyes gazing ocean-deep and resolute into mine until I thought I would never surface.

Her lips, ice cold, touched mine. I closed my eyes.

When I opened them, I was standing in the hall at the high school, scanning the sheet of paper taped to the auditorium door. My name wasn't on it. I stared at the words as if I were reading them wrong. *Cynthia Foster: Joan.*

Of course Cynthia had got the part. Of course I hadn't. How had I even dared to think I might?

"I really thought you were going to get the part."

I turned. Cyn was smiling at me. Pretty, popular Cynthia Foster with her long blonde hair. "You did?" I asked.

She shrugged. "I hope this play won't make me too busy for the debate team."

I was still sinking, sinking into a morass of disappointment.

"Hey, want to come over after school?" Cyn asked. "I could use some help with this damn play."

We fell into being best friends as if it had never been otherwise.

Chapter Twenty-three:
Whatever Gets You Through the Night
(January 1976)

I hurried out of the late-afternoon cold into the little bar. Cyn had said Chauncy's, near Lincoln Center, was one of the places the cast and crew of *Hope Springs Eternal* liked to go after work. Apparently she still felt comfortable going there now.

I pulled off my gloves and stuffed them into my coat pocket. Predictably, Cyn wasn't here yet, though she lived a short walk from the bar. Aside from the bartender, a broad-shouldered guy with curly dark hair, there were a handful of people drinking and smoking in the brown leather booths. A somber, dark-haired man in jeans and a pullover sweater was nursing a beer and reading a newspaper in a booth near the front of the place. He looked familiar. Oh, great—this was Martin Yates, Cyn's married lover.

I'd only seen a handful of episodes of *Hope Springs Eternal*, since it aired when I was at work, and anyway I'd never been a fan of daytime dramas. ("Don't you dare judge me," Cyn had said. "Being on a soap opera is fucking hard work! Besides, it's a paycheck." I hadn't bothered to bring up the fact that, with her trust fund, she hadn't needed the money.) From what I'd seen, Yates wasn't a bad actor. He and Cyn had, fittingly enough, played adulterous lovers, until Cyn's character took a header down a flight of stairs, and the writers killed her off.

Well, this was awkward. I didn't relish having to talk to the guy before Cyn got here. I was tempted to pretend I hadn't noticed him, but he looked up, and his gaze latched onto me. He waved me over.

"Joanna?" he asked, and I nodded. He smiled and held out his hand for me to shake. "I'm Martin. I guess Cynthia's running late." His hand felt very warm. "Can I buy you a drink?"

"I'm already up. I'll just get something at the bar." I took off my coat and left it in the booth. I hoped that by the time I returned, Cyn would have arrived.

No such luck. I sat across from Martin with my mug of beer. He smiled at me, but neither of us seemed to know what to say. Just great.

"So, you're a schoolteacher?" Martin asked.

"Junior High. I teach English and drama in Washington Heights."

"And you've been Cynthia's best friend since high school."

I nodded, though I was a little surprised she'd told him that.

"She talks about you a lot," he said. I had the feeling he wanted me to like him. Why would he care? Middle-aged soap opera actor screwing around on his wife. How sleazy. At least he wasn't the only guy Cyn was currently involved with. She usually preferred musicians to actors—especially after she'd broken up with Ian, an alcoholic actor she'd met in a production of *King Lear* (she'd played Goneril, he'd played the Fool).

I wracked my brain for something to talk about. Cyn hadn't told me much about Martin except that he was kind of old, but good in bed. I ran my hand over the cracked leather of the booth. "So do you like acting in a soap opera?"

He barked out a laugh and sipped his beer. "Now there's a question. Depends which day of the week you ask me."

The door opened, and Cyn strode toward us, pale blue knit hat crammed over her long blonde hair. "Sorry I'm late!" She grinned at me and briefly leaned down to hug me—she was icy cold—then gave Martin a quick kiss on the lips and took a swig of his beer. "So you've already met. Good." She shivered. "Man, it's fucking freezing out."

"Want a whiskey?" Martin asked.

She pondered. "Irish coffee would be better."

He headed for the bar.

I thought Cyn would want to sit next to Martin, but she said, "Scoot over, Jo," pulled off her hat and leather coat, dumped them next to me, then slid into my side of the booth. She wore a sleek red turtleneck and black trousers, which made me feel dowdy in my sensible schoolteacher outfit of rust sweater and tan skirt. She glanced over at Martin at the bar. "So, what do you think?"

I shrugged. "He's good-looking, I guess."

"You guess! Well, he looks better out of his clothes."

"Cyn!" I said, and she laughed.

"So when am I going to meet the guy you're seeing?" she asked.

"Oh, I don't know. We've been so busy."

She shook her head with an injured air. "I'm busy too, but I still make time for you!"

I didn't want Cyn to meet Joel, for fear she'd sabotage our relationship like she had with my college boyfriends Lenny and Neil. Not that I was sure Joel was the guy for me, though he was earnest and good-hearted. He wasn't very political, but he was a Democrat. He wanted to get married and have kids sooner rather than later. He seemed the exact opposite of every guy Cyn had ever been involved with. Sometimes I envied her adventures, though more in the abstract than any of the actual guys.

Martin returned and placed a steaming cup of Irish coffee before Cyn. "Joanna won't let me meet her boyfriend," she sulked.

"Oh, please," I said. "I never said that."

"What's his name again?"

"Joel," I said.

She rolled her eyes. "Joel and Jo—isn't that sweet?"

"Shut up."

"So what does your boyfriend do, Joanna?" Martin asked.

"He teaches science at the same school as me."

"A teacher," Cyn said. "Just like your dad." She pretended to yawn.

"Teaching is a noble profession," Martin said. "I'm grateful to my kids' teachers. We're entrusting them with the future of the country."

His whole expression changed when he spoke of his children—it softened, suffused with warmth. Had Cyn mentioned that the guy had kids? It made his philandering seem even sleazier, but at the same time, there was something appealing about him just now. Stop that, I thought.

"So how's that bitch Clarissa?" Cyn asked.

"Now, now," Martin said.

"And is Babette still babbling on about her wedding?" She turned to me. "Babette plays Marty's wife. They used to fool around, but now she's engaged to this super-straight guy who looks like an insurance salesman."

Martin ducked his head. "Jesus, Cynthia."

"Who is Jo gonna tell? It's not as if she knows your wife."

He was visibly squirming. I almost felt sorry for him.

Cyn glanced around the bar. "I thought I might run into someone else from the company here. I'd just as soon not. Especially that bitch Clarissa."

"You know she doesn't come here," Martin said.

"Or Amy Gundersen. She has the hots for you, you know." She said it as if this Amy person was beneath contempt.

Martin shrugged. "She's a nice girl."

"You would think so." She sipped her Irish coffee. "So my agent thinks I'm a shoo-in for that hair commercial."

"Of course you are," Martin said.

Cyn tossed her hair on cue. "And I'm auditioning next week for some new play my agent says is going to be a big deal."

"That's great," I said. Though I enjoyed teaching, I'd never stopped envying Cyn her acting career. Whenever I saw her act, though, I felt like she was playing herself, not disappearing into a character. Maybe that was all she needed to do, with her charisma. When she was on the stage or on screen, you couldn't take your eyes off her.

"Tim makes fun of me for trying out for commercials," Cyn said.

I was surprised she would mention the other guy she was seeing in front of Martin, but he seemed unfazed. She had told me Tim was a skinny, pale guitarist and poet who'd written a song about her.

"You should come with me the next time Tim's band plays at CBGB's, Jo," Cyn said. "It's a wild scene, all these artists and musicians and writers. You'd love it."

"What, I'm not invited?" Martin asked with a wry smile.

"Sorry, Marty, it's just not your scene," Cyn said, not unkindly.

"I'm over the hill, that's what you're telling me?"

There was something about the way he said it that made me blurt out, "Are you Jewish, Marty?"

He gaped at me, then laughed. "On my mother's side. Takes one to know one, I guess." Apparently Cyn had told him I was Jewish. What else had she told him? "My old man was Irish Catholic."

"Quite a combination," I said.

"Joanna, Tim played me this record by a singer named Patti Smith," Cyn said, as if neither of us had spoken. "She does a version of 'Hey Joe' that's all about Patty Hearst. You know…" She took a sip of Irish coffee, then began to serenade me, "Hey Joe, where you goin' with that gun in your hand?'"

I was about to say that "Hey Joe" (at least the Hendrix version) was such a misogynist song, I was curious to hear a woman singing it—but Martin waved his newspaper at us and said, "What's a day without a Patty Hearst reference? A day without sunshine."

I laughed, and he looked gratified.

"I sort of enjoyed the SLA," Cyn said loftily. "They had style."

"They were a bunch of crazies," Martin said. "Do you think Squeaky Fromme had style, too?"

Cyn stuck her tongue out at him.

"The SLA lost me early on, when they shot that black school superintendent," I said.

"I don't remember that," Cyn said. "Was Patty involved?"

I shook my head. "It was before they kidnapped her."

"Oh."

Cyn had been against the war, like me, but she'd been too involved with theater in college to do more than go to a few rallies and marches. When she'd heard the cops were tear-gassing protesters, she stayed away because she said she couldn't risk messing up her voice. She was totally uninterested in my political involvements of the past few years—The League for Peace and Justice and the women's movement. (When I'd been involved in a consciousness-raising group, she'd said, "What could be more boring than listening to a bunch of women moaning about housework and husbands?")

Martin polished off his beer. "Either of you ladies need anything?" We shook our heads, and he headed back to the bar.

Cyn watched him go, then grinned at me. "So, you like him, don't you?" she whispered.

"Do *you*?"

"What do you mean?"

"The way you kept needling him! He looked pretty uncomfortable."

She looked triumphant. "Ah, you *do* like him!"

I didn't want to. It would be unfeminist of me to like a man like him. "Why, do you want my blessing or something? You're not serious about him, are you? He's married, and anyway you're seeing Tim too."

She laughed. "You're getting the totally wrong idea. I was thinking you might like to…" She turned and looked at Martin at the bar. "Have you ever participated in a *ménage à trois?*"

It took a moment to sink in. "Jesus, Cyn," I whispered furiously, "tell me this isn't what I think it is."

She smirked. "What do you think it is?"

I glanced over at Martin. He was chatting with the bartender. "That I'm here so he can get a look at me! Cheating on his wife with you isn't enough—he's got to have two women at once?"

She shrugged. "Oh, it's a fantasy of his. You know, because he's middle-aged and all, and wants to live it up while he still can. But I thought it might be fun."

"And you told him I'd be the ideal candidate?"

"Jo! I wouldn't do that without asking you first."

I wasn't sure I believed her. "So I'm here to get a look at *him?*"

"You don't think he's sexy? I thought you'd like him."

"Even if I did, I'm already seeing someone, remember?"

She grinned brattily. "So what? I won't tell on you."

Martin returned with another beer. I flushed as he slid into the booth. *Had* Cyn suggested me for some kind of three-way? Jesus. He looked from Cyn to me and back again. "Everything okay?" he asked with a slow smile, and I held my breath.

"Everything's fine," Cyn said. "I'm off to the john." She headed for the back of the bar, leaving me alone with Mr. Middle-aged. To my dismay, I found myself moved by Martin's physical presence, his fingers curled around the beer mug, his strong chest and upper arms beneath his sweater. I pictured myself in bed with him, and the thought made me throb between the legs. *Stop* it. Then I imagined Cyn in the bed—the two of them locked together, me a third wheel watching their fun, or, worse, Cyn telling me what to do, Cyn touching and kissing me for Martin's delectation, Cyn running the show. No.

Martin was gazing at me with frank interest. "You sure nothing's wrong?"

"Why do you ask?"

"You had quite an intense look on your face just now."

I started to laugh and shook my head. This situation was too ridiculous.

He smiled quizzically. "You're not at all what I'd expected."

"Why? What did Cyn say about me?"

"Oh, she has nothing but great things to say about you. It's just, the two of you are so different."

"I know, I know," I said wearily.

"It isn't a bad thing," he hastened to say.

I sipped my beer. "Isn't it?"

"I was wondering…" He looked down at the table, then at me again. "I was wondering if I could call you sometime."

To set up the three-way? But wouldn't Cyn take care of that? Damn her. "Why?"

The question seemed to take him aback. "We could meet for a drink someplace. Talk."

"Without Cyn?" Well, this was a first.

"Believe me, she wouldn't mind." His lips twisted with what looked like shame. "It's not as if she and I have anything deep and meaningful going on. Her dance card's pretty full."

"And yours isn't?" I sounded aloof, but I couldn't think straight. On the radio at the counter, "That's the Way (I Like It)" leered propulsively with its horns and its *uh huh, uh huh*s. I glanced over to see if Cyn was coming back yet.

Martin let out a sigh. "Look, if I'm offending you, feel free to forget it. But I think you're beautiful, and I'd like to get to know you, Joanna."

He looked so beautiful sitting across the table, dark-eyed, dark-haired (Jewish, Irish), his face all serious planes and shadows, his hands cradling the beer mug.

"I have a boyfriend," I said faintly.

"I know." He kept looking at me with that steady gaze. All at once I didn't want him to stop. Cyn would be back any minute. I hunted in my purse for a pen and scrawled my number on a napkin, then pushed it toward him. He reached for it, and his hand touched mine. Tentatively we smiled at each other across the table.

He pocketed the napkin as Cyn returned. She eyed us. "What'd I miss?"

"Not a thing," I said. Martin sipped his beer imperturbably.

Cyn sat beside me. She wasn't smiling. Could she sense what had happened? She couldn't expect fidelity from a married man, and anyway she'd screwed two of my boyfriends. This was only fair. No three-way. Something for me, for once. I didn't think it was okay to fool around with a married man, but he was already cheating on his wife. What would it matter?

"So when will you find out if you've got the shampoo ad?" Martin asked.

Cyn absently wound a lock of her hair around her finger. "Not sure."

Her long blonde hair. She had always kept it long, ever since I'd known her. Even when she'd played Joan of Arc. But that wasn't right, was it?

What wasn't right? Something about her hair. Something about her playing Joan of Arc. Something about me…playing Joan of Arc.

I glanced over at the bartender. His name, I suddenly remembered, was Jim. He had served me drinks many times. With Martin. With Babette and Susan.

The room spun, then snapped into focus.

"Jo, are you okay?" Cyn asked.

Martin's poker face slipped then, as if I were suffering from an attack of conscience and it was all his fault. I started to laugh. "Oh, Marty," I said. "You want me now, because I have a boyfriend? Now it can be casual, right?"

He looked at me like I was nuts, which was understandable.

"What are you talking about?" Cyn asked. "What the fuck is going on?"

"What's going on? You stole my life." I grabbed her arm. It felt slight and breakable beneath my fingers. "Listen, I'm glad you're alive. I'm so glad. I wish you could stay that way, but I'm beginning to think it's either you or me."

Her eyes filled with horror and confusion. "Let go of me!" she yelled and yanked her arm away.

Then I was sitting on the bed in my apartment, with Cyn—her short-haired ghost in jeans and an Argyle sweater—seated beside me. She was looking around the room as if she were having trouble situating herself. Then she glared at me. "Why did you have to ruin everything?" she asked. "I hadn't even finished my Irish coffee. I thought we were having fun."

"Maybe *you* were having fun. You tricked me. I thought we were going back to Venice. But you had to do it, didn't you? You had to find a way to have sex with Marty."

She smirked. "He wasn't much. You're not missing anything. Anyway, how dare you be angry with me? You just basically admitted that you'd rather see me dead. And now I am, again! You got your wish."

I got to my feet. "That's not what I said. I said it was either you or me. Am I wrong? You got the part of Joan. You got the part of Jean Christopher. My god, you even went out with my ex-boyfriend Ian. Nice touch, by the way, that you met him playing Goneril—no one would ever buy you as Cordelia. And you lived in this apartment! You had to have every little bit of my life."

"I did a better job with it than you ever could."

I hauled off and slapped her. My hand connected with her cheek with the cracking sound of thin ice. The air shivered and was still. My fingers burned with cold.

Cyn raised her hand to her cheek, though I was pretty sure she hadn't felt a thing. "Who do you think you are, a character from that lousy soap opera?"

"You took my job at that lousy soap opera!" This did remind me of a confrontation from *Hope Springs Eternal*. At any rate, Cyn and I were playing our parts as scripted, the way we always did. I had never been more weary of the dance we kept doing, and my part in it.

"I tried to arrange it so you could sleep with that actor," Cyn countered.

"You just wanted to get me into bed, and you threw in Marty to hide that fact. Admit it!"

She wouldn't look at me.

"I bet the three-way wasn't even his idea. God, you are so controlling! Now I remember why I had to leave you."

She stared up at me then. "How dare you say that to me?"

"I'm sorry, but it's true. You always have to have everything of mine—or, if it's something you don't want, you don't want me to want it either. Nothing is ever enough for you!"

Cyn got to her feet and faced me. "Stop blaming me for everything! It's not my fault you gave up acting when I got the part of Joan. It's not my fault you got together with that boring science teacher."

"Joel…" I tried to remember him. What was his last name? I remembered the taste of his mother's pot roast, redolent of carrots and onion. But Joel was already fading. I wondered if in this life he was teaching in Washington Heights, and if he was dating one of the other teachers. He had wanted to marry me. In my other lives, I'd had people—Jeremy, Cyn, Joel—who loved me, and I'd loved them. Even Martin had wanted school-teacher Joanna, and had dared to act on it, apparently because I was in a relationship, which was rather silly and sad, but predictable. He had called me beautiful. He hadn't returned my call tonight. Tonight? Yes, it was still the same night.

"Jo and Joel," Cyn sneered. "What a joke. As if I ever would have picked someone like that for you."

And here I was again, stuck with a vengeful ghost who I was pretty sure loved and hated me in equal measure—and the feeling was mutual. But it wasn't Cyn's fault that I'd spent the end of last year and the beginning of this one in a morass of despair.

"You're right," I said, and she blinked in surprise. "My choices in that life weren't your fault. Or in this life either, for that matter."

"We could go back again," Cyn said. "You can do things differently. You can still be an actress. You can still have it off with that actor dude, though why you'd want to is beyond me."

As of this moment, Cyn didn't have my life. I did. That was something. Maybe it wasn't too late for me to do something about it.

"We're not going back," I said. "It's time for me to run the show."

She laughed derisively. "I'll believe that when I see it."

Chapter Twenty-four:
Someone Saved My Life Tonight
(January 1976)

"Who are you calling?" Cyn asked as I sat on the bed and reached for the phone early one evening. Then I picked up the envelope from the bedside table. "You're calling him again? I thought you learned your lesson."

It had been a week since I'd phoned Martin. Since then I'd talked to my agent and managed to set up an audition for next week (for a bit part in an episode of a cop show), and I'd forced myself to leave the apartment every day—though Cyn stuck to me like glue wherever I went.

"I just want to know what's going on with him," I said. That wasn't the whole truth, though I was still curious about Martin's black eye, and why Amy's part was still being played by the dreadful Annabel Becker.

Cyn sat beside me on the bed. "He doesn't care about you."

I paused with my hand on the receiver, still in its cradle. "That may be." I remembered what Martin had said in that other version of my life: *I think you're beautiful, and I'd like to get to know you.* A come-on, sure—but his words had stuck with me. In this life he'd asked me more than once what was going on with me. What would have happened if I'd told him the truth? Maybe it was time I found out. I turned my back on Cyn and lifted the receiver.

"He's just going to disappoint you again," she said. "I'm your only real friend."

"So you always like to remind me." Even if it were true, a life shared with Cyn's ghost was no life at all. I needed a living friend. Maybe it was Susan I should be calling—but in spite of everything, Martin knew me better than anyone besides Cyn. Or, at least, he had tried to know me.

I dialed the number. After two rings, it picked up. "Hello?" A woman's voice, brusque and unwelcoming. I was tempted to hang up.

"Gloria?" I asked.

There was a pause. "Who is this?"

"It's Joanna Bergman." Silence on the other end of the line. "Gloria? Are you there?"

"I'm here, Joanna." There was a flatness to her voice that was completely different from her lively warmth at the party at the Brand.

"How are you?" I asked, though that was clearly a stupid question.

Another pause. "I'm not so great. How are you?"

"I'm…" I turned and looked at Cyn, her eyes lit with voracious interest. "I'm not so great either."

"That's right, you lost your job." She didn't sound particularly sorry about that.

"Is Marty there?" I almost couldn't get the words out.

"Marty doesn't live here anymore." She gave a laugh. "That's a movie, isn't it?"

"Alice," I said.

"What?"

"*Alice Doesn't Live Here Anymore*." I loved that movie. I couldn't believe we were talking about a movie at a time like this.

"I tried to call you the other day," Gloria said, "but your line was busy."

"You did?" That couldn't be good. "How come?"

"You haven't talked to Marty?" She sounded skeptical.

I wished there were a way I could get off the phone gracefully, but on the other hand, I was dying to know what was going on. "I called him last week, but he never got back to me."

"Well, I threw him out." She uttered the words with gusto.

"What happened?"

"What do you think happened? I found out he was cheating on me with this chick from the show. Amy Gundersen."

Hearing it confirmed felt like a punch in the stomach. "Are you sure?"

"He admitted it. She wasn't the first, either. Did you know about him and Babette?" She barreled on before I could reply. "Of course you did. Everyone knew but me, right? And there were other women besides! He actually seemed to think it would make me feel better to know that he slept with Heather O'Connor while he was having the affair with Babette."

"Heather O'Connor?" The girl who'd shared Clarissa's dressing room before me. I remembered Heather swinging her hair from side to side in slow motion in her shampoo commercial. Martin had never had a nice word to say about her.

"And what about you, Joanna?"

"What about me?" I asked faintly.

"Did you sleep with him too?" She uttered the words calmly, without melodrama.

"No." In that moment at least, I was glad I hadn't.

"Because I happened to see a couple of love scenes between the two of you, and they seemed awfully passionate."

"That was acting, Gloria." I told myself I was only saying that for Gloria's sake, but on the other hand, if it hadn't been just acting, surely Martin would have slept with me.

"So nothing ever happened between the two of you?"

Oh, it hurt so much that he had slept with Babette and Amy and even Heather O'Connor, and not me. But it was far worse for Gloria. "We kissed a few times. I would have done more, but he wasn't interested. For what it's worth, I'm sorry."

"You didn't sleep with him?" Gloria asked. "You wanted to, but he wouldn't?"

"That's about it."

"Babette said she thought something had gone on between you and Marty."

I suppressed a groan. "Did you call Babette?"

"She kept saying, 'I'm getting married, all that is behind me.' As if that absolved her of everything! She didn't seem to know about Heather O'Connor. That seemed to really surprise her." She gave a malicious laugh.

"So you said you threw Marty out. Where is he staying?"

"So you can get another crack at him?"

"Gloria—"

"Enough." All at once she sounded very tired. "He's staying with David Halpren. Do what you want." She hung up on me.

I hung up the phone. "My god."

"You ratted him out to his wife!" Cyn sounded scandalized. "That's cold, Jo."

"Jesus, I need a drink." My hands were shaking. "I've got to talk to Marty."

A corner of Cyn's mouth crooked upward in disdain. "You think things have changed? That because his wife threw him out, he's gonna give you what you want?"

"It's not about that right now."

"You're saying you'd kick him out of bed?"

"I'm saying he's my friend." Before I could stop myself, I phoned David.

"Joanna! How nice to hear your voice," he said. "You've been much missed."

I wasn't sure I believed that, but it was a pleasure to hear David's bland, sonorous voice. "Thanks. How are you?"

"Fine, fine! I've landed a role in an off-Broadway production, a comedy by a very talented young playwright..." He babbled on enthusiastically, while I listened with half an ear.

Finally I said, "So I hear Marty is staying with you."

There was a pause. "Yes, he's going through rather a rough patch at the moment."

"Is he there, by any chance?"

"I'm afraid not. He's not working tomorrow, so he's almost certainly at Chauncy's. He'll probably pour himself back into the apartment a few hours from now."

"That bad?"

"Bad enough. Do you want me to tell him you called?"

And end up waiting by the phone again? "Maybe I'll go see if I can find him at Chauncy's."

"I'm not sure I'd recommend it. These days he's less than charming when he's had a few."

∞

The entire brisk walk to Chauncy's in the bitter evening air, Cyn kept after me: "This is a bad idea. You should go to some other bar, meet some new people."

My breath came out in frosty gusts. I said nothing, though I didn't understand why Cyn didn't want me to go to Chauncy's all of a sudden. I fizzed with adrenaline. Maybe Martin wouldn't be there, but others from *Hope Springs Eternal* might be.

"Are you listening to me, Joanna? Those people aren't your friends. Especially not *him*."

"Shut up," I muttered as we reached the door. Cyn was silent then, and I went inside.

Chauncy's was half-full. Jim was tending bar, and Terry the stage manager was sitting at a booth near the door with a couple of the cameramen. On the radio on the bar top, a woman wailed over a wailing guitar. And there, at the bar, sat Martin with a mug of beer. A shock of gladness and fear went through me.

Jim poured Martin a shot of whiskey, and he threw it back. Then Jim said something, and Martin laughed. I headed for the bar, but Terry stopped me. "Look who's here!" he said. "How are you, Joanna?"

As I exchanged pleasantries with Terry and the cameramen, Martin turned, and his smile faded at the sight of me. Slowly I approached him. He looked haggard and sallow.

"Hi, Marty," I said.

He regarded me warily. "You women don't waste any time," he said and barked out a laugh.

"Good to see you, Jo!" Jim said, looking uneasy. He turned up the radio, and "Don't Go Breaking My Heart" lilted through the bar.

"Gloria call you too?" Martin asked hoarsely, then gulped some beer. "You women work fast, all right—bunch of vultures." He started to cough dryly. I couldn't remember him ever having had so much as a cold. *Too mean to get sick, my wife always says.*

"I was sorry to hear about you and Gloria," I said softly.

"Sure you were, sure you were." A grimace of a grin spread over his face. "Hey, I know why you're here."

"What are you talking about?"

Jim slunk off to polish a glass.

"You want to join the chorus, lecture me about my crimes against womankind. Tell me how I should've resisted every female who ever threw herself at me. Excuse me if I'm not made of stone. Little did I know I was better off when I was a pimply teenager no girl would look at twice. Women! Jesus Christ, all I ever wanted was to keep everybody happy."

"You're kidding, right?" I asked, though I found it hard to take a breath. "I know you're going through a rough time, but this male chauvinist martyr routine doesn't become you."

"Here we go," he said, more loudly. "Go ahead, tell me what a selfish bastard I am. What, you've got nothing to say? Then what do you want from me, Jo?"

"Excuse me for thinking you might need a friend right now," I said, fighting to keep my voice from shaking. "You were the one who was so big on our friendship, right? Well, never mind. I won't make that mistake again."

His expression, a smug, arrogant mask, didn't change. I wasn't going to let him see me burst into furious tears. I turned and made for the door, past Terry and the cameramen, who were watching with looks of concern. Only when I'd yanked open the door did I hear Martin say, "Jo, wait." Or maybe I'd imagined it. I hurried out into the cold.

"Come on," Cyn said. "Let's go home."

"Fine. Just don't say I told you so."

I'd only taken a few steps before the door swung open and Martin was at my side. "Joanna, wait!" he said. When I kept walking, he grabbed my arm.

"Let go of me!" I yelled, and he did. I couldn't look at him; I was still on the verge of tears. I took a deep breath and tried to compose myself. Finally I looked up. "What?" I demanded.

"I'm sorry." The mask was gone, replaced by that shamefaced look I knew so well. "I had no right to talk to you that way."

"No, you didn't."

"It's just, Babette really let me have it after Gloria called her. And then you showed up, and I thought—"

"That I wanted to join the chorus? I tried to call you, and Gloria told me she'd kicked you out. I was worried about you."

"Thanks." He smiled wanly, then hugged himself with a shiver. "Jesus, it's cold. I'd offer to buy you a drink, but I don't really want to go back in there."

I studied his face; he looked exhausted. "I don't think you need another drink. How many have you had?"

He shrugged. "Not as many as I was letting on."

"Have you had anything to eat?"

He shook his head. For a moment I thought he was going to start to cry. "This is the worst time of day for me, when I should be home with my family. Oh Jo, I really screwed up."

I put my hand on his shoulder. "Come on, let's get something to eat."

∞

"I'm sorry I never called you back," Martin said, pouring soy sauce on his rice. "The night you called, everything was hitting the fan. Amy kept calling the house. It was a disaster."

We were at a little Chinese place near the studio. It was full of people gabbing and smoking and eating. Martin sat facing the street and kept looking uneasily toward the windows.

I crunched into a greasy egg roll. It was wonderful to eat Chinese food with a living person for a dinner companion, even though Martin looked miserable, and Cyn loitered by our table as if hoping to be invited to sit down.

"I saw that someone else has been playing Amy's part on the show," I said. "What happened?"

"What happened? Amy turned out to be freaking insane. One day I'm leaving the studio, and this skinny kid's waiting for me. 'Are you Martin Yates?' he asks. I say yeah, and *pow!*" He mimed a right hook. "He punches me in the eye! Then he says, 'Stay away from Amy!' And he ran off."

"Was Amy there?"

He shook his head. "So I've got this massive black eye I have to explain to my wife. Then Amy starts phoning my house and babbling about how I shot the fucking seagull."

"What?"

"You know, the line from *The Seagull?* She calls and tells Gloria, 'Tell Marty he shot the seagull. Tell him Nina called. Tell him he shot the seagull, just to pass the time.'"

"Jesus Christ."

"By that point, I was all out of explanations." He rolled his eyes grimly, then picked up a sliver of beef with his chopsticks and ate it.

"Marty, I should tell you—Gloria asked about you and me."

He abruptly stopped chewing, then resumed and swallowed. "She kept asking me the same thing. What did you tell her?"

I lowered my voice. "That we'd kissed a few times. I said I would've gone farther, but you said no. I didn't want her torturing herself imagining stuff that didn't even happen."

"I'm glad you told her, Joanna. I'm sorry if it was hard on you." His eyes were grave and kind.

I busied myself attempting to eat chow mein with my chopsticks. Half the noodles fell back onto my plate. "So, you and Amy?" I said finally.

"Me and Amy." He heaved a sigh. "At first she came on all casual, like the only thing she cared about was acting. Then she turned possessive. She wanted to know exactly what I had done with you and Babette and every female in the cast, and she'd cry and say she couldn't stand the thought of me going home to my wife. So I called it quits, and all hell broke loose." He popped a spear of broccoli into his mouth.

"I could say it served you right, but that would be kind of hypocritical of me."

He shook his head. "It did serve me right. I had no business getting mixed up with her. Anyway, she completely went to pieces. She kept going up on her lines and crying in her dressing room and following me around."

"So they fired her?"

"She quit, with no notice whatsoever. They had to get a girl to fill in at the eleventh hour."

"I saw. She's terrible."

"They contacted another girl who'd auditioned for the role before, but she wasn't available. She finally started taping this week. She's good."

"Don't sleep with this one, Marty."

He looked stunned—then he burst out laughing, which triggered a coughing fit. He drank some water, and finally it subsided. He looked worn out and miserable. "Believe it or not, kid, a new conquest is the last thing on my mind." He spoke softly but deliberately. "I'm a failure, Joanna. I failed my wife, and I failed my kids. I'm a liar and a cheat. I'm a lousy excuse for a human being. I don't know why you'd even want to be in the same room with me."

Even though a lot of what he said was true, it only made me wish I could say something that would make everything all right. "Sure, you've made a lot of mistakes, but I still consider you my friend, Marty."

"I've tried to be," he said. He looked desperately sad, but Cyn looked even worse, staring at me as if she were on the edge of starvation. I wished she would just go away, and in spite of everything that had happened, I hated myself for that wish.

Then Martin said, "Listen, enough about me and my problems. How've you been?"

It was my cue, unexpected as it was. My mouth opened, and the words tumbled out. "Marty, I really need to tell you something."

He looked taken aback. "Jo, if this is about you and me…"

I shook my head. "No, it has nothing to do with that. It's the stuff I couldn't tell you about before. Maybe you don't remember."

"You said it was a problem with an old friend," he said.

Cyn shook her head frantically at me. I ignored her. "I can't believe you remember that," I told him.

Martin gazed at me steadily, the way he used to—that wonderful listening gaze. "I know something's been going on with you. I've known that for a long time. I'd like to help if I can."

"Thanks. Although, maybe I shouldn't lay this on you now?"

"Honestly I'd welcome the distraction."

Cyn spoke urgently in my ear. "What are you doing? There could be pigs in here."

I looked around the restaurant at the gray-haired, mustached guy shoveling chow mein, the blonde girl spooning up soup, and the middle-aged black couple holding hands across the table. It seemed unlikely that any of them were Feds with tape recorders stashed beneath their tables, but Cyn did have a point. "It's a long story," I said. "I'd just as soon not tell you here. Would you come to my place after dinner?" I hoped it wouldn't sound like a come-on.

He shrugged. "I'm in no hurry to bunk down for the night on Halpren's couch. He's probably happy to have the place to himself."

I sipped jasmine tea from its tiny cup. I had lost my appetite. Cyn was racketing in my ear: "You wouldn't really tell him, would you? Think of how he'd look at you."

∞

After dinner I walked back to my apartment between the two of them—Martin coughing from time to time, Cyn loping along in worn jeans, hands thrust into the pockets of her peacoat, short hair gleaming in the streetlights. "You can't tell him," she said. "They'll clap you in a loony bin. Is that what you want?"

"You're awfully quiet," Martin said. "This must be some story."

"It is," I said.

"You don't have to tell me if you don't want to."

"You don't have to tell him," Cyn implored.

"I want to," I said.

∞

When we got to my place, I made Martin a cup of Lipton's tea with honey and a slug of whiskey for his cough. I poured myself a little whiskey to steady my nerves. "This is hard," I said when we were sitting on the sofa. "I don't know where to start."

Cyn paced back and forth across the living room floor.

"Start anywhere," Martin said.

"Okay." My heart was pounding, and my hands were cold and clammy. I took a sip of whiskey and set the glass on the table. "When I was in college, at the School of New York, my best friend and I were obsessed with ending the war."

He nodded. "What year was this?"

"1971. Cynthia Foster was my best friend." It felt monumental, saying her name aloud. It felt like an explosion ought to burst at our feet. Cyn stood there hugging herself as if she were freezing. *Don't tell don't tell don't tell*, the terrified voice said, and I could no longer tell if it was Cyn's voice or my own. "We both thought the revolution was coming. After all, it was happening all over the world! Cyn and I, and these two guys we knew, decided we had to do something to oppose the war—something more than just going to endless demonstrations. Obviously we weren't the only ones who felt that way. We wanted to, you know, bring the war home."

Martin gave a laugh. "What did you do, blow something up?" Then his eyebrows lifted. "Go on."

"We decided to target a draft board near campus. Cyn wanted me to go with her, and I agreed. The guys were going to call it in, so the street could be cleared and no one would be hurt." Saying the words aloud to someone who hadn't been there made it sound like fiction, not something that had actually happened to us. No, not something that had happened to us—something we had made happen.

The incredulous look in Martin's eye reminded me of my dad about to give me a lecture. "But that was no guarantee. Someone could've been hurt. *You* could've been hurt, or killed. You could have been arrested."

"I got the flu at the last minute, and I was overjoyed, because it meant I could get out of it."

He nodded emphatically. "You were using your head. And what about those guys, sending the women to do the dirty work while they stayed out of harm's way and made a phone call?"

"The guys wanted to place the bomb. Cyn talked them into our going. Like the women in *The Battle of Algiers*. You know, the film by Pontecorvo."

"*The Battle of Algiers?*" he spluttered. "Stupid, irresponsible college kids. This wasn't a movie, Jo!"

"I know," I whispered. "Anyway, I didn't go. I thought Cyn might call it off, but she went anyway." I looked over at where Cyn had been standing. She had disappeared. I could still feel her fear. "The bomb exploded while she was placing it under a mailbox. She was alone. She died alone. No one else was hurt. Some windows shattered, and the mailbox..." The full weight of all the times I'd experienced Cyn's death threatened to overwhelm me. I drank down the rest of the whiskey. "The police questioned me, but I said I had nothing to do with it. For some reason, they believed me. Nobody was charged."

Martin was silent. The outraged look on his face was gone. He just looked sad. "What a terrible thing," he said at last. "Your friend was so young. What a senseless waste. But Jo, that was five years ago. You talk as if it just happened."

This was the point where I ought to stop. I took a deep breath and forged on. "Because it's happened to me over and over again. Every time it's different."

He scrutinized me. "You mean you keep replaying it in your mind, imagining how you could have done things differently?"

"No. I mean I've been living it over and over, and every time it's different. One time I died at the draft board with Cyn. Another time I watched her die, and then I ended up in prison. Another time..."

The look on his face stopped me cold.

"What are you saying, Jo? That you're having hallucinations or something?"

"I think it's real, Marty. I know how this sounds. But I went to the library and checked out details of the stuff that happened. I know about cities and places I've never been to in this life. Cyn makes it happen. Or no, that's not quite right. She and I make it happen together, somehow."

"Cyn *makes* it happen?"

I wanted to take it all back. "You think I'm crazier than Amy Gundersen."

"What do you expect me to say, Jo?"

The air felt cold in my lungs. My last hope—daring to tell someone, being heard and understood—was falling away.

Martin reached out and gave my hand a squeeze. "Don't clam up on me now. Tell me all of it."

So I did—or nearly. I didn't tell him Jeremy's name or Alex's. But I told him about Cyn haunting me. I told him about Brightdale. I told him about robbing a bank. Somewhere in the midst of it, Martin stopped looking at me as if I were nuts. He was captivated.

"Are you a lesbian, Jo?" he asked when I told him about living with Cyn in Venice.

"I thought I was, in that version of my life. I guess I must be bisexual." I felt my face flush. "*You* and Cyn were lovers in another version."

"What?" he exclaimed, with a hilarious look.

"She had my part on *Hope Springs Eternal.* I think you had an affair with her instead of Amy."

"Huh. Well, if these are hallucinations, they're the most entertaining hallucinations I've ever heard."

I considered telling him about the *ménage à trois* idea, and how he'd asked for my phone number when Cyn left the table. Somehow it seemed wrong to get into that now, when he was dealing with the breakup of his marriage. "At first it was beyond my control, getting shunted off into these other versions of my life. Now I seem to have some control over it. But the thing is, Cyn's been with me all the time since I left the company, and I don't want her to be. It's like being dead too, Marty. It's like being a ghost."

He glanced around the room. "Is she here right now?"

"I don't think so, but she was with us for most of the evening."

"Did you happen to drop a lot of acid back in college?" he asked, deadpan, and we both started to laugh.

"Not once, Marty! Cyn did, a couple of times, but I was too scared."

"Does anyone else know about this?" I shook my head. He regarded me levelly. "Listen, I don't think you're crazy. Maybe this is your way of coping with your grief and your guilt for surviving when Cyn didn't. Do I think you might want to see a psychiatrist? Possibly. I know you want me to say I believe everything you've told me is literally true, but this is the best I can do. Can you be satisfied with that?"

"I guess so." Was I disappointed? Not exactly. I had told him, and he was still here. I didn't think he would abandon me. I hoped he wouldn't. I was still afraid I might end up in a psych ward. "You won't make me see a shrink?"

"*Make* you? Of course not. It's your choice." He finished his cup of tea and set it on the table. "It must have been awfully lonely keeping quiet about all of this. I'm glad you felt you could trust me with it."

Relief kicked in, as if I'd been swimming for miles with no land in sight, and suddenly I'd reached the shore. "I'm so glad I told you. I can't believe I did." We just looked at each other then, a long moment of knowing each other. "I love you, Marty," I said. It just slipped out.

"I love you too, Jo," he said matter-of-factly.

"You want some more tea?"

He nodded. "It seems to help."

I made us both tea with honey and whiskey. I turned on the TV, and we watched Johnny Carson, then the late movie,

293

which, hilariously enough, turned out to be *The Canterville Ghost.* "When I was about nine, I had a huge crush on Charles Laughton," I said.

"You did?" Martin made a face.

"*Young* Charles Laughton," I qualified.

"Ah."

He fell asleep halfway through the movie. Martin looked serious in sleep, like a rabbinical scholar or a character from Dostoyevsky. For the first time I noticed a few silver threads amid his thick, dark hair. There was a troubled set to his features, as if all that was wrong with his life had settled even more heavily upon him in sleep. A wave of protectiveness went through me.

I turned off the TV. The apartment was warm, but I set a blanket and pillow next to him on the couch in case he woke before morning. Then I went to bed. I didn't sleep deeply. Knowing he was in the next room kept my nervous system alert, but it also comforted me. A living person was in my space, and maybe I was one of the living too. Cyn was still making herself scarce. Could she actually be gone?

Chapter Twenty-five:
Don't Interrupt the Sorrow
(January 1976)

I woke in the morning to the sound of the shower running. Martin coughed, the sound echoing off the shower walls. It was odd and comforting to have someone in my apartment, someone who wasn't a ghost. Then I remembered the look on Martin's face when I'd told him about Cyn's ghost and everything else. Surely he thought I was a fruitcake. But he'd stayed. Where was Cyn? Was it possible that telling Martin everything had made her go away? Somehow it seemed too easy—not that telling Martin had been easy in the least.

The shower squeaked off, and I sat up and smoothed my hair. Should I get dressed? My long flannel nightgown was certainly modest enough. I looked at the bedside clock. It was a little past nine.

I heard the bathroom door open. Martin coughed some more. He approached my door and stopped. "I'm awake," I called.

He opened the door. "Good morning," he said a bit hoarsely.

"Come in."

He was unshaven, wearing yesterday's jeans and sweater. His feet were bare. He rubbed his hair with a towel. He looked a little disoriented, maybe from waking in a strange place. "Sleep well?" he asked.

"Not too bad. How about you?"

He didn't answer right away. Then he said, "Your couch is more comfortable than Halpren's. But I had a weird dream about your friend the ghost."

"You dreamed about Cyn?"

He sat on the edge of the bed. "I dreamed I woke up, and she was looming over me. She said, 'Leave Jo alone. She belongs to me.'"

My scalp prickled. "You saw her? She talked to you?"

He looked more and more disconcerted. "It was just a dream."

Was it? I had stopped wondering long ago if anyone but me might be able to see her. "Then what happened?"

"I told her, 'I'm sorry about what happened to you, but if you're Jo's friend, you should let her get on with her life.'"

I gave a laugh. "Oh boy, I bet she loved that." I wondered whether he would have been able to remember such specific wording if it had been merely a dream.

"She told me to mind my fucking business."

"That sounds like her. Then what?"

He busied himself folding the damp towel. "She started taking her clothes off. Or maybe they were already off? I said thanks, but no thanks."

"You did?" A guy saying no to Cyn seemed almost more implausible than Martin seeing her ghost.

"Hell, even in a dream, all I wanted to do was talk about how I'd cheated on my wife and needed to get my head on straight. Finally your friend got bored and went away."

I couldn't help but smile. But had he really seen Cyn? "Do you remember what she looked like?"

He set the towel beside him on the bed. "Short blonde hair, blue eyes. Skinny. Pretty, but kinda cold."

"That's her, Marty."

"You must've told me what she looked like."

"I didn't." I got out of bed and opened the closet door.

"Whatcha doing?"

I reached up and pulled a small white box from the top shelf. It was labeled PHOTOS in faded pencil. I sat on the bed and peeled up the yellowed Scotch tape that held the box shut. "I haven't looked at these in years." I hunted through photos of my family and friends, though it was hard not to stop and look at each one. Then I found a photo of me and Cyn. We both had long hair and wore minidresses, mine green, Cyn's blue. We stood side by side in front of the living room table in my parents' house. My mom had taken the photo on my eighteenth birthday. Cyn turned eighteen two weeks later. We both were smiling.

"Is this who you saw?" I asked, handing Martin the snapshot.

He studied it. "I'm not sure."

I hunted through the box some more. I skipped past a photo of myself with my gangly, grinning prom date, and one of myself with four high-school girls, two of whose names I couldn't remember. Then I found a black-and-white shot of Cyn. Jeremy had taken photos and developed them in a darkroom on campus; he'd taken this one in Cyn's apartment. Cyn sat in an old wooden chair she'd found on a street corner. Books were piled on a tiny table next to her. The one on top was Fanon's *The Wretched of the Earth*. Cyn's hair was shorn, and she stared seriously into the camera. She had on worn jeans and a peacoat. It was like looking at the photo of a ghost.

"Jesus Christ," Martin said. "Are you sure you didn't tell me what she looked like?"

"I'm sure, Marty."

He stared at the photograph. "God, this is strange. I wonder if hallucinations can be catching? Then again, I suppose if anyone you knew was going to see her, it would be me."

"How come?"

"Because we're—I don't know how to say this—bound together by make-believe? I've missed that, since you left the company."

I nearly choked up hearing him say that, after the miserable, isolated months I'd spent in this apartment. "I've missed it too," I managed to say. "But are you saying we're sharing a hallucination? You still think I made her up?"

"I honestly don't know what to think."

Just then the child on the other side of the wall started to scream. "No, no, no, I don't wanna, I don't wanna!" he wailed, interspersed with murmurs from his mother. The kid sobbed piteously.

Martin turned and stared at the wall for a long moment. "Christ," he muttered, looking stricken.

"You okay?" I asked. He seemed even more disturbed by the child's weeping than by Cyn's visitation.

"I get to see my kids tomorrow," he said in an unsteady voice. "Michael thinks it's his fault I moved out, that he must've been bad. Can you imagine? And Rosie's furious with me because I made her mom cry."

I put my hand on his shoulder. I wanted to tell him everything would work out, but that seemed unlikely. The child's sobs ebbed and ceased.

Martin let out a sigh. "You want to go get some breakfast?"

"Sure, after I take a shower."

When I'd blow-dried my hair and put on jeans and a sweater, I found Martin sitting on the couch watching *The Price Is Right* with a bleak expression on his face. "A new car!" Bob Barker proclaimed, and the audience cheered.

Martin got up and switched off the TV. "You have any plans today?"

I shook my head.

"What do you do all day, usually?"

"Watch soap operas with Cyn."

He goggled at me. "Seriously?"

"What? They're very addictive. Anyway, I want to find out who killed Jean Christopher." I hadn't said *who killed me*. Maybe that was a good sign.

"I can tell you if you want to know. We shot the scenes the other day."

Part of me wanted to be surprised along with the other viewers, but I supposed it was better hearing it from Martin. "Tell me."

"Clarissa did it."

I burst out laughing. "Perfect!"

He grinned. "Isn't it? The scenes where Sylvia confesses are a bit over-the-top, but great. She didn't mean to kill you. The two of you were arguing, she got mad and gave you a push, and you fell down the stairs."

"But Clarissa's not leaving the show, is she? Is Sylvia going to prison?"

"Clarissa's not going anywhere. I think Eric Read is going to pay off a judge or something."

"That's good."

"You think so? Clarissa wasn't particularly nice to you."

To my surprise, I found that I thought of Clarissa with something like affection. With respect, at any rate. "I still wouldn't want her to get written out. I wouldn't wish that on anyone, especially someone who's been with the company as long as she has."

"Speaking of being written out, have you been looking for work at all?"

"Actually I have an audition next week, my first since getting fired. It's been hard to bounce back."

He eyed me intently. "Jo, I didn't shoot the seagull, did I?"

"What?"

"I'm not proud of what happened with Amy. She came to the show a promising young actress, and she left a mess, reneging on her contract. I'm not saying that was all my fault, but clearly a lot of it was. I would hate to think I'm the reason you haven't been looking for work."

"Your conscience can be clear on that score," I said.

"Are you sure?"

"Absolutely."

"Good. Because sitting in your apartment all day can't be good for you. Especially if it's haunted." He looked around the place uneasily. "Come on, let's get out of here. I'll buy you breakfast."

I glanced at the darkened TV and felt a stab of regret at the thought of missing any of my stories—but it seemed as though my own story had resumed. It was strange leaving the apartment without Cyn by my side, though.

∞

She was sitting on the bed when I got home. I wasn't sure whether I was disappointed or relieved to see her—maybe both. She was staring down at the photos I had left out. She had on the blue minidress from the photo of the two of us, and it contrasted oddly with her short hair. "Where were you?" she asked.

I dropped my purse on the bed and sat down. "Don't you know?"

"I wasn't invited."

"Since when has that ever stopped you?"

She shrugged, dejected. "Things have changed, now you have a new best friend."

I was about to say that Martin wasn't my best friend. Then it occurred to me that maybe he was. "I hear you tried to warn him off last night," I said. "And when that didn't work, you resorted to your usual tactics."

"Meaning?"

"You tried to fuck him. But he turned you down. That must've been a surprise."

Cyn gave a snort of laughter. "This business with his wife has completely emasculated him. Anyway, what about what you did last night? Selling me out again. Winning some dude's devotion by telling him all our secrets."

"It wasn't like that, Cyn. I had to tell someone. I trust him."

She let out a *Pfft!* sound. "Oh, what's it matter? You've got a new best friend, and he has a penis. I can't compete."

"What does his having a penis have to do with anything, when we're not sleeping together?"

"Oh, please."

"He was pretty freaked out about seeing you, after I showed him your picture. He almost didn't want to let me come back here. I told him my apartment isn't particularly haunted, that you've gone all sorts of places with me—but that didn't make him feel any better. I told him I'd be all right."

Cyn was looking at me strangely. "So where did you go?"

"We had breakfast at Barney Greengrass—eggs and lox and bagels and orange juice and coffee. This older woman sitting at the next table kept staring at me. Then we heard her tell her husband, 'But I saw her die!' And Martin told her, 'She's alive! It's a miracle!'" I laughed and laughed.

Cyn was stony-faced.

"Of course, I don't think it took Martin's mind off anything, but at least he gets to see his kids tomorrow. I think he's gonna start looking for an apartment near the studio."

"Near you, you mean."

"That too, I guess." I couldn't help but smile at the thought.

"You guess!" She shook her head. "Well, I can't protect you, that much is clear."

"Since when have you ever tried to protect me from anything?"

She was silent. Finally she said, "Come here. I need to show you something." She reached for me, but I jumped off the bed.

"Oh no, you don't! You're not taking me anywhere. Not when my life is finally getting back on track."

"Back on track because of *him*?"

"He has a name, Cyn. And no, not because of Marty, but because I told him the truth about my life. Because I no longer feel so alone."

She flinched. "So I count for nothing?"

I hated to see the pain on her face. Would we never stop hurting each other? "I need living friends, Cyn! And even if I didn't, you've proven you don't have my best interests at heart. I can't trust you."

She looked me straight in the eye. "You can now. This is for your own good. One last trip."

"One last trip?" I felt a strange lightness at her words. "Do you mean that?"

She nodded.

"This isn't some kind of trick? Because you know that wherever you take me, you can't keep me there. I will come back here, to my life."

"You can't stay where I'm taking you. I just hope it might change your mind about him."

She had said the one irresistible thing; I had to find out what she meant. Slowly I sat on the bed. "Okay," I said. "One last trip, for old times' sake."

She gave a laugh, though her expression was elegiac. "I won't be with you where you're going."

I sat cross-legged and let her take my hands in hers. They felt cold and insubstantial. Nothing happened. She tried to lean her forehead against mine. It felt like a cold mist against my face. I closed my eyes. "Where are you taking me?" I asked, my heart pounding.

"Someplace bad. Someplace I hope you never end up."

My eyes flew open. "Cyn!"

She smiled grimly. "*He'll* be there."

I let my eyes close again and listened to the traffic noises from the street below. I thought those sounds would cease when I got where I was going, but they never did. I became aware of the shower running, and I opened my eyes. They ached from crying. I was sitting cross-legged on the large unmade bed in our Upper-West-Side apartment. I had on green sweatpants and a Keep Abortion Legal t-shirt. It was a muggy August night. I was glad Grace was sleeping over at Doris's. I didn't want her to see me like this.

The shower squeaked off, and I swiped at my eyes. I reached for the book of Toni Cade Bambara stories on my bedside table, sat up against the headboard and pretended to read.

I didn't look up when the bathroom door opened. Then I felt his eyes on me, his waiting presence, and I did. Martin stood in the doorway with a towel wrapped around his waist. With his wet hair shot through with silver and his stomach softer than it once was, he was still fatally attractive, damn him. I tried not to see his damp, wiry body, which he diligently kept fit with trips to the gym and morning jogs. Not for my benefit as much as for the viewers—and not just for the viewers, apparently. I wasn't in remotely as good shape. He'd always said he didn't care, that I was beautiful just as I was. The liar.

He stood there looking at me, his eyes full of worry.

"What?" I demanded.

"Are you ready to talk to me?" he asked quietly.

"Oh, now you want to talk?" My voice rose to a shriek.

He let out a heavy sigh. "I'll take that as a no." Christ, we sounded like characters on *Hope Springs Eternal*. But it felt more like *Scenes From a Marriage*.

He pulled the towel from his middle and rubbed his arms and back with it. The sight of his flaccid cock sent a wave of rage through me so strong, it left me shaky. Martin opened a dresser drawer, pulled out blue boxer shorts and stepped into them. Then he approached me and reached out to touch my shoulder.

"Don't touch me!" I cried, flinching away. My histrionics seemed overdone even to me, but I couldn't seem to help myself.

"I'm sorry," he said. "If you want to talk, I'll be on the couch. Me and my aching back."

"I won't," I muttered.

He looked like he was about to say something, then he shook his head and slunk from the room. He didn't shut the door. I leapt up, made for the door, and slammed it hard, then sat on the bed again. I stared at the darkened TV set atop the chest of drawers. Babette's voice went through my head yet again. *I'm sorry to have to be the one to tell you, Jo,* she had said on the phone, two days ago that seemed like weeks. *I really thought he'd changed. What an idiot he is!* We both knew I was the idiot.

Chapter Twenty-six:
Accidentally Like a Martyr
(August 1989/January 1976)

"You've got to talk to him eventually," my best friend Ana said on the phone a week later.

"Why?" I asked.

"Well, either you're gonna work things out or you're gonna break up, but either way, you've got to talk to him."

"And here I was hoping you'd tell me I should write him off and join a lesbian commune."

Ana laughed. "Last I checked, you weren't actually a lesbian."

In another life, perhaps. "Details!" I looked up, and Grace was standing in the bedroom doorway, her lovely little face pinched with worry. "Hey, Ana, I better go."

"Me too. The place just exploded with customers."

I thought of She Who Bookstore with a sharp yearning—a safe haven. "I'll try to come by tomorrow."

When I hung up, Grace sat next to me on the edge of the bed. Her forehead scrunched up the way it did when she was trying not to cry. "Hey," I murmured, "what's up, kid?"

"Mom…are you and dad getting a divorce?" she asked, her voice thin and plaintive.

"What?" I put my arm around her. She was a slender wisp of a ten-year-old in jeans, sneakers, and a Mickey Mouse T-shirt.

"I don't want you to get a divorce. I don't wanna be a child of divorce like Mike and Rose."

"A child of divorce?" It sounded like a line from an After School Special. I had played a drug counselor in one of those a few years back.

"You're not answering me!" Her lip trembled. She had Martin's wavy dark hair and delicately bumpy nose, my eyes. It occurred to me that maybe Grace—her eventual creation—was the reason I'd felt drawn to Martin to begin with. If so, there were worse reasons.

I pulled her close. "I won't lie to you, honey. Things aren't great right now. But whatever happens, it won't change how your dad and I feel about you. Everything's gonna be okay." Now *I* sounded like an After School Special, or maybe a scene from *Hope Springs Eternal*. Love welled up in the pit of my stomach. For Grace if for no other reason, I needed to talk things out with Martin.

The doorbell rang. Grace sniffled and disengaged herself, then ran for the door.

After a minute I got up and walked into the hall, where Grace stood whispering with her best friend.

"Hi, Doris," I said.

"Hi, Ms. Bergman," Doris murmured, barely looking up from the intensely whispered conversation. She had long, straight, black hair and an arrestingly pretty, heart-shaped face. She had on a sundress and sandals, and was both taller and more mature-looking than Grace, though Grace was a month older. Doris's mother was from Japan, her father a WASP dentist from Ohio. When Grace and Doris became best friends a year ago, Grace read everything she could lay her hands on about Japan, though Doris seemed entirely uninterested in non-American culture.

"Call us when you finish dinner, and your dad or I will come get you," I told Grace.

Doris startled me with an appraising glance that made me wonder what Grace had told her about Martin and me. "My mom said my dad can bring Grace back after dinner," she said.

"Oh, okay." I reached out to rub Grace's shoulder. "Have fun at the movie."

"I'll be right back," Grace told Doris, and she went into the living room. "Bye, Dad!"

"You off to the movies?" I could hear the smile in Martin's voice. "Have fun, sweetheart."

I'd planned to shut myself in the bedroom when the girls had gone and work on the syllabus for the Women Playwrights class I'd be teaching this fall. Instead, when Grace and Doris left, I went into the living room, which was pleasantly cold from the window A/C. Martin was sitting on one end of the old orange suede sofa, frowning down at what was probably the next day's script. He wore a white t-shirt and old jeans; his feet were bare.

I looked at the family photos arranged on the breakfront. Photos of Grace at every age, alone, with me and Martin, with my parents. Proud Martin surrounded by his beautiful kids: Mike and Rose, dark-haired, dark-eyed young adults, and Grace, the adoring little sister. Martin's Emma Goldman-loving grandmother as a bright-eyed young woman, standing with her tall, stiff, glossy-haired, mustached young husband. The same woman, many decades later, with dyed red hair, a housedress on her ample body, sitting on a sofa next to a curly-headed, pre-adolescent, impish Martin. Our wedding photo: Martin handsome in a dark suit, I so young and slender in my simple, off-white lace dress (how had I not realized back then how beautiful I'd been?), the two of us smiling into each other's eyes, so solemnly, stupidly happy.

"God, this script is terrible," Martin said, and I turned; he was looking up at me.

I was tempted to leave the room without replying, but I sat beside him. "Let's talk," I said.

He immediately tossed the script onto the coffee table. Then we just looked at each other, like scene partners who'd forgotten their next lines. "I don't know where to start," he said finally, "except to say again that I'm truly sorry."

He appeared truly sorry, but what good did that do? "The whole thing is such a fucking cliché," I said. The furious tears sprang to my eyes, but I fought them back. "And the worst part of it is, I had to hear about it from Babette. Why couldn't you have just told me?"

"I was ashamed. I felt like an idiot." There was that grimace of contrition and self-loathing that I remembered from years ago, when he and Gloria were splitting up. Back then I'd felt sorry for him.

"You *are* an idiot," I said. "But I'm an idiot for thinking you could change."

He looked faintly reproachful. "I did change. Mostly because I couldn't stand living like that anymore. The lies and the sneaking around and the guilt…"

"I suppose it's amazing it took you this long to revert to type. Though I really have no way of knowing whether this was the first time."

"It was the first time. I realize there's no reason for you to believe me." He let out a sigh. "The whole time I was on location, I missed you and Grace so much. I felt lost, somehow."

I hated the stirrings of sympathy I felt at this admission. "I missed you too, but I didn't feel the need to sleep with some guy. And excuse me if I don't feel sorry for you, getting paid to go work in a beautiful place."

He raked a hand through his hair. "Sure, Bermuda was beautiful, but I was lonely and bored out of my mind. I kept thinking, How the hell did this show turn into a freaking comic book? The action sequences were fun, but that was just one day." Sam Jameson had chased the bad guys across a pink sand beach and knocked out one of them with a single punch. It had looked silly but fun. "I didn't know how good I had it back when Prudence was writing the show. I thought of you, back in the city, and how what you were doing was so much more satisfying."

"For god's sake, Marty! You always use this to justify your indiscretions. It's the same as when you were with Gloria—you're not doing enough theater, you're sick of the show, so you end up in bed with someone. Did it ever occur to you to just do more theater?"

He hung his head. "You're right. I fell into my old pattern."

"To spite me, because I was directing *Ghosts*?"

"Of course not! I'm proud of the work you do."

"And why Stephanie? You don't even like her. Or was that a lie, too?" I pictured Stephanie Andrews, with her masses of frizzy blonde hair, big blue eyes, and toothy smile, Stephanie who played plucky young heroine Andrea Robins who'd married her true love in Bermuda (after she'd been kidnapped by and rescued from a spy ring). Stephanie who was always romping across the screen in shorts or lingerie or a bathing suit, always looking young and golden and resoundingly healthy. I had never looked like Stephanie, even when I was her age. And here I sat feeling shlumpy in my sweatpants and t-shirt.

Martin's lips twisted in disgust. "Stephanie can't act, but she gets all the air time, while the little I get is out-of-character crap."

"Babette learned to act eventually. Maybe Stephanie will, too."

He stared at me. "Are you actually defending her? Is this some feminist thing?"

How much easier it would have been if I could have mustered the desire to slap Stephanie's face, pull out her blonde hair by the roots. But she wasn't the one who'd betrayed me. "I barely know her. But I'd be a hypocrite if I hated her for doing something I would gladly have done with you when you were married to Gloria."

"That was different. You and I cared about each other. I don't feel anything for Stephanie, and the feeling is mutual."

"So fucking her was your way of getting back at her for having so much air time?"

He gave a surprised blink. "I don't know. It just happened. We were drinking rum in the hotel bar one night, and she ended up in my room. We were both smashed. Believe me, it was nothing to write home about. I was so drunk, I kept slipping out…"

I pictured her luxuriant permed hair spread across the pillow as he moved on top of her. I felt sick and aroused at the same time. "Enough. I don't need to hear any more."

His face sagged with shame. "We've kept out of each other's way ever since. It's been awkward. I don't know why she felt the need to blab to Babette. Maybe instead of confessing to you, she figured she'd confess to my on-screen wife. Bottom line, it meant nothing, Joanna. If I could take it back, I would."

"I believe you mean that. But you did it all the same. Do you know how that makes me feel? Like no one is young enough or pretty enough for you." My throat grew tight with threatening tears, but I kept going. "No one is enough for your fragile fucking ego. And I have to play the part of the poor, betrayed wife. It's humiliating! Maybe I should sleep with some cute young actor, see how you like it."

He winced. "I halfway expect you to say you're going to leave me for Ana. I've halfway expected that for years."

"Are you serious?"

"You're bisexual, right? You told me that once. You hang out with all these feminists and lesbians and lesbian-feminists."

In another life, nearly forgotten, I had been lovers with Cyn. Martin and I hadn't talked about any of that in years.

I didn't think either of us knew if any of it had been real. I brushed away the memory. "Ana's been with Rachel for as long as I've known her. And don't turn this around on me. I'm not the one who cheated. How can you be so insecure?"

"I'm well aware that you can do better than me," he said quietly. "I've always known that. You're still so young. You're beautiful and intelligent, and you have way more going for you than I do."

It hurt to hear him call me beautiful, when that was so far from how I felt. "I'm pushing forty. For all I know, you want to trade me in on a younger model. Wife number three."

His eyes widened in dismay. "God, no. Do you know how miserable that sounds? You and the kids mean everything to me. I know I fucked up. I'm so sorry I hurt you. I love you. Please, Joanna…" He leaned toward me and tried to kiss me. I slapped his face. I'm not sure which of us was more surprised. He looked stunned. Then he grinned grimly.

"Why are you smiling?" I demanded.

"Feel free to do it again."

I slapped him harder. My hand stung. He rubbed his cheek, his eyes dark and unreadable. Then he took my hand and pressed his lips to the stinging palm, once, twice, and my pelvis tightened. I lunged at him and smashed my mouth against his. He tried to kiss me gently, but I bit his lip. He let out a yelp and pulled back—then he smiled again, that wolfish smile I hadn't seen in what felt like a long time. "Come here," he said.

Minutes later we were in our bed. His body still felt right. His hands, his mouth, the weight of him on me. Even now, angrier with him than I had ever been. Even now, even now.

Afterwards we lay sweating, our breath slowing, I wet and sloppy between the legs. I was on my back, he curled towards me. "This doesn't change anything," I said.

"I know," he murmured. "But please don't give up on me." His face was so open, so utterly unguarded. I knew I should get up, or at least turn away from him. Instead I turned to face him and cupped the cheek I had slapped.

Abruptly I was sitting on my small bed with Cyn's ghost. "You are hopeless, Jo," she said. "He screws you over, and you still let him screw you." She looked impossibly young. It occurred to me that if I were to look in a mirror, I would, briefly, perceive myself as nearly as young, until the memory of being older slipped away.

I could still feel the fading pleasure and slight soreness between my legs. "We had a daughter," I whispered. I wanted to block Cyn out, hold onto the memory of our daughter's face. Our life together. I had been an actress and a director, a teacher and an activist. I had been a mother. A wife. But there were too many details, too much to make sense of. Operation Rescue Ronald Reagan George Bush Webster Decision Central Park Jogger *When Harry Met Sally* "Talkin' bout a Revolution" *And The Band Played On* Tiananmen Square *Roseanne Do the Right Thing Honey I Shrunk the Kids*? Everything canceled everything else out. I couldn't keep my daughter's name, but I tried to hold fast to the feeling of loving her.

"You couldn't possibly have known any of that," I said. "It's the future."

"I'm outside time, Jo."

"So it was real?"

"You had another best friend," Cyn accused. "That dyke on the phone."

"Did I?" I remembered the feeling of that, too—a close woman friend who I trusted completely.

"And my god, you looked like your mother." Cyn looked down at the photo of us in our minidresses, then looked at me. "You already look older than you did in that picture. But just now, you looked so *old*. I didn't know you." She stared at me as if I were the ghost.

"I still don't see how you brought me there."

"It wasn't just me," she said impatiently. "I've told you, it's never just me. It's both of us together."

"Both of us together," I repeated. I didn't know if it was more frightening or less that it hadn't been all Cyn's doing, that I'd had a hand in seeing my future. Or, at least, a possible future.

"Like I said, I'm outside time," Cyn said. "We could probably see you as a little old lady. We could see you die of old age."

I shuddered. "No. I don't want to."

"God, it was strange, wasn't it? The future. I can't make sense of it. It was like another planet." Briefly she hugged herself as if she were freezing. "But now do you see why I wanted to take you there?"

"It's just one possibility of what could happen, right? It's not a done deal."

"There's one way to make sure it doesn't happen. Steer clear of him. Don't turn into your mother. Is that really what you want, to turn into your mother? To be…" She struggled for words. "Middle-aged," she finally spat out.

It dawned on me then that Cyn hadn't wanted me to see the future because Martin would cheat on me, but because she thought I would find the prospect of myself as an aging wife and mother as alien as she did. "What's the alternative, Cyn? If we'd stayed together, in that version where you lived, we'd have wound up middle-aged together. Do you want me to grow older alone, or not grow older at all? Because if it's the latter, only dying will take care of that."

She stared at me in incomprehension. I thought about Martin cheating on me in the future. If we did get together someday, there was no guarantee that would happen. It seemed pretty damn likely, though. Martin had failed me—would fail me. And yet.

Cyn gave a heavy sigh. "All I can say is, the life I saw you leading just now sure isn't the life I would've chosen for you."

"I know that. But you can't choose for me. You're never going to get any older. You never get to grow up." The words stuck in my throat.

"I can't just sit on the sidelines and watch you making terrible mistakes—or watch you get it right, either." She spoke slowly and laboriously. "I thought we could both live, but we can't, and it's exhausting to watch you keep living while I'm dead. I am so fucking tired, Jo."

When had she begun to fade? Sitting cross-legged on the bed in her blue minidress, her image was indistinct like a TV screen riddled with snow. "You are?" I whispered, breathless at the sight of her.

"Don't sound so glad," she said.

"I'm not!" Suddenly I was afraid to take my eyes off her for an instant.

"You kept asking me if I wanted to rest." Her eyes were locked on me as if that were the only thing that could keep her from vanishing. "Well, today is your lucky day, Joanna. But you're going to have to let me go."

"Let *you* go?"

She gave a laugh that sounded tinny and strange. "Do you think I could have done any of this without you? You're the one who brought me back. You remembered me."

"I never forgot you! I never got over losing you."

"I think maybe now you *can* get over it. Not because of that dude," she added. "I want it on record that he's not good enough for you."

"Duly noted." All at once I felt panicky as it sunk in that it was in my power to let her go. That any power she'd had over me—in death, in life—had been power I'd given her. I reached for her hands and held them as tightly as I could, but they felt like pins and needles, half there. Cyn looked down at our joined hands as if she couldn't quite feel them, and she smiled.

"Remember the day you got the part of Joan?" she asked. "That was a great day, the day we became friends."

"I was so proud you wanted to be my friend. I was so surprised."

She looked up at me. "You were? Why?"

"You were Cynthia Foster, the belle of the ball, with that athlete boyfriend of yours."

"I can't even remember his name, can you?" She shook her head ruefully. "His claim to fame was that he was tall and had muscles. But you—you already knew what you wanted to do with your life."

"I was terrified the day of that audition."

"Oh, you were always terrified," Cyn said with another tinny laugh. "But you knew who you were. In every version of your life, you knew! I admired that. Sometimes it drove me nuts, but I always admired that."

"You always seemed so sure of yourself."

"I was sure of you," she whispered.

Tears came to my eyes. "Cyn…"

Her eyes, blue-gray and beautiful, gazed into mine. "You won't forget me again?"

"I never forgot you. I never could." My throat grew tight. "What I wanted to forget was how I failed you. Can you forgive me?"

Her smile deepened. "If you can forgive me, Jo."

"Of course I can." Tears rolled down my face. Cyn wasn't crying. She looked clear and resolute. I thought of Jean Christopher's dying words. They weren't my words, but they would suit. "I'm so glad we met, in spite of everything," I said.

Cyn nodded. She looked unafraid. "Goodbye, Jo."

"Goodbye, Cyn," I said, and let go of her hands.

∞

I sat on the bed and stared for a long time at the snap-shot of me and Cyn. Then I looked through the box of photos. I found a picture of myself and Jeremy. Who had taken it? Alex, probably. We stood together a bit awkwardly, Jeremy's arm about my shoulders. I was smiling over-effusively, Jeremy warmly. He had dark, curly hair and kind eyes.

I picked up the photo of short-haired Cyn and gently touched her black-and-white cheek with my fingertip. Then I took that photo, and the one of myself and Cyn, and tacked them to the wall above my dresser. We had loved each other. I would not forget.

Chapter Twenty-seven:
The Unknown Soldier
(September–October 1976)

"Why'd you leave *Hope Springs Eternal?*" Jeremy asked, and took a drag of his cigarette. "I couldn't believe it when they killed you off."

"I got canned," I said with what I hoped was a nonchalant shrug. "I don't think I'll ever really know why."

"That's too bad." Looking embarrassed, he glanced down at the paperback of *We Become New: Poems by Contemporary American Women* that lay on the coffee table, picked it up, and perused the cover with a growing frown. I watched him with a feeling of upheaval, like someone with a secret love watching a friend happen upon the beloved's picture. Some of the poems in that book lit me up inside—poems by Judy Grahn, June Jordan, Adrienne Rich, Marge Piercy, Audre Lorde, so many electrifying, truthful voices.

Jeremy looked up, brightening, and put the book back on the table. "Hey, I saw your shampoo commercial!" he said.

A couple of the women in my theater group had challenged me about being in that commercial, even after I'd retorted, *Look, it pays the damn bills.* "I used to look down my nose at that kind of work," I said. "But it means I don't have to go back to secretarial work. Not at the moment, anyway."

It was a Sunday afternoon in late September. Jeremy had arrived a few minutes ago, and the sight of him on my sofa wasn't getting less weird. I sat perched on one of Martin's chairs and tried not to stare. Jeremy was familiar and unfamiliar with his dark, curly hair and dark eyes that were kind but

317

reserved, his slim body in jeans and blue flannel shirt—a body I had known intimately and not at all.

He tapped ash into the ashtray. "Listen, I was so glad you called, Joanna. I was sorry about the way I behaved last time."

"I was afraid you might've been angry with me for not agreeing to help out, after..." I trailed off.

"After Alex was arrested? No, I get where you were coming from." Apparently now that Alex was no longer underground, Jeremy thought it was okay to say his name.

I had allowed myself to spin a few fantasies about Jeremy's visit: that we would end up together, that it would be easy and sweet and uncomplicated. It had taken me an hour to figure out what to wear. I'd ended up in jeans and an orange peasant blouse.

"Do you know how Alex is doing?" I asked.

"I've had a couple of letters from him since he was convicted. Did you know he got ten years minimum?" He watched my face as the words sank in. "So did Sharon Gilmore."

"Patty Hearst only got seven." Patty had finally been sentenced and was about to start serving her time in Pleasanton, California. In that other life, Jeremy and I would've been serving our time along with Alex and Sharon. Jeremy didn't know how lucky he was.

"The two black revolutionaries who participated in the bank robbery got twenty-five to life," he said bleakly.

I shook my head. "Of course they did." I couldn't remember the names of the other men who'd participated in my version of the bank robbery—had they been the same guys in this version?—but I thought one of them had named himself after a jazz musician.

Jeremy took another drag of his cigarette. I didn't relish the fact that my apartment was filling with cigarette fumes, but I was loath to ask him to stop when we finally seemed to be on better terms. "They only ended up charging Alex and Sharon for the bank robbery," he said. "They'd wanted to charge Alex for some of the other actions, too."

"The draft board?"

"No, the bombings of Shell Oil and the police station in San Francisco, stuff like that. But apparently they had to drop those charges because the government's case was tainted by misconduct—wiretaps and dirty tricks." He spoke all in a rush, gesturing with his hands, his eyes bright. There was little doubt that he still had revolutionary daydreams. I had finally allowed myself to consider the possibility of revolution again, albeit a very different kind from our old fantasies, but somehow I didn't think Jeremy would want to talk about the women's movement.

"How much do you know about Sharon?" I asked. My recollection of her was hazy, but I didn't think I'd liked her much.

Jeremy shrugged. "She and Alex have been together a long time. She's a very committed revolutionary." He paused, then added, "I guess I shouldn't compare her to Cyn."

It was both comforting and disconcerting to hear him say her name. "I know what you mean."

"Alex was crazy in love with Cyn, you know. She was so aloof with him, it made him nuts!" He smiled ruefully. "And I wanted to be just like Alex, so I thought I had to be in love with her too."

How crazy was it that it still hurt to hear him say that? "Right," I said, because I didn't know what else to say.

"But I was always sweet on you, you know." He looked me straight in the eye.

My face grew hot. "I felt the same way about you."

"Really?" He shook his head, grinning shyly like the boy I once knew. "We really fucked that one up, didn't we?"

"We sure did!" What would he say if I told him that in another life, we'd been lovers for years? Somehow it seemed impossible to tell Jeremy any of the things I'd told Martin.

"Are you involved with anybody?" he asked.

"No…I've been pretty busy lately," I hastened to say. "My friend Susan keeps threatening to set me up with someone." It felt like a lie to say I wasn't involved with anyone, Martin and I spent so much time together. Gloria had filed for divorce, and Martin was seeing a psychiatrist. He told me he'd sworn off women for the duration, but I told myself he must be sleeping with someone, because that was better than believing he wasn't and being disappointed later. As for the future I'd seen, maybe it had been nothing more than some kind of waking dream, nothing real. I'd wracked my brain trying to remember how Martin and I had become a couple in that future, but it was a blank.

"I see," Jeremy said. Then he burst out with, "I live with a woman. I didn't tell her I was coming here." And there it was, that shamefaced expression Martin had worn so often.

"Why didn't you tell her?"

"She doesn't know about Alex or Cyn or any of it. She's a Buddhist. She wouldn't understand."

That sounded like a flimsy excuse, but I didn't feel like calling him on it. What would be the point? "That must get lonely for you," I said.

He shrugged. "Sometimes, I guess."

We were silent then. I wished I smoked too, to have something to do to fill the silence. Jeremy stubbed out his cigarette and walked over to the stack of albums against the wall. The LP in front was Phil Ochs' *Rehearsals for Retirement*, and he picked it up. I remembered him looking at Cyn's copy the night we met.

Jeremy read aloud the words emblazoned on the gravestone on the LP cover: "Phil Ochs (American), Born: El Paso, Texas 1940. Died: Chicago, Illinois 1968." He shook his head. "Bizarre, isn't it? Now that he's killed himself."

"It's such a terrible waste." After I'd heard the news that he'd hanged himself at his sister's house in Far Rockaway, I'd played the album for the first time in years and cried as I listened to his plaintive, hopeful vibrato. "He was Cyn's favorite."

"I remember." He put the LP back in the front of the stack. "So have you been back to the draft board any time recently?"

For a moment I thought he couldn't be serious. Then I realized I couldn't tell him the whole truth. "No," I said finally. "I've never gone back there."

"I avoided the place for a year. The first anniversary of her death was the first time I went. It was still a draft board then. You've really never gone? You should go sometime."

"It's not still a draft board?" I gave a startled laugh. "Of course it's not! There's no draft."

"Actually it stayed open for a while after the draft was abolished. The building's vacant now. At least, it was the last time I was there." His eyes grew large and haunted. "The first couple of times I went, I expected cops to leap out at me. Maybe in a way I was hoping that would happen."

"I understand." We shared a long look that acknowledged the painful past we had in common. Maybe that was all that was left between us. In that moment, it still helped.

Jeremy stayed a few minutes more, and we talked about how we hoped Carter would beat Ford in the election. Then he said he had to get to the hospital. I walked him to the door. "It was good to see you, Jeremy."

"It was good to see you too, Jo. Don't be a stranger." He kissed me on the cheek a bit awkwardly, and I smelled his cigarette breath. Then he gave me a quick hug.

When he'd gone, I stood there feeling deflated. So much for easy and sweet and uncomplicated. Oh well, I needed to prepare for a TV movie audition and work on the piece about Emma Goldman my women's theater group was doing.

321

There was a brisk knock on the door, and I thought it must be Jeremy again. I opened the door, and my stomach did its predictable flip at the sight of Martin, in his red shirt and jeans.

"Marty! Hi."

"Hi, kid," he said quietly. He walked in and looked around as if he expected to see something incriminating. Then he scrutinized me. "You look nice," he said, but he sounded crestfallen. "I think I saw your friend just now."

"You did?"

"Your old boyfriend, right? He was getting on the elevator when I got off."

I was about to say that he hadn't been my boyfriend—but he had been, in that other life. I wasn't sure if that counted. I had told Martin about robbing a bank and living with a fellow revolutionary, but I'd never told him it was Jeremy. "I can't believe you remembered that. You saw him for all of a minute or so, and that was last year."

He barked out a laugh. "I could tell he recognized me. That's when I recognized him." His gaze latched onto the ashtray on the coffee table. "Wow, it stinks of cigarettes in here," he said, waving his hand. "Your friend smokes, I guess." He said *friend* with derision.

I resisted the urge to go empty the ashtray. "It's funny, because he didn't smoke when we were in college. I mean, he smoked grass, but not tobacco. And now that he's a nurse, you wouldn't think he'd have started."

"He's a *nurse*?"

"What's wrong with a guy being a nurse?"

"Nothing, I guess." With a scowl he sat on the sofa and moved the ashtray to the far end of the table.

I went to the window and yanked it wider. I wondered if something had happened with Gloria to put him in this mood. "So, what's up?" I asked.

"I wanted to see if you wanted to go to the movies."

"Sure! What movie did you want to see?"

He gave a sigh. "I don't know."

"Actually I was going to call you and see if you'd help me run lines for that TV movie audition."

"Sure," he said absently. "Anytime."

I sat next to him. "What's wrong?"

He shot me a look, as if it ought to be obvious. Then he leaned in and kissed me. After a stunned moment I kissed him back. I expected him to pull away. Instead he pulled me closer, his tongue in my mouth, his hand in my hair. His slight stubble prickled my face. I couldn't catch my breath. I couldn't believe that this was happening, that it was suddenly possible. I clung to him and kissed him hard, and he responded with equal passion, as if he had always wanted this. Then he began to kiss my neck, and my body grew heavy with wanting, even as a single word resounded in my head: *Idiot*. His hand moved in slow, hot circles over my breasts, then reached under my blouse.

"Wait," I managed to say, though it felt like I was speaking from the depths of a dream. He looked at me with half-closed eyes. "Marty, what brought this on?"

He gave a breathless laugh. "Do I have to spell it out?"

It was hard to think straight, but his weird behavior when he'd arrived began to make sense. "You were jealous of Jeremy?"

Abruptly he looked wide awake. He let go of me and sat back on the couch, his chest still rising and falling with his beautiful heavy breathing. "Yes, I was jealous. I saw that kid, and I guess I panicked."

I suppressed a smile. "But you and I are friends. That's what you said you wanted."

"Things have changed since then."

"Well, you might have clued me in!" It wasn't easy to make myself talk to him, when all I wanted to do was grab him before the moment passed. Before he changed his mind.

"I wanted to be sure," he said. "I guess I waited too long, huh? I must admit, I'd thought you might get involved with one of those women in your theater group, but I didn't think of that guy. It makes sense you'd want to be with someone your own age."

A flash of Martin's voice: *You're bisexual, right? You told me that once.* "Marty, there's nothing going on between Jeremy and me. But that doesn't mean you and I should get involved."

His face darkened. "You're saying you don't want me anymore? You wanted me when I had a wife, but you don't want me now?"

I had to stop myself from reaching for him and reassuring him. "It's not that. I'm just not sure I can trust you."

"You trusted me when you told me about Cyn."

"As my friend, I trust you completely. But—"

"As a man, you trust me as far as you can throw me. I understand. You're not wrong." He met my gaze, and I saw he took this judgment to heart. "But I don't want to be that guy anymore. My shrink says I slept around because I was dissatisfied with my acting career. I created drama and challenge in my life where it was lacking in my career. I got a little more excitement than I bargained for."

"So now that you're done looking for excitement, you want me?"

He threw up his hands. "Jesus! Why are you twisting my words? All you have to do is say you're not interested."

"Of course I'm interested! I just don't want to get hurt."

"That makes two of us," he said quietly.

That was a new idea: that I could hurt Martin. Why was it always so hard for me to believe I had any power over the people who meant the most to me?

"Listen, I want to be someone you can trust," he said. "I want it to be just you and me."

I studied his face. That Martin would say such a thing to me seemed even more improbable than all the vastly improbable things that had happened in the past year. "Can you do that?" I asked.

He gave a laugh. "Kid, I certainly hope so. If I can't change, I'm never going to have a moment's peace."

"I suppose you could find someone who's into non-monogamy."

He shot me a despairing look. "Is that what you want? Non-monogamy?"

I shook my head. "I'm not built that way."

"Thank god."

"Really?"

"Yes, really." He smiled for the first time since he'd shown up at my door. All I wanted to do was take him straight to bed. But I could well imagine what Babette and Susan would say. Hell, Martin was still doing love scenes with Babette on *Hope Springs Eternal*, and while Babs was married now and I knew things were long over between her and Martin, it was a reminder of how things used to be. A reminder of how things might be again.

"Marty, there's something I need to tell you. Before Cyn left for good, she showed me my future. Or she and I saw it together. It was years from now, and you and I...we were a couple." It seemed wrong to tell him we were married with a child. Like cheating, somehow. It had to be only one possibility of the future. "And you cheated on me."

His eyebrows raised. "With who?"

I gave a snort of laughter. "You would ask that! I don't remember much, just flashes of it, and the way it felt. I was so angry and so hurt."

He was quiet then. I could see the wheels turning. I suspected he wanted to ask more about the future. Instead he said, "You saw us together in the future, and you never thought to tell me?"

"It wouldn't have been fair. You've been going through so much. I couldn't lay all that on you. Besides, I don't know if it was even real."

"Real enough for you to use it as a roadblock now." He shook his head. "I can't trust anything Cyn showed you. She told me to stay away from you. It seems like she kept you from being close to anyone."

"You're right, and I let her do it. But she's gone now."

"Is she?"

"It doesn't mean what I saw won't happen."

He let out a defeated sigh. "What else can I say? I know I'm a bad risk. But I really do love you, Joanna."

Was I actually going to talk my way out of something I badly wanted? With a palpable sensation of falling, I knew that if Martin failed me (he would fail me), I would forgive him as Cyn had forgiven me. "I really do love you too," I said. Slowly I put my arms around him and kissed him.

∞

I was too keyed up to relax when we got into bed, though Martin's naked body felt shockingly good against mine. I couldn't stop running my hands over his sleek skin. I kissed his neck, his shoulders, his hairy chest, and delighted in his look of rapt arousal, the way I made his breath hitch.

He eased me onto my back and slid his hand between my legs, and I let in a sharp intake of breath. "Is this okay?" he whispered.

"Yes. But I keep expecting someone to yell, 'Cut!'"

We both started to laugh, and I felt myself relax. "I'm nervous too," he said, and his eyes were full of tenderness.

"Come here," I said, and we kissed. He kept touching me, and I kissed him deeply and at length, my legs spread wide as the pleasure built. Then I broke the kiss with a gasp.

When I came back to myself, breathing hard, I found him watching me with evident satisfaction. "Beautiful," he said, with a smile that in and of itself would've sent me over the edge. He kissed me again and climbed on top of me.

For an instant I flashed on Jeremy looking delightedly down at me, and then Cyn, fierce, fucking me with her fingers—and then an older Martin with silvering hair and a thicker middle, making love to an older Jo who had, I suddenly remembered, a C-section scar. I felt tenderness towards the people he and I might become. Then Martin pushed inside me, and there was nothing but this present moment with him.

∞

"So, do you still want to go to the movies?" I asked afterwards, my head against his chest.

His chuckle rumbled against my ear. "No," he murmured. "I like it here."

"So do I."

A while later, when it was starting to get dark, he asked, "Are you hungry?"

"Mm hmm. But I don't want to get out of bed."

"I'll go forage in the kitchen." He sat up and stretched, and I reveled in the sight of his beautiful muscled nakedness in the half-light. He got out of bed and switched on the lamp. While I snuggled under the covers, he walked over to my dresser and peered at the photos on the wall above it. "There she is: your not-so-friendly ghost. Christ, she's giving me the creeps." He picked up his shorts from the floor and stepped into them, as if Cyn could see him.

I sat up in bed. "She wasn't too fond of you either, but she's gone. That's what the pictures are for."

"To keep her away?"

"No. To remember her."

He sat on the edge of the bed. "You didn't sleep with her, right? I mean, you did in that other whatever-it-was, but not in real life."

"That other whatever-it-was felt real. All the other versions felt real."

"You're not answering the question."

The idea of a jealous Martin wasn't going to get old anytime soon. "No, we weren't lovers. Maybe if she had lived, we would have been. But we loved each other. She wasn't easy to love, but I loved her."

His listening gaze made me feel like I could tell him anything.

"You know, I think I ought to visit the place where she died." I didn't know I was going to say it until the words were out. "I've never gone back there since it happened. I was always afraid to go back there, and now I'm even more afraid, because that place was the catalyst for those trips I took, most of them. But I think I should."

He stared uncomprehendingly at me. "We've just gone to bed together for the first time, and this is what you want to talk about? You're ready to take another trip?"

"Marty..."

"It feels like you're trying to push me away, and it feels shitty. And the idea of you going off into some other version of your life scares the hell out of me."

I had put that pained grimace on his face. "Marty, that's not what I meant at all. It's just, you're the one who brought up Cyn, and a friend of mine was telling me about the draft board. The building's vacant now."

"A friend of yours," he said, and his eyes lit up. "A friend of yours told you about the draft board. God, I'm an idiot! Your friend from college. It was Jeremy, right? He was part of the bombing."

My brain froze like I'd forgotten my lines. I wanted to pull the covers over my head. "It feels like you're interrogating me."

His shoulders relaxed slightly. "I'm sorry. I don't mean to. But am I right?"

"Okay, yes, Jeremy was part of it. Please don't ask me for details! I didn't tell you because I didn't want to incriminate him. Now will you please come here?"

He got back into bed, and we clung to each other. It still seemed amazing that we were together, even though we were arguing. I closed my eyes and let out a long breath. Then I looked up at him. "I'm going to tell you something else, and I need you to not freak out."

He gave a laugh. "Oh, wonderful! Go ahead."

"In the version of my life where I robbed a bank—"

"You do realize how that sounds?"

"I know, I know. The thing is, in that version, I lived with Jeremy for years. But the Jeremy you saw getting on the elevator has no clue, and there's nothing going on between us. Though I find it a bit bizarre that I'm the one giving you assurances, after the cavalcade of women you've been involved with."

Martin took it all in impassively. "I know I have no right to feel possessive. I'm sorry if it's a colossal turnoff."

"Actually it's kind of the opposite. Except for the part where you're tying yourself into knots unnecessarily," I added gently.

"Just tell me this: is Jeremy into anything that could get you into trouble?"

"I don't think so. It's not as if I'll be seeing him again anytime soon."

"Okay." He cupped the side of my face and kissed me. "So you want to go to the place where Cyn died. How come?"

I pondered this. "To pay my respects. To move forward with my life. To prove I'm not running from what happened."

"Then I'm coming with you," he said.

"Cyn would've hated that."

"Tough."

"I think I should do it alone."

He pulled me closer. "Kid, you've been doing it alone for years. Let me help."

∞

We took the subway to the Village the following weekend. I huddled in my seat, my clammy hands clasped together. By the time we reached our stop, my heart was pounding. "You don't have to do this today," Martin said.

"Yes, I do," I said, and the doors slid open.

We climbed the stairs from the subway. It was Saturday afternoon. The weather was still mild, but there was a hint of autumn in the air. The sidewalks bustled with students, and I remembered walking here with Cyn. Every step I took was suffused with her. We marched past brick buildings and elm trees. I was so nervous, I felt disembodied. "It's up ahead," I said. "The next block."

A taxi careened around the corner. Then we crossed the street, my heart beating faster with each step.

"We're here," I whispered, and Martin took my hand.

The windows of the brick building were boarded up, and I sucked in a breath. For a moment I thought we'd gone back to 1971, after the bomb blew out the windows. I gripped Martin's hand, and the moment passed.

There was something uncanny about seeing the building vacant. The draft had been abolished. The war was over. We had won, after all. But it hadn't brought back any of the dead.

In front of the building there was a mailbox, blue metal. I couldn't look at it straight on. Next door was the Chinese laundry, and, on the corner, the bakery. A couple of girls went inside, and sugary smells wafted out the door. "We used to get coffee here," I said. I was surprised at how ordinary my voice sounded.

Martin wouldn't let go of my hand, as if something might pull me away from him. "I can feel it," he said. "This is—was—a bad place." He looked haunted. He had never been more beautiful to me.

I squeezed his hand. "Thank you for coming here with me. It helps more than I could've imagined."

He quirked a smile. "That's what I've been trying to tell you. And you're welcome."

It dawned on me that nothing was going to pull me out of this life. I belonged in this one, finally. And Cyn—where was she? I listened hard for her voice and tried to sense her active, argumentative, hungry presence. She wasn't here, not in that way. I didn't have to seek her out. She was with me. I lived for her as well as for myself, even though I couldn't pretend she'd agree with my choices.

The back of my neck prickled, and I became aware of eyes on me. Feds? In a flash the old paranoia was back. Had they figured it out at last, my connection to the bombing? But it was just those girls, SNY students by the look of them, who'd come back out of the bakery. One had brown skin and braids, the other red hair and freckles. Both wore jeans and t-shirts and carried book bags. The redhead held a small paper bag from the bakery. The girls were staring at us, but when I looked at them, they put their heads together and started whispering, darting occasional glances our way.

"They're amazed you're holding hands with Sam Jameson," Martin said in my ear. "Not to mention the fact that you're alive."

The girls walked demure and silent past us. Then, with peals of laughter, they took off running pell-mell down the sidewalk, book bags bouncing from their shoulders. *Best friends*, I thought, watching them disappear into the distance.

I looked up at Martin and smiled. "I know the feeling."

About the Author

Gwynne Garfinkle is a Los Angeles native, a fiction writer, poet, and erstwhile rock critic. Her collection of short fiction and poetry, *People Change*, was published in 2018 by Aqueduct Press. Her work has appeared in such publications as *Strange Horizons, Uncanny, Escape Pod, Apex, GigaNotoSaurus, Mermaids Monthly, Not One of Us,* and *Climbing Lightly Through Forests.* She has an MFA in Creative Writing from Antioch LA. Follow her on Twitter or Instagram (@gwynnega) or visit her website: gwynnegarfinkle.com.